VANISHED IN THE MIST

LENA DIAZ

DISAPPEARANCE AT ANGEL'S LANDING

NICHOLE SEVERN

MILLS & BOON

First Published in Great Britain 2025
by Mills & Boon, an imprint of HarperCollins*Publishers* Ltd
1 London Bridge Street, London, SE1 9GF

www.harpercollins.co.uk

HarperCollins*Publishers*
Macken House, 39/40 Mayor Street Upper,
Dublin 1, D01 C9W8, Ireland

Vanished in the Mist © 2025 Lena Diaz
Disappearance at Angel's Landing © 2025 Natascha Jaffa

ISBN: 978-0-263-39727-7

0925

MIX
Paper | Supporting responsible forestry
FSC™ C007454

This book contains FSC™ certified paper and other controlled sources to ensure responsible forest management.

For more information visit: www.harpercollins.co.uk/green

Printed and Bound in the UK using 100% Renewable Electricity at CPI Group (UK) Ltd, Croydon, CR0 4YY

VANISHED IN THE MIST

LENA DIAZ

This book is dedicated to my fierce sisters, Lisa Detmers and Laura Brown, for facing cancer head-on with dignity and courage. I thank God for your strength and am so grateful you're both cancer-free now. Love you so much.

Chapter One

Shanna Hudson didn't believe in ghosts. She didn't believe
in the boogeyman. And she certainly wasn't going to quake
in fear over the so-called Phantom the locals claimed lived
in the remote area of the Smoky Mountains above the town
of Mystic Lake, an hour outside of Chattanooga, Tennessee.
But as she stood in the late afternoon sun at the end of her
sister's dock overlooking the vast lake with the same name
as the town, a tingle of uneasiness skittered up her spine.
Not because of the myths and legends that surrounded this
place, but because of one indisputable fact.

People had died in this lake.

So many had died or disappeared over the years that
Mystic Lake was officially one of the deadliest lakes in
North America, second only to Georgia's Lake Lanier.
Both of those lakes were deadly for the same reason: the
hazards beneath their deceptively calm surfaces from when
they'd been created by flood waters that submerged whole
towns decades earlier.

There was one notable difference, though. Lake Lanier
had been created on purpose, with the building of a dam
to provide hydroelectric power and water to nearby towns.
Mystic Lake's inception was an act of nature, the result of

a devastating confluence of storms that permanently re-routed a small river down the side of a mountain and buried a town, drowning most of its residents.

Shanna shivered as she looked out across the dark water and wondered just how many poor souls had met their end here. And how many cars, homes and entire trees lurked in the depths today, ready to snag a boat or tangle in a swimmer's hair to add to the lake's tragic history. From what her sister, Cassidy, had told her, the townspeople did what they could to make the lake safe. Known hazards were hauled out when feasible and budgets allowed. Warning signs had been posted in particularly treacherous areas. But there was no way to eliminate all potential threats. The lake was too deep, too big. Its waters covered thousands of acres of land and extended through the foothills for miles. Yet, in spite of the dangers, both locals and tourists flocked here to boat, fish, or swim, believing the worst wouldn't happen to them.

Until it did.

In the decades since the lake had existed, not a single year had passed without at least one person dying in a mysterious boating accident or by drowning. Usually, it was a handful, sometimes even more.

She shook her head, still amazed that her sister had finally worn her down enough to get her to come here. But Cassidy's most recent request had been different. Instead of pressuring Shanna to travel to Mystic Lake in her official capacity as a private investigator, Cassidy had offered her lakeside cabin for a week's vacation while she and her husband went on a Caribbean cruise they'd won in a contest. Being teachers, it was hard to get permission to take a vacation in April, just weeks before the school year ended. But they were top performers and this was a special circumstance, so their dream trip had been approved.

Shanna was happy for both of them. They deserved this time away. And the invitation to Shanna to enjoy their cabin while they were gone had come at a time in her life when it was too tempting to pass up. The lure of escaping the mounting pressures of running her PI company, which was located in Morgantown, West Virginia, particularly after her last, exhausting case, had been too tempting to turn down. Well, that and because her ex-boyfriend was struggling to accept the *ex* status of their relationship. Maybe her being out of town for a week would help Troy come to terms with their breakup. If not, if his stalking behavior continued to escalate, she'd have to escalate her response, too, by involving the police. Again.

She patted her right pants pocket, reassuring herself that her gun was there. Not that she expected to need it. But she wasn't taking any chances, especially if Troy figured out where she'd gone and decided to make a surprise appearance. The ability to bring her gun was her sole reason for driving the nine hours rather than fly. She hadn't wanted to deal with the hassle of declaring her weapon to airport security and being forced to store it in a checked bag, where it might be *supposedly* lost.

Guilt rose inside her, crowding out her concerns about her ex. Shanna had refused her sister's many requests that she look into the disappearance of one of Cassidy's high school students almost a year ago. And yet, here she was, for purely selfish reasons. But she'd always been clear with Cassidy when turning her down. Shanna didn't have contacts in this area, no confidential informants or insider knowledge to help her solve the case. And besides that, her West Virginia PI license wasn't valid in Tennessee.

Could she have looked into the case in an unofficial civilian capacity rather than as a private investigator? Yes.

Of course. But she had no reason to expect that she'd do a better job in this unfamiliar area than the local police had. Plus, there was another reason she'd turned down her sister. It was the same reason that she'd refused to come here after Cassidy first moved to Mystic Lake two years ago, when she'd gotten married.

Shanna was afraid of the water.

Not the drinking kind or the showering kind. Her fear focused on anything large, deep, or scary, including lakes, ponds and even swimming pools, like the one where she'd nearly died as a young teen. She'd sworn off ever allowing herself to be that vulnerable again by going near or in the water. And until today, she'd kept that vow.

Part of keeping it meant refusing to search for her sister's missing student, Tanya Jericho. After all, Tanya was believed to have perished in this lake a few weeks after her sophomore graduation, in May of last year. Since her body had yet to be found, she was still labeled as missing eleven months later. Investigating her disappearance would have meant spending time around the water, probably even going out on the lake in a boat. Since Cassidy knew about Shanna's fear, she never should have asked her to work the Jericho case. Although, to be fair, her younger sister might not realize just how debilitating Shanna's fear could sometimes be. Cassidy was too young to remember what had happened all those years ago. Only Shanna, her parents, her therapist, and the police knew the full terrifying truth about that day at the pool.

Squaring her shoulders, she turned her back to the water. Immediately breathing easier, she headed up the gently sloping hill to her sister's log cabin. When she'd arrived earlier, she'd parked her silver Lexus beside it, but had left her suitcase at the bottom of the porch steps. She'd wanted to deal with the lake head-on, right away, instead of allowing dread to build up. Now, if Cassidy called and asked her, she could honestly say she'd faced her fear and was fine. More or less, even though her heart was racing and her palms were sweaty. No one needed to know that part.

She smiled at the clay pots with pink and white flowers spilling over their sides that hung from the porch railings. Unsurprisingly, the cabin's foundation was also surrounded by flowers and shrubs. Her little sister and her husband both loved anything to do with nature. With it being full-on spring, they wouldn't miss an opportunity to take advantage of the mild weather to grow something. There were probably plants inside the house too with detailed instructions on how Shanna should care for them this week.

She hauled her suitcase up to the wide wooden porch that ran across the front of the cabin and used the key that Cassidy had mailed her to unlock the door. Even after having been told it was a one-bedroom, one-bathroom cabin, she was still surprised at how small it was as she stood in the opening. Her sister and her husband's high school teacher salaries meant they weren't exactly flush with cash. But they could have afforded something bigger than this. They'd probably opted to devote the bulk of their mortgage money on expensive lakefront property rather than get a larger house in town on a much smaller, more affordable, lot. The view and unspoiled location would have been too hard for them to resist.

What mattered, of course, wasn't the size of the cabin. What mattered was that Cassidy and her husband, Gavin, seemed happy. And they'd made a welcoming, cozy home here. The soaring vaulted ceiling saved the place from feeling claustrophobic even though it was probably a quarter the size of Shanna's two-story brick home in West Virginia.

True to her sister's personality, the wide open room with the sitting area to the left, the kitchen to the right with the table in the front corner near the door were all so clean they practically sparkled. The windows framed an impressive view of the lush, green Smoky Mountains. And the cabin was high enough on the hill that Shanna could focus on the Smokies, rather than the lake, when peering out those windows. It was the perfect setting for her planned week of solitude and peace. And once her sister returned, they could spend some time catching up before Shanna left for home.

The stress she'd been struggling with from her most recent case, her arguments with her ex and even her few minutes on the dock all seemed to lighten as she stepped across the threshold. It was as if she'd left her worries outside. It felt good. Really good.

She drew a deep breath, smiling as she turned and shut the door. But when she saw what was on the back of the door, the stress came hurtling back, like a fist slamming into her chest. A faded eight-by-ten piece of paper was taped to the door. Across the top, printed in large black letters was a heart-wrenching, ominous word.

MISSING

The color picture beneath the caption framed the smiling face of a young girl with long red hair and a smattering of freckles across her pale cheeks. Her bright blue eyes stared back at Shanna, making her throat tighten. This was the girl her sister had wanted her to try to find. Had Cassidy simply forgotten to take down the flyer? Or had she put it there to make Shanna feel guilty? Maybe it was worse than that. Maybe her little sister had tricked her and this wasn't a simple vacation opportunity. The couple was probably hiding in the bedroom right now, waiting to ambush her and beg her to look for this girl. No, not *this girl*. She was a real person and deserved to be thought of by her name, the name printed beneath her picture.

Tanya Jericho

She let out a shuddering breath and turned away, her good mood having completely evaporated.

"Cassidy? Are you here?" She headed to the door in the middle of the back wall and yanked it open. "Cassidy? Gavin?" She strode into the bedroom and glanced around, fully expecting one or both of them to be there. But aside from the king-size bed, with its patchwork quilt and the usual assortment of nightstands and a dresser, the room was empty. She checked the closet and surprisingly large, attached bathroom as well. Both were devoid of a sneaky sister or her equally sneaky husband.

Okay. Maybe assuming the worst about them was unfair. A faded poster of a girl who'd been missing for almost a year wasn't enough evidence to prove her sister had an ulterior motive for inviting her here. Shanna strode back into the main room of the cabin, circling the two-tiered kitchen island to get a drink of water while trying to quiet the suspicions in her mind. But when she rounded the island, what she saw on the countertop by the sink had her tensing up again: a half-inch-thick manila folder. Her sister had promised to leave a note about the local sites, hiking trails and restaurants. Nothing about the thickness of that folder had her believing that's what she'd find. Drawing a bracing breath, she took the folder to the table and flipped it open.

And swore, viciously.

She'd been tricked. Shanna didn't have to be a private investigator to reach that conclusion. It was spelled out clearly and succinctly on the very first line of the first page in the folder.

Hey, sis. I'm so sorry that I tricked you.

Shanna swore again and plopped down in one of the chairs at the table to read the rest of the note. Her sister explained that she was desperate to help the Jericho family and the only way she knew how was to ask her brilliant private-investigator sister to look into Tanya's disappearance. Cassidy begged her to please read everything in the folder, which had been given to her by the missing teen's parents. The stack of pages contained background information on their daughter, what they'd documented and collected about the investigation that the police had done, as well as their own attempts to find out what had happened.

If you read this and are still set against helping, I'll understand. You can enjoy the cabin regardless and have the vacation you deserve. I had to try one last time to get your help or I wouldn't be able to live with myself. Forgive me, please? Love you.

Shanna sighed. Of course, she'd forgive her sister…eventually. Honestly, in her place, she'd have probably done the same thing. But what Cassidy didn't seem to get was that Shanna hadn't made her decision lightly to not investigate the girl's disappearance. She'd agonized over whether or not to come here and help. But in a town built around and dominated by a deadly lake, she'd decided it was best to trust in the local police rather than try to interject herself into the investigation.

Thankfully, her sister had given her an out, telling her it was okay to stay and use the cabin anyway. Cassidy and her husband hadn't lied. They really were on a cruise, as the note went on to explain. To do right by her sister, all Shanna had to do was read the folder. Then she could set it aside without any guilt and get on with her plan to do absolutely nothing but sleep, read and eat for the next seven days.

Her gaze, seemingly of its own accord, slid back to the picture of the young woman on the flyer.

So young. So innocent.

Shanna had been that young once, that innocent. And what had happened to her had been horrendous. But she'd survived, because of the help of some really good people. Who was helping Tanya? Who was helping her parents?

Shanna started to shake. *No.* This wasn't her problem. It wasn't Shanna's fault that this girl was missing. It wasn't her duty to help every single person who got into some kind of trouble. She was only one person. There was only so much *she* could do.

Anger came to her rescue, giving her the strength to surge to her feet and snatch the missing poster off the door. She was about to slap it on top of the stack of documents in the folder when she noticed dark shadows of words bleeding through to the front of the flyer. Someone had written on the back and she didn't have to guess who.

Cassidy.

She fisted her hands at her sides. *Ignore it. Don't turn it over. Don't read it.*

Oh, for the love of…who was she kidding? She was an investigator for a reason. Her curiosity was her superpower, driving her until she uncovered every little crumb of evidence to solve a case. Unfortunately, it was also her kryptonite. She let out a strangled groan and flipped over the flyer. Her sister's neat teacher's handwriting flowed across the page.

There is one more thing I need to tell you, and it's a doozy. I really hope you can forgive me.

"Oh, Cassidy. What else have you done?"

To make sure you have the best possible chance at finding out what happened to Tanya, I—

The cabin door suddenly opened and a man stepped inside, eyes wide with surprise as he stared at her.
Shanna clawed for the pistol in her pocket.
The man leaped at her, tackling her to the floor.
Bam! The gun went off.

Chapter Two

"Get off me!" the woman yelled, twisting and bucking beneath Kaden Rafferty as he wrestled the pistol out of her right hand.

He sent it sliding across the hardwood floor out of her reach and grabbed her now-free wrist before her fist could make contact with his jaw.

"Knock it off, all right?" he practically growled. "Obviously there's been some kind of misunderstanding here."

"Misunderstanding?" She bucked against him again, her knee nearly connecting with a vulnerable part that had him settling his full weight on her to stop her from trying that move again.

"Lady, if you'll just quit fighting me I'll let you go. You're obviously in the wrong cabin and—"

"Wrong cabin?" Her blue eyes blazed up at him, hot with anger. "You're the one in the wrong cabin. Or maybe the right one if you were hoping to break in and steal something. You just didn't expect anyone to be home."

"You're right about one thing. I was told that no one would be here."

She jerked her wrists, struggling against his hold. "Who told you that? Your partner in crime? Let me guess. He's waiting outside with a truck to load up whatever you both plan on stealing."

"Not unless my partner in crime is a high school teacher named Cassidy Tate."

The mad-as-hell brunette suddenly grew still, her brow wrinkling in confusion. "Cassidy Tate? How do you know her?"

"Remember the part where you accused me of breaking into this cabin? If you think back, instead of trying to get your gun to shoot me again—"

"I didn't shoot you."

"Not for lack of trying."

She rolled her eyes.

He prayed for patience. "I didn't kick down the door. I used a key. The one Mrs. Tate mailed to me last week when she hired me."

The woman blinked, her eyes widening. "Cassidy hired you? To do what?"

"You know her?"

"Not as well as I thought I did. She's my sister."

"Ah. That explains it."

Her eyes narrowed suspiciously. "Explains what?"

"She was stubborn and feisty on the phone, calling several times over the course of three weeks insisting that I consider her proposal. Somehow, she convinced me to help her, free of charge in exchange for lodging and food. That stubbornness must run in the family."

She swore.

He couldn't help smiling. The salty words coming out of that pretty mouth weren't the way he'd have expected this beautiful woman to speak. She was nearly as tall as he was, which put her at close to six feet. Her slim, athletic body, delicate facial features and long, thick brown hair were an appealing combination. The only things destroying her supermodel potential were her generous breasts, which were currently burning a hole in his chest. She didn't have that waiflike half-starved look that so many models had. And he most definitely approved.

She was gorgeous, especially when she wasn't trying to punch or shoot him. She'd stopped struggling and her face was turning a delightful pink. She was either still mad and planning her next attack, or she was embarrassed about something.

"Why did Cassidy call you?" She was markedly calmer now as she waited for his reply.

"She wanted me to come here to search for a missing girl."

The woman groaned. "What's the girl's name?"

"Tanya Jericho."

She squeezed her eyes shut for a moment, and her brow wrinkled as if she were in pain. Then her body went lax and soft beneath him as all the fight drained out of her. "I'm guessing you're the doozy she mentioned in her note."

"Doozy?"

"Will you please let me up? You're right. There's been a misunderstanding."

Her soft curves were starting to do alarming things to him now that she wasn't trying to kill him. He was eager to let her go before she noticed his body's response. But he wasn't even close to trusting her.

"You don't have another gun in your other pocket, do you?"

"I wish."

He smiled again. The woman was delightfully sassy. Too bad she was so bloodthirsty. "I'll release your wrists on the count of three. Don't try to pull any sucker punches when I let go."

"Just get up already."

He chuckled and rolled off her, then leaped to his feet and swiped the pistol off the floor before she could get it.

She stood and frowned, then shrugged as if she didn't care even though she'd been clearly going for her gun.

He shoved it into his back jeans pocket, shaking his head.

"Don't look at me that way. I wasn't going to shoot you." She frowned and glanced around the cabin. "Where did that bullet end up, anyway?"

He pointed toward the wall to the right of the door. "Judging by the splintered wood, I'm guessing it's buried inside that log."

She winced. "Cassidy is going to kill me. Then again, it serves her right for this little stunt she pulled." She cleared her throat and offered her hand. "Let's start over. I'm Shanna Hudson, Cassidy's big sister."

He shook her hand. "Kaden Rafferty." He motioned over his shoulder. "I hear there are bears around here. Mind if I shut the door?"

She blinked. "Bears? Oh. Yes, please do." She sat at the table.

He shut and locked the door, then took the chair across from her.

They sat in silence for a long moment, then she let out a deep breath and picked up a piece of paper that must have fallen to the floor earlier. She turned it over and read a paragraph on the back, then set it on the table.

"What's your superpower?" she asked.

"My superpower?"

"The reason Cassidy made that deal with you, free work

in exchange for food and a roof over your head. I'm a private investigator. And you are?"

"Ah. I see. She tricked both of us into coming here to investigate the case of this missing girl. But she didn't tell either of us the other one was coming. Am I getting warm?"

"Burning up."

He grinned. "Then I guess my superpower is that I own a search-and-recovery company. We operate out of Charleston, South Carolina. This is my first time coming to Mystic Lake, Tennessee."

She crossed her forearms on the table. "What type of search and recovery does your company do?"

He sat back. "It's not your turn."

"My turn?"

"To ask another question."

"This isn't a game."

His amusement fled. "No kidding. I'll be dead serious then, and tell you that almost being shot wasn't in my plans when I drove eight hours pulling an extremely expensive boat and giving up a lucrative contract to take on your sister's request pro bono."

Her eyes widened and her cheeks flushed pink again. She glanced past him, presumably at the splintered log, before she looked back at him. "I'm sorry. I truly am. We've both been played. You weren't told I'd be here. And I didn't know anything about you. I hadn't finished that part of the note that my sister left before you opened the door. I honestly thought you were an intruder and that my life was in danger. Otherwise, I'd have never drawn my gun."

The sincerity in her voice assuaged his anger and had him nodding his acceptance of her apology.

"You were going to ask me a question," she said. "Please. Go ahead."

He cleared his throat. "Yes, well. The trip here was a long one and I only stopped once, to gas up. I also drank way too much water along the way."

A bubble of laughter escaped her as she pointed toward the far wall. "Go through that door. Once inside, the bathroom's the second door on the left."

Chapter Three

When Kaden returned to the table, the beautiful brunette was deeply immersed in whatever she was reading in the folder. He sat down across from her. When she didn't look up, he asked, "It's Shanna, right?"

She started, as if she'd forgotten he was there. His ego took a hit. Not that he thought he was God's gift to women. But he'd been told he was decent-looking and being outright forgotten by a beautiful woman wasn't typical for him.

"Are you married?" He glanced at her left hand. No ring. But some people didn't wear them these days.

She blinked. "Uh, no. You?"

"Nope. No girlfriend, either, at the moment. Is there some jealous guy I need to worry about?"

Her eyebrows raised. "Why would you need to be worried?"

He motioned toward the doorway in the back wall. "There's only one bedroom in this cabin and one bed. Since we're both staying here—"

"There's a bed-and-breakfast in town. You can stay there."

"I prefer the cabin."

"You're going to the B and B. It's my sister's cabin. It wouldn't make sense for me to leave it for a stranger to use."

"Except that your sister invited me and gave me a key."

She frowned and closed the folder. "Why would you want to stay where you aren't wanted?"

"Ouch. You don't mince words, do you?"

"Not normally, no. What's the problem? Do you need money? I can pay for the B and B if that's the issue. It's not your fault that my sister, ah, overbooked her cabin." She pulled out her cell phone. "I'll even call and reserve a room for you."

He stood. "Don't bother. I won't use it." He moved to the front door.

"Wait. Where are you going?"

"To put my boat in the water. I saw a public ramp a couple of miles down the road."

"There's a ramp not far from the B and B, too. I drove around town scouting things out before I drove to the cabin. It's a decent ramp, spacious, lots of parking. Wouldn't that make more sense?"

"Not when I'm planning on tying my boat up at the dock I saw outside this cabin after I finish my work every day. I'd like to park my truck and trailer here since I'll need the truck off and on this week. I'd ask you to drive them back to the cabin for me since I'll be driving my boat. But since you're in denial, I'll hire someone else to do it." He opened the door.

She jumped up and followed him onto the porch. "Hold on a second."

He stopped and leaned against the railing.

"You said you'd come back here, after you're through with work. What's that about?"

"I would expect that's obvious. I'm going to start my

search for Tanya Jericho. There are still several hours until sunset. Might as well start now."

"Using your boat?"

"Since she allegedly disappeared either on or near the lake, yes. I'm going to search for her using my boat. *Underwater* search and recovery is my company's specialty. It's why your sister sought me out."

Something dark seemed to pass across her eyes, like a shadow. Fear? Confusion? Whatever it was, it had her silent and deep in thought.

He didn't wait. He jogged down the porch steps to his truck.

The sound of swearing told him she'd come out of her trance or whatever it was. He tried not to laugh as she ran after him. Forcing a straight face and a bored look, he turned around and leaned against the driver's door as she stopped in front of him, slightly out of breath.

"What now?" he asked.

"You haven't even read the folder. You don't know where to look."

"I'm assuming your folder is like the one that your sister sent to me. I've already read it and pinpointed the first grid area I'm going to search."

"Just like that?"

"Just like that." He opened the door and hopped into the driver's seat.

Her soft hand was suddenly on his, stopping him. "The police had divers in the water, several times. No one ever found anything."

"That's where my—what did you call it?—*superpowers* come in. I have the latest handheld sonar technology that's specifically programmed to pinpoint anything under the water that has the characteristics of a submerged body." He gently removed her hand. "I really need to get going. It'll take a while to get my boat in the water, arrange for my truck to be driven back here, drive my boat to the area I want to search, and then spend a few hours actually search- ing. If I don't get going soon, I won't have enough daylight left to make starting the search today worthwhile."

She moved back so he could shut the door. But as soon as he started the engine, she knocked on his window.

He sighed and rolled it down. "Now what?"

"You don't have to hire someone to drive your vehicle to the cabin. I'll do it and then you can… You can pick me up on the—the boat here at my sister's dock." She swallowed as if that hesitant statement had been hard to say. Then she added, "I'm going with you on your search."

"No. You're not."

She stared at him in confusion. "Why not?"

"Because you have something else to do."

"What would that be?"

"You were calling the B and B to try to evict me. I'm not sharing my boat if you're bent on not sharing the cabin."

"Oh, for crying out loud. That's childish."

He arched an eyebrow.

She crossed her arms, clearly struggling with her de- cision. She didn't seem to be afraid of him anymore. But something had her clearly worried.

After nearly a full minute of silence, he decided he'd waited long enough. "Like I said, daylight's wasting. I need to go."

Something akin to panic crossed her face as she glanced from him to the boat behind his truck. She cleared her throat and seemed to gather herself. "Okay, okay. We can share the cabin. Just give me a minute to get my purse and—"

"Another gun you probably have hidden inside? I don't think so." He revved the engine.

Her hands fisted at her sides. "You're the only one who has a gun. Mine. Which you *are* going to give back to me at some point. But right now, I need to lock up the cabin. Not that there's a lot of crime around here, but some hiker could come along and decide to help themselves to anything inside. I can't leave Cassidy's home unprotected."

He pretended to consider her statement when what he really wanted to do was laugh. She was so fun to tease. "Okay. Lock it up. Hurry." He shifted into Reverse and began to carefully back the trailer up so he could turn around.

She swore a blue streak and ran for the cabin.

Chapter Four

Shanna stood at the edge of her sister's dock watching Kaden's impressive blue-and-white boat, or maybe it was a yacht, bobbing up and down in the water as he reached his hand out to help her board.

"That's—that's a really big boat," she said, stalling. "What kind is it?"

"A Scout 530 LXF. Thirty-three-footer. Are you coming on board?"

She ignored his outstretched hand. "Do you have another life jacket? For me?"

"Of course. I'd never allow someone to go out on one of my boats without one."

"*One* of your boats? How many do you have?"

"Enough so that my company can work several contracts at a time. Otherwise, I'd never earn enough to cover expenses, let alone turn a profit." He motioned toward her. "Now, if you'll just—"

"Is it like the one you're wearing? The life jacket you have for me? That one looks awfully thin."

He glanced down at his jacket. "The thinner ones are more comfortable than the bulky ones and don't hamper movement the way those do. But they're just as buoyant. If you'll step over the side, we can—"

"Are you positive it will keep someone afloat if they fall overboard? Mystic Lake is well-known for people going under and never coming back up. There's something…odd about this lake. Something—"

"Mystical?" He smiled.

Her face warmed. "That's not what I'm saying. I just—"

"Want to be sure you're safe?"

"Right. Yes." She cleared her throat, desperately trying to calm her racing pulse. *Breathe. In, out, in, out.*

He dropped his hand. "Shanna?"

"Yes?"

"What are you afraid of? The boat? Or me?"

She blinked. "What makes you think I'm afraid?"

"It's a balmy spring day and you're shivering like it's ten below zero. You're also extremely reluctant to board even though you said you wanted to come along."

"I do. I want to help, to tell my sister I did everything I could to find Tanya. I mean, she tricked me, tricked both of us. But she must be truly desperate to have done that. There's no way I can ignore her request now and go back to my original plan. Especially when a total stranger is willing to help. I *have* to do this."

"Your original plan?"

"Do nothing. Sleep late. Ignore the world for a week."

"Got it. No shame in that. I'm sure you work hard and could use the break. Go on up to the cabin. Relax. Leave the search to me and I'll update you when I get back. I've got this." He turned away.

"Wait!"

He sighed heavily and glanced over his shoulder. "Yes?"

Her stomach knotted as she tried to ignore the sound of the dark water lapping against the dock. "It's not the boat. And it's definitely not you."

He frowned in confusion.

"That I'm…afraid of." Her face flamed with embarrassment. "It's the water."

He blinked, understanding dawning in his expression. "You're afraid of the water, and you still want to come with me?"

The wake from a passing boat had the dock bobbing slightly. She stiffened, the traumatized teenager deep inside her desperate to turn away, to run to her sister's house and hide beneath a mountain of blankets. But the memory of the missing poster and the sound of her sister's voice pleading for help over the phone was battering her with guilt.

Please, Shanna. Tanya's parents need to bring her home. They've accepted that she's no longer with us. But they can't rest until they've given her a decent burial. Help them.

She swore beneath her breath, then stretched out her hand. "I'm ready."

He stared at her a long moment, as if weighing her resolve. Then, instead of taking her hand, he straddled the side of the boat, one foot on the dock, the other on the deck, and clasped his hands around her waist. He lifted her up and over the side so quickly that she didn't have time to be afraid or protest. He steered her into the interior behind the glass windows and had a life jacket on her almost as fast as he'd lifted her onto the boat.

She marveled at his strength, considering she was in no way tiny at five-eleven. He was probably six foot two, maybe taller, his broad shoulders and impressive biceps speaking to the strength she'd felt in those arms. That strength was reassuring, since he was the one who would be guiding the boat. Unfortunately, logic was doing nothing to stop her roiling nausea.

Deep breaths. Deep breaths. Don't look at the water.

As he adjusted the straps on her vest, she finally found her voice again.

"Thank you," she whispered.

"No worries." His deep voice resonated with empathy and understanding, sending a pleasurable tingle up her spine that had nothing to do with nausea and everything to do with how appealing he was. "You're safe. The boat's high-powered, with several engines. More than enough horsepower to get us back if an engine fails. It's sturdy, easy to maneuver. Everything you might need is down those steps in the cabin. A galley, bedroom, head."

"Head?"

He chuckled. "I'm guessing you don't speak *boat*. The head is the bathroom. The galley's the kitchen. And you can remember the overall areas of a boat by thinking of it like a compass, with north being the front. North, south, east and west are bow, stern, starboard and port."

"Got it. I think. Wait. There's a bedroom? Earlier you were arguing that we'd have to share my sister's house, implying that we'd have to share the only bedroom, too."

"Don't get me wrong. This is a hell of a boat, with all the luxuries I could possibly want. But staying on it a whole week? I prefer the freedom of movement of an actual house, at least when I'm not out on the water searching. I can certainly sleep here at night. But I'd prefer to share your sister's place during the daylight hours, if you're open to it, especially since she promised the kitchen would be stocked. I have drinks and snacks on board, but little else."

"So you were teasing earlier?"

His deep brown eyes sparkled with amusement. "I certainly wouldn't mind sharing your bedroom, and your bed, if you ever want to." He winked, making her face heat again, and her belly tighten for an entirely new reason. How could she want him when she barely knew him and felt so awful right now? "But, no," he continued. "I wasn't serious when I teased you about sleeping in your sister's cabin."

She couldn't help smiling in response and shaking her head. But even that small movement made her nausea worse. She drew several quick breaths, desperately fighting the urge to throw up.

His expression turned serious as his brow furrowed with concern. "You can lie down on the bed if you'd like. But I recommend you sit outside. There's built-in seating. It's secure. And the fresh air should help ease your nausea."

"That obvious, huh?"

"You've gone from Casper the Friendly Ghost white to Shrek green."

She laughed, then pressed a hand against her protesting stomach and desperately tried to ignore the gentle rocking motion of the boat and the sparkling of the sun off the water surrounding them.

"Sit. Once I drive us to the desired location, I'll launch off the stern to conduct my search. You won't have to do anything but relax and work on your tan."

"In jeans?"

"I didn't bring any bikinis for you. But I'm fine with you just wearing your birthday suit."

She laughed again, then groaned, her stomach protesting her every movement. "What did you mean by launch?"

Another small boat passed with two fishermen on board. They waved as they went by and Kaden waved back, then motioned toward the rear of the boat as he turned his attention back to Shanna. "The deck at the stern. That's where I'll go into the water, scuba dive."

She felt the blood drain from her face. "Oh. Okay."

"That's the underwater part of search and recovery."

She gave him a weak smile. "Earlier you mentioned sonar. I guess I figured it was built into the boat and you wouldn't need to dive."

"You're partly right. The main equipment maps out images below the water to help with navigation so I don't run aground. It also helps me locate large objects, like a submerged car. But it's not that effective with smaller objects, such as human remains. Detail work requires a diver. So does recovery, for anything we're looking for."

She winced. "Makes sense. I'm not thinking things through very well. Usually I'm better than this."

He lightly squeezed her arm. "You're facing your fears to help your sister and Tanya's family. You can't get much better than that."

She stared up at him, marveling at his patience and kindness. And how had she not realized how good-looking he was until now? He was clean-cut, with short brown hair and whiskey-brown eyes. Ruggedly handsome was the cliché that came to mind. He wasn't one of those pretty boys, the ones with a perfect tan and long lashes that graced the cover of a magazine—like her ex, Troy. Instead, Kaden seemed like an incredibly capable man, the kind who could build a fire by rubbing two twigs together in a rainstorm, build a shelter without any tools that could withstand the worst that nature could throw at him. That was far sexier than any cover model could ever be. He didn't seem much older than her, maybe thirty-two or-three. And yet, he wore the confidence of a man with far more years of experience. Kaden Rafferty was *hot*.

She shook her head in wonder. "How are you not married? Or escorting some beauty-queen girlfriend around on your arm?"

He laughed. "Beauty queen? Is that the kind of woman you think I'd be attracted to?"

"Well, yes, actually. Like attracts like, or so they say. And you're not exactly plain-looking."

A sexy smile curved his lips. "Neither are you."

She blinked, her mouth falling open and her entire body flushing with heat.

His smile widened, revealing straight white teeth and an adorable dimple in his left cheek. "Are you flirting with me, Ms. Hudson?"

If she didn't feel so bad, she'd be jumping him right now. She cleared her throat instead. "Unfortunately, Mr. Rafferty, I feel too bad to flirt right now."

He gave her a sympathetic look. "You'll feel better once you see how smooth she rides."

"She?"

"*Discovery*. The boat."

"Right." She cleared her throat. "It's a good name. For what you do, discovering lost things beneath the water. Just, ah, one more question." She pressed a hand to her throat. "If I need to throw up, where should I—"

He grabbed her hand and rushed her down the steps.

Chapter Five

Kaden glanced through the cockpit window toward the prow of the boat, where Shanna was sitting. Her complexion had been alarmingly pale when she'd emerged from the head earlier. But after brushing her teeth with one of the guest sets he kept on board, and drinking down a bottle of water, she'd regained some of her color. He'd tried to get her to lie down, no longer sure that her being outside, where she could see the water, was going to help her feel better. But she'd insisted she'd feel trapped down in the cabin and would rather face whatever was coming. Then she'd straightened her shoulders like any good soldier and marched to the prow, where she'd been ever since. Anyone looking at her would think she was enjoying herself, unless they caught a glimpse of her hands. She was clinging so tightly to the arms of her seat that her knuckles were white.

He wondered what had happened in her past to make her so afraid. Seeing her physical reactions to the lake, and the fact that she still insisted on being part of the search for Tanya, he couldn't help but be impressed that she refused to give in to her fears. Most people he'd met would have made a beeline for her sister's place rather than purposely place themselves in the position that she had. Heck, he probably would have stayed there himself if he felt physically ill near water.

Shanna was courageous and full of determination—both traits he greatly admired. It also didn't hurt that she was as beautiful, or more, as any so-called beauty queen that she'd mentioned earlier. But he had a feeling that comparison wouldn't go over well with her. So he kept that thought to himself.

A flash of white off the starboard side had him turning the wheel to port and gunning the engines to get around yet another reckless boater. That made three near misses in the last ten minutes. As soon as the danger passed, he glanced at Shanna. If she'd reacted, she wasn't showing it. He certainly didn't want to scare her any more than she already was. But it was hard to keep clear of all the wannabe captains around here who'd likely watched a required thirty-minute video on boating safety before being handed a key to a rental boat.

The lake finally began to widen, so he steered toward the middle, putting more of a buffer between him and the fools closer to shore as he passed the marina that had likely rented them those boats.

He'd researched this area before driving here. From what he'd learned, the main tourist season would start in the summer, about two months from now. But obviously, the people out on the river, or fishing from the shore, or just plain drinking and partying on the docks, didn't care which season it was. They were enjoying the mild weather and didn't appear to be worried about the stories—both real and imagined—of all the accidents and disappearances on Mystic Lake. Heck, knowing human nature, the mysteries surrounding this place likely increased tourism instead of putting a damper on it.

If he'd realized this many people would be out here, and how reckless they'd be, he'd have brought a smaller boat so he wouldn't have to struggle to get this one's thirty-three-foot length clear when a speedboat got too close. Thankfully, where he was headed was a much more shallow section of the lake that was less frequented by boaters. Just a few more turns and he'd be away from the crowd, assuming at least some of his online research was reliable.

He made the first turn, relieved to see a noticeable drop in the numbers of other boaters, just as he'd hoped. Still, he kept in the middle of the channel and watched for the crazies and drunks. When he made a second turn, the lake opened up, and was much wider and calmer with no other boats around. There were houses here and there tucked up in the trees along both shores. But most of the docks were empty, devoid of partiers and tourists. Most likely these homes belonged to locals and weren't being rented out to sightseers. Those locals were most likely finishing up their day at work or even preparing to make the long trek home from neighboring Chattanooga. That should make the search much safer, at least for a little while, which was always his primary concern. There were a lot of potential dangers on the water and under the water, in Mystic Lake more than most.

He slowed to four knots and checked the depth-meter gauge. Back by the marina, it had read close to fifty feet. Here, it was reading twelve. But every once in a while it would bump down to four or five for several seconds before going back in the twelve-foot range. Variations in the bottom of the lake bed were to be expected. But jumps that sharp and fast indicated something else, likely debris beneath the surface.

It wasn't unexpected, given the lake's history. There

could be trees, automobiles, even crumbling buildings down there, all of which made the dangers significantly higher than one of his usual trips. He'd have to be extremely careful, not just to protect his investment in the *Discovery*, but to look out for Shanna. He didn't want to add any trauma on top of what she was already experiencing by involving her in a boating accident.

The GPS meter showed he was close to his destination, the area where Tanya had told her parents she was going to sit and read at some picnic benches under the trees at the lakeshore the day she disappeared. Looking at the bank off to starboard, he could understand why the bookish, smart sophomore, who was said to be a loner, would choose that area. It was serene and beautiful, dotted with purple and yellow wildflowers this time of year, with a dozen picnic benches scattered under the trees. The road that led here ended off to the right, a dead end. This was where access to the lake ended by land.

The closest house he could see was a good hundred yards away, high up the mountain. Still, if she'd been his daughter, he'd have been uneasy knowing she was out here all alone. Not because of the myths and legends, but because of the very real dangers to young girls—*other people*, especially men. The same things that attracted Tanya to this area could attract those who were up to no good. The kind of men who might stumble across a lone female and suddenly become her worst nightmare.

He cut all but one of the four engines. Hopefully, what had happened to Tanya was much more benign. It would be far better if she'd simply drowned, although that was tragic in itself. But to learn she'd been taken by some stranger and likely had awful things done to her before being killed would be a much worse fate. He couldn't even begin to imagine the agony a parent would feel learning something like that. It might be kinder for them to never know what had happened rather than to have the worst confirmed.

"Is something wrong with the boat? I think most of those massive engines off the back have quit running."

He glanced to port, where Shanna was standing in the cockpit opening, clinging to the nearest railing. He offered her a reassuring smile.

"I cut most of the power. The water near that bank off to our starboard side, to our right, is our destination. I'll use one engine to turn into the current while I drop anchor so we don't run into the shallows."

She looked confused, but nodded as if she understood. He wondered if she'd ever been on a boat before. If not, her fear of the water wasn't because of a boating accident. Something else must have happened.

"We got here sooner than I expected," she said. "I thought it would take a lot longer."

"It would have by car. From what I saw on the maps I studied, the main road from town winds around these mountains quite a bit. By water it's straighter, much shorter. Even going slower than a car, a boat would beat them every time out here." He checked his depth gauge again, making sure they were clear of underwater hazards before slipping past her to take care of the anchor.

Once he was back at the helm, Shanna stood beside him, shaking her head in wonder. "I had no idea they made boats this fancy and sophisticated. All of these huge screens and digital instruments look like something out of a sci-fi movie. One that has leather seats and white oak cabinetry everywhere. If I didn't hate the water, I'd probably want something just like this."

"Thanks. I think. She's a stunner for sure, quite the investment in my company. The luxurious features are a bonus, especially when we end up on an extended salvage operation. But it's the horsepower, reliability and generous-sized scuba deck that sold me on her."

"Scuba. You mentioned that before. Are you going to dive right here and search for—for signs of Tanya, assuming she went into the water as the police believe?"

"Yes and no. I won't actually dive unless my scanner indicates a potential hit."

She leaned past him, eyeing the twenty-four-inch Garmin navigation screen. "Scanner? You have cameras to see underwater?"

"Not a typical camera, no. Unless you're in the Bahamas or some other tropical paradise, where the water is crystal clear, you won't be able to see more than a few feet or a few yards. A camera doesn't do you much good under those conditions. *Discovery*'s scanners use sonar, like a bat, and draw a picture on the screen that's similar to a topographical map."

"The kind that shows how high or low land is, like mountain elevations?"

"Exactly that, yes. The instrumentation, including the depth-meter gauge, is sophisticated enough to give a pretty good picture—more or less—of what is at the bottom. Specifically, obstacles, hazards and, if we look in the right place, the item we're searching for."

"Like cars or boats? Is that what you search for most of the time?"

"Those make up a lot of our contracts. But we also get contracted for plenty of other things, like mapping out bodies of water to look for potential hazards to be removed before opening up for water traffic. We've discovered old cemeteries too, from the 1800s, as one example, that the government was forced to dig up and restore somewhere else, and have assisted treasure hunters by eliminating some areas from their searches. The list goes on and on."

"Basically, if anyone needs any mysteries figured out under water, you're the go-to guy."

He smiled. "Go-to company, at least. We're building quite the reputation, which is why your sister zeroed in on us after she went searching the internet for help."

"You haven't mentioned searching for bodies."

"We don't typically do that. But we do come upon them from time to time. It's unavoidable when locating vehicles that went off bridges, for example. That special sonar I mentioned before is what I'll use today to try to locate Tanya. Give me a minute to change and I'll show you." He headed down into the cabin and a few minutes later emerged in a pair of dark blue swim trunks.

Shanna's eyes widened as she took in his change of clothing. His naked chest in particular seemed to hold her attention. When her roaming gaze finally met his, her cheeks flushed a light pink. She cleared her throat and quickly looked away, clearly embarrassed to have been caught staring. Since her staring seemed appreciative and admiring, he didn't mind one bit. It was good to know that she wasn't completely immune to him, especially since he was definitely not immune to her.

"So what's this scanner thing you said you would show me?" she asked. "Or was that a pickup line?"

He grinned. "If it was, did it work?"

For the first time in far too long, she smiled, a true smile that actually reached her deep blue eyes. "The change of clothes worked far better than the scanner line."

If her face got any redder she'd look sunburned. But she didn't back down from her statement or turn away.

He laughed when what he really wanted to do was kiss her. But this wasn't a date. And he didn't want to risk making her uncomfortable if he was misreading her signals. She was already uncomfortable enough on the water. Worrying about a man she'd only just met making a pass at her wasn't a burden he wanted to add to her already full plate.

"The scanner, the sonar, is out here." He stepped around her and headed to the stern, crouching to pop open one of the built-in storage bins. He grabbed a towel, then pulled out the lime-green container that resembled the kind of box that might house a drill. But this was far better and more complicated than any power tool. He opened it and took out the rectangular green-and-white device, holding it up by the long handle attached to the bottom.

Shanna frowned as she stood beside him. "It looks like a computer tablet with a handle."

"That's pretty much what it is, except that it's waterproof. Shanna Hudson, meet my newest and by far coolest toy, AquaEye."

"Aqua what?"

"AquaEye. It's a handheld sonar device made by a company called VodaSafe. But what makes it so special isn't the sonar alone, it's the amazing software that goes with it. This piece of equipment is the main reason your sister asked me to come here."

"She researched search-and-recovery companies and picked you because you have a handheld sonar?"

"Pretty much. Let's say that someone drives their car off a bridge, like I mentioned earlier. Law-enforcement rescue divers go in and try to find the driver and save them. Of course, by the time they get there it's normally a recovery, not an attempt at rescue. But that's what they do. They take the body. My company is left to pull the car out. But finding the car in the first place isn't always as simple as going into the water where the vehicle was believed to have gone. A vehicle can end up being a long distance from where it went in, depending on the depth, currents and obstacles, or lack of them. In some cases someone might have last been seen driving their car and no one even knows they ended up in the water. The police might call us in that situation to search lakes and ponds near major roadways to see if the car went into any of them. Either way, my company locates the vehicle and then works to tow it out of the water."

"But Tanya didn't have a car. And she didn't take either of her parents' cars. So why does that handheld thing make a difference here?"

"This handheld device makes a world of difference because it's specifically programmed to look for sonar signatures that could indicate human remains."

"No way."

"Way. It's cutting-edge. When I heard about it, I got one for us to beta test. I'm not in the business to find human bodies. But there are many times when we locate a vehicle for the police and expect a body to be inside but don't find one. All we typically can do at that point is give the coordinates of the vehicle to the law-enforcement divers so they can perform the search for the person who went into the water with it. Once their part is done and the body is recovered, again, we recover the vehicle. After so many experiences like that, I was frustrated at always having to pull back and wait for law enforcement to stumble around trying to locate the victim. It can be a long, slow process, taking days or even weeks. I wanted to be more proactive and provide better information to them so they could find the remains more quickly."

"How would my sister have known about this…sonar

device, and have asked you to come here to search for Tanya?"

He tapped the AquaEye. "The local news in Charleston did a story about this equipment and highlighted my company as a beta tester. That's why we came up in online searches when your sister was trying to get someone to help here at Mystic Lake. This sonar, and its unique programming, just might give us a chance to bring Tanya's remains home so her family can finally have closure."

She shook her head, her eyes full of wonder as she looked up at him. "A hottie with heart. Imagine that."

He almost choked, then cleared his throat. "Can't say I've ever been called that before."

"Trust me. You have. Just not to your face."

"You must be feeling a lot better. You're smiling again."

She sobered and glanced around, making him regret saying anything. She had a beautiful smile and he hated seeing that haunted look in her eyes.

"I almost forgot we were on the water," she whispered.

He gently tilted her face up toward him. "I'm sorry that I reminded you." In spite of his best intentions, he couldn't resist temptation anymore. He took a chance that he was reading her right and pressed a quick kiss against her forehead. "I'm not the only hottie around here." He winked.

She let out a burst of laughter, then covered her mouth.

Relief swept through him. He'd read her right. And he was glad to have gotten her to laugh again. And glad that she hadn't slapped him for kissing her, even if it wasn't on the lips. He was starting to look forward to returning to her sister's place later. Spending some time with this interesting, beautiful woman in close quarters wouldn't exactly be a hardship. And maybe sometime soon he could give her a real kiss instead of a peck on the forehead. But returning to the cabin wouldn't happen until he finished his work here, so he'd better get to it.

After shrugging into his life jacket again, he opened the starboard-side panel near the rear of the boat to give him access to jump into the water.

"Wait," Shanna called out, her eyes dark and shadowed again as she clung to the railing beside the opening, surprisingly close to the water in spite of her fears. "You're going into the water without a tank and wetsuit and whatever else?"

"I'm not planning on diving just yet. I'm going to swim around at the surface and hold the sonar just below the water to see if it pinpoints any areas I need to search more thoroughly. If it gets a potential hit, that's when I'll get my scuba gear. I honestly don't expect any hits right away. It's been almost a year since her disappearance. Her body, if she went into the lake around here, could have moved quite some distance due to the currents. That's why I perform grid searches. I start at the last known location, or in this case, the last suspected location. Then I spread out from there, tracking on my maps where I've searched and where I still need to search."

"Makes sense. But…if you're swimming, and you need help, I can't… I don't know how to…"

"You can't swim?"

She shook her head. "No. I mean yes. But I haven't, not in a long time. And, honestly, even if I needed to, I don't know that I could. I'd probably drown because the panic would make me freeze." Her cheeks flushed red. "I'm really sorry. I'm not much help out here."

He lightly squeezed her hand. "No apologies. You're doing great. I'm the one who should apologize. When you insisted on coming along I automatically assumed you could swim, or that you could in spite of your anxieties. I should have asked to be sure." He glanced at her life jacket, reassuring himself that it was still secured the way it should be.

"I wanted to come. That's on me. But I wasn't thinking about being your wing man if something happened. I should have been more upfront."

"Don't worry about me," he told her. "The life jacket will save me, if I need saving. All you need to do is sit there and wait."

"But if something does happen—"

"It won't."

"But if it does—"

"Then you'll call nine-one-one. If your phone doesn't have service out here, you can call from the hard-wired satellite phone in the console, beside those fancy screens I showed you earlier. That's it. Nothing else. Promise me you won't go into the water, no matter what."

She looked past him, her face going pale again. "Trust me. I won't." She made her way to one of the seats and sat down. She was holding on so tightly, he could see her knuckles turning white again. "Okay. I'm ready."

He almost decided then and there to cancel the trip, to bring her back to the cabin and return on his own tomorrow. But he'd already seen how stubborn she could be. She'd probably hate him for it. Besides, she'd gone through self-torture just making this trip. She'd likely not forgive him if he didn't at least try to find Tanya after she'd ridden all the way out here.

With one last reassuring smile, he slid into the lake. He treaded water, using his legs to kick just enough to keep his head up. He clutched the sonar device in his right hand and held it slightly below the surface, scanning back and forth.

His first scan was toward shore. When he held up the device to look at the screen, it was clear. No hits. He turned and submerged the device again, sweeping it left and right. Then he lifted it out of the water to look at the screen. This time, it showed an X. He stared at it in surprise. Was it malfunctioning? He truly hadn't expected any hits in this first grid. But he had to rule it out before moving to another area.

As Shanna had said, the police had searched this part of the lake last spring when Tanya was reported missing. They hadn't found anything. He hadn't expected to, either. If the sonar really was picking up human remains, then maybe her body had been pinned by some underwater hazards that the divers hadn't risked searching. That was the only thing that he could think of to explain it still being in this area after so long. Still, that seemed unlikely. Even cars, as large and heavy as they were, usually scraped along the bottom, pushed by currents, ending up surprisingly far away in most cases than where they'd gone into the water. Tanya had been missing since mid-May, nearly a year ago. How could she be right here where she'd first been reported missing? Unless this wasn't where she'd originally gone into the water.

"Is everything okay?" Shanna called out.

He gave her a reassuring nod. "Just double-checking the equipment," he called back, before submerging the scanner and trying again. When he pulled it back up, the X was still there. Something was beneath the surface, about eight feet down. Could it be a tree branch, or rocks, throwing off the sonar? It was still new, still being tested out. But whatever the device was picking up, it was too close to ignore. He had to check it out. And he didn't need his scuba gear to head down eight feet for a quick look. He did, however, need to take off his life jacket or he wouldn't be able to submerge.

He quickly took it off and instead strapped the AquaEye to it so he wouldn't lose it.

"Kaden, what are you doing?" Panic gave Shanna's voice a sharp edge. "Put your life jacket on."

"Be right back," he called out, figuring the quicker he got this over with the faster he could reassure her. Then he drew a deep breath and dove beneath the surface.

The water was darker, murkier than he'd expected, with visibility incredibly limited. He immediately regretted his decision to dive without first getting his equipment, which would have included an underwater flashlight. But he was already at the bottom, so he made the best of it, feeling around to see what might have tripped up the sonar.

Something slimy brushed against his hand. He jerked to the side and squinted in the cloudy water, but didn't see the fish or plant that he assumed he'd touched. The water was so gloomy and dark. It seemed to weigh him down, pressing against his chest, making his lungs burn for air far sooner than they should have. He could normally hold his breath for a good two minutes, even longer if he absolutely had do. He'd been an avid swimmer and diver since he was a kid. But something about this lake seemed…different. Even when he'd been driving his boat through the water, it had seemed as if he was moving through thick sludge in spite of the lake not appearing to be polluted or muddy. He'd definitely had to push the engines more than he'd anticipated. It was almost as if the lake was a living thing that resented his intrusion and was fighting against him.

He shook his head in disgust. The fanciful stories he'd read online about this place were messing with his head-space. He needed to focus, find whatever the sonar had seen down here before he was forced to surface for air.

He sifted his hands through the muck on the bottom, digging through rocks and sticks, pieces of wood. The bottom truly was littered with debris, the kind that could easily catch a swimmer's long hair or loose clothing and add them to the long list of others who'd disappeared in this water.

And if he didn't surface soon, he'd become one of those statistics.

His hand touched another piece of wood. It was hard, unyielding and mired in sticks and muck, just like everything else in this area. He tugged it loose and decided to bring it up to gain a better understanding of the kinds of debris he'd need to be aware of while diving in this lake.

Seconds later, blessed cool spring air rushed into his aching lungs. He bobbed on the surface, treading water, his arms and legs feeling heavy and weighted down. It was the oddest feeling, as if something was trying to suck him back under.

"Kaden! Over here."

He turned, surprised to see Shanna waving at him from the boat a considerable distance away, at least three times the distance from where he'd gone into the water. And there wasn't even much of a current to have pushed him that far.

"Kaden, grab your life jacket. There!" She pointed.

He turned again, to see it floating a few yards away, the sonar device still attached. He lunged for it, grabbing it and holding on. The strange weakness in his limbs was disconcerting and made no sense. It took all his strength to hold on to the jacket and kick toward the boat.

As soon as he reached it, he let out a shaky breath and tossed the life jacket and muck from the lake bed onto the deck.

Shanna's face was pale. He must have scared her by being gone longer than he'd intended. He really should have suited up and gone in with a flashlight and tank. With her fear of the water, it hadn't been fair to leave her alone. From the way she was shaking, he must have terrified her.

"I'm so sorry I worried you." He pulled himself onto the deck. The moment his legs cleared the water, the strange lethargy evaporated. "How long was I under?" He stood and closed the opening before turning around.

Shanna wasn't looking at him. Her body was shaking as she stared down at the bundle of debris and muck he'd tossed onto the boat. Except that it wasn't just debris.

It was a human hand.

Chapter Six

Shanna wrapped her arms around her waist as she sat at a picnic table a good thirty feet from the shoreline, watching the activity on the lake. The police had told Kaden yesterday that it was too late in the afternoon to begin their search of the lake where he'd made that horrific discovery. So they'd all agreed to meet out here this morning.

Neither Kaden nor she had been interested in dinner yesterday, so he'd stayed on his boat to do whatever maintenance boaters did after going boating. He'd spent the night there while Shanna had slept at her sister's cabin. This morning, the two of them had shared a quick, lean breakfast of toast and juice in spite of the kitchen being well-stocked as Cassidy had promised. Neither of them had gotten their appetite back yet. Then he'd left in his boat and she'd left in her car, both of them ending up at the same spot. This place, where he'd discovered that awful, severed hand yesterday afternoon.

There weren't any local police divers, so rather than wait for the state police to arrive with their dive team, Kaden had volunteered to begin the process of recovering the remains. As he dived yet again, this time in scuba gear, three Mystic Lake police officers, including the chief, assisted from their much smaller boat, holding a rope tied to Kaden and tugging it now and then. In answer, Kaden was supposed to tug back so they knew he wasn't in trouble.

She shivered as he disappeared beneath the water for the dozenth time. At least he had people with him to help if he ran into trouble. The only thing that Shanna could have done the previous afternoon was to call 911 if she felt he needed help. If he really had been in trouble, he'd have likely ended up drowning since there was nothing she could have done to save him. She felt so danged useless, frozen on that boat staring at the water and counting down the seconds since he'd disappeared beneath the surface. She'd wanted to dive in, to look for him. But she couldn't seem to move, no matter how hard she'd tried. Fear had held her in place.

Four minutes.

She would have sworn an oath that Kaden had been underwater for four minutes when he'd made that dive without any diving equipment. She'd been on the verge of making that 911 call when he'd finally surfaced. Later, he'd assured her that he couldn't have been down that long. He'd have run out of air. But she'd checked the time on her phone throughout his dive. It had definitely been four minutes. Or, at least, her phone told her it had. Maybe yet another of the anomalies around this allegedly cursed lake was that it somehow messed with electronics. It was either that, or divine intervention had protected him.

She shook her head at her fanciful thoughts, torn between her being determined to wait until all of the bones were recovered, so they could officially confirm that it was Tanya, and wanting to head back home. One thing was for certain. She wasn't ever going out on that lake again. The largest, deepest body of water she ever planned to get close to in the future was a bathtub.

"Hey, there," a friendly voice said as one of the female police officers sat beside her at the picnic table. "How are you holding up?"

Shanna gave her a weak smile. "Okay, I guess. I'm sorry, I forgot—"

"My name? I wouldn't expect you to remember. We only spoke briefly when all of us met up here a couple of hours ago to start the search. I'm Officer Grace O'Brien. That's Chief Dawson and Officers Ortiz and Collier on the boat out there. And you're the private detective that Cassidy has been hounding to come here for quite some time."

Shanna winced. "Guilty as charged."

The policewoman surprised her by pressing Shanna's hand in camaraderie. "Try not to feel guilty. There's no evidence that Tanya Jericho's disappearance was anything sinister that needed your expertise as an investigator. You should feel proud today, proud that you and Mr. Rafferty are likely bringing closure to the Jericho family by bringing Tanya home. Or, at least, helping them accept that she's truly gone so they can lay her to rest."

Shanna nodded her thanks, but guilt was riding her hard. She doubted it would go away until or unless she could confirm that her refusal to help before now hadn't contributed to whatever had happened to Tanya, and whatever the young woman may have suffered.

She watched as Kaden handed a dark plastic bag to one of the officers on the police boat. Then he dived beneath the water yet again. "You really think it's her? Tanya?"

"You don't?"

"I hope it is. Not that I want her to really be…gone. But if it's not her, that means we still don't know what happened, where she is. Her family won't get that closure you mentioned. And someone else's family is going to get some really bad news."

"We don't have anyone else missing, at least not recently. And no one's ever been reported missing in this section of the lake. An unfortunate number of swimmers and boaters do go unaccounted for around here, more than in most lakes—"

"Second only to Lake Lanier, which is allegedly haunted."

O'Brien nodded, her expression solemn. "You've done your homework. Despite our regrettable statistics overall, we've had a pretty good run this past year. The last known person to go missing was Tanya Jericho, last spring. So unless someone else went missing and no one reported them, those remains are hers."

"There was still some tissue on the bones that I saw. If it is her, wouldn't the remains be completely skeletonized by now?"

O'Brien narrowed her eyes, as if taking her first close look at Shanna and trying to figure something out. "You seem awfully nervous about the recovery of that body. I thought as a private investigator that you'd have seen dead bodies before. But the questions you're asking make it seem otherwise. Which is it?"

"I've seen a few bodies in my line of work, more than I'd like. That's not why I'm nervous."

The officer waited, but Shanna wasn't about to discuss her embarrassing fear of water with a woman she'd just met. Or her ridiculous concern for Kaden, a man she'd also only just met, even though it already seemed as if she'd known him for years. Or maybe it was that after being so worried about him yesterday when he'd been underwater so long she felt vested in his safety and far more concerned than made sense, given their short acquaintance.

"I'll take your silence as a reminder to mind my own business." O'Brien smiled. "Not the first time I've been told that. Instead, I'll answer your earlier question. With my background from having been an FBI special agent, I can tell you that while bodies in the water do usually decompose quickly, that's not always the case. In special circumstances, it can take much longer, from a few weeks up to a year or even longer. There are a variety of factors, like temperatures, whether they were clothed when they went into the water, marine-life activity. Around here, I'm learning there's also the Mystic Lake factor to consider. The water is…different than most lakes. It's almost like it's…thicker. We've had champion swimmers tell us that swimming out here is really challenging, that the water seems to weigh you down. Whatever it is that makes it unique could potentially impact the decomposition, likely due to the currents and different chemicals and other elements that make the water the way it is."

"Thicker?"

O'Brien nodded. "That's the word we hear the most. It's a better explanation than to say there are unknown forces at play, like the lake itself is sinister in some way. So we lump all of that together and call it the Mystic Lake factor."

"Doesn't sound very scientific for someone who used to work for the FBI."

"Yes, well, things change once you've been here for a while. Or, I should say, this place changes you."

"How long have you been here?"

"Well, Alannah, my daughter, is five months old. Aidan and I were married a year before I got pregnant and I was here several months prior to that. I guess it's getting close to three years. Longer than I'd realized. But even though I'm a transplant, I became indoctrinated pretty quickly from the day I arrived, working on a case for the FBI. I've learned quite a bit about the myths, rumors and downright lies made up about this place to know what's what."

"So you don't give credence to the legends?"

O'Brien gave her a sharp look, then looked out at the water. "I didn't say that."

Kaden popped up on the surface close to the police boat and handed another black bag to police chief, Beau Dawson.

"How long will it take your coroner—or medical examiner, I guess, in the state of Tennessee—to conduct the autopsy and confirm the victim's identity?"

The policewoman sighed. "Unfortunately, Mystic Lake doesn't have a medical examiner. We'll have to transport the remains to Chattanooga for an autopsy. A drowning victim who's been under water for a year or more isn't likely to come up high on their priority list. If they've got a caseload queued up, it might be several days."

"What about the Jerichos? If they hear about a body being found—"

"Already taken care of. Officer Fletcher—Liza—is over there now, letting them know what's going on. Since you and Mr. Rafferty located the remains while searching for Tanya, Liza is telling them that you're here looking into the case. I hope that's okay."

"Yes, of course. I should have spoken to them already. But I didn't expect…" She motioned toward the water. "This. Not so quickly, anyway. I was going to call and arrange a meeting later today, introduce myself. But this happened yesterday late in the day and…" She shook her head.

As they both watched, Kaden disappeared back underwater. Shanna looked away, too unsettled by what was happening out on the lake to keep watching. O'Brien glanced at her curiously, but didn't pry.

About twenty minutes later, the whine of boat engines had Shanna looking up again. "Looks like they're done. Kaden's boat is heading down river. But he's on the police boat, in his regular clothes again, coming here."

O'Brien nodded "Officer Ortiz is likely piloting Mr. Rafferty's boat to the marina, or wherever Rafferty wants it docked. The chief will need formal statements from you and Rafferty, which is probably why he's on the boat with Dawson and Collier heading to shore. Are you going to give him a ride to the station, or should I?"

"I've got my car. He can ride with me."

"Okay, thanks. I'll ask Liza to pick up Ortiz and Collier once they have both of the boats docked and bring them to the station. I'll meet you there." O'Brien headed toward the lake.

As the boat got closer, Shanna noticed the piles of dark bags at one end. How tragic that a person's entire life was now condensed down to those sad little bags.

A minute later, the boat idled up near the water's edge. Dawson and Kaden took turns hopping over the side of the idling boat onto the grass.

With them off the boat, the last officer, Collier, turned it and took off in the direction that Ortiz had gone with Kaden's boat.

Chief Dawson stopped to talk to O'Brien a short distance away. Kaden, his hair wet and disheveled, headed toward Shanna. His face was grim as he looked down at her, as if trying to figure out the best way to tell her what he'd found.

"It's Tanya, isn't it?" she asked, already nodding.

His jaw tightened. "No. The... What I found down there

wasn't Tanya Jericho. There wasn't much left, not enough to make an ID. But Chief Dawson was certain the pelvis bones were that of a male. Even if he's wrong, judging by the length of the femur and the tibia, the victim was at least ten inches taller than the missing teen."

Disappointment had her shoulders slumping. "I suppose it would have been a miracle to find her on our first try. You said as much earlier. It makes sense that it's not her. If it was, I'd have expected the police to have found her when she originally went missing. After all, you discovered that body really close to the area where her parents thought she'd gone that day. Do the police have any idea who he might be? Officer O'Brien didn't seem to know about any missing-persons reports that might account for another accidental drowning out here."

"Whoever he is, there's more to his death than an accidental drowning. That hand I found didn't detach from the rest of the skeleton on its own. There were tool marks on the bones."

Shanna stared at him with growing dread. "Are you saying that someone…cut off his hand?"

He gave her a tight nod. "Hopefully the autopsy will tell us that it happened after he died. Regardless, drowning victims don't have their skeletons chopped up. This guy, whoever he is, was murdered. Which begs the question of—"

"Whether Tanya was murdered, too."

Chapter Seven

Following Officer Grace O'Brien, Chief Beau Dawson, and Shanna into the Mystic Lake police station, Kaden paused just inside. If it wasn't for the gold letters above the glass door he'd just come through, he wouldn't have known this building housed the police. He certainly hadn't realized it when he'd arrived in town yesterday, admiring the row of quaint shops fronting the cobblestone street out front that bordered the lake. His assumption was that this was the tourist-focused part of town and that the government offices and other businesses were clustered somewhere else.

"Not what you expected?" Shanna's words echoed his thoughts.

"I suppose it's got everything a police department needs. A set of holding cells to the right, vending machines and the chief's office to the left. A glass-walled conference room along the back wall. The small cluster of four desks here in the squad room. It's just so—"

"Small?"

He smiled. "My Realtor sister would call it cozy. Only four officers plus the chief to take care of the entire town seems like it would be a struggle. Then again, I haven't seen that many people since arriving. I wonder what the population is in Mystic Lake."

The chief, obviously having heard them since he was only a few feet away talking to O'Brien, seemed amused as he joined them. O'Brien headed into the conference room.

"Less than two thousand locals," he said. "A third of those only live here part-time, in vacation and hunting cabins high up in the mountains. Two to three officers per thousand is usually enough in a small town like this, where the crime rate is low. But I wouldn't mind having a few more permanent officers to help when we get a flood of tourists during the summer months. We make up the difference by contracting with other law-enforcement agencies to temporarily beef up our staff during the busy times, or to help cover us when our staff takes vacations. Which reminds me, we don't have a contract with you for your services. But we'll definitely reimburse you for what you did for us today. Send me the bill."

Kaden nodded his thanks.

The chief studied him for a moment. "You don't plan on billing me, do you?"

"No reason to. I knew what I was in for when I agreed to come here at Cassidy Tate's request. I'm covering the cost of this trip, searching for Tanya Jericho pro bono. I just wish it was her we'd found today."

Dawson nodded. "Tanya's an only child. Her family's been through hell. I'd like nothing more than to bring their daughter home. But thanks to you, we'll at least have answers for another family, once we figure out who you found. On the way here, I sweet-talked the Chattanooga medical examiner to put a rush on trying to ID the remains once we transport them. But as you can imagine, with no personal effects or even clothing to help with the identification, it's going to be hard to figure out the identity of our John Doe. None of our locals have gone missing, so it's likely a tourist who went swimming or fell off a boat and never came back up. Unfortunately, we get some of those cases most years and rarely recover a body."

Shanna addressed the chief. "How will you determine the victim's identity with mostly bones to rely on? DNA?"

Chief Dawson shook his head. "Unlikely. At least, not initially. I imagine we can extract DNA from the bone marrow, or even some of the hair that was found with the skull. But unless the victim had a reason to have his DNA in one of our national databases, that won't be how we figure out who he is. Dental records, same story. Unless we have something to compare to, they won't help us ID anyone early on in the investigation. It will require old-fashioned door-to-door knock-and-talks to see if anyone in town has a friend or relative they don't see or hear from often and don't even realize could be missing. They can check, see if they can contact him. If not, we'll add that name to a list to research. Hopefully, if the guy's not a local and went swimming on his own without anyone knowing, he'll be listed in a missing-persons report in a neighboring county. The medical examiner will give us information like height, race, age range. It will likely take quite a bit of time, unfortunately, to figure out his identity."

The sad look on Shanna's face had Kaden wondering how she dealt with investigating other disappearances without it crushing her spirit. Maybe those weren't the types of cases she was normally involved in.

As if noticing her sadness as well, the chief added, "Don't give up hope. We're only getting started. Chattanooga PD has agreed to send over some forensic divers tomorrow morning to sift the lake bed near where the remains were found. They might find a wallet or a phone, something to help us figure out who this guy might be."

He motioned toward the glass-walled conference room where O'Brien was waiting. "If you two are ready to give your formal statements about what happened yesterday, that will help get things rolling."

Kaden motioned for Shanna to precede him.

Instead, she looked up at Dawson. "May I assume some quid pro quo? Once we provide statements, can you help us by handing over anything you have on Tanya Jericho's investigation?"

His eyebrows raised but he nodded. "I'll get one of our officers to print out everything we can share."

"We need the whole—"

He held up a hand to stop her. "Ms. Hudson, there are some things that I can't turn over. Not a lot, nothing that will impede your investigation. But there are a few details we'll keep confidential to help us rule out false confessions in the future, in the unlikely event that her disappearance was sinister in nature."

She blinked. "So you have considered it could be murder. I'm surprised to hear that. Cassidy said your office dismissed the possibility."

"And I'm trusting you not to tell her otherwise." Dawson's face was grim. "You make a living as an investigator. As does Mr. Rafferty, to an extent. You should both understand how important it is not to muddy the investigative waters. We're considering everything in Ms. Jericho's disappearance. But we don't want rumors to spread and hurt her family, or our investigation. Telling your sister, who is extremely close to the Jericho family, isn't a good idea. Are we clear?"

She hesitated, then nodded. "Clear."

"Then I'll get Officer Ortiz to make those copies."

Just as he spoke, the door opened and officers Ortiz, Collier and Fletcher stepped inside. Ortiz stopped, his gaze shifting back and forth suspiciously. "Why is everyone staring at me?"

"I've got an opportunity for you," the chief said.

Ortiz groaned and Collier laughed.

"Thank you, Collier," the chief said. "You just volunteered to transport the remains to the medical examiner. They're stored in a body bag in the back of my police SUV." He tossed his keys to a very unhappy looking Officer Collier. "Might as well take care of it right now."

"Yes, sir," he grumbled, as he turned and headed out the door.

The third officer, Liz Fletcher, didn't say a word. Instead, she headed into the conference room to wait with O'Brien.

"Smart woman," Dawson said. "Ortiz, you could learn from Fletcher's example."

Ortiz smiled good-naturedly. "I'm sure I could, sir." He handed a set of keys to Kaden. "Your incredible yacht is parked at the Tate cabin, as you requested. If this lake wasn't landlocked, I swear I'd have taken off to unknown destinations with her. She's amazing."

Kaden pocketed the keys. "She's a working boat, not a yacht. But I can take your subtle hint. I'll offer you a ride before I head back to South Carolina."

"Was I subtle? I sure didn't mean to be." Ortiz laughed. "Go ahead, Chief. Hit me with my so-called opportunity."

Kaden pressed his hand against the small of Shanna's back and loudly whispered, "This is *our* opportunity, to make an escape before he realizes we're the reason for his assignment."

She smiled and hurried with him toward the conference room while Ortiz's shoulders slumped at what the chief was telling him.

Chapter Eight

Kaden was surprised to see that the sun was already setting by the time that Shanna parked her car beside his truck at the cabin. But recovery work always seemed to take longer than expected. Diving was something he truly enjoyed, in spite of the grim reason for it today. And time seemed to fly whenever he was in the water. Add to that the interviews at the police station, and the day was essentially over.

"You coming?" Shanna paused in front of the car.

He hopped out, then looked down the hill toward the dock. He was relieved to see his boat solidly tied where Officer Ortiz had told him it would be. Ortiz had even hung the bumpers over the side to keep the boat from getting damaged from rubbing against the dock.

"It *is* a beautiful boat," Shanna said, following the direction of his gaze. "Even though I never want to get on it again."

"Want to talk about it?"

"Your boat?"

"The reason you're afraid of the water."

"Nope."

Disappointment shot through him. He respected her desire for privacy. But he also knew burdens were easier to bear when they were shared.

When he realized she was carrying the box of police file copies that Ortiz had given them, he took it from her.

"I can carry that," she insisted.

"My mama taught be better."

She smiled. "I'll bet I'd like your mom."

"I know you would. You're a lot alike. Smart, funny and beautiful."

"Are you flirting with me, Mr. Rafferty?" she teased, echoing his earlier question to her on his boat.

"Just making an observation," he replied.

Her laughter was a light tinkling sound that sent a frisson of pleasure straight to his groin. He enjoyed everything about her. But the logical part of him kept sending up warning bells. When this week was over, they'd both go their separate ways. They had to. Their entire lives and careers were based in two completely different parts of the country. He had no desire to leave his business in South Carolina to head to…where had she said her business was? West Virginia? He imagined she wouldn't want to pull up roots and start over in Charleston, either. And he didn't get the vibe that she was the type to engage in a fling without a commitment. Which meant he needed to keep a tight rein on the wicked attraction searing his veins every time she smiled, laughed, or impressed the hell out of him with her bravery and intelligence.

Once inside the cabin, he set the box on the kitchen table, then made sure to lock the door. When he turned around, Shanna was standing a few feet away with her hands on her hips.

"That reminds me." She nodded toward the lock he'd

just turned. "It's high time you gave me back my gun. It's not just bears I need to be concerned about around here. There's a killer on the loose." She held out her hand.

"Do you honestly think I would have gone into the police station with a gun?"

She considered that question, then slowly lowered her hand. "I guess not. And it's not like you'd have had it on you when you were diving."

"It's on the boat. I'll go get it."

She put her hand on his arm, stopping him as he reached for the lock. That hand was soft and warm. And if he didn't stop thinking like that he'd never survive the remainder of the week, not without a lot of cold showers.

"Keep it," she said. "You plan on continuing to sleep on the boat, right? You'll need protection."

He unlocked the door. "It's your gun. As long as you don't plan on trying to shoot me again, I'll return it. Lock the door behind me. I've got my key." He headed outside.

An hour later, they'd both finished another light dinner, this time sandwiches they'd made in the well-stocked kitchen. After cleaning up, they sat at the table with both of their case folders, as well as what the police had given them today.

Kaden motioned toward the stacks of papers and photographs. "That's a lot of dots to connect. How can you possibly perform the investigation in a week? Less, since this is day two and it's almost over. Maybe you should leave it to the police and let me finish searching the areas of the lake most likely to produce results. If you try to make heads or tails of all of this, you won't have any time left for your planned vacation."

She sighed. "You're right. I can pretty much kiss my vacation goodbye. But I couldn't give up on the investigation now, not after seeing Tanya's pictures and reading just a few of the interviews. I'm already emotionally invested. I'll do what I can until Cassidy and Gavin return. After that, I have no choice but to return to West Virginia. We have other cases my investigators are working on and I'll need to review those and brainstorm additional avenues to explore. It might be another month before I can come back. But I'm determined to see this through to the end, whatever it takes and however long it takes."

"I would think a PI would make a point of not getting emotionally invested in their work. That could lead to a lot of heartbreak, and a heck of a lot of stress above and beyond the norm."

She shrugged. "I try not to. Most of my investigations are financial in nature—follow the money. Or the usual husband-and-wife-cheating-on-each-other scenario and someone wanting evidence for the divorce hearing. Those don't bother me. But when the person at the heart of the investigation is completely innocent, like Tanya, a sophomore in high school, it's pretty impossible not to get caught up in the emotions around that. Especially empathy for the loved ones left behind. It takes its toll. That's why I don't take those cases very often." She held up her hands as if in surrender. "I appreciate the advice. But it's already too late on this one. I'm all in." She cocked her head, studying him. "It can't be easy for you either, finding what you found. And then helping the police to recover…the rest."

"That was a first, for sure. Usually law enforcement wants to immediately take over the recovery process if there's a person involved. Can't say that I want to do ever do that again."

She crossed her arms on top of the table in one of the few spots not covered with papers. "But you still plan on continuing? Searching for another victim… Tanya?"

He arched an eyebrow. "I'm already invested."

She smiled. "Touché."

"Besides, spending more time with you will more than make up for whatever else I go through."

"Ha. I'll poll you in a few days to see whether you still feel that way. I've been told I can be way too bossy and too aggressive. Although the person who most often told me that used a much less polite word."

"Mind if I ask who that person was?"

Her posture stiffened.

"Forget I asked," he said. "None of my business."

Her gorgeous blue eyes stared into his. "Actually, it is your business. I mean, I hope it doesn't really impact you, but if you do plan on continuing to work with me—"

"I do. I can't go near the crime scene tomorrow since the police divers will be there. And it won't take long to sweep that section of the river once I'm allowed access again. Might as well spend my extra time helping you, if I can."

She nodded, looking grateful. "Then you need to be aware of a potential…complication. The person I've had a lot of troubles with—"

"Who thinks you're too aggressive?"

"Yes. His name is Troy Warren. My ex-boyfriend. We dated for only a couple of months. The warning signs were there from day one. But my hormones convinced me to ignore the red flags."

He chuckled. "Good-looking guy, I take it?"

"I thought so. But it only took a few weeks for his ugly to come out. He's…controlling, to put it mildly. Called me all the time. Texted nonstop. Got jealous when I went out with friends, regardless of whether they were male or female. Kept showing up at my office to check on me."

Kaden could feel his inner caveman wanting to come out, to find this Troy and give him a lesson on how to treat a woman. He reached across the table and took her hand in his. "Did he hurt you, Shanna?"

She stared at their joined hands, then gently pulled her hand back. "Only once. I had him arrested, filed a restraining order. That was the day I broke up with him, obviously. As so many do, though, he's largely ignored the order. I had him arrested just a week before I came here because he kept texting, calling and showing up outside my house. He made bail and disappeared. Haven't heard from him since. Honestly, the silence, not knowing where he is, has me more jumpy than when he was openly harassing me. Which is why I felt I should warn you. I don't know if his violence would escalate beyond what happened, given the chance. But since you're around me you should be careful, just in case he does show up here. I'll text you his picture."

"Is that why you brought your gun?"

"It definitely factored into my decision."

He wanted to reassure her that he'd protect her. But it was a catch-22. Although they clicked together as if they'd been friends a long time, the truth was that they didn't know each other all that well. Acting as if he wanted to be her bodyguard at this point could make him seem like the controlling one, like the ex she'd fled. Making her uncomfortable around him was the last thing he wanted to do. Which meant the next time he was tempted to take her hand in his, or even kiss her forehead as he'd done earlier, he'd have to quash those desires. She was coming off a bad relationship and didn't need to worry that he was coming on to her. That, and their lives being based so far apart meant one thing. Shanna was off-limits. He knew it. But his heart, not to mention the rest of his body, was going to take some convincing.

Her gaze searched his. "I'm sorry. That was a lot to lay on you. If you want to head back to Charleston now and leave all of this to me, I totally get it."

He was shaking his head before she finished speaking. "You haven't managed to chase me away just yet. And both of us have businesses to get back to. A week is all we've got. Let's make the most of it and see if we can figure out what happened to Tanya. Her parents deserve to know." He motioned toward the ominous stacks of paperwork. "My investigations are completely different than the type you do. You're the lead here. How do we start?"

"Thank you, Kaden. Thanks for your support, especially even after you're aware of the potential danger." This time she was the one who reached across the table and took his hand in hers.

A spark of desire shot straight through him. But he did his best to keep any sign of that from his expression. "Of course. We're in this together. For a few more days, anyway."

She pulled her hand back. "I'll check with the police back home tomorrow to see if they've located Troy yet. At least if they have, that's one less thing to worry about."

"You mean besides a killer being in Mystic Lake, a killer whose identity we have no clue about? Let alone the identity of his victim?"

"Right. Besides that. Heck of a vacation, huh?"

"At least it won't be boring."

They both laughed and she began scooting some of the piles of papers to the side. Then she retrieved a yellow legal pad and pen for him from the brown leather satchel she'd set beside the table earlier, after they'd finished eating. For herself, she pulled out a laptop and set it in front of her.

He motioned toward the legal pad and computer. "If that's what you brought when you were planning to do nothing, you need some serious coaching on how to relax away from work."

"My satchel of supplies and my computer are my security blankets. I always take them with me. Always be prepared, right?"

"Are you quoting the Boy Scouts to me?"

She blinked, then grinned. "I guess I am. It's a good motto."

He laughed and nodded his agreement.

She picked up one of the larger stacks of papers and set it in the middle. "This is the official copy of Tanya's investigation file from the police. On most of my investigations, like the divorce cases, I have the luxury of time on my side. But we don't here, so we'll have to take some substantial shortcuts and hope we don't miss anything. Where I'd usually try to start the investigation pretty much from scratch, not relying on someone else's work, on this one we'll need to rely a lot on the foundation the police built. We'll note any inconsistencies or holes that will need more follow-up. But we can't start from nothing and hope to make enough headway to make a difference fast. I'll need you to be my devil's advocate, the person to question everything I do so you can help me see any gaps."

"Makes sense. But I'm at a disadvantage. I read everything your sister sent and used that to formulate a plan of where I'd scan the lake. I'm not sure what to do aside from that. Do we go talk to Tanya's family? Her friends at school? Try to get a better timeline of what happened the day she disappeared?"

"All of that, to an extent. But, again, we have to take some shortcuts. The police investigation, at least initially, would have been focused more on quick action to find someone they believed could still be alive. That's very different from what we're doing now, trying to find a body."

She swallowed, obviously feeling sad about Tanya, then continued. "We're more in the cold-case phase of the investigation and need to look at it that way. We'll build on what was done, and try to narrow everything down as much as possible to see who we actually need to reinterview, so as to cause the least distress to the family."

"Officer Fletcher mentioned she'd notified Tanya's family that we're looking into her disappearance," he reminded her. "Do you still want to talk to them?"

"Probably. But let's review the reports from all of their previous interviews to be sure it's necessary. I'd rather not bother them if we don't have to. Let's organize everything into piles that are logically related. All interview reports can go in one stack. Any physical evidence reports, like logs of what may have been seen or taken from Tanya's bedroom, her school locker, anything the police may have collected from the outdoor area where we were today, let's stack those together. Photographs should go in a separate stack too. Once we get all of the information sorted, we can go through each group together."

"And after we do that? What's next?"

"Normally, interviews and reinterviews. Then, I'd dive into cell-phone records, the missing person's computer, a health-tracking device if they wore one to see if we could get location data from it. Really, any technological devices associated with the missing person to help formulate who they've been talking to, what was going on in their life at the time they went missing and where they might last have been. I'd also look for a journal, or diary. Those can be a gold mine of information about daily activities and people the missing person has been interacting with, people her parents might not even know about. Many young girls keep diaries or journals without their parents ever knowing."

She powered up her computer.

He chuckled. "Doesn't sound intimidating at all. I'm sure if we don't take time to eat or sleep, we can get it done."

"Right? I know it's a lot. And that's not even all that I want to do on Tanya's case. We'll have to prioritize, decide what we think we can accomplish versus what we'll have to set aside. At least for now." She tapped her computer keys, presumably entering a password. "I definitely want to research her social-media accounts looking for anything suspicious, maybe someone bothering her online, or references she made, posts, telling us her plans in the weeks and days leading up to when she went missing so we can establish a solid timeline. I'd love to check any forensics reports too, see what the police may have found that Cassidy and Tanya's parents don't know about. But we're going to do all that as one step, or as few steps as possible. I don't want to overwhelm you, so I'll stop right there."

"Too late. I'm totally overwhelmed. I wouldn't have thought of half of that on my own. The main thing I wanted to know when I started my own research before coming here was whether she could swim, and whether she was the type to get near the water."

Her eyebrows raised. "Those are exactly the sorts of questions we need to explore. You might have more of an instinct for this sort of work than you realized."

"Doubtful. I'm just the kind of guy always focused on water. That's my job."

She shivered. "I'm grateful there are people like you to do that. I sure couldn't. Looks like we're a good pair. Our skills complement each other's. Maybe we'll get lucky and solve this together. But we honestly won't have a chance if the police didn't do a lot of the important groundwork—like cell-phone records and forensic searches of her cell phone and other technology. That stuff takes a lot of time. If our base of information from them *is* solid, and if we build an accurate timeline, then our work should point us to where we should search. If it all goes back to the lake, then it's on you to find her remains. But if this isn't a simple drowning in a place that likes to keep its bodies and hold on to them, then it could be something else entirely."

"Murder. Possibly connected with the body we found."

"That's a leap I wouldn't normally consider this early in an investigation. But, yes. I think we have to explore that as a potential theory as part of our short-cuts."

He sat silent for a moment, taking it all in. "Then we need to look into our John Doe. Search for connections between him and Tanya. Right?"

"Absolutely." Glancing at the dark windows that formed the corner of the cabin where the table was positioned, she asked, "What time do you normally turn in for the night?"

If he hadn't cautioned himself about trying to quash his burning attraction for her, he'd make some lame sexy joke in answer to that question. But he had to focus. Keep the personal stuff out of this.

No matter how much he longed to make it far more personal and a hell of a lot more intimate.

He checked the dive watch that he always wore, and winced. "It's a lot later than I realized. But it doesn't matter. I'm keyed up and won't be able to sleep anytime soon. If you're okay staying up for a while, count me in."

"I was hoping you'd say that." She moved half of the stacks of paper toward him and pulled the others closer to her. "We'll get as much done as we can tonight. Then, tomorrow, be prepared to get going really early."

"Where to?"

"The scene of the crime."

Chapter Nine

Shanna shook her head in exasperation and shifted on the picnic bench to make herself more comfortable. "I can't believe there are, what, twenty-five, thirty rubberneckers out here at the scene of the crime? You'd think the police would rope off the entire area to keep people from potentially interfering as the divers search for evidence and more remains this morning."

"Isn't a rubbernecker someone who slows traffic because they're gawking at a car-accident on the side of the road?" Kaden asked, from his seat beside her.

"I'm pretty sure it applies to anyone who's being nosy, watching some event that has nothing to do with them and getting in the way. Not that they can see all that much, anyway, with all the mist on the lake this morning."

He chuckled. "The mist is already clearing. As to the audience, the police officers are watching the crowd, just like us. I'm sure they'll make sure no one interferes." He pointed to her laptop screen, which displayed pictures she'd uploaded from the police investigation folder last night. "Having so many curious onlookers out here is a blessing in disguise. I've already identified five of them by comparing them to those pictures. Most appear to know each other, probably locals. I'll do what I can to get pictures without being obvious. If John Doe's killer is out here watching the recovery like you think he might be, we should come out of here with his picture. If nothing else, it might help the police with their investigation. And if the same person did something to Tanya, it can helps ours too. Win-win."

"Are you always this happy at nine o'clock in the morning?" she griped.

"Are you always this grumpy?"

She cursed beneath her breath, making him laugh.

"Oh, got another one." He wrote a name on his legal pad.

She glanced at it. "Jessica DeWalt. Wait. Isn't she the head cheerleader from the local high school?"

"*Was* the head cheerleader. She graduated the same school year that Tanya went missing. There are several graduates from last year's senior class here, all of whom were interviewed by the police last spring. The odd thing is that they're not mingling together. They're standing or sitting around in different areas. It's a small town, even smaller school. You'd think they'd all know each other, wouldn't you?"

"Probably." She glanced around at the other picnic tables scattered around the sloped hill above the lake where the Chattanooga police divers were searching. After a few minutes of casually looking, she nodded. "You're right. It's as if they're purposely avoiding each other. You saw the football team's quarterback over there, right? By that tree? He and the cheerleader would have to know each other."

"Sam Morton. Maybe they didn't like each other at school. That could explain it."

"Maybe." She opened a new document on her computer and made some notes before pulling up the pictures again.

"Give me your list. I'll focus on trying to ID everyone while you subtly take more photographs."

"You got it." He held his phone in one hand while he made scrolling motions with the other, as if he was surfing the internet. But every now and then he'd zoom in on someone and take their picture.

"Are you sure you haven't done this kind of work before?" she asked. "You're pretty good at it."

"If that's a job offer, I'm not sure you can afford me."

She laughed, then sobered as a diver surfaced and motioned for one of the forensics guys on the dive boat to take something from him. "I think they found another bone."

Kaden nodded as he snapped a picture in their direction, then pulled up the photograph and zoomed in. "Wait. That's not a bone. That's—"

"A steel rod. Like the kind they implant in bones when they've been shattered. Which means—"

"They'll be able to trace it."

"Or we can." She minimized the photos and typed in the address for the Mystic Lake High School website.

He hovered over her shoulder, watching the screen.

"Take pictures," she reminded him. "We need to identify all the onlookers." She blinked, then looked up at him. "I'm being bossy and aggressive, aren't I?"

He slowly shook his head. "No. You're being the boss, as you should be. You're heading the investigation. I'm your helper. Forget what Troy told you. Those are monikers insecure jerks put on women to try to make themselves feel more superior. Don't let him get to you."

Her eyes actually started tearing up. "Remind me again why some lucky woman hasn't snapped you up as a husband yet?"

He opened his mouth as if to respond, then seemed to think better of it and simply shrugged.

Her face heated. She'd expected one of his flirty replies. Maybe she was making more of the attraction between them than there really was. Or maybe the attraction was mainly on her side and he was just the kind of guy who was nice and made you feel good about yourself, without meaning anything deeper by it. She cleared her throat and started typing again. "We need more pictures. Please."

"Peyton Holloway."

"What?"

He held up his phone, showing the photograph he'd just snapped. "Prom queen. Another recently graduated senior. Most of the people out here this morning are older, the retiree type who can check out what's going on without worrying about missing work. Sure is odd that the younger ones watching the recovery of a body in the lake are mostly kids from Tanya's school. You'd think they'd be at college, or working right now."

Shanna swiped through several more screens on the school website. "Here's the one I was looking for. Tristan Cargill."

He set his phone on the picnic table and looked over her shoulder again. "Another senior who graduated last year. I haven't seen him here. Why did you bring up his photograph?"

"I remembered reading his interview, the opening discussion where the police make small talk to establish rapport. He was in a boating accident several months before graduation, shattered his left leg. He was in a wheelchair for a while but was walking with a cane when it was time to head down the aisle to get his diploma."

"Shattered his leg?" Kaden took his phone and zoomed

in on the picture he'd taken of the diver handing what he'd found to a forensics tech. "It might be long enough to stabilize a femur. Or a tibia. But I sure hope our John Doe isn't another teenager."

"Preaching to the choir."

Neither of them spoke for a while. They sat quietly, openly watching the flurry of activity taking place on the lake. When the news came, in the form of Officer O'Brien hurrying over to them as she put her cell phone away, it was no surprise to learn that their John Doe had been identified, by following up on the serial number on the steel rod.

It was Tristan Cargill.

"What are the odds?" O'Brien said. "A local high-school kid is found murdered in the same area where another missing high-school kid is believed to have disappeared? I don't think Jericho's disappearance should be treated as a potential drowning anymore."

"I agree," Shanna said. "Although it still might be, it's not much of a leap to think the two could be connected."

O'Brien looked around. "Everyone here is a local. If the killer came back to visit the scene of his crime today, he's no stranger. He's one of us." Her eyes took on a haunted look. "And if Tanya was killed, murdered, and it's the same perpetrator, we may have another serial killer on our hands. We may be looking for more bodies."

"Another serial killer?" Kaden glanced at Shanna. "You don't seem surprised to hear that there's already an active serial killer in this area."

"That's because he's not active. That case is closed. My sister told me about it."

"That's right," O'Brien said. "The killer, well, he's not a threat to anyone anymore. And that all happened long before Tristan Cargill was killed." She looked around at the curious faces turned their way, then lowered her voice. "I hope no one else heard that. I need to perform the notification before Tristan's family finds out from someone else." She started to turn away, then paused. "We'll obviously be actively working on Tanya's disappearance again to see if there's a link between these two cases. I recommend that you both back down, go home. If the killer knows you're looking into any deaths for which he's responsible, it could be dangerous for you. Cassidy will understand you stopping your search." Without waiting for a reply, she hurried toward her police SUV, which was parked where the road ended.

Shanna began furiously typing on her computer.

Kaden sighed. "You don't plan on stopping, do you?"

"Nope."

"I didn't think so. Guess I'll hang around, too, to keep you out of trouble."

She rolled her eyes and continued typing.

"What are you doing there?" he asked.

"Jumping to conclusions and letting my theory lead me instead of the evidence."

"Isn't that what we're not supposed to do?"

She stopped typing. "Yes. We're short-cutting, remember? Seeing where we can go with what we have. Two teens from the same school in a tiny town go missing or are murdered within days, weeks, or months of each other depending on the medical examiner's conclusions about Tristan Cargill's time of death. We'd be idiots for not thinking they could be related. O'Brien thinks the same thing. You heard her."

"She's also part of the same police force that hasn't found Tanya and wouldn't have found John Doe on their own. Emulating them and jumping to conclusions doesn't sound like the right way to go here, at least not based on your earlier cautions."

Her face heated. "I hate having my own words thrown back at me."

"Then you're really not going to like this. I have a theory too."

"Okay. What is it?"

"We already discussed how odd it was that so many of the school's recently graduated seniors were out here. What if the killer is one of them?"

She glanced around, a chill going down her spine. "I couldn't even begin to pick one of them as a suspect. They're all so young, innocent looking. But it's not like killers go around with an M tattooed on their foreheads so we can pick them out."

"That would make it too easy," he teased, then motioned behind her. "Maybe we can do one of those shortcuts you mentioned and talk to someone who likely knew all the other teens, including Tanya and Tristan."

She glanced over her shoulder. A young brunette was standing off on her own by a thick oak tree, her hand to her throat as she watched the divers at the lake.

"The prom queen," Shanna whispered. "The most popular girl in school. She had to know both of our victims."

"Looks like she's leaving."

"Watch my laptop." Shanna jumped up and hurried after the departing girl.

Chapter Ten

"This was a bad idea." Kaden shifted on his feet and leaned against the porch railing of Cassidy Tate's cabin. "We're wasting time we could be spending following other potential leads while waiting for a prom queen who isn't going to show."

"Her name is Peyton Holloway. She'll show."

"What makes you so sure?"

"Because of the deal I made with her by the lake. She was extremely agitated to be seen talking to me after I was seen talking to the police. I left her alone only after she promised to come here."

"And you believed her?"

"Since I warned her that I'd pressure the police to bring her in for questioning if she didn't, yeah, I'm pretty sure she'll be here."

"Brutal." He grinned.

"Whatever works. As nervous as she was it seems as if she may know something. I just hope it's a lead that will take us to Tanya."

He straightened away from the railing. "Looks like we're about to find out. That's the blue Mazda she drove earlier coming up your driveway."

Shanna looked past him. "Score."

The sedan seemed like a toy as it pulled up beside Kaden's huge black Ford F-250 truck. He turned back toward the cabin. "I'll get us some drinks. As pale as she is, looks like she'll need one. Or two."

"No alcohol," Shanna warned. "She's not legal."

"Well, I need one." He headed inside.

A few minutes later, a very nervous young woman was sitting on the edge of one of the recliners in the Tate cabin's main room with Shanna and Kaden sitting across from her on the couch. But other than saying hello, she'd barely spoken.

"Ms. Holloway," Kaden said. "Would you feel less nervous about answering questions if I leave?" He started to get up, but she waved him back down.

She drew a shaky breath. "I'm sorry. It's just... I guess I'm in shock. When I heard that policewoman say they'd found Tristan, I—I couldn't believe it. I didn't even know he was missing."

When she didn't continue, Shanna asked, "Why were you so afraid to speak to us back by the lake?"

Her dark brown eyes widened in surprise. "I wasn't afraid. I just didn't want to. You have no idea what the police put us through after Jericho went missing. I'd rather avoid that again if I can. The reason I agreed to speak to you is because you're Mrs. Tate's sister. She did a lot for me in school. I probably wouldn't have graduated without her help."

"She'll be happy to hear about your appreciation. You said the police put 'us' through a lot. Who did you mean by 'us'?"

"Um, you know. Us kids, from school. I swear the cops

grilled everyone who'd ever passed Jericho in a hallway to see if we knew anything. It was ridiculous."

"Jericho. Is that how the kids referred to her at school?"

"Huh? No. I mean... I don't know. I didn't even know her. We never associated with each other. Not once."

"Her name is Tanya."

"Sure. Okay. What did you want to ask me?"

Kaden sat back against the couch and crossed his arms. He didn't want to assume anything about Peyton just because she was one of the popular kids at school. But the way she was referring to Tanya, as if she was beneath her, tended to confirm the clichés rather than dispel them. He couldn't help wondering whether Tanya was bullied by some of the popular kids, maybe even Peyton Holloway.

"You said you didn't know that Tristan was missing. Since you used his first name, can I assume he was a friend?"

"He is...was."

"But you didn't know he was missing."

"Well, no. But, I mean, since graduation a lot of us kind of...went our own way, you know? It's what people do."

"You graduated last May?"

"Yeah. Almost a year ago." She shook her head. "Wow. Time flies."

"When is the last time you saw Tristan? Or heard from him?"

She chewed her lip a moment. "I guess...it would have been at the graduation after-party." Her knuckles whitened as she clasped her hands together.

"I'm sorry, Peyton," Shanna said. "I understand the events at the lake were quite a shock. But I need to understand the lay of the land around here, being an outsider and all. My sister, Mrs. Tate, wanted me to look into Tanya's disappearance and I'm hoping you can help by answering our questions."

Peyton chewed her bottom lip. "How did he die?"

"The cause of death will have to be determined by a medical examiner."

Her hands fisted in frustration. "What do you want from me?"

Kaden gave her a reassuring smile. "I'm sure you're a busy woman and we appreciate your time. Ms. Hudson and I are trying to locate Tanya Jericho to help give her parents closure. You were one of the key leaders at school, from what we've heard. So we're hoping you can tell us what you know about Tanya."

As he'd hoped, hearing him call her a leader had her puffing up with self-importance. "Yes, well, I had some influence, for sure. But like I said, that girl—Tanya—wasn't one of us. I mean, wasn't in my circle of friends. I doubt I can really tell you anything about her."

"What about Tristan Cargill?" Shanna asked. "Did he go swimming in that area a lot? Or boating?"

"No. Never. That's not an area where we, I mean he, would ever hang out. Wrong side of town, you know?"

"No. I don't know. Can you explain it to me?"

Peyton let out an impatient breath. "That's not one of the nicer parts of the lake. And it's dangerous, with steep drop-offs. My friends and I hung out in the more, you know, exclusive areas."

"Then why were you and so many of your high-school classmates out in that area today?"

"The same reason everyone else was. To see what was going on. You hear lots of police sirens and stuff, you go look. It's a small town."

"Okay, I get that. You said you didn't hang around Tanya. What about Tristan? Did he?"

She made a derisive sound. "You know he's rich, right? I mean, his parents are rich. They have homes all over the country and only come here in the cooler months. For the most part, Tristan has always lived here alone. Well, except before he turned eighteen they always had a housekeeper. I mean, it's not like his parents could leave a minor unsupervised for months, right? Anyway, no. Tristan never hung with Jericho, I mean Tanya, either. You know, the more I think about it, the more I think that cop I heard by the lake was wrong. The body they found must be Tanya. There's no reason for Tristan to have even been there. He's on his gap year."

"Gap year?" Shanna asked. "Like when someone skips a year after high school before starting college?"

"Exactly. Wish I could have done that but my parents would never go for it. He was due to head off to Europe a few weeks after graduation. That's the last I heard about him." She clasped her hands tightly again and looked down at the floor.

Kaden exchanged a knowing look with Shanna. Peyton Holloway was hiding something. The question was whether it had anything to do with Tristan's disappearance, or Tanya's. Or neither. Nothing she was sharing seemed like anything they could base an investigation upon. Then again, he wasn't the PI. Maybe Shanna was getting more out of this than he was.

Shanna continued to press for more details, but the young woman wasn't very forthcoming. Then Shanna suddenly threw Peyton a curve.

"When was the last time you saw Tanya?"

Peyton stiffened in her chair. "Tanya? I don't…like I said.

We weren't friends. It's not like we hung out together. Ever. Look, I've answered your questions even though I don't know anything." She stood. "It's getting late. I need to go."

Shanna checked her phone as she too stood. "It's only lunchtime. You have an appointment?"

"Appointment. Right. Yes. I have to, ah, be somewhere."

"Of course. Sorry to have kept you. Thank you for helping."

"Helping?"

"With our investigation into Tanya's disappearance."

"Oh. Right. Sure." Peyton couldn't seem to get to the door fast enough, pulling it firmly closed behind her as if to ensure that Shanna wouldn't follow her.

Shanna turned around at the door. "I screwed that up."

Kaden crossed to her. "What do you mean?"

"Without being obvious, look past me through the windows. She's on the phone, isn't she?"

"She's backing out but, yeah, looks like she's talking to someone. Hands-free phone, I'm guessing."

Shanna swore. "She's hiding something. And now, she's telling whoever else knows her secret that we're on to them. I should have been more careful, not gone full bulldog on her trying to rattle her. It could have been more helpful to have a bug in her car before she called whoever she's speaking to now. We might have learned quite a bit."

"You're talking about planting a listening device in her car? Isn't that illegal?"

"Not if I got approval from law enforcement as part of the murder investigation. I should have talked to the chief before pressing so hard."

"I don't think we've learned anything useful enough to convince the police to get a warrant. Or did I miss something?"

She headed into the main part of the kitchen area. "How much did you drink before I came inside with Peyton?"

"I was kidding earlier. I didn't get anything."

"Perfect. Are you willing to be our designated driver today?"

"You do know it's not even one in the afternoon, right?"

She grabbed a beer from the refrigerator. "I'll take that as a yes." She opened the bottle and took a deep sip. When she set it on the countertop, Kaden leaned on the raised part of the counter across from her.

"What did you learn from that interview?" he asked.

"That depends."

"On?"

"On whether Tristan Cargill went missing before or after Tanya."

He stared at her a long moment. "You suspect Tristan had something to do with Tanya's disappearance?"

"I think it's possible that he had some part in it, yes."

"And then what? Someone found out and killed him, as revenge?"

"Maybe."

"O-kay. And why would they do that? Who would do that? Not Tanya's parents. They're both pushing for answers. If they found out that Tristan killed Tanya, I can't see them killing him and then hounding the police to keep investigating. They'd want his death covered up, not exposed."

"Agreed. I doubt they have anything to do with Tristan's death. And I'm not saying with any degree of confidence that Tristan killed Tanya. I'm just considering that he might have known something about it or have been involved in some way. You heard Peyton talk about having friends in high school. But when I questioned her about them, she said they'd all gone their separate ways, lost touch. You don't get to be a prom queen without being an outgoing, people person, someone who's popular and makes friends wherever they go. She'd have to have had a personality transplant after high school to immediately give all of that up. If she truly hasn't kept tabs on her high-school friends, there has to be a compelling reason. And I'm betting that compelling reason is whatever made her nervous whenever I brought up Tanya."

"I'm following but not following."

She took another swig of beer. "I'm all over the place. I know. This isn't my normal way of investigating, being in a rush, trying to jump from point *A* to point *G* without covering the letters in between. I'm babbling and going off on all kinds of tangents."

"How about we sit, take a deep breath, then talk it through."

"Good idea." She reached for the beer again.

He took it from her and set it in the sink. "Let's keep that brilliant mind of yours operating on all cylinders since we have a limited amount of time. Okay?"

She rolled her eyes but headed to the table, where they sat across from each other.

"Go ahead," he said. "Slowly, for those of us not used to doing investigations like this. What are we looking at so far?"

"So far." She crossed her arms on the tabletop. "All right. Let's talk it through. We have a sophomore, a fifteen-year-old about to become a junior. She's smart, a bookworm, creative, introverted. The reports we read say she didn't have any close friends. Her parents and her books were her only real support system."

"Aside from your sister, right? Cassidy was her teacher and concerned about her."

"Cassidy said that Tanya was very private, hard to get close to. She worried about her not having friends so she'd spoken to her parents several times, becoming close to them. Cassidy is one of those teachers who is usually the favorite, the teacher all the kids adore. But in Tanya's case, she, well, wasn't. I think that's why Tanya's disappearance hit her so hard. She'd tried to be her friend, to be there for her, but never quite managed to break through Tanya's wall."

She gave him a sad smile. "We're back to a young girl pretty much on her own. She goes missing a few weeks after graduation. And after that, one of the most popular seniors, Peyton, cuts off contact with all her friends. Not only that, her main friends from school were at the lake today and ignored not only her, but each other. So it's likely that her friends did the same thing, dropped all of their close acquaintances after graduation. There aren't any huge, traumatic events in town that I've heard of from Cassidy that happened around that time. The only traumatic event was Tanya's disappearance and the fallout from that."

"The police grilling Peyton and her friends, among others."

"Exactly," she said. "And now one of those former friends has died. Not just that, he was murdered. Peyton spoke about him like she still cared for him, and yet she hadn't talked to him in almost a year. Add to that her nervousness, fear really, every time I mentioned Tanya and, well, you can see where I'm going."

"It's all connected."

"Seems like it," she said.

"What if those conclusions we're jumping to are completely wrong?"

"What if they aren't?"

He smiled. "Okay. So other than me performing searches on the lake, once I'm allowed back in that area, you and I are going to spend the rest of our time looking into a group of teenagers to see, what, if one or all of them are killers?"

"Now, that would be jumping to conclusions."

"Normally I consider myself an intelligent man. But keeping up with the twists and turns of your thought process is blowing my confidence."

She laughed. "I'll take that as a compliment. I'm just thinking out loud here. No hard facts, just a lot of assumptions and potential connections, far more questions than answers. All I'm really concluding is that we need to look for a connection between Tristan and Tanya. And follow up on Peyton to see what connections she might have had with either of them. I'm not saying that she or her other friends are killers. Honestly, it doesn't sound plausible since nothing in any of their backgrounds—at least according to the police reports we read—raised any red flags. None of them have police records or have done anything outrageous."

"That we know of."

"Agreed." She shrugged. "But my experience, or instinct, or whatever you want to call it, tells me we've found a thread to follow that might lead us where we want to go. We should focus on Peyton, Tristan and Tanya, and look for where their paths crossed in the days leading up to Tanya's disappearance, and Tristan's death—once the medical examiner can give us a date range on that."

"Is there another angle we should pursue, in case that one is a dead end?"

"I didn't find anything in the files we read last night that leads me to any other avenues to explore. If I had another month to research and interview people, I'm certain

I could come up with something more promising. But time being what it is, this is the best we've got."

"You're the expert. I'll follow your lead. Until Chief Dawson gives me the green light to continue my grid search, I'm free to be the Watson to your Sherlock. What's our next step?"

She grabbed her purse from one of the end tables. "We're heading into town. I'll drive. I'm tired of climbing up in that behemoth truck of yours."

"I don't mind being chauffeured. What's the plan once we get to town?"

"Lunch and eavesdropping."

When they reached her silver Lexus, he held the driver's door open. She smiled her thanks but hesitated, her smile fading as she looked over the car's roof toward the woods behind the cabin.

Kaden turned and scanned the trees as well, but didn't see any cause for alarm. "What is it? Did you hear something?"

Her gaze was still on the woods. "I didn't hear anything. It's just… For a moment, I thought I… The breeze, it smelled like…cologne."

He glanced toward the woods again, studying the shadows. But it was no use. In spite of the bright sunlight today, the gloom of the forest was nearly impenetrable. "Get in the cabin. I'll check it out."

She grabbed his hand. "No. You're not going into the woods alone just because all those flowers my sister has in her yard reminded me of someone. She could practically start her own perfume factory with everything she's planted out here. Come on. Let's go. We have an investigation to run."

When she tried to pull her hand back, he tightened his

hold. "Is it Troy? Is that what you're worried about? You think he might have figured out where you are?"

She blinked in surprise. "You remembered his name?"

"Troy Warren. I remember." He glanced at the woods again. "Get in your car. Lock the door. When we get to town, the first thing we're doing is stopping at the police station."

Chapter Eleven

With Troy Warren's picture given to the police, and after Chief Dawson assured them he'd send some deputies to search the area around the cabin for signs of an intruder, Kaden was more at ease. But he was still on high alert just in case Shanna's ex was here in Mystic Lake. Kaden had no intention of letting her out of his sight now, even if that meant sleeping on the couch for the rest of his time here.

As Shanna turned her car into a parking lot behind a large two-story building, Kaden couldn't help but laugh.

"Stella's Bed and Breakfast. Guess you changed your mind about me sharing the cabin, even during the daylight hours."

"I wouldn't dream of kicking out my new assistant, Dr. Watson. My sister's notes about places to go around town included the restaurant attached to the B and B. Aside from a few sandwich shops or the restaurant at the marina, it's pretty much the only place to eat around here. It's supposed to be really good, though."

"Seems unusual to attach a restaurant to a B and B." Kaden got out of the car and headed toward the building with Shanna.

"True, but my sister said the restaurant is the real money

maker for Stella and her husband, Frank. The rooms don't fill up much except during the summer."

"Sounds like Stella is a good businesswoman to have diversified."

"Thanks for noticing," an older woman said as she opened the door for them. "Now, if you'll share that observation with my husband, I might comp a dessert for you. Table for two? You must be Cassidy's sister. Shanna, right? And this handsome man must be your plus-one."

Before Kaden could set her straight, Shanna said, "Yes, ma'am. I keep him along as eye candy."

Kaden choked, then coughed and cleared his throat.

"Does the eye candy have a name?" Stella stepped in after Shanna while Kaden held the door for them.

"He can hear you, you know." Kaden followed them toward a table.

Stella turned around, grinning. "Well, that's one advantage you have over my Frank. He can't hear a thing without his earpiece. You got a name or should I use the one Ms. Shanna called you?"

He held out his hand. "Kaden Rafferty, ma'am."

She pushed his arm away. "Save the handshakes for the men. We're all about Southern warmth here. Give this old woman a hug, young man." Without waiting, she wrapped her arms around his waist.

He froze in surprise, then narrowed his eyes in warning at Shanna, who was obviously struggling not to burst out laughing. He put his arms around Stella and lightly returned the hug.

She pulled back and patted his chest. "He's handsome and strong, Ms. Shanna. And too polite to refuse to hug an elder, even though she's invading his space and making him uncomfortable."

Kaden cleared his throat again. "You're not making me uncomfortable."

Stella rolled her eyes. "I'm sure you're more comfortable hugging pretty Ms. Shanna. You're sweet to indulge me. But we have to get back to business now, before she gets jealous. I'll bring you both some of my famous blueberry muffins hot out of the oven. We serve them all day. Have a seat right over here, in the middle of the room, and take a gander at the menus. This here will give you the best location for listening in on everyone's conversations."

Shanna's eyes widened. "Excuse me?"

Stella waved her into her seat. "Now, don't you be getting upset. I mean no harm. But you're an investigator, right? Cassidy told me about you enough times for it to click. You're looking into that awful business with that young man who drowned at the lake, aren't you? Can't say it's the first drowning around here and it won't be the last. But it's always sad. Anyway, you do what you need to do. Listen in, see what you can figure out about whether he was with someone or not whenever he drowned. I hate to say it but not everyone is a Good Samaritan and will risk themselves to save someone else. If he was with a friend and they refused to help or at least call for help, they deserve punishment fitting that. I'll send Daphne over in a few minutes to take your order."

Kaden sat across from Shanna, shaking his head. "Wow. That was…wow."

"She's a whirlwind, for sure." She arched a brow. "And quite friendly with my plus-one."

He grinned and looked around. "Guess we got lucky getting a table. There aren't many left."

"I figured it would be extra busy after this morning's police activities. Everyone's gathering to talk theories and gossip." She pulled two pocket-size notebooks out of her purse and slid one, along with a pen, across the table. "I came prepared."

"I'm not surprised." He picked up the pen and little pad of paper. "Let the eavesdropping begin."

They both had cheeseburgers, although Shanna ordered hers without bread and he added bacon. But the clock was ticking and they were both mainly focused on gathering information.

As Shanna had predicted, the town gossips were having a field day about the discovery of remains in the lake, and the even more shocking revelation that the person who'd died was one of the town's own. From what Kaden had heard from a group of men sitting behind him, the Cargill family wasn't exactly beloved here in Mystic Lake. They had one of the largest mansions on one of the tallest mountains and, whether true or not, at least gave the impression to many of the townspeople that they thought themselves above them socially, not just literally.

Tristan only associated with the most popular kids, allegedly using his family's wealth as a carrot to buy his way into the school's inner circle despite being somewhat of a nerd. It became clear that the town had given a collective sigh of relief when Tristan headed to Europe for his so-called gap year. No one, it seemed, had any idea that he'd ever returned.

Except for whoever had killed him.

The police had done well to keep the fact that Tristan had been murdered a secret. So far, at least. The people at the tables near Kaden all seemed to believe it was yet another mysterious accident that could be attributed either to the ghosts of the original people killed when the town was formed, or someone called the Phantom. He underlined *the Phantom* several times, determined to follow up and try to figure out what that was all about.

Across from him, Shanna had her own list going, but hers mostly consisted of names with little comments beside each one. She'd listed Tristan and Tanya in the middle of the page and had drawn lines to each name she added, forming what appeared to be a tree of spaghetti with lines crossing over each other as she apparently linked each name to other names in her tree.

A few minutes after Daphne had taken away their plates, Stella seemed to appear from out of nowhere, leaning over Shanna's shoulder.

"You forgot Jack," she said.

Shanna started, then looked up. "Sorry, what?"

Stella patted her shoulder. "Didn't mean to startle you, honey. Just looking at your little tree there and I noticed you're missing Jack Neal." She tapped an empty spot on the page. "There. Put his name there. He's the local bully around here." She frowned. "Well, one of them. He's sitting over at that table in the far corner with Sam Morton, the former high-school quarterback."

Shanna and Kaden both looked toward the table that Stella had indicated. The plates of food in front of the two young men didn't appear to have been touched. Instead, they were in deep conversation, ignoring everyone around them.

"Wonder what they're talking about," Shanna said. "Seems serious."

Stella shook her head, a look of disgust on her face. "Knowing those two, nothing good. At least, in the old days they'd be up to some foolery. I haven't seen them together in a long time. Either they're discussing plans for a party or whose car to egg next. Then again, they haven't caused much trouble since graduation, so maybe they've reformed."

The look on her face showed her doubt in her own statement. She obviously wasn't a fan of either of them. She tapped Shanna's paper. "Jack Neal. Add him to your list. I see you already had Sam on there."

"Right." She added the name and drew a line from Jack to Sam.

"Now, draw a line from both of them to Tristan. You're looking for connections, friends, right? Or at least who they associated with on a regular basis?"

"Yes. Exactly." Shanna drew the additional lines. "Am I missing anyone else?"

Stella considered a moment, then shook her head. "You've got all the names of the popular crowd and a pretty good representation of who was besties with whom."

Shanna shook her head, a smile curving her lips. "Maybe I should have saved Kaden and me some trouble and just sat down with you today. It would have been faster."

"Maybe. The memory isn't what it used to be. I wouldn't have thought of Jessica DeWalt, former cheerleader, and you've got her. Never saw her in here as often as the others. Haven't seen her around in a while. What's that line you drew from Tristan to Tanya? Far as I know they weren't friends."

"The line means there's something they have in common, that both of them appear to have, ah, drowned in the lake."

"And you're wondering if there's another connection? Like foul play?"

Shanna motioned for her to keep her voice down. "I don't know that at all. I'm just keeping an open mind until we find Tanya."

Stella put a hand on her hip. "Now, don't you go telling half truths, Ms. Shanna. That'll put you on my bad side quicker than anything."

Her face reddened, like a child caught with their hand in a cookie jar. It was a struggle for Kaden not to laugh. She really was adorable.

"That's not my intention," Shanna said. "I'm just…trying to be quiet about it. I don't want to spout any theories without proof. And, honestly, we really don't have a theory just yet. Other than that it's odd for two kids from the same school to die the same way, allegedly, anyway. We won't know for sure, of course, until we locate Tanya."

Shanna pointed to the page. "I haven't heard of any friends for Tanya. Do you know of any?"

Stella pursed her lips as she studied the page. "Poor little Tanya was pretty much a bookworm. Nice to everyone but never hung out with other kids that I know of. Her parents and her studies were what kept her company. The others on your list, well, they were the popular ones, though I never did understand why. You could put everyone's name from their graduating class on that chart since they all knew the popular kids. If you're looking for close ties, then you've pretty much covered the main clique that hung together. Let's see, the prom queen, the quarterback, the rich kid, the cheerleader and, of course, Jack, the resident bully. That's the gang. But I don't think Tanya should be on that page at all. She was a sophomore. The rest were seniors. They wouldn't have hung out with her. Whatever happened to that child has nothing to do with Tristan or the kids he hung with. Then again, I'm not the investigator. So what do I know?" She shrugged and stepped back, as if to leave.

"Stella," Kaden said, stopping her. "I don't suppose you

can help me with a name." He turned his pad of paper toward her and pointed.

Her eyebrows raised. "The Phantom? What's a myth for tourists have to do with what you're investigating?"

"Humor me?"

She glanced around the room. "Guess everything's under control for now. I'll give you a few more minutes."

Kaden rushed to pull a chair back for her. She raised her eyebrows and sat.

"Your mama taught you manners, young man. Reminds me of another big, strapping fellow around here. Handsome, like you. Now, who am I thinking of?" She frowned and tapped her fingers on the tabletop. "Aw, yes. Aidan O'Brien. Even now, he's more of a recluse, doesn't come around much or have much use for most of the people here in town. But he always treats me like a queen." She patted Kaden's shoulder, as if he'd somehow passed a personal test of hers.

"He's Officer Grace O'Brien's husband, right?" Shanna asked.

"He sure is. Father of little Alannah. Such a sweet child. Pretty, too. When she grows up she's going to have her daddy sweating when all the boys start coming around." She chuckled. "But that's not why you're here. What was it you asked about? Ah, yes. That silly Phantom story."

Kaden smiled, not buying her claim that she'd forgotten anything, even for a minute. This woman might be approaching seventy, but her mind was every bit as sharp as someone decades younger.

She crossed her arms and sat back in her chair. "You might do better asking one of the natives for more information. I'm a transplant, only been here a few years past a decade. Even this B and B has been here far longer than me, built before I ever knew Mystic Lake existed." She smiled. "But I can tell you what I've heard. Mainly it's the kids who spread the rumors. I've never seen one piece of evidence that this Phantom exists. I swear every year the next class of kids at school adds more to the myth, embellishing and pretending they've seen this Phantom out in the woods by the lake or hiding up in the mountains. They'll tell you he's half-man, half-fish, that he has gills and can swim underwater. Every time someone falls off a boat around here and never resurfaces, they blame it on this Phantom, say he's the one who pulled them overboard and held their bodies under water."

She shrugged. "Others swear he lives in the caves in the mountains, that he uses old forgotten mines around town to move around without being detected. Some kids have said he's got a beard to his belly and is covered with fur, like Sasquatch. All I know for a fact is that sometimes people's food, clothing and other supplies disappear from their vacation homes or hunting cabins up in the mountains. Heck, I've even had stuff go missing here, but I've always figured it was the local kids, not some ghost. Beau, Police Chief Dawson, does his best to look into those reports. When he does catch someone, it always ends up being exactly what you'd expect. Kids up to no good."

Kaden rested his forearms on the table. "So you don't think the Phantom actually exists? He's not someone we should be looking at who might have something to do with the death of Tristan? Or Tanya's disappearance?"

She waved her hand in the air as if waving away the theory. "You'd be wasting your time in my opinion. I think this whole Phantom thing was made up as a way for kids to scare each other, like telling ghost stories around a campfire. Or, even more likely, a way for unscrupulous adults to build up yet another story about Mystic Lake to make it seem mysterious. Tourists love things like that. And tourists mean money for the town. Hard to blame anyone when you put it in that perspective. A harmless made-up myth to help them put food on the table."

She shoved back her chair and stood. "That's about all the time I can spare right now. Frank will be yelling for me to come help with the dishes soon. And I need to keep after the waiters and waitresses to keep the fear of Stella in 'em." She winked and hurried toward the doorway that led into the kitchen.

Kaden sat back. "I can't see Dawson using his limited resources to chase a legend and search what's likely to be hundreds of caves up in the mountains. And sending his people into old abandoned mine shafts would be far too dangerous."

"Aimlessly searching through the woods for Tanya wouldn't be the best use of our time, either. As much as I loathe the idea of causing the Jerichos any more pain, I feel we should talk to them. Maybe they can shed some light on whether there could potentially be any link from Tanya to Tristan or the other popular kids."

Kaden cocked his head, considering. "If Tanya had no friends because she was shy, socially awkward, but was desperate for company, what might she do?"

Shanna shrugged. "Crash a party? That's the best way to meet a lot of other kids in one location outside of school. But that doesn't really work in this case since she disappeared a few weeks after school was over, after graduation."

"When do people plan all those post-graduation parties? While school is still in session. She could have overheard someone in the hallway talking about parties happening in the weeks after school was out and decided to show up at one uninvited. But someone didn't like that she was there."

"And they killed her because of it? That seems weak."

"Because you're assuming they did it on purpose. Maybe it was an accident. The police theory was that she went to that picnic area we were at this morning and ended up going down to the lake, maybe fell in and drowned. What if there was a party out there and she was pushed in, instead of falling in? The area is remote enough that it's unlikely anyone would have seen it happen."

She slowly shook her head. "Where did you come up with that idea? There's nothing to base it on."

"It's based on the belief that she was in that area, the picnic grounds, before she disappeared, which is based on interviews with her parents. Add to that we both know it could be the perfect party spot for a bunch of high schoolers. They could even light a bonfire out there without getting much attention. Think about it. Tristan was found in the lake right there. And we feel that Tanya could be there, too. If she never associated with this so-called clique, but one of them and her are found in the same area, an end-of-the-year bash and her crashing it fits."

"Okay, yes, it could fit. But it's still completely speculation."

"True, but there is one other thing that makes it sound plausible, or at least something to further explore. Stella told us the group that formed the most popular clique at that school quit seeing each other for the most part after graduation. Peyton told you that graduation night was the last time she's pretty much seen the others. If something bad happened out by the lake, it makes sense why they'd all take a vow of silence, or whatever, then stay away from each other in the hopes that none of them would talk."

She shot a look at the corner table. "Maybe we should ask Sam and Jack about any end-of-the-year parties, or at least, whether they frequented that area where Tristan's remains were found. I'd rather get more information from them before I bother the Jerichos."

They both stood and gathered their notes.

French doors off the side of the restaurant burst open and an older man hobbled inside, eyes wide, face pale. "Somebody help! There's a woman lying in the ditch. I can't pull her out." He headed back outside, leaving the doors open behind him.

Shanna exchanged a startled glance with Kaden. Then they were both running outside as she used her cell phone to dial 911. It seemed as if the entire restaurant was emptying behind them as they raced across the grassy side yard toward where the much slower white-haired man was pointing.

Kaden was the first to reach the ditch and saw the nude body of a young woman half in and half out of the water. Her fingers clutched the green grass as if she was trying to pull herself up onto the bank. But the rest of her, from her hips down, was still beneath the water. Her eyes were closed.

He slid down the incline and pressed his fingers against the side of her neck, which he noted had two burn marks. A Taser? Stun gun? He couldn't find a pulse, and she was cold. He quickly pulled her out of the water. Then he put her on his shoulder and climbed up to the level grassy area.

After gently laying her down, he swiped her long dark hair back from her face.

"No-o-o-o!" The scream resonated through the crowd.

He jerked his head up to see Peyton Holloway framed

in the French doors of the restaurant, her mouth now covered with her hands.

Shanna dropped down beside Kaden as he began chest compressions on the young woman.

"Police are on the way," she said. "They don't have an ambulance or hospital around here. They're sending a medevac chopper from the local marina. Apparently, the owner doubles as a chopper pilot and Stella rides with him to take patients to the hospital in Chattanooga. I asked one of the patrons to get Stella. I'm surprised she's not here already with all the commotion going on."

He nodded, silently keeping count of compressions. Once he hit thirty, he pinched the woman's nose closed and blew a quick deep breath into her mouth, watching to ensure that her chest rose. After a second breath, he felt her carotid again. Still no pulse. He started compressions again.

"Out of the way, people. Move." Stella suddenly burst through the crowd, her knees popping as Shanna helped her down across from Kaden. She was carrying a red box with the picture of a heart on it and a jagged electrical line going down the middle—an automated external defibrillator.

Stella glanced at the woman's face, then gasped. "It's Jessica DeWalt." She shook her head in sympathy as she quickly affixed two patches on the woman's chest, one below and one to the side of where Kaden was doing compressions.

"Okay," she said. "Kaden, stop. Shanna, back up. Make sure neither of you are touching her."

Kaden grabbed Shanna around her waist and scooted her back several feet.

She smiled her thanks, tears in her eyes as she looked at DeWalt, the young cheerleader with her entire future ahead of her.

A light on the AED went green. Stella pressed it, sending electricity sizzling through the leads to the pads on DeWalt's chest. Her body jumped, but her eyes remained closed. Her chest was still, no breaths filling her lungs.

Stella pressed a stethoscope against the woman's chest. "She's cold."

"Hypothermia?" Kaden asked.

Her haunted gaze met his. "Even in the mountains this time of year, I don't think it's cold enough for that. I think we're too late."

Kaden immediately began compressions again. "Recharge, Stella."

"It's charging. Just a couple more seconds." The light turned green. "Everyone clear."

Kaden sat back and watched Stella deliver another shock. She listened with her stethoscope again and shook her head.

"Charge it." He continued compressions. How old was this woman? Eighteen? Nineteen? Too young to die. Stella was wrong, had to be. The cold mountain water running through the ditch must have cooled her body, putting her into shock. How many times had he heard about someone being submerged in an icy cold lake and later being revived? The cold water had slowed down their brain activity, allowed them to survive.

Twenty-eight. Twenty-nine. Thirty. He stopped and blew two deep breaths.

"Clear," Stella said, the urgency gone from her voice.

He pulled back, waited for the zip of electricity to flow into the woman's body.

Kaden watched as Stella listened through her stethoscope, then shook her head.

"Damn it. Again, Stella. Again." He began compressions as the machine charged.

"Kaden." Shanna's hand touched his shoulder. "She's gone. Jessica's gone."

He shook off her hand. "Stella? Is it ready?"

"Ready," Stella said. "Clear."

He leaned back, holding his arms out to make sure that Shanna was safely out of danger as well.

A blast of air was accompanied by a loud *thwap-thwap-thwap* sound. Kaden and Shanna looked up to see the medevac chopper hovering out on the street in front of the B and B as it slowly lowered.

The sound of a ragged cough had Kaden jerking his head back around.

"My God," Stella whispered. "She's breathing." She stared at him in shock.

Kaden looked down, his own breath catching as he looked into a pair of light brown eyes. "It's okay," he whispered brokenly. "You're safe, Jessica."

Her eyes welled up with tears.

"A blanket," Stella ordered. "We need to warm her and—"

Kaden was already pulling his shirt over his head. He placed it over the small woman, covering her from chest to thigh.

"Back up, folks. Back up." The man from the chopper rushed over with a rolling gurney.

Kaden started to rise, but the girl grabbed his hand, clinging to it. "D-don't let h-h-him get m-me. D-d-don't—"

"Shh," Shanna whispered, crossing to Kaden's other side and gently feathering the girl's hair back from her cheeks. "You're safe. No one is going to hurt you again. The chopper pilot—"

"Mr. Thompson," the man said, his voice calm and soothing. "Jessica, it's Bobby. We're taking you to the hospital, okay?"

She frowned. "Billy Bob?"

He grinned. "Stop with the Billy and Billy Bob stuff. I prefer Bobby and you know it."

A tear slid down her cheek.

Thompson grimaced. "I'm teasing. Call me whatever you want, sweetie. We're going to take care of you. Let, Mr. ah—"

"Rafferty. Call me Kaden."

Bobby nodded. "You need to let Kaden's hand go, Jessica, so we can take you on a chopper ride."

She nodded, still crying, but finally let go of Kaden's hand.

"Stella, where's she hurt?" Bobby asked, motioning toward the gurney. "Do we need the backboard and neck brace?"

Kaden's breath caught. He'd been so intent on getting her out of the water and reviving her that he hadn't considered the possibility of broken bones. *God, please don't let her be paralyzed.*

"Grab the brace and backboard as a precaution." Stella leaned over, meeting the girl's tortured gaze. "Jessica, are you hurting anywhere? Any broken bones?"

"N-neck. Burns."

Stella checked Jessica's neck. Then her gaze shot to Kaden.

He nodded, silently mouthing the words *stun gun.*

"Ch-chest hurts," Jessica whispered. "On…fire."

Guilt slammed through Kaden. Had he been too rough with his compressions? Broken some ribs?

Stella, as if sensing his turmoil, gave him a reassuring look. "We'll take care of that. Bobby's going to put a brace on your neck to make you comfortable." She moved to give Bobby room, holding the girl's head still as he put the neck brace on her. As he positioned the backboard beside her, Stella asked, "Do you hurt anywhere else?"

"All… All over. Sore. C-cold." Her voice was strained, her brow furrowed in obvious pain.

"We're going to roll you on your side really carefully and put a hard board under you to protect your back, okay? I'll hold your head while Kaden and Bobby roll you and slide the board under."

"O-okay. Th-thank you." Her voice seemed to be getting weaker.

Stella gave Bobby a sharp look and whispered, "Hurry. I'll get her vitals in the chopper."

Kaden helped with Bobby's directions. Soon, Jessica was on the backboard and they were strapping her onto the gurney.

Kaden pushed the gurney while Bobby guided it and helped rush Jessica to the chopper. In a matter of seconds, she was loaded, along with Stella, and the chopper began its ascent.

The sound of sirens filled the air as a police car raced up the road on this side of the lake, coming from the direction of the marina toward the B and B.

"The cavalry is finally here," Shanna said. "I'd hate being them right now, with so much happening. They have to be stretched pretty thin."

Kaden nodded, looking at the crowd gathered outside the restaurant. "Where did Peyton go?"

Shanna slid an arm around his waist, startling him. He looked down in question.

"I don't care about Peyton right now." She pressed a hand against his chest, her soft warm fingers against his bare skin heating him like fire. "How are you? That was an awful, traumatic thing to go through. Are you okay?"

He slowly shook his head in wonder. "You're worried about me? You went through it, too."

"It's not the same. You had her life in your hands. And even though Stella and I were ready to let go, you didn't. You saved her, Kaden. You saved a life." She stepped closer, pressing her cheek against his chest as she hugged him.

In spite of his vow to keep things cool between the two of them, he was powerless to stop himself as he tightened his arms around her and rested his cheek on the top of her head. The feel of her in his arms, her warmth cradled against his naked chest, made the agony of almost being unable to save a dying girl begin to fade. As Shanna had reminded him, the woman hadn't died. They'd given her a chance at a future. And that was the best feeling of all.

"Get a room," a man's voice said close to them, laughter heavy in his tone.

Shanna stiffened, then quickly pulled away, her cheeks flushing a light pink.

Kaden frowned at an amused-looking Chief Dawson. "You're late. And your timing sucks."

Dawson's smile faded as he glanced around at the chattering onlookers. "Yeah. I know. When the call came in about another body being found, Officers Fletcher and Collier were searching around Mrs. Tate's cabin for signs of the Warren guy. Ortiz and O'Brien were responding to a medical emergency and I was at the lake with the Chattanooga diving team. Days like this, I sure wish I had more than four deputies. I saw the chopper head out. I'm hoping that's a good sign? I don't need to call the medical examiner? Again?"

"Jessica DeWalt is alive," Kaden said. "Or, she was, when we loaded her onto the chopper."

"DeWalt." Dawson shook his head, clearly surprised to hear that name.

"Kaden saved her," Shanna said.

"With help," he corrected. "It was a team effort. There wasn't any blood or obvious injuries that I saw. But there were two parallel burn marks on her neck."

"Stun gun?"

"I think so, yes."

Dawson swore. "What else?"

"When I found her, she was naked, lying in the ditch, unresponsive. We had to revive her. Thank God that Stella was here with a defibrillator."

Dawson raked his hands through his short hair. "What's going on around here? DeWalt's a kid. Why would anyone want to hurt her?" He let out a deep breath, then motioned toward Kaden's chest. "We're about the same size. I'll grab you a shirt from the go bag in my patrol car."

Chapter Twelve

Shanna threaded her way through the still-crowded restaurant while Kaden finished briefing Dawson on the other side of the room. The chief had asked everyone to stay, so his recently arrived deputies, Christopher Collier and Liza Fletcher, could interview them as potential witnesses. But Shanna couldn't seem to locate the people *she* wanted to speak to.

"Hey, everything okay?" Kaden stopped beside her.

"I guess so, except that I can't find Peyton, Sam, or Jack. Do you know whether they were already interviewed?"

He motioned toward Collier and Fletcher, sitting at a table near the French doors. "They've only spoken to a few people so far. I don't remember seeing the ones you mentioned over there yet. But I was speaking to Dawson, so I could have missed them. I wanted to give you an update about the search by your cabin. Nothing was found. No indications that anyone had been in those woods anytime recently."

"That's a relief. I guess. Honestly, I'd rather know for sure where Troy is these days rather than him being in the wind. But as long as he's not here in Mystic Lake, that's good."

"I'd feel better if you stick close to me for now on. It's not just Troy that we need to be on guard against, it's whoever is terrorizing this town."

"No need to convince me. I'm happy to have a tall, buff man as my bodyguard."

He grinned. "And I'm happy to keep an eye on you."

She smiled and motioned toward the chief, who was talking to one of the potential witnesses. "Has Dawson gotten any updates about Jessica?"

"Not yet. He already notified the family. They live close by and are on their way to the hospital right now. He'll text me once he hears anything on her condition."

"Good. Are we free to leave?" she asked. "He doesn't need to question us further?"

"We can go. You have somewhere specific in mind?"

"Talking to the remaining members of the popular clique is near the top of my list. But I'd like to see the Jerichos first. They deserve to be updated about what happened here in case the rumors start up about connections to Tristan, and then potentially to Tanya. I don't want them caught off guard like when they were told by the police that we were here working their daughter's case."

"You have their address?"

"I'm hoping they haven't moved since last spring, when Tanya went missing. I programmed their address from the police files into my phone for when it came time to go see them. It's time."

RAYMOND AND LYDIA JERICHO were nothing like Shanna had expected, or at least that's what she thought when she and Kaden had first arrived at their home. From Cassidy's comments about how devastated they were, Shanna had assumed they'd be broken, barely able to function. They were definitely somber. But they were also polite and welcoming.

In spite of Shanna and Kaden's insistences that they didn't need anything, Lydia had brought them ice-cold glasses of sweet tea and placed crystal bowls of pretzels and nuts on the coffee table in front of them, along with little cocktail napkins. It wasn't until Kaden began explaining what had happened at the B and B that the cracks in their facades began to show. Shanna realized they were putting on a brave face for the world. But the truth revealed itself in how Raymond's hands shook as he sat quietly listening. And in the streaks of white that peppered Lydia's dark hair that shouldn't have begun to gray for many more years. Inside, their battered souls were being held together with tattered threads of hope that wouldn't sustain them much longer. They were a dam ready to break. And she desperately didn't want to be the one to burst that dam wide open and destroy them.

Shanna stood. Kaden gave her a surprised glance then stood as well.

"You're leaving already?" Lydia rose and took Shanna's hands in hers. "I thought you wanted to discuss Tanya, that you had questions."

Shanna lightly squeezed the woman's cold, thin fingers. "I did. We do. But now isn't the right time. We can come back later and—"

Lydia's hold changed, gripping hers with surprising strength in spite of how frail she appeared. "Please. Don't leave. Not yet. Ask us any questions you have. We want to help. We want your help." Her mouth formed the ghost of a smile that probably hadn't curved her lips in months. "We're stronger than we look, Ms. Hudson. If there's any chance you can find our little girl, no matter what has happened to her, we want her found." She let go and sat beside her husband, who put his arm around her shoulders, and waited.

Kaden gently took Shanna's hand, and lightly tugged her down beside him as they sat once again. Feeling as if she needed as much support as poor Mr. and Mrs. Jericho, right now, Shanna subtly moved closer to Kaden, taking comfort in his strength and warmth.

"Go ahead." This time, it was Mr. Jericho who spoke. "Please."

For the next half hour, Shanna carefully led the grieving parents down the path she wanted to take. But she did it by having them tell her about Tanya, her likes and dislikes, what she preferred to do with her free time. While Shanna mentally logged the details that would help her understand a typical day for the missing girl, and the people she associated with on a regular basis, Kaden sat quietly beside her. He seemed content to trust her as an investigator and only spoke up a few times to clarify his own understanding of some details that had been shared.

While Shanna was getting a good picture of Tanya and how she liked to spend her time, her parents hadn't said anything about the popular crowd, like Peyton and the others. The few classmates the Jerichos mentioned were other smart kids in the academic top ten. Tanya had plenty in common with them. But there'd been nothing said about them going anywhere together. No trips into Chattanooga for a girl's day of shopping, or to see a movie. No trips to a concert or a ball game. No stories about any of them ever visiting her at her home, or vice versa. Was it because Tanya didn't want any friends? Or was it because the friends she had, she didn't speak about to her parents.

The Jerichos seemed like nice people who loved their

daughter more than anything. But that kind of love, while well-intentioned, could also feel smothering to a girl on the cusp of becoming a woman. Did Tanya have a crush on some boy and was afraid to tell them because they'd be worried about the impact on her grades, potentially ruining her chance to go to college on a full scholarship? Or was it something insidious, like bullying? Shanna had been that smart, studious girl at school, too. She knew how awful other kids could be, singling her out for being different, for not fitting in. Would Tanya tell her parents about things like that? Or would she keep that a secret, be too embarrassed to tell them. Or too scared that if she did, they'd try to help her by going to her teachers about it, making her even more of a target for bullies?

Somehow, Shanna had to find out what secrets Tanya kept from her parents, assuming there were any. And the only person who could tell her that was Tanya.

When there was a break in the conversation, Shanna smiled. "Mrs. Jericho—"

"Lydia. Please."

"Lydia. Would you mind if we—Kaden and I—sit in Tanya's bedroom for a few minutes? Alone? It would help us get more of a feel for her true personality by experiencing the feeling of her room, how she decorated it, what she looked at every day. Would that be okay?"

The woman frowned and glanced at her husband. He gave Shanna a knowing look, as if he understood her true goal. And supported it. Perhaps he knew more about Tanya than her mother and was unwilling to say it in front of her. He squeezed her shoulder and smiled. "It's okay, Lydia. They're trying to find our little girl."

She chewed her lip, obviously struggling with the idea of them being in Tanya's room.

Raymond nodded at Shanna and Kaden. "It's the last room on the left, down that hallway behind you. Take as long as you need."

Lydia frowned. "Ray—"

"It's okay. Here, I'll help you clear away the food and drinks."

Shanna nodded her thanks as she and Kaden hurried out of the room.

Once inside Tanya's bedroom, Kaden quietly closed the door behind them and raised an eyebrow. "Looks like a princess theme park threw up in here. I've never seen so much pink and purple in one room. What are we searching for, Sherlock?"

"Secrets, dear Watson."

"Like a diary?"

"Exactly like a diary."

"On it." Kaden flipped the pink comforter up on top of the mattress.

"Careful," Shanna whispered. "We need to leave the room exactly like we found it. I don't want to upset Lydia."

"I'll put it back once I search under the mattress."

"It won't be under the mattress, assuming she has one. That's too easy." She headed for the tall bookshelf on the other side of the room, its shelves sagging beneath the weight of all the books stacked on them. "It will be somewhere else, like maybe—"

"Here?"

She turned around to see him pulling out a small book from beneath the mattress. It was purple with gold-edged pages and a gold lock on the front holding it closed. "No way."

He thumped the cover with big gold letters that spelled out *Diary*. "Way."

"Gimme, gimme."

He grinned as he handed it to her and rearranged the comforter to look as if they hadn't touched it.

Shanna tugged at the lock. "It's cheap and will break easily. But I don't want to do that to something that might end up being a keepsake. We need a key, or something similar that I can use to—"

"Jimmy the lock?" Kaden held up a pocketknife and flipped open one of the smaller blades.

Shanna shook her head. "I'm not feeling needed here at all."

"What kind of Watson would I be if I wasn't helpful? Want me to open it?"

She crossed her arms. "Go ahead. Don't scratch or break it."

He inserted the knife tip into the tiny lock and turned. The cheap closure snapped open just as if he'd used a key.

"That was a little too easy for you." She took the now open diary from him. "Perhaps I should run a background check to see if you've been cat burgling on the side. I'll take a quick look through this. Can you check out the bookshelf? Maybe she hid pictures or books behind the ones in front that can tell us things she's been doing that she might not have told her parents."

"You picked up on that, too, huh. They seem well-intentioned. But I imagine a fifteen-or sixteen-year-old girl might feel smothered by all that close attention."

She stared at him, surprised to hear his words echoing her earlier thoughts. "Having been that young girl in a similar situation, I absolutely agree."

He tilted some books on the top shelf, looking behind them. "Did you keep a diary, too?"

"Oh, heck no. I wouldn't dare have put my secrets down in writing for someone to find."

"Then what makes you think Tanya did?"

"Honestly, it was a toss-up as to whether we'd find a diary here. I was more interested in looking through the books to see if she wrote her thoughts in some of those or slid pictures and notes in them. But everyone is different. A lot of girls do keep diaries. I just hope hers isn't a cover and has some real information." She continued to turn pages, skimming through it.

"A cover?" He slid the books back and started checking the next shelf.

"Well, if your mom keeps close tabs, you might put a fake diary under your mattress. The real stuff would be..." She looked up as he turned toward her. "Don't you dare tell me you found something."

"I can put it back if you want."

She blew out an exasperated breath and held out her hand.

He gave her two pictures, then bent down to examine the larger books on the bottom shelf.

Shanna's heart seemed to squeeze in her chest as she looked at the photos. They were slightly blurry, as if they'd been taken from far away or in a hurry and Tanya had zoomed in. Both showed the five popular kids that she and Kaden were looking into. The first one was of a bonfire in the woods. The second was at an outdoor pizza joint. There wasn't a sixth seat waiting for Tanya to take it. She obviously wasn't part of the group. Did she long to be one of the popular kids? Part of their inner circle? Or had she taken the picture for another reason? Like maybe she couldn't stand the group and was trying to figure out how to pay them back for some slight, real or imagined.

Shanna snapped her own pictures of Tanya's photos using her phone. After finishing flipping through the diary and concluding that it was indeed likely a made up rosy story of her life for the benefit of her snooping mother—because no one's life was this sanitized and happy—she slid the diary back where Kaden had found it. Then she crossed to the bookshelf.

"Where did you find these?"

He was crouched down, studying the lowest row of books. "Top shelf, middle. Page eighty-three of *The Scarlet Letter.*"

"Go, Tanya. I loved that book." She pulled it out and inserted the pictures in the right spot.

"Seriously? You liked it? Wasn't it required reading in high-school English class?"

"Yes, but I still loved it." She narrowed her eyes at him. "Please tell me you read *Wuthering Heights.* And liked it."

"I'll plead the Fifth."

She shook her head. "I don't even know what to say."

"I sense five whacks across the knuckles with a wooden ruler in my future."

"Now where can I find a wooden ruler." She blinked at one of the books on the bottom shelf. "Is that a school yearbook?"

He tilted his head to read the spine. "Looks like. From last year."

They exchanged a sharp look.

Kaden pulled out the book and set it on the bed. Shanna flipped it open, then sighed. "Oh, Tanya. Poor thing."

"What? I don't see anything."

"Exactly. No one signed her yearbook. At least, not the inside cover." She flipped to the end. "They didn't sign the back cover, either. Even casual acquaintances sign each other's yearbooks."

"Maybe her mother didn't want her messing it up by having people write in it." He motioned around the room. "Look how spotless this bedroom is."

"Good point. Where's the senior student section?"

"She was a sophomore. Oh, you want to look for the popular clique."

"Exactly." She thumbed through the pictures, stopping at the section for last names starting with a *C*. "No way."

Kaden leaned over her shoulder. "Four stars below Tristan Cargill's picture. I'm guessing that means she liked him?"

"Did you even go to high school?"

He laughed. "Guess I missed some of the more important parts of my education."

"I'll say. Yes, she liked him. *Really* liked him. Although I don't see how. Sounds like he was a jerk, God rest his soul. Ugh. I shouldn't criticize the dead."

"I don't think he cares at this point."

She lightly punched him on the shoulder. "Who's next in the alphabet?"

"Jessica DeWalt. I'm guessing we skip her since she put the stars on a boy's picture. Sam Morton is the next guy in the clique."

"Morton, Morton." She flipped several more pages, then stopped.

"There," Kaden said. "Bottom right."

"Oh, wow. I wouldn't have recognized him. He sure changed since high school. A lot more clean-cut. A lot less hair."

"And five stars. Looks like we have our connection."

"Looks like. Just for kicks, I'll check out Jack Neal. Want to bet how many stars before I get to his photo?"

"Wasn't he the one Stella said was a bully?"

Shanna turned one more page, then froze. "Oh, my."

Kaden shook his head as he studied the picture. "What the heck did he do to her?"

"Whatever it was, it was bad. I mean, you don't draw devil's horns and knives piercing someone's skull unless you're really upset at them." She took a picture of that as well and then handed the yearbook to Kaden to return it to the shelf.

"I think we've got what we came for," she said, when he joined her by the bed again. "We know there was a connection between Tanya and the others. Or, at least, Tanya wanted there to be a connection. The real question is whether they all knew it and took advantage of her in some way."

"Like hurt her? Or killed her? You really think a group of seniors would murder a sophomore because, what, she was bugging them too much or got caught spying on them?"

"In my line of work, honestly, it wouldn't surprise me. Just like people go nuts with road rage and do things they'd never dream of under normal circumstances. People can be horrible to each other, given the right conditions."

"Or wrong ones," he said.

She nodded her agreement. "Hopefully we can find out the truth about Tanya's last day by aiming targeted questions and putting pressure on Peyton, Sam and Jack."

He got up and held open the bedroom door. "Assuming we can find them."

Chapter Thirteen

Having left Shanna's car parked farther down the mountain in the hopes that Peyton wouldn't notice it, Kaden now stood with Shanna on the road in front of the Holloway home. To call the massive, two-story structure a log cabin seemed like an oxymoron. There was certainly nothing rustic about it. It was elegant, stately and, in spite of its size, it seemed to complement its natural surroundings as if it was always supposed to be here. Situated near the top of one of Mystic Lake's higher mountains, it had nearly 360-degree views from expansive windows on both levels. A wide, wraparound porch gave it a homey feel and easy access to every part of the property.

"Well," Shanna said. "I can see why Peyton hasn't moved out of her parents' house yet. If I lived in something this sweet, I'd never want to leave."

"It's stunning, for sure. But I'd rather struggle not to capsize in hurricane swells than have to tackle that steep, narrow road up the mountain every day. Can you imagine making that drive in ice and snow?"

"Actually, yes. I do live in West Virginia."

"Touché. Your house is at the top of a mountain, too?"

"It would be, if I had the type of money to afford it. But

looking up from the foothills isn't exactly a hardship. And I can drive up the mountains anytime I want for that top-of-the-world feeling. Let me guess, you live right on the water in Charleston?"

"When your bread and butter involves boating, it's the sensible thing to do."

"Tell you what. If you ever visit me in the winter, you can close your eyes while I drive us to the best sightseeing elevations."

"And if you visit me in Charleston, I'll…" He hesitated, remembering her most deep-seated fear. "I promise not to take you anywhere near the water."

She rolled her eyes. "You live on the water. What are you going to do, waste money on a hotel just because of my ridiculous phobia?"

He took her hand in his and pressed a kiss against her knuckles. "It's not ridiculous. Even if you never tell me the cause, or don't even know why you're afraid, the fear is real and nothing to be ashamed of. I would be more than happy to wine and dine you at the most expensive accommodations Charleston has to offer, miles from the coast. You're worth it."

She stared at her hand in his, her eyes suspiciously misty.

He grinned. "Did that sound as sappy to you as it did to me?"

The corner of her mouth twitched. "A little. But it's still the best pickup line anyone's ever tried on me." Her smile faded. "If only you lived in West Virginia."

He squeezed her hand and let go, not voicing what they both were thinking.

If only he didn't live near the one thing that terrified her, the one thing he relied on day in and day out to earn a living.

Hoping to get them back on track, he motioned toward the house. "I don't see any cars. But I doubt they park on the street or even in the driveway with that four-car garage off to the right."

"There's only one way to know for sure." She jogged across the road and started up the walkway toward the house.

Kaden swore and hurried to catch up. In spite of her earlier speech about being glad her ex wasn't in Mystic Lake, he'd heard the wobble in her voice. She wasn't convinced that the police were right, that Troy hadn't been outside of their cabin. Until Kaden knew for certain, he'd play it safe and assume the creep was in town. Which meant sticking close to Shanna so her ex wouldn't get a chance to hurt her.

He scanned the bushes along the home's foundation as they climbed the porch steps. The bushes made great hiding places for someone up to no good. But in an exclusive area like this, odds were that a cowardly stalker ex wouldn't risk being seen. There were security cameras on every porch, every garage. No one was coming up this mountain road without being caught on several security videos. Hopefully Peyton wasn't one of the ones keeping an eye on those videos and wouldn't know they were there.

When Shanna rang the doorbell and the musical chimes played a tune, she burst out laughing. "AC/DC? 'Highway to Hell'? Do you think the parents know?"

"If they do, they've got a great sense of humor."

"If they don't, I'll bet their daughter secretly laughs every time someone comes to visit."

After a few more rings and several knocks went unanswered, Shanna's shoulders slumped in disappointment.

"Our plan to try to catch Peyton off guard is a bust. No one's home, not even her parents. Or the maid. Or the butler."

"My, aren't you the snob," Kaden said. "I doubt they have a butler."

She laughed. "Maybe not."

The sound of a car engine coming up the gravel road had both of them turning.

"Blue Mazda," Shanna announced.

"Peyton. If she sees us, she'll probably turn around and take off." He motioned toward the bushes beside the porch steps.

"Oh, heck no." She held up her hands as if to ward him off. "I'm not hiding down there with all the creepy-crawlies."

"Then we'd better run." He grabbed her hand and they took off across the wrap-around porch, not slowing until they rounded the corner at the back right side of the house.

Shanna lightly punched his arm and then bent over, struggling to catch her breath. "How are you not breathing hard?"

"You need to work on your cardio exercise."

"Whatever." She peeked around the corner, then hurriedly ducked back. "She's coming up the driveway."

Moments later, a low hum sounded as one of the garage doors raised.

She looked around the corner again. "The car's parked. There, she's coming out, heading toward the house." She jerked back, both of them being quiet as the sound of shoes crunching on gravel announced Peyton's location.

This time, Kaden leaned around the corner to take a look. "Clear," he whispered. "Go."

As quietly as they could, they raced across the side porch, rounding the corner to the front as Peyton pushed open the door. She blinked at them, her eyes widening in dismay, before she rushed inside.

Kaden reached the door just as it was about to close. He shoved both hands against it and angled his shoe in the opening to keep her from closing it.

Red spots of anger dotted her cheeks. "Let go of the door. Back off or I'll call the police."

Beside Kaden, Shanna held up her phone screen showing the copy of the bonfire picture that he'd found hidden in Tanya's bookshelf. When Peyton saw it, all the color seemed to drain out of her face.

Peyton's throat worked. "Where—where did you get that?"

"Kaden found it in one of Tanya Jericho's books." She lowered the phone. "Would you like to explain the picture to us or the police? Choose."

Peyton slowly opened the door.

Shanna set her phone on the coffee table, turning it around so that Peyton could see the damning picture.

Peyton stared at it, twisting her hands together on the couch across from the one where Shanna and Kaden were sitting.

"You lied to us," Shanna said. "At my sister's cabin, you swore you'd never even met Tanya, that you and your friends never hung out with her. And yet, here's a selfie she took with you and your friends in the background, out in the woods having a bonfire. Explain that."

Peyton's chin lifted defiantly. "You just explained it yourself. It's a selfie. She must have been in the woods, snooping on us, and took that. We didn't even know she was there. She's hiding in the bushes. Can't you tell?"

"Oh, I can tell. And I agree that she probably followed your group. Maybe she heard about the bonfire and wanted to join you, make friends with the popular kids. Is that what happened?"

"What? No. We didn't know she even took that picture. I mean, we never saw her. We didn't know she was spying on us."

Shanna zoomed the photo. "That story doesn't fit what I see in this picture. You, Tristan Cargill and Jack Neal are all looking directly at the camera. You saw her."

"No. No, we didn't. We were just looking in that direction. It's a coincidence." Her knuckles were turning red and raw from rubbing and squeezing her hands together.

"Peyton," Kaden said. "What did you do when you and the others saw her taking your picture? Did you yell at her? Run after her?"

Peyton shook her head, looking down at her hands. "No. We didn't know she was there."

"This picture tells me otherwise."

Peyton looked away.

Kaden gave Peyton a hard look. "Did you chase her? Knock her down? Warn her that you'd hurt her if she ever followed you again?"

"No. I wouldn't do that. I'm not like that."

"What about one of the guys?" Shanna asked. "Sam Morton was a football player, big, intimidating. Maybe he got rough trying to scare her and knocked her around. I can see that. I'll tell Chief Dawson to bring Sam in for an interview and—"

"No. Don't. Sam's a good person. He'd never hit a woman. He's not the one… He didn't…" She squeezed her hands harder.

"Ah, I see," Shanna said. "Tristan. Spoiled little rich kid

beats up the annoying girl who dared to intrude on your little party in the woods. I can see him doing that and—"

"That's not what happened. Tristan didn't... I mean..." She swore beneath her breath.

Shanna exchanged a knowing look with Kaden. They were close to a break. She could feel it. "Peyton," she asked, "If it wasn't Sam, or Tristan, was it Jessica?"

"It was Jack, okay? There. I said it. He's the one who did it." She pressed a hand to her mouth, a horrified expression on her face as she dropped her face into her hands.

"What did he do?" Shanna went for the jugular, not giving Peyton a chance to regroup. "Did Jack beat her? Do something worse?"

When Peyton remained silent, Shanna nodded at Kaden, trying to let him know that she wanted them both to jump in and fire questions, increase the tension. They both did exactly that, taking turns, barely giving Peyton enough time to answer before asking another one. Kaden had a real knack for knowing where Shanna was heading and playing right along. He was the perfect Dr. Watson.

He tapped the bonfire photo again on Shanna's phone. "The date stamp on this tells us this was a week before your graduation. A few weeks before Tanya went missing. She didn't say anything to her parents about it. And they certainly didn't mention anything about bruises or cuts, no black eyes, so no one hit hurt. Not that anyone could see anyway. Peyton, what did he do that's so bad that you're afraid to tell us? Did he rape her?"

Peyton's head jerked up. "What? No, nothing like that. It's just that..." She bit her lip, glancing back and forth between them with a panicked expression on her face. "None of us hit her or—or...did anything to her. We saw her taking the picture and Jack wanted to erase it. That's all. We—

we were smoking weed, okay? Jack's the one who got it for us and he was scared he'd get in trouble with his parents if they found out. His dad would beat the crap out of him if he ever knew he did drugs. And the rest of us were worried she would show the picture to the cops. That's it. That's all."

But that wasn't all. Shanna could see that Peyton was still covering up something, hiding the full truth. It was obvious in the way she was wringing her hands, the tortured look in her eyes, how she could barely look at either of them. Shanna glanced at Kaden, and waited, letting him continue since he was doing so well.

He motioned toward the phone. "I don't see any drugs in that photo."

Peyton glanced at the screen, then looked away. "Maybe not that one. But there were others. Jack chased her down, took her phone, deleted everything. I mean *everything*. All her photos, not just the ones she took of us. She—she begged him not to, said she'd delete the ones of the bonfire. But he held the phone up to her face so it would unlock and he deleted everything in her photo app. And he warned her not to follow us ever again. I don't… I don't know how you got that picture. I thought they were all gone."

Shanna shook her head. "Maybe Tanya's just smarter than you and your friends. Haven't you ever gone to the recently deleted photo folder on your phone to recover pictures?"

Peyton's face reddened. "What are you talking about?"

Shanna sighed. "Never mind. What happened after Jack deleted the pictures?"

"I don't—"

"No more lies, Peyton. What happened after Jack caught up to Tanya?"

Her lower lip quivered. "Nothing. I mean, like I said, he warned her to stop following us around. She was a pest, you know? Always trying to talk to us at school, asking us over to her house, wanting to go shopping in Chattanooga with Jessica and me." She made a disgusted sound. "Like we'd ever do that."

Kaden stared at her. "You were upset at her for trying to be your friend?"

Peyton lifted her chin at a defiant angle. "You had to be there to understand. We weren't trying to be mean or anything. We just...had nothing in common with her, okay? She was a kid, a sophomore. I guess she was desperate or something, trying to fit in, and thought we could help her. She was trying to use us to become popular. It was ridiculous. She wouldn't stop. Just kept bugging us, following us around at school and—"

"She followed you again, didn't she?" Shanna asked. "After the bonfire, after Jack deleted those pictures and warned her. Was there another bonfire? More weed? Maybe the night she disappeared? And you caught her again?"

"Of course not." Peyton started to shake.

"She saw you illegally drinking alcohol?"

"No."

"Something worse? Heavy drugs? Meth?"

A single tear coursed down her cheek as she shook her head no.

"Peyton." Kaden took the lead again. "What did Tanya see the night she went missing that she shouldn't have seen?"

She shook her head again. "It wasn't like that. That's not what—"

"Happened?"

She drew a ragged breath.

Shanna stared at her, waiting. But when Peyton remained silent, she nodded at Kaden to try again.

"You know where she is," he said, his voice kind but laced with steel. "Tell us."

Another tear spilled down her cheek and dropped to her lap. "You're wrong," she whispered, sounding desperate. "I don't know where she is. That's the honest truth."

Shanna glanced at Kaden. He shrugged, clearly unsure whether to believe the girl or not. He motioned for her to take it from here.

"But you do know what happened to her," Shanna pressed, her voice hard without any sympathy like Kaden's had been. This girl might very well be a murderer. Or she could be covering for someone who was. Shanna didn't feel an ounce of sympathy for her.

Peyton's eyes closed, her breaths coming in labored pants.

"She's dead, isn't she?" Shanna demanded.

"Oh, my God." Peyton covered her face in her hands, silent sobs shaking her shoulders.

Kaden winced, obviously pained at seeing the young woman so upset. He'd done an amazing job helping Shanna push Peyton to this point. But he wasn't the seasoned investigator that she was and appeared to have reached the end of his tolerance for playing the bad guy to Shanna's bad girl. He began to rise, as if to try to comfort Peyton. But Shanna put her hand on his and shook her head.

His jaw tightened, as if he was waging an internal battle. But he finally gave her a curt nod and settled back against the couch.

This time, it was Shanna who stood, moving to the other side of the coffee table and sitting on it across from Peyton. She covered the young woman's clasped hands with her own and leaned in close. It was time to take this to the finish line.

"Whatever happened, it's over, in the past. It can't be undone. But if you tell the truth, tell us where to find Tanya, we can at least bring her back to her family. Her parents need to know. They need to give their baby girl a proper burial."

Peyton choked on a sob.

"She was fifteen," Shanna whispered. "If you disappeared when you were only fifteen, don't you think your parents would deserve to know what happened? To know where you were?"

"Stop," Peyton pleaded. "Stop."

"The only one who can make this stop is you, by telling the truth. Tanya's parents need to find their baby girl. Where is she, Peyton? Where's Tanya?"

"I don't... I don't know where she is. I really don't." Her words were a ragged whisper, sounding as if they'd been wrenched from her soul.

"But you know what happened to her, what was *done* to her."

Silence.

"Is that why you don't want to tell us? Because it wasn't Jack who hurt her? It was you, wasn't it? That's it. You hurt Tanya."

Peyton's head jerked up. "No. No, it wasn't me."

"Then who was it?"

Her lips trembled, her face so pale her skin seemed translucent. "All of us."

Shanna stilled, so shocked and dismayed that she couldn't respond.

Kaden came to her rescue, sitting beside her a few feet from the prom queen. "Peyton?" His voice was gentle, compelling, but somehow brooked no refusal in spite of that. "End this. Now. Tell us the truth. Who is *all of us*?"

Her face seemed to crumple as she answered. "Jack. Tristan. Jessica. Sam. And…" A fresh flood of tears flowed down her cheeks. "Me. We did it. All of us. We killed Tanya Jericho."

Chapter Fourteen

Shanna always hated this part of an investigation, the point where she had to involve the police and relinquish her control over the case she'd been working on. But at least Chief Dawson was letting her and Kaden sit in on Peyton's interview.

Not that he really had a choice.

For some reason, once Peyton had broken down and told Shanna and Kaden that she and her friends had killed Tanya, she'd clung to Shanna and sobbed on her shoulder. From that point on, Peyton had refused to let go of Shanna's hand. And she'd threatened to call a lawyer and not say anything else unless the police interviewed her at her home and allowed Kaden and Shanna to be there.

So now, Shanna sat on the couch beside Peyton, offering comfort to the girl who was apparently, at least partly, responsible for the death of the young girl they were trying to find. Sometimes life really sucked.

Across from her, Chief Dawson asked Peyton questions, with Officer Fletcher recording the session off to the side as unobtrusively as possible. Kaden sat beside Dawson, his gaze locked on Shanna most of the time, silently offering her the support that he seemed to instinctively know that she needed. She smiled her thanks, but then something that Peyton said had both her and Kaden looking at her in surprise.

Chief Dawson leaned forward, his forearms resting on his thighs. "Wait a minute. Now you're changing your story and saying you and your friends did *not* kill Tanya Jericho?"

"What? No. No, I'm just explaining what happened."

Shanna exchanged a quick look with Kaden, who shrugged, as confused as she was.

"Let's back up," Dawson said. "Two weeks after graduation, the third week of May and the night that Tanya Jericho went missing, you said she again followed you and your friends to one of the bonfires you liked to hold out in the woods by the lake."

"Yes. I've told you that like four times already."

"It's important to get this right. It's a different bonfire than the one in that picture that Ms. Hudson showed me, correct?"

Peyton clutched Shanna's hand more tightly. "Yes. This was a different one, the last bonfire we ever held because— because of what happened that night."

Dawson referred to his notes on the coffee table in front of him. "Got it. You were all five partying as in drinking and getting high on marijuana. You heard a noise and realized Tanya was watching you. That made you mad."

"Well, yes. Of course. We'd told her to stop following us around and spying. We'd all graduated by then and thought it was ridiculous for a kid to be following five adults around like a lost puppy."

The empathy Shanna had begun to feel for Peyton after she'd broken down earlier was rapidly drying up. Did the girl have no clue how bad she sounded? She'd admitted to murder and here she was, victim-blaming. The whole thing made Shanna want to pull her hand free and join Kaden on the other couch. But she couldn't risk doing anything that might stop the confession. They still needed the final clue, the location of Tanya's body.

Tension showed in the lines around Dawson's mouth as he continued to politely question Peyton. But his professionalism kept him from revealing any anger or disgust as he worked at getting the truth. "Where exactly was this last bonfire held?"

"In the woods, by the lake."

"Near where our divers have been searching? Where we found Tristan Cargill?"

She frowned. "No, of course not. I'll never understand why Tristan was found over there. All of us, including him, stayed on our side of town."

Dawson blinked, looking confused. "Where is our side of town?"

"You know, past the marina, but on the other side of the lake. On the same side as Stella's B and B but way down."

"So it's past the campground."

"A few miles past, yes. But—"

"On the other side of the lake. Got it. Is there a landmark you can give me?"

"I don't know about any landmarks right there, but it's past the Andersons' place and the mountain that looks like it's been split in two."

"Cooper's Bluff?"

"Yeah, yeah. That's it. Maybe a mile past that."

"All right. We'll get you a map in a bit and maybe you can show me. Let's get back to what you were saying earlier. At this bonfire, when you saw Tanya, Jack dragged her into the clearing by the fire. And the rest of you…spoke to her. Correct?"

Her hand squeezed Shanna's again. She was shaking, ever so slightly, her face pale. Maybe the way she was talking was more false bravado than lack of caring about her victim. Shanna squeezed back and Peyton gave her a grateful look, leaning into her side.

"Correct," Peyton said. "But you're—you're making it sound better than it was. We were mean, Chief Dawson. We said terrible, hurtful things. I'm not saying I wouldn't have said them sober, but I don't think me or the others would have been quite as…horrible if we weren't drinking and smoking."

"But no one hit her, or assaulted her in any way?"

She cleared her throat, her gaze falling to her lap. "Not at that point, no."

"Walk me through it, right up to where you said she was in the water. That's where you lost me earlier. After you had the shouting match by the bonfire, Tristan grabbed her and—"

"No. Tristan *shoved* her. His leg was hurt, remember? He was using a cane to walk so he couldn't grab her arm. He would have fallen. He bumped her, really. Hard. It was Jack who grabbed her and dragged her toward the lake."

"What did you and the others do when Jack was dragging her toward the water?"

"Well… Jessica, I think she was the least drunk of all of us. She was mad. At us. She kept telling us to leave Tanya alone. She hung back by the fire."

"But she didn't physically try to stop any of you, or help Tanya?"

"No." Her voice was quiet, sad. "Neither did I. I stopped at the edge of the water."

For the first time since she'd begun her confession, she sounded as if she felt ashamed of what she'd done.

Or what she hadn't done.

"Peyton," Dawson said. "This is important. Did all three of the boys—Tristan Cargill, Sam Morton and Jack Neal—did all three of them help pull Tanya into the water?"

"Yes," she whispered.

"And what did Tanya do?"

"She…" Peyton squeezed her eyes shut, all her earlier annoyance gone. It was as if she was finally facing the horror of what she and the others had done, and realizing just how awful they'd been.

"What did she do?" Dawson pressed.

"She was crying. She—she cried for her mom, asked them to let her go. She promised she'd never try to…try to be our friend again." Peyton let out a keening sob and covered her mouth. "Oh, my God. What did we do?"

"We'll take a break soon," Dawson said. "Hang in there. Once they got Tanya into the water, what happened next? Did they hold her under? Choke her? Hit her? What exactly did they do?"

She frowned, staring off into the distance as if trying to focus on the memories. "It all happened so fast. They pulled her out, pushed her. Then, she just disappeared."

Kaden exchanged another searching glance with Shanna. That's the part all of them were trying to understand.

"When you say pushed her," Dawson said. "Do you mean they pushed her head under the water?"

"No. No, nothing like that. They were trying to scare her. They reached one of those sharp drop-offs in the lake, about fifteen feet from shore. Then they just…pushed. She fell backward into the water and went under. That's it."

"She fell underneath the water and didn't come back up?"

"Exactly."

"Did anyone dive in to help her?"

Her chin wobbled. "We couldn't. We were drunk, high, scared. You know what happens at Mystic Lake. People go in and they don't come out. The lake took her. I swear we only wanted to scare her. But we killed her. She drowned, and it was our fault."

She broke down, crying again as she curled up against Shanna.

Shanna fought tears in her own eyes, hating this tug of war with her emotions. She hated what Peyton and her friends had done. But Peyton's anguish was real. She hated herself in that moment, and she was all alone in her grief and shame. Shanna wrapped her arms around her, whispering soothing words against the top of her head.

"I think it's time for that break," Kaden said.

Dawson nodded. "Agreed. I've got to get Jack Neal and Sam Morton into custody as quickly as possible before they compare notes and concoct some bogus story to try to cover what they've done. Peyton, you were seen at the restaurant when we found Jessica DeWalt. So were Sam and Jack. Until Mr. Rafferty called to tell me you were here, we'd tried to find all three of you and couldn't. Where did you all go after you left Stella's?"

Shanna gently helped Peyton to a sitting position and wiped the tears from her cheeks. "Where are Sam and Jack?"

"I—I don't know where they are. I heard about Tristan and called them. We were upset and wanted to get together to talk about it. I couldn't… I couldn't get in touch with Jessica." She wiped the streaming tears from her eyes. "I don't understand what's happening around here."

"Did you meet with them at the restaurant?" Dawson asked. "I just need to know where they are."

"No. I mean yes. I…saw Mr. Rafferty carrying Jessica and I—I ran and found Sam and Jack. We agreed to meet in the woods behind the public boat ramp. We thought we were cursed, or something. I mean, how could that happen to Tristan and Jessica? It doesn't make sense, unless it's the universe getting back at us for being so horrible."

"You haven't seen them or heard from them since the boat ramp?"

"No. I heard the police, you, wanted to talk to me, so I—I hid until I thought you'd given up and then came home."

"All right." He checked his phone. "The time is seventeen thirty, five thirty in the afternoon. The first interview with Peyton Holloway is concluded." He motioned to Fletcher to turn off the camera.

"What happens now?" Peyton asked, sniffling and straightening on the couch.

Dawson pulled out a pair of handcuffs. "I need you to stand up and turn around."

ONCE PEYTON WAS in the back of Officer Fletcher's police car heading down the mountain, Kaden stood with Shanna and Chief Dawson by the chief's SUV.

"What's going to happen to Peyton?" Shanna asked.

"She'll be arraigned before a county judge, who will decide whether or not to set bail. However, even if she makes bail, I'd rather not let her out. Five friends and one wannabe friend go into the woods. Nearly a year later, most of those people are either missing or dead. Peyton is alive and unharmed so far and I want to keep her that way."

"You're talking protective custody?" Kaden asked.

"I am. I've issued a BOLO to neighboring law-enforcement agencies, be on the lookout, for Sam and Jack's vehicles. There's only one road in and out of this town, so I've got eyes on that, not to mention security cameras. But so far, there haven't been any sightings. We'll perform a cursory search of the boat ramp as soon as I leave. That's all we can do with the sun going down soon. A more thorough, organized search with local volunteers will take place tomorrow."

"Chief," Shanna said. "If you do find Jack Neal, there's something you should know. Kaden and I got a look earlier today at Tanya's last high-school yearbook. She'd defaced Jack's picture, adding devil horns and knives in his head. From what I've heard, she was a smart, sweet young girl. I can't imagine her doing that unless he'd done something really bad to her. I'm not sure if erasing the photos on her phone qualifies, like we told you earlier, especially since it appears that she was able to recover her pictures."

His jaw tightened. "I'll keep that in mind if I do get a chance to interview him. Is there anything else?"

"Not from me," she said.

"I've got a question," Kaden said. "I'm sure you have this covered already, but I have to ask. Do you have someone at the hospital guarding Jessica DeWalt, just in case there really is someone after all these kids?"

Dawson winced. "She didn't make it. Sorry. I know you both did everything you could to give her a chance. She passed away a couple of hours ago. I received the notification right before you called about Peyton and haven't had a chance to update you."

Kaden stared at him a long moment, shocked to hear about the girl's death. He gave Dawson a terse nod to thank him for the update.

Shanna leaned against his side, her arm around his back as if to let him know she was there for him. It was amazing how well she understood him. She obviously realized what a sucker punch it was to find out that the young woman he'd tried so hard to save hadn't been saved after all and was trying to offer him comfort. He glanced down at her, the burden in his chest lightening, if only a little, as he met her knowing, sympathetic gaze.

"I appreciate what you've both done to light a fire under this investigation," Dawson said. "I assure you it's no longer cold. It's all hands on deck. Shanna, take that vacation your sister promised. It might be hard to enjoy it at this point, but at least you can relax and chill out for a few days before you have to head back to West Virginia."

"What is it with all you police trying to get me to quit? I'm going to see this through until we bring Tanya home."

His jaw tightened. "I've got three young people dead now—Tanya, Tristan, and Jessica. And you have some crazy ex-boyfriend after you. I strongly recommend you go ahead and head back home, tonight. Get out of town. No one will think less of you. You've done what you could."

She put her hands on her hips. "I don't see you telling Kaden to tuck tail and run."

"That's because I'm selfish. I need his help."

"The search for Tanya's remains," Kaden said. "You want me to check the lake out past Cooper's Bluff with my sonar?"

"I'd sure appreciate it, if you're inclined to do so. I can't pull the Chattanooga dive team off the crime scene for Tristan Cargill just yet. They have to finish searching for additional bones and any evidence that might be at the scene. It could be days before they free up. Even then, there's no guarantee I'm next in line for additional dive-team assistance, not when the person I want them to dive for has been missing for nearly a year and we can't say for sure exactly where her remains might be. It sounds callous, I know, but they have to prioritize resources and have already spent a lot of time here in Mystic Lake. But if your fancy sonar finds something, they'll know it's not a wild goose chase and might help us that much sooner."

"When do you want to head out?"

"As soon as the mist burns off the lake tomorrow morning."

Kaden glanced at Shanna. "Are you leaving, as he suggested?"

"Hell, no."

He sighed. "I'll help you, Dawson. But only if you put Shanna in protective custody while I'm on the boat."

She gasped and pulled away from him. "No one's locking me up."

He faced her and put his hands on her shoulders. "I know the police didn't find any proof that Troy Warren has been near your sister's cabin. But I'm not willing to risk your safety if he's just good at covering his tracks. I'm assuming the worst, that he's here, somewhere in Mystic Lake. I'm not leaving you alone."

"Kaden, I can take care of myself. I—"

"She can join us on the boat," Dawson said. "I plan on going with you as your backup. No one should ever swim or dive in Mystic Lake without someone around to help if something goes sideways—as it often does around here. Two people to back you up is even better. Shanna can call for help while I dive in after you if necessary."

"Okay," Shanna said, her face pale in spite of her brave words.

"No," Kaden countered, still holding Shanna. "Not happening. There's no way you're getting back on my boat. It was hard enough for you last time, especially with how the trip ended. I'm not going to put you through that again. We already know how this trip will end, if we're lucky. It'll end in the discovery of more remains."

Dawson looked at Shanna, his confusion evident. "If you're worried about seeing a dead body, keep in mind we're talking bones at this point."

Shanna started to speak again but Kaden cut her off. "Her reasons are personal. She's not getting back on my boat. Period."

She shoved his hands off her shoulders. "Isn't that my decision?"

"No."

She raised her hands in the air and rolled her eyes.

Dawson smiled. "Okay, none of my business. I get it. But, there's a simple solution. Shanna, if you won't leave town or let me put you in a holding cell for your protection, there's someone else who can look after you while we're on the boat. Aidan O'Brien, Grace's husband. Trust me. No one's going to mess with Aidan. You'll be completely safe with him at your sister's cabin."

Kaden shook his head. "I don't like it. I've never met the guy. You may trust him, but I don't."

"Um, hello." Shanna waved her arms in the air again. "Quit talking about me as if I'm not here. This isn't either of your decisions. It's mine." She turned to Kaden. "I appreciate you being okay with me not getting back on your boat. Since Chief Dawson is going to be your backup, I'll agree to that. But as for my protection, I'm a big girl. Have you forgotten I have a gun?" She glanced at the chief. "That's okay, I hope? I didn't even think about checking the Tennessee laws on gun ownership before coming here."

Dawson smiled. "We live in the wilderness with bears and so-called phantoms roaming the woods." He winked. "I'd be surprised if any adults living around here *don't* have a gun."

She nodded. "That settles it."

"No," Kaden said. "It doesn't."

She pressed a hand against his chest. "Kaden, your protectiveness is sweet and I really appreciate that you care. But you're going overboard with this. The police don't think Troy is in town. Even if he is, I'll be just fine by myself in Cassidy's cabin. Chief, I appreciate you suggesting that Mr. O'Brien can protect me. But I'd feel awkward with someone I don't know there and honestly don't feel it's necessary."

The chief shrugged, appearing weary of arguing anymore.

"Shanna," Kaden began again, "I don't want—"

"It's not what you do or don't want that matters this time. I really can take care of myself. And something you don't realize is that Cassidy has real working shutters on all her windows. Solid wood to keep out dangerous storms, or bears. Thick enough to stop a bullet, just like the walls... as we both know."

Dawson frowned in confusion again.

Kaden reluctantly smiled. "Yes. We do."

"I'll be okay, really. I'll be locked up tight where I'm comfortable and can make myself useful with my laptop and the investigative folders to continue looking into the case. Someone is after Peyton and her crew. If I can help come up with a list of potential suspects, then that's what I'm going to do."

"I really don't want you there alone," Kaden told her.

"And I don't want the Jerichos to wait days or weeks for the Chattanooga dive team to find their daughter. I want this over with before we both have to go back to our respective businesses. Please. Trust me. While you help in your way, I'll help in mine. Okay?"

"You'll stay inside? Locked up tight, no matter what? No going into town to conduct interviews?"

"I won't open the door until I hear your voice. Even if I think Troy's out snooping in the woods, I won't go looking for him. Shooting him would just result in more paperwork for our friend Dawson."

Dawson chuckled. "Thanks. I think."

Kaden shook his head. "You're really something, you know that?"

"So I'm told."

He squeezed her hand, then faced Dawson. "I'll do it. I'll take the boat out, work with the sonar."

Relief flashed across Dawson's face. "Thanks. Thank you both."

"How big of a search area are we talking about?" Kaden asked. "Any idea?"

"Too big to search without narrowing it down. I asked Fletcher to work with Peyton at the station, get her to mark the target area on a map. Hopefully, she'll cooperate. As soon as I've got some coordinates, I'll text them to you so you can plan your approach. Your boat is still docked at the Tate cabin, right?"

"It is."

"I'll meet you there in the morning once we have those coordinates. My police SUV parked outside will be yet another deterrent against anyone up to no good." He hopped into his SUV. "Kaden, is that your Lexus parked down the road?"

"It's mine," Shanna said.

"Hop in. I'll take you to it."

Chapter Fifteen

Shanna turned from the kitchen sink as Kaden stepped inside the cabin with his overnight bag. He immediately shut and locked the door, then surprised her by sliding one of the kitchen chairs under the doorknob.

She tossed the dishcloth she'd been using onto the counter, having just finished cleaning up from their dinner. "Paranoid much?"

"I'm getting that way." He set his bag down on the table.

"Something happen while you were getting your stuff from your boat?" She looked toward the front windows, then remembered that he'd insisted on shutting and locking all of the shutters over them when they'd first arrived and after he'd searched the tiny cabin to make sure that Troy, the Phantom, or any other possible bad guy wasn't inside. "What is it?" She glanced at the covered windows again, starting to feel uneasy. "Did you see someone outside?"

"I checked the perimeter before coming in. It seems to be all clear." He shoved his hands in his pants pockets. "Dawson called. As expected, the initial search of the public boat ramp down the road from Stella's came up empty. No sign of Sam or Jack."

"Hopefully they're safe and just hiding out somewhere

like we talked about. What about Peyton? Did she narrow down the area where they had that last bonfire? Will you and Dawson be able to take the boat out in the morning to search for Tanya?"

"She cooperated, gave a specific location. Dawson's meeting me here around nine."

"That's good news."

"Yes." His expression was tense, in spite of what he'd said.

"Kaden? Is something else going on?" She pressed a hand to her chest. "Did Dawson...did they find another body?"

He shook his head, then slowly crossed the room, stopping so close to her that she had to tilt her head back to look him in the eyes.

"Kaden? What's wrong? You're worrying me."

He drew a ragged breath but didn't say anything.

She frowned in confusion. She'd never seen him this way, so tense, so...keyed up. Then again, they hadn't known each other all that long. And how was that possible when she felt as if she'd known him forever? They'd been together almost 24/7 since the moment they'd met, spending far more time than if they'd been casually dating for weeks, or months. Maybe that's why she felt so in tune with him. And yet, this morose, tense man standing before her was a side of Kaden she'd never seen. She didn't understand his mood, or know what had caused it.

She touched his chest to get him to look at her.

He jerked as if she'd branded him, giving her his full attention. Slowly, ever so slowly, he placed his hands on either side of her against the countertop, trapping her with his body, his heat, his jaw so tense he seemed to be in pain. And then, she knew. She understood.

Her pulse quickened, her belly tightened deliciously as she slid her fingers across his shirt over his heart. It was pounding just as fast as hers. He was a man on edge, struggling for control.

She smiled.

He swore even as he feathered his hand across her cheek, sending a shiver down her spine. That slow caress continued down the side of her neck. Her skin flushed hot and cold everywhere he touched. Since when had her neck ever been that sensitive?

His throat worked as he leaned down, closer, his mouth angling toward hers. She stood on tiptoe to meet him halfway. Suddenly he let her go, swearing again as he strode away from her, stopping in front of one of the shuttered windows beside the couch.

She blinked in surprise and settled back on her feet. Disappointment and confusion warred with each other as she pushed away from the kitchen counter and followed him. "What was that about?"

He slowly turned around, his hands shoved in his pockets as if to keep himself from reaching for her. His eyes had darkened to the color of midnight and practically blazed with heat. "Do you have any idea how beautiful you are?"

Her breath caught at the hungry look in his eyes, the rough rasp in his voice. Her pulse began to race, her belly tightening with desire. It was a heady feeling, knowing he wanted her as much as she'd been wanting him for what felt like forever. But she'd just embarrassed herself by responding when it seemed that he was going to kiss her. She wasn't putting herself out there again. The ball was in his court. It was up to him now.

He drew a ragged breath, then shook his head. "I'm sorry. I know I'm being a jerk. I don't mean to be, I just…

do you have any clue how utterly frustrating it is that we're both going to sleep in the same tiny cabin tonight and knowing I shouldn't touch you?"

She had to curl her hands at her sides to keep from reaching for him. "Shouldn't? Why?"

He frowned, as if the answer was obvious. "Why? I live in Charleston. My business is there."

"So?"

His frown deepened. "You live in West Virginia."

"Yes. And? What's the problem?"

"What's the problem? Seriously? Our businesses, our livelihoods, are a day's drive apart. We could never be... It wouldn't make sense to... Ah, hell." He yanked his hands free and scrubbed his face that was already showing signs of needing a shave. "I'm sorry. This is... I never should have said anything. I was just sitting on my boat and thinking about you here, and me, tonight, and I couldn't... I wanted... Damn. I'm trying to be a gentleman."

She took a step closer, then another, until her breasts pushed against his chest.

His Adam's apple bobbed in his throat as his gaze dipped down.

"Kaden?"

He shuddered and seemed to struggle to force his gaze up until he was looking at her face. "Shanna?"

The way his voice caressed her name had her flushing hot all over. This time, she was the one who traced the outline of his cheek, feathered her hands down the side of his neck, then across his lips. A bead of sweat ran down his cheek even though it was cool inside the cabin.

"Shanna, I don't... It wouldn't be right to start...something between us that has no future. You get that, right? I don't want to hurt you, or treat you with anything but respect. You deserve to be protected, cherished, not used for a night when there's no possibility of a future relationship."

She stared up at him, searching his smoldering gaze. "You want me."

He swallowed. "Yes."

"And I want you."

His nostrils flared, but he remained silent.

"But you're holding back because you feel I deserve respect, and to be...cherished?"

His hand shook as he reached for her. Then his fingers curled against his palm and he dropped his hand to his side without touching her. "You deserve so much more than I can ever give you."

She stared at him in wonder. "Wow. Why couldn't I have met you when I was sixteen?"

He frowned. "Sixteen?"

"When I was a champion swimmer with a gazillion swim-meet medals to my name. Did I ever tell you that?"

He slowly shook his head. "No. I thought you were terrified of the water."

"I am. But back then, I wasn't. I loved the water, swimming, diving, anything I could do to feel it rush through my fingers as I pulled myself forward faster and faster. I wanted to be an Olympic champion. But it wasn't meant to be." She cupped his cheek in her hand, unable to resist the desire to touch, to treasure.

To cherish.

"What happened?" His dark eyes searched hers, the desire tempered with concern.

Because he cared about her.

It was a heady knowledge to have.

She slowly slid her hand down the side of his neck, as

he'd done to her earlier, delighting at the feel of his pulse speeding up beneath her fingertips.

"For my sixteenth birthday, my parents threw a pool party at our home and invited all my friends. Once everyone left, I was in the pool getting all of the floats out, when one of my friend's brothers who'd come with her to the party suddenly appeared in our backyard. He'd made advances earlier. But I told him I wasn't interested."

Kaden's eyes darkened, the heat tinged with anger as he gently took her hand in his. "Please tell me he didn't... that he didn't—"

"Attack me?"

He nodded.

"He kissed me, or tried to. But I turned my head and told him to leave. The rest of it happened so fast I don't remember all the details. He...shoved me under the water, grabbed my breast. I kicked and swam away. But he was a strong swimmer, too. He dove, pinned me to the bottom of the pool, yanked down my bikini bottoms and..." She drew a shaky breath. "I haven't spoken about this to anyone besides my parents. And the police. And my therapist. Ever. Not even with my little sister, Cassidy."

His hand was shaking now as he held hers, his thumb gently rubbing her palm in a soothing motion. "And you don't have to tell me this, either. I don't want you to relive something so awful."

"I want to tell you. I want you to understand. He didn't... The boy didn't do what he wanted. My dad saw him from the kitchen window and dove into the pool. He jerked him off me and hauled him out. That's when it happened."

He frowned, his thumb stopping its soothing motions against her palm. "What happened?"

She drew a bracing breath before continuing. "When I

pushed off the bottom of the pool to swim to the surface, my hair got caught in the drain. I don't think that would happen in a modern pool, but it was an old house, with an old pool. My hair was long and…well, I woke up in the hospital. My dad had realized what was happening and grabbed a knife from the kitchen to free me. I don't remember that part. I'd lost consciousness by then. But I do remember waking up with a really bad haircut."

She chuckled but he didn't smile back. His expression was a mixture of anger, shock and sympathy.

"That's why you're afraid of the water," he said.

"Apparently. I haven't been able to get near it since without feeling nauseous. My therapist at the time told me it was like riding a horse, that I needed to hop back on to get over my fear. But every time I tried… I couldn't. So I gave it up. I never went near a pool again."

"Please tell me the jerk who attacked and almost killed you got what was coming to him."

"We had a security camera that caught everything. But I didn't want to go to court, be victimized all over again. I'm sure his lawyer would have made me out to be some temptress or something equally stupid to justify his client's actions. We settled out of court, kept it quiet, even though I promise you my dad wanted to kill him." She smiled. "But that's not why I told you. I told you because I trust you enough to tell you the worst thing that ever happened to me. Well, aside from Troy. He's the second worst thing to happen to me. But that's different. And I don't even want to go there right now. Kaden, you say I deserve to be protected, cherished. You make me feel that way, already, just by being here, wanting to keep me safe. And by denying yourself something I would freely give, because you care about me. You're worried that it will hurt me to spend a night in your arms when there's no possibility of a future relationship. But isn't that my decision to make?"

"Shanna—"

"We don't know what the future holds. But I do know how I feel tonight, right now. I care about you, too. Hold me, Kaden. Cherish me. Make me forget everything else if only for a night. Erase the hurts, the pain, the struggles. Love me, Kaden. Even if one night is all we ever have."

He made a strangled sound deep in his throat. Then she was in his arms, cradled against his chest as he carried her into the bedroom.

Chapter Sixteen

We're here. Dawson's getting ready to head back to town.

Shanna read Kaden's text then tossed her phone onto the kitchen table and jumped up to put her shoes on. Last night in Kaden's arms had been incredible. Saying goodbye this morning had been torture. Waiting all day, closed up in the cabin with just her investigative folders and the internet to keep her company, had been a study in boredom. Normally an investigation got her excited, pumped. But she'd grown used to Kaden being around. Without him, she'd been…lost.

What that meant to her future happiness once they parted wasn't something she even wanted to contemplate. After all, Kaden had warned her. She knew there was no future for them, and agreed that giving up their businesses and moving wasn't going to happen. But that didn't make it any less hard to even think about saying goodbye.

Which was why she refused to think about it right now.

She shoved that unpleasant thought to the back of her mind and hurried out the front door and down the porch steps to the side where the vehicles were parked. She had a big smile on her face for Kaden. But his back was to her and it was Chief Dawson who saw her first. His eyes widened, then he grinned knowingly as she forced herself to slow her bouncy steps and dim her smile.

"Hello, Shanna. Good to see you again."

"Chief." She barely managed a nod before heading to Kaden. She stopped a few feet away as he turned around.

His mouth curved in a sexy, glad-to-see-you smile. "Hey, there."

"Hey, yourself. I thought you, um, both of you would never be done with your search. How did it go?"

His smile faded. "Not too well. But it wasn't a complete bust."

"What do you mean?"

He motioned toward Dawson.

Dawson leaned back against his SUV. "We found the clearing that Peyton described. Apparently, her group isn't the only one that has bonfires out there. I'm guessing the current senior class does as well since there are plenty of signs of recent activity. Finding something of evidentiary value there is a nonstarter. But it does corroborate Peyton's story, which helps with building a chargeable case. But Kaden's sonar search didn't come up with anything, not for lack of trying. He scanned all over that cove and ended up diving for several hours to check out some of the structures under the water in case sediment had covered up any remains."

"What? Kaden, you dove into the debris? Isn't that one of the main things people say is deadly in that lake?"

Dawson winced. "Didn't mean to get you in hot water, buddy."

"I was careful." He shrugged. "It had to be done. And I'm going back tomorrow. Tanya has to be there. We know we're searching the right place. But it's a difficult area to search. The sonar isn't working its magic. It could take days, maybe longer. I'll help as long as I can. But I have to get back to my company by the weekend. Dawson's going to put in a request to the Chattanooga dive team if I'm not able to find her before I leave."

Shanna wanted to ask him not to go back. But the reality was that part of the reason she was so drawn to him was because he was such a decent man. He was losing money being here when he could have been working for a paying customer in Charleston. And he was donating his time, and lost income, because he felt it was the right thing to do. How could she fault him for that? Or be angry? Or ask him to reconsider? Instead, she'd have to trust his expertise and experience to do what needed to be done without getting injured. Or worse.

Maybe she'd call Dawson in a private moment and put the fear of Shanna into him if he didn't make sure that Kaden came back unscathed from his diving trips.

Dawson exchanged an uneasy look with Kaden.

Shanna glanced back and forth between them. "What? There's something else?"

Kaden nodded. "The reports coming back from the search at the public boat ramp aren't encouraging. Sam and Jack weren't found, but their cars were. They'd been parked deep in the woods, off a trail. Dawson's theory is that they were forced against their will to go with someone through the woods to the road and taken away in another vehicle."

Shanna's stomach churned at the news. "Someone's after all of them isn't he? Peyton's little clique of friends."

"It's getting nearly impossible to think anything else is happening. The question is who, why, and how do we stop them?" Dawson glanced at the sky overhead. "We've got a couple more hours of daylight. The state police are bringing in lights and more dog teams to help search through the night. I'm heading over there once I leave. We have to find those boys before they end up like DeWalt and Cargill." He shook his head. "This just keeps getting worse and worse. And once the public hears about Peyton and the others and their involvement in Tanya's murder, they'll be putting a paranormal spin on this whole dang thing which will only make our jobs more difficult."

"What do you mean?" Shanna asked. "Blame it on the so-called Phantom?"

"That's one possibility. But I can see them saying that Tanya's spirit is haunting the lake, taking its revenge. That's exactly the kind of story the local kids like to spread around. Everything bad that happens here is blamed on the lake. If I don't find the guy responsible for the murders and disappearances, this episode will go down as yet another part of the legends that overshadow this town." He straightened away from his car. "You two be careful, just in case that Warren guy ends up making an appearance. With the run of bad luck we're having right now, it wouldn't surprise me."

As Dawson's SUV headed down the road, Kaden scanned the woods around the cabin.

"Stop worrying," Shanna said. "Troy may be a bully but he's also a coward. He's not going to hang around with a policeman close by. Or big, strong Kaden Rafferty."

He gave her a lopsided grin that had her pulse leaping.

"Big, strong Kaden Rafferty isn't going take a chance, either way," he teased. "Let's get you into the cabin behind a locked door. I want to hear about your progress on the investigation. Got any new leads?"

She grimaced. "Not really. The main thing I've been able to do is rule people out, not in. My potential suspect list is woefully short." She turned to jog up the stairs.

"Shanna! Get down!" Kaden yelled.

She dropped to the ground just before a bright flash of light zipped past her. She stared in shock at the haft of a large knife sticking out of the railing near where she'd been standing.

A loud bang had her whirling around, still on the ground.

"Get in the cabin," Kaden yelled. "Now."

He was on the ground a few yards away, wrestling with a man holding a gun.

"Shanna, go!" Kaden yelled, slamming an elbow against the side of the man's head.

Her fight-or-flight reflexes finally kicked in as she recognized whom Kaden was fighting.

Her ex. Troy Warren.

She took off, leaping up the stairs two at a time, her shoes squeaking on the wood as she slammed against the doorframe, going too fast to make the turn. She grunted at the pain and bolted into the cabin.

The sound of another gunshot outside had her cringing and praying that Kaden was okay. She grabbed her gun from her purse and ran outside, rushing down the steps, not even slowing down as she sprinted toward where the men were rolling around on the ground, close to Kaden's truck now.

Kaden threw a punch that slammed against Troy's jaw. Blood flew from his mouth, but he didn't stop wrestling for control of the gun.

Shanna stopped a few yards away, pointing her gun skyward, waiting for a clear shot.

Kaden caught sight of her and swore.

The distraction cost him.

Troy slammed an elbow against Kaden's face, and jerked the gun around toward him.

Shanna didn't have a clear shot, but she couldn't wait. She fired up in the air. *Bam! Bam!*

Troy screamed and threw himself against a truck tire.

Kaden grabbed his wrist and wrenched it up against the truck's frame.

Troy screamed again, blood gushing from where the frame had sliced his wrist. The gun went skittering across the ground.

As Kaden scrabbled forward to grab it, Troy took off toward the woods, cradling his wounded hand.

Shanna lowered her gun, lining up the sights at Troy's back. Just as she was about to squeeze the trigger, the gun was plucked from her grip.

Kaden swore. "What are you trying to do? Send yourself to prison over that sleazeball?"

She blinked, then blew out a shaky breath. "I wasn't thinking."

"Damn straight, you weren't. You should have stayed in the cabin, not offered yourself as a target. You took ten years off my life when you came back out here."

She put her hands on her hips. "A simple thank-you would be fine, instead of a lecture."

His swear-laced reply had her gasping in outrage. "Kaden Rafferty. How dare you—"

His mouth came down hard against hers as he pushed her back against the side of the cabin. He ravaged her mouth, setting her nerve endings on fire like molten lava. She whimpered deep in her throat and grasped his shirt, desperately trying to pull it free from his pants.

He broke away, swearing again. "You're dangerous."

"You're a tease."

"For the love of… Get in the cabin, Shanna. Call the police and—"

The sound of a siren had both of them looking down the road.

Shanna crossed her arms. "Looks like Dawson heard the shots."

"Good." He handed her gun back to her. "You can unlock the door once he gets here. In the meantime, barricade yourself inside. Warren's wounded but he's not down for the count."

He checked the loading of Warren's gun, then took off toward the woods, where he'd disappeared.

"Kaden, don't you dare go into those woods on your own. Let the police handle it."

He made a disgusted sound and jogged into the forest.

In desperation, Shanna yelled, "Don't you dare leave me alone to face some murderous psychopath while you go off chasing my idiot ex!"

Silence.

Then, Kaden slowly stepped out from the trees, his jaw set and the gun down at his side.

Dawson's SUV slid across the gravel driveway, barely stopping a few feet from Kaden's truck.

Kaden ignored him as he stalked forward to where Shanna stood at the bottom of the steps. "You don't play fair," he accused.

"As long as you're safe, that's what matters."

"Kaden, Shanna, what's going on? I heard gunshots." Dawson ran up to them, his weapon out and down at his side. "What happened?"

Kaden stared at Shanna and shook his head in disgust.

"You do realize he almost killed you, right? And now, he's free to try again."

"Who's free to try again?" Dawson demanded.

Shanna smiled up at Kaden. "I have faith in you. You'll keep me safe."

Dawson rolled his eyes and stepped away to make a call. "Ortiz, yeah, I'm at the Tate cabin. Someone's been here shooting up the place. A knife's buried in one of the porch railings and there's blood and evidence of a scuffle beside Kaden's truck. I need backup... Yesterday. I'll update you on the situation and who we're after just as soon as I can get Kaden and Shanna to stop flirting with each other and answer my questions."

Kaden glared his displeasure at Dawson.

Shanna burst out laughing.

"At least tell me how many bad guys I'm after," Dawson said. "And which way they went."

Kaden arched an eyebrow at Shanna. "I've got backup. Now, will you lock yourself inside the cabin?"

"What?" Dawson asked. "I'm not backup. You are."

"I'd be happy to," she said. "Go get him." She jogged up the steps and headed into the cabin, locking the door behind her.

It couldn't have been more than fifteen minutes later when a knock sounded at the door.

"Ms. Hudson, it's Officer O'Brien."

Shanna hurried to unlock the door and pull it open. But her greeting died on her lips when she saw the urgency in O'Brien's face. "What happened? Is Kaden—"

"Mr. Rafferty and the chief are both okay. The chief phoned in an update as I was pulling into the driveway. You're going to be hearing a lot more sirens, other people arriving, in just a few minutes. I've been asked to make sure you don't leave this cabin, that you stay locked inside. Even if, um, even if I have to handcuff you to the refrigerator, or whatever I can find to make sure you can't leave the cabin. Ma'am." Her face turned a slight red.

Shanna narrowed her eyes. "The chief wouldn't have told you that."

"Not in those words, no."

"Kaden did."

O'Brien gave her a pained smile. "Will you promise you'll wait until Mr. Rafferty or one of us police tell you it's okay to come out before you do so? Please?"

Shanna sighed. "Fine. Okay. I promise I won't come out until I'm given permission." She rolled her eyes. "But only if you swear that Kaden's really okay."

"He's uninjured, from what I've been told. I haven't seen him yet. I only spoke to him on the phone."

"Fair enough."

The policewoman gave her a relieved smile, then hurried outside, pulling the door closed behind her.

Shanna turned the lock, then settled down to wait, her foot tapping an impatient tune against the wooden floor.

"WAKE UP, BEAUTIFUL. We're leaving."

"Hmm?" Shanna slapped at the hand pulling on her covers and snuggled into her pillow.

An impatient sigh sounded. "Come on, sleepyhead. Your chariot awaits."

"Chariot?" She yawned, wondering what kind of dream had chariots and grumpy-sounding princes in them.

"Unbelievable," her prince complained.

Her world suddenly tilted and her head fell back against something hard. And warm. The ground began to shake. She grabbed for her pillow.

"Ouch, dang. Sheathe those claws." Her world tilted again and her bottom pressed down on something hard and cold.

Her eyes flew open. She blinked and looked around. What the? She was in the bathroom? On the floor?

"Ew," she exclaimed, trying to jump to her feet. Her legs got all tangled up in her comforter. Her comforter?

Laughter sounded above her.

She looked up into Kaden's amused eyes as he bent down and began pulling the comforter off her shoulders.

"Kaden?"

"Shanna?" He freed her and tossed the comforter into the tub.

"Why am I in the bathroom, on the floor? With you?"

"Because I couldn't wake you up. Do you always sleep like the dead?"

"I have no idea. Help me up. Why were you trying to wake me, anyway? Wait, Kaden. You're here."

He was laughing as he helped her stand. "I don't remember you being this confused this morning when you woke up."

"That's because I woke up on my own, not when some rude person dropped me onto the bathroom floor. Gross, by the way, regardless of how much of a clean freak my sister might be."

"I didn't drop you. And you have approximately five minutes to do whatever you need to do in here before we leave."

"Leave. Wait, that's what the prince said."

He frowned. "Prince?"

Her face heated. "Never mind. It must be late or I wouldn't be this tired. Not that I can tell the time with all the windows blocked out." She blinked at him, her stomach clenching with sympathy. "Your right eye's turning black."

"Warren got a lucky shot in earlier. Poor jerk."

"Poor jerk? He's a stalker and an attempted murderer. I have absolutely no sympathy for him. Wait. You caught him? Dawson's taking him to jail?"

His jaw tightened. "Not exactly." He glanced at his dive watch. "I'll explain on the way. I've already packed you a bag. Just…wash your face or whatever you need to do and get dressed. You have four more minutes. After that, I'm hauling you out of here, even if you're naked." He checked his watch. "Make that three minutes."

"Ugh." She stomped her feet in frustration and shooed him away with her hands. "Get out. I need a minute."

"I figured you would." He smiled, but it didn't quite reach his eyes, or ease the tension along his jaw.

Before she could ask him again what had happened, he left, pulling the door closed behind him.

True to Kaden's threat, he was back to get her in just a few minutes. Luckily she'd already emptied her bladder and brushed her teeth. She was tying her shoes when he knocked, then shoved open the door.

"Let's go."

She called him some unsavory names that had his mouth twitching with amusement, but he didn't complain. He didn't say anything at all. He just grabbed her hand, and hauled her through the cabin and out the door, barely giving her a chance to grab her purse.

The sky was black as velvet, not a star in sight. Clouds must have moved in while she was sleeping. Seeing the driveway and yard empty now, except for Kaden's truck, her sedan, and his boat trailer sitting near the end of the cabin sent a shiver up her spine. It was too dark, too quiet, especially given the chaos she'd heard outside earlier when all the police had been there.

Refusing to answer any questions, he lifted her into the truck and shut the door. After rushing around the hood, he hopped into the driver's seat, tossed a black leather carry-on bag into the back and locked his door. His tires spit gravel as he turned around in the yard, then he sent his truck barreling down the road toward town.

"Slow down, Mario Andretti," she complained, clinging to the armrest, "or we'll end up in a ditch."

He checked the rearview mirror and the side one before easing up slightly on the gas.

"Well, that was fun," she said, letting her death grip on the armrest go. "Fastest I ever got ready. Hope you don't mind the lack of makeup. Lucky for you I have some in my purse so I won't scare everyone who sees me in the morning. It's too late for me not to scare you."

As if against his will, his mouth curved in a smile. "You're adorable when you first wake up. But your disposition could use some sweetening."

She snorted.

He laughed.

"Since this is the road into town," she said, "and according to the clock in your truck it's past, oh wow, two thirty in the morning, we're either going to the police station—"

"Nope."

"Or...out of town?"

"Too far a drive right now through a creepy, dark two-lane road for an hour to reach Chattanooga. I'm half-asleep myself. We'll figure out our next steps in the morning, after we get some rest and both have a clear head."

"Ah. We're going to Stella's, the B and B."

"Best hotel in town."

"The only hotel in town."

He smiled. "I called ahead. The desk clerk said he'd leave our room key under the cookie jar on the counter."

"That sounds really secure."

"I'll clear the room before we go inside. And the police station is just across the lake. If we need them, they're less than a minute away."

"You sound like a cop yourself lately. 'Clear the room.' I think you've been around far too many police officers this week."

"I couldn't agree more."

"All right. The B and B. We've got about fifteen minutes before we get there. Well, the way you're driving, maybe only ten. Plenty of time for you to tell me what happened after I humored you by locking myself in the cabin. Speak, Kaden. I'm about out of patience."

By the time he made the turn at the end of Main Street and headed around the end of the lake in town, she was numb with shock over what he'd told her.

He and Dawson had tracked Troy into the woods and found him tied to a tree, his throat slit.

Beside him was Sam Morton. Tied to the same tree, covered in blood. But it wasn't his. It was Troy's. Sam had numerous cuts and scrapes, and was covered in bug bites. But there was nothing more serious wrong with him, physically at least, except for stun-gun burns on his neck.

Just like Jessica.

He'd seen the killer slice Troy's throat and was hysterical and blubbering behind a gag over his mouth when Dawson and Kaden found him.

When they'd calmed Sam down, he told them he and Jack had been taken at knifepoint and with the threat of a stun gun by the killer behind the public boat ramp, as the police had theorized. He'd forced them to hike endlessly through the mountains. Eventually, he'd brought them to a side-by-side, a four-wheeler hidden in the woods. He'd tied them to the seats and blindfolded them before taking them on a long, winding ride that seemed to take hours.

Sam didn't know where Jack was. Jack had been taken away while Sam was left handcuffed to a tree. This morning the killer brought Sam to the woods behind Cassidy's cabin. He'd heard in town that Shanna had some stalker bully after her. In his own sick way, the killer had planned to kill Sam—someone he considered to be a bully, too—and leave him as an offering of justice for Shanna.

When Troy showed up, he became the perfect target. Instead of killing Sam, the killer had murdered Troy. After slicing Troy's throat, he'd warned Sam, "This is what happens to bullies." Then he'd taken off before Kaden and Dawson could catch him.

Shanna shivered as Kaden pulled the truck into a parking space behind the B and B.

True to his word, the clerk had left the key under the cookie jar. And Kaden, with a gun in his hand that must have been given to him by Dawson, made her wait just inside the door while he checked out the huge walk-in dressing room closet, under the bed, the attached bathroom—anywhere he thought a killer could possibly hide. Only then did he allow her to move freely around the room.

She immediately sank onto the bench at the end of one of the two double beds, her horrified and confused mind full of questions. But she only asked one.

"Kaden."

"Hmm." He'd just finished putting their toiletries in the

bathroom and set the bag on a chair in the dressing room before sitting beside her.

"Who is this man who exacts his own form of perverted justice against people that he thinks are bullies? Who is he?"

His voice was subdued, tired, as he answered. "He told Sam he was the Phantom."

"Oh, my God." Her shoulders began to shake with her sobs as the events of the last few days shredded her composure.

Kaden pulled her onto his lap and cradled her, whispering soothing words against the top of her head as she cried against his neck.

Chapter Seventeen

Kaden listened to Dawson on the phone as he stood at the B and B's bedroom window, watching the sun come up over the lake trying to burn through the heavier-than-usual mist rising from the water.

"Sounds like a depressing lack of progress." Kaden tried to focus in spite of his right eye having swelled half-shut from that one lucky punch Warren had landed. "I'd have figured with the state police searching for Jack through the night that they'd have at least found some indication of where he might have been taken."

"Give me a break. Last time we saw each other was only, what, five hours ago? No, they haven't found Jack and, yes, they're still searching. Their search is focused on two areas now, the woods behind the boat ramp and behind the Tate cabin. But so far, no dice. Did you even get any sleep last night?"

"Not much." He glanced toward the bathroom as the door opened and Shanna came out, her hair damp from her shower and her body wrapped in one of the B and B's fluffy white towels. His mouth went dry as he watched her cross the room. With a sleepy smile and a wave, she headed into the large closet to get dressed.

"Kaden? Kaden, you still there?" Dawson asked.

"What? Oh, sorry. I was…distracted."

Dawson laughed. "I'll bet you were. How's Shanna doing?"

"What you'd expect. She was upset last night but she's strong. She's more determined than ever to find some kind of evidence today that will tell her where Jack's being held. She was combing through topography maps on her laptop before I even woke up, trying to figure out—in her words—where she'd hold someone captive if she was trying to hide in these mountains."

"More power to her. Have her pass along any theories she comes up with."

"Will do." Kaden leaned closer to the window. "The mist doesn't seem to be burning off as quickly as usual. Seems strange, given the warmer spring temperatures."

"They don't call it Mystic Lake just because of the mystical stories about it. That mist has a mind of its own. You never know when it will roll in or roll out. Are you okay staying at Stella's for a few more hours, at least until I get a safe house lined up and transport arranged? I sure don't want her out roaming around with this killer on the loose. He's got some weird thing about bullies and I don't know whether his sick offering yesterday is his only interest in her."

"She's not going anywhere alone, that's for sure. I'll do what I can to keep her occupied while we wait on you."

"I'll bet." Dawson started laughing.

"Grow up." Kaden ended the call, smiling.

He let the curtain close and pocketed his cell phone as he turned around, expecting to see Shanna waiting for him. But the room was empty. He smiled again. As long as it had taken her to shower and put her makeup on, he shouldn't be so surprised it was taking her this long to put on a pair of jeans and a blouse.

He sat on the bed, browsing through the notes she'd made this morning on her laptop. It surprised him to see a list of mines in the area, and a list of known caves around the lake. Maybe since Sam had told them the killer was calling himself the Phantom, she was looking into the legends Stella had told them about.

A few pages into her notes, he saw something else that surprised him. Questions she'd written. He read the first one.

Why didn't Kaden find Tanya's remains in the lake near the bonfire clearing?

He grimaced. He'd wondered that himself. But the water was especially deep there, and riddled with old decaying buildings and even trees that made the sonar ineffective. It was going to take a lot more dives to thoroughly search that area. He read the next notation.

KISS. Keep It Simple, Stupid.

The words were bolded and underlined. That was Shanna. She didn't pull any punches. Most of the remaining questions were typical of what they'd both been asking for days, without any answers. The last question was *Where is Jack?* Beneath that she'd written:

Tanya.
The bonfire clearing.
Jack.
Tristan. The cove.

He frowned. Did she think the killer had taken Jack to the bonfire clearing after Dawson and him had called off the boat search near there yesterday afternoon? And drowned him like he and the others had done to Tanya? It was a disturbing theory. He was really hoping that Jack would be found alive and wouldn't become another deadly Mystic Lake statistic. Hopefully, he'd be given clearance soon to search the cove again where he'd found Tristan, the one her notes mentioned. He'd use the sonar first, just in case the worst had happened and there was another fresh body down there, not buried beneath a year's worth of sediment and debris.

Jack's body.

He set the laptop aside and looked at the closed closet door. It was quiet. Too quiet. The hairs on the back of his neck stood up and a feeling of dread shot through him. He jumped to his feet and crossed the room, briefly knocking on the door before yanking it open.

The closet was empty.

Chapter Eighteen

The knife nudged Shanna in the back.

"Hurry up." The man calling himself the Phantom pushed her, making her stumble in the dark tunnel, lit only by the flashlight he was holding. "I don't like being downtown. Too many people. Don't make me cut you again, or wrap your mouth in duct tape again."

Like he'd done in the closet at the B and B. One minute she'd been pulling her shirt over her head. The next, a draft of cool, musty air had her turning to see a man coming through an opening in the wall. Before she could even scream, he'd pressed a stun gun against her neck. And before she could recover from the electrical shock, he'd shoved a cloth in her mouth and covered it with duct tape. Thankfully he'd removed it once he was far enough away from the B and B to worry about being heard. She could breathe much better without that rancid cloth in her mouth.

The sound of water dripping somewhere up ahead had her stopping. "Is—is there water down here?"

"It's a mine, in a mountain full of waterfalls and creeks. What do you think? Now, go." Once again, the knife pricked her in the back.

She jerked away from its sharp tip and forced her legs

to move, to trudge forward in spite of the panic flowing through her veins.

Drip. Drip. Drip.

Please don't let this lead to water. Don't let it be water. Please.

Finally, the tunnel began to even out, head more in what seemed like an uphill direction. She drew a relieved breath, then another. He wasn't taking her to an underground pool of water to drown her. So where was he taking her? And why?

Focus. Think.

She tried to picture the maps she'd reviewed earlier of the old, abandoned mines in the area. But the maps were from before the deadly storms had diverted the river and flooded the old town that used to be here. Were they even reliable?

Think, Shanna. Talk to him. Get the information you need.

"If—if you tell me where we're going, maybe I can go faster. It's hard to follow the path in the dark."

"Just keep going straight where my flashlight is shining. It doesn't curve again for a quarter mile. I'll tell you when to turn."

She kept going, doing her best not to stumble. She didn't want to make him mad or fall and break a bone. Staying healthy and able to run at the first opportunity was her only chance. A quarter mile to the next turn? There were only two mines she remembered on the map that were that long. The two of them had only made right turns since coming down the secret passageway at the B and B and entering this shaft. And the musty smell was still strong, The old Cooper's Bluff mine. That had to be it. The other long mine would have taken them off to the left. If they were in the Cooper's Bluff mine, then they were heading…

She started to shake. A whimper caught in her throat. She knew exactly where this mine would end.

Keep it simple, stupid.

The bonfire clearing.

Where Tanya had disappeared. Where Jack had likely disappeared. And now—now, where she would disappear.

They were heading to the lake.

"Up ahead, there's your right turn."

After making the turn, she drew several bracing breaths. How far was the bonfire clearing from here? Miles. Too far to walk. Maybe he wasn't taking her where she thought. Maybe—

"That patch of light. That's our exit."

Sunlight. The green of trees. This was her chance. She sped up.

He jerked her backward, a rock-solid arm around her neck. The cold steel of the knife pressed against her cheek. "You remember that knife back at the cabin? The one that other guy threw? He missed. I never miss. You try to take off and I'll kill you. Got it?"

"G-got it," she whispered, struggling to answer without getting cut.

He let her go, and shoved her again. She could feel the heat of him behind her as he kept close, no doubt pointing the knife at her back. She'd have to bide her time, wait for the right opportunity to escape. For now, she'd do what he said.

Kaden.

Unbidden, his image rose in her mind. What was he thinking right now? He had to have discovered that she'd gone missing. And she knew he was probably tearing the place apart searching for her. But the hidden door in the closet was locked from the other side with a thick steel bar. There was no way he'd be able to go through it even if he knew it was there. He wouldn't have any way of figuring out where she went. He didn't know about the tunnel under the B and B. According to the Phantom, no one did. But him.

She was truly on her own.

Bright sunlight temporarily blinded her as she stepped out of the mine shaft. Her captor chuckled as he jerked her arms behind her, using his duct tape again to tape them together. When her sight cleared, she realized he was wearing sunglasses. He must have put them on just before exiting the mine. She blinked and looked around. They were in the woods, in a small clearing. And on the other side of the clearing was a side-by-side, the exact same kind of four-wheeler that Sam had described.

Without a word, he lifted her onto the front passenger seat, then secured her with a seat belt. He held up the knife again, inches from her face, then chuckled and shoved it into a sheathe attached to the doorframe beside him.

"There's no one around to hear you scream, so don't bother. If you do, though, I'll gag you again so I won't have to listen to it."

"Where are we going? Why are doing this to me?"

He looked at her as if he thought she'd lost her mind. "We're kindred spirits. I'm helping you."

"Helping me?"

"Saving you from the bullies." His mouth scrunched in a sneer. "No one saved me. But I saved you. You should be thanking me for getting rid of that ex of yours."

He set the vehicle in motion, racing down a well-worn path through the woods, a path that wasn't on any of the tourist maps of the area. "They never thank me," he complained. "Not once."

They? Never? How many people had he done this to?

Practically feeling the heat of the anger seething in him, she said, "Thank you. For—for saving me."

He gave her a suspicious glance. "You're thanking me?"

"Of course." She smiled, or tried to. "Troy made my life hell. I'm sure he would have…would have hurt me if you hadn't been there. You protected me."

His chin lifted and his back straightened as if with pride. "Dang straight I did."

"Can you… Can you tell me where we're going? Please?"

His mouth curved in a benevolent smile. "I'm taking you where you've wanted to go ever since you got here and started snooping around. I'm taking you to Tanya."

Chapter Nineteen

Kaden brought the axe crashing against the Sheetrock, knocking a hole in the closet wall. Dawson immediately stepped forward, helping him break through.

"See a passageway?" Kaden asked.

Dawson shook his head. "Are you sure that Shanna didn't get past you, go out into the hallway?"

"She was in the closet. Someone's got her, that Phantom or whoever. There has to be a secret passage in the wall."

"Hey, hey, what the heck are you doing to my hotel?"

They both turned to see Stella standing in the doorway. "State police are running all over downstairs thumping on walls and now, you two are up here busting holes. What's going on?"

"He's got Shanna," Kaden told her, his voice tight and raw. "Someone took her."

"From the closet?"

"She went inside and never came out. There's a hidden door in here somewhere. Has to be."

She whirled around and left.

"Move your hands," Kaden ordered.

Dawson jumped back and Kaden brought his axe crashing down a foot to the right of the first hole. "Check it."

"Nothing. Just lumber, no gaps."

"It sounded hollow when I banged on the wall before. Maybe it's on this side."

Again, Kaden swung the axe. Again, there was no opening.

"Make room for Frank."

Kaden frowned and glanced over his shoulder. Stella ushered her husband into the tight space. He, too, was holding one of the fire axes, like the one that Kaden had grabbed from the wall in the hallway. Without a word, he shoved past Kaden and began pounding on the wall with the dull end of the axe, knocking holes as he went, in a straight line, from right to left.

Kaden swore and started doing the same thing, but from left to right. The sound of metal on metal had him whirling around.

Frank motioned toward the last hole he'd made. "Metal bar on the other side. This must be the door."

With Frank, Dawson and Kaden ripping and breaking through the Sheetrock, the passage was quickly revealed.

"Stairs," Stella announced from over their shoulders. "Well, I'll be. They go straight down. What do you think, Frank? The Cooper's Bluff mine shaft? You think it runs all the way to the B and B?"

He nodded. "Could be."

"We'll need flashlights," Kaden said.

"Hang on." Stella ran from the room.

"Dawson—"

"Yeah, yeah. I'll grab my guys from downstairs. Be right back."

Stella ran into the room, passing Dawson as he ran out. "Here, Kaden. That's the only one I could find." She gave

Frank a stern look. "Someone hasn't been keeping up with the batteries around here. The others are dead."

Frank rolled his eyes.

"Tell Dawson he'll need more flashlights," Kaden said. "I'm not waiting for him." He ducked under the metal bar that was no longer holding anything, since the Sheetrock and wood around it had been obliterated, and jogged down the steep set of steps.

Chapter Twenty

In spite of the frightening speed at which her captor raced his four-wheeler through the woods, it seemed as if they'd ridden forever until he finally began to slow. Although she'd tried to keep her bearings, to figure out where they were going, the thick canopy of trees blocked out most of the sun. It was impossible to be sure in what direction they were headed. But judging by the turns they'd made, they seemed to be going in a somewhat straight line.

That meant most likely they were still heading out of town, parallel with the lake. But where, exactly? She clenched her fists in frustration. Her one chance at escape may have been when they'd exited the mine. She should have made a run for it. Even half-blind from the sunlight she might have had a better chance than now, with her arms duct-taped behind her. He had no plans of ever letting her go. That was obvious, since he hadn't blindfolded her, as he'd done with Sam. He wasn't worried about leaving a witness behind.

Earlier she'd hoped that Kaden would find her, that he'd somehow manage to rescue her. Now, with time potentially running out, she hoped for the opposite. She prayed he wouldn't put himself in danger for her. Somehow, she'd managed to fall half-in-love with him in an incredibly short amount of time. Love at first sight? Such a cliché, but she felt it deep within her soul. She couldn't bear the thought of him getting hurt, or killed, because he tried to help her.

The vehicle finally slowed, then stopped. He grabbed his knife and pulled her out. Then he slashed her bindings as he'd done shortly after entering the mine.

She rubbed her aching wrists. "Thank you. That feels so much better."

"I only did it so you can keep your balance. I don't want to have to keep picking you up and pushing you along." He prodded her forward. "Not too much farther. You'll see."

Going as slowly as she dared, stalling for time, she tried to get more information.

"Is there something I can call you other than the Phantom? It seems so…impersonal. We're friends, right? You saved me from a bully."

He gave her a sideways look. "The Phantom is all you'll get. It's been my name for the past twenty years. No reason to change now."

"Twenty years. You've lived in Mystic Lake that whole time?"

"Mostly. Why?"

"I'm just…making conversation. Have you…saved… others? Like me?"

His eyes narrowed. "Why all the questions?"

She shrugged. "I just… I want to know more about you. You're my hero, right?" She nearly choked on the words, struggling to keep a straight face. "But I don't even know how you heard about me, or knew about Troy."

"That guy at your cabin? The one who threw a knife at you?"

"Yes."

He shrugged and jerked her arm, forcing her to move faster. "I'd heard around town about you and that boat guy looking into my business. Didn't know about this… Troy. I went to your cabin to send you a warning. I was going to leave that other bully's body as a message to tell you to keep your nose out of my business or you'd end up like him. But when I got there he was threatening you. That's when I knew what I had to do." He nodded sagely, as if his explanation made perfect sense.

"And what is that?" she asked.

He frowned and shoved her again. "Just like you said. That guy was bullying you. That's when I knew he needed to learn the lesson and that you were the one who needed saving. What are you, stupid or something?"

"I'm sorry."

He grunted and trudged along, every once in a while jerking her arm to make her go faster.

She skirted close to bushes and low hanging branches, hoping to catch some fabric on one of them as a bread crumb, a clue, for someone to find if they did come looking for her. But every time she got caught he stopped and carefully removed any trace of fabric, smiling as if he knew her game.

A few minutes later, she tried again to learn something, anything that might help her figure out what was going on and what kinds of weaknesses he might have. She needed leverage of some type if she was going to either talk her way out of this situation or plan an escape.

"Did you, ah, teach a lesson to anyone else that I might have heard of? Besides Troy. Did you teach Tristan a lesson? Jessica?"

His smug smile was his only answer. But she understood the answer as if he'd shouted at her. He'd killed both of them. Her insides ran cold. She was in the woods with a psychopath. And he'd turned his latest attentions on her.

She started to shake.

He glanced sideways at her again, not slowing. "Something wrong with you? You're shaking like you're cold. You sick or something?" He jerked her to a halt and whirled her to face him, holding up his knife. "I don't want you to get me sick. There ain't any doctors up in these mountains and most of the cabins will be filled up with tourists in the next few weeks and months. Medicine's going to be scarce and hard to find without risking being seen." He pressed the knife's tip against her throat. "Answer me. Are you sick?"

She lifted her head ever so slightly, trying to avoid the sharp blade. "No. I'm not sick. I swear. I'm just…nervous. You know, around new people."

He narrowed his eyes again as if weighing her words for truth. Then his dark eyes widened as if in understanding. And he smiled. "You're scared ain't ya? Scared of old Phil?"

"Phil? Is that your name?"

He roared with rage and slammed a fist against her jaw.

She whirled around and fell onto the ground, gnashing her teeth against the pain to keep from crying out. She didn't want to give him that satisfaction.

He stood over her and leaned down until he, and his knife, were inches from her face. "I told you my name is the Phantom."

She should have said something, begged his forgiveness. But her jaw ached and throbbed. And she was so angry she didn't think she could speak right now without telling him exactly what she thought of him. He'd probably slash her throat to shut her up. So she remained silent.

He finally straightened and stepped back. "Get up."

She was eye level with a sensitive part of his anatomy, thankfully covered by grimy jeans. She wondered if she could slam her fist against him hard enough to drop him to his knees before he could stab her.

He grabbed her arm and yanked her to her feet, then slashed the knife against her left arm, leaving a streak of red across it.

She swore and grabbed her arm.

He laughed, then sobered, pointing. "Move. We're almost there."

Hate wasn't usually in her vocabulary. But she didn't feel an ounce of remorse about hating this man right now. She marched forward, holding her throbbing arm. One benefit was that it hurt so much she barely noticed her aching jaw anymore.

A moment later, the trees seemed to fall away as they entered a clearing. She stopped so quickly he ran into her, then swore.

"I didn't tell you to stop. Move."

She stayed rooted to the spot, staring at the remains of the last bonfire that had been held here, and at the lake beyond. She'd been right after all. KISS. Keep It Simple, Stupid. Everything came back to where it had all begun, this place. Where Tanya's life had ended and the bullies who'd killed her began to disappear or die, one by one. He hadn't admitted it, but she'd heard enough, seen enough to no longer have any doubt. And if she didn't do something she was going to become his latest victim.

The water sparkled off to her right. How many times had she dived into a pool, felt the thrill of the water rushing over her, the satisfaction of well-toned muscles pulling her through it like a fish. All she had to do was run, jump in, and swim away. This Phantom—Phil—was tall and strong. But he was older than her, past middle age. And she was fast in the water, or had been. Olympic champion hopeful fast.

Go. Run. Jump.

She tried to make her legs move. But she was frozen in place. Images of the last time she'd been in the water flooded her vision. Her hair, pulling her down. Trapped. Bubbles of air escaping her lungs, rising to the surface above her. And when she couldn't hold her breath another second, the burn of chlorine spilling into her lungs as they filled with water.

Her hands fisted at her sides as she stared at the lake. But she couldn't make herself move.

He grabbed her arm, swearing when she fell. "What's wrong with you?" He grabbed her again and yanked her up, then pushed her away from the water, past the bonfire area, circling behind a large boulder.

She stopped in confusion.

"In there," he said, motioning her toward a tree in front of one of the boulders.

"I don't... What do you mean? There's nowhere to go."

He chuckled. "Sure there is. That tree is hollow. Duck down. You'll see. The cave is dark, so anyone looking at the hole in the tree won't see it. I discovered it years ago." His mouth scrunched up in a sneer. "Go on. She's waiting."

"She?"

"Tanya. You're about to join her."

He was going to kill her. Right now.

She lashed out with her foot, trying to sweep his legs out from under him.

He jumped to the side, laughing, then shoved her down and pushed her inside the hole in the tree.

She brought her hands up to protect her face from being

slammed into the back of the tree. But she kept going, falling forward to the ground.

He was right. There'd been a hole in the back of the tree. She was on the cool, damp ground. A cave?

It was so dark, she could barely make out the rock walls around her. The cave dipped down, several feet below ground level. That explained why no one else had ever found it. No one would expect a large cave to be hidden behind a half-rotten tree and a boulder that was about six feet by six feet.

She sensed more than saw him standing beside her. He moved past her and she heard the sound of…keys? There was a loud click and the squeak of metal. A moment later, he was back, his hot breath making her shiver with revulsion as he leaned in close. The flashlight snapped on, startling her as it painted his face in light and shadow, like a creepy mask in a horror movie.

He laughed and aimed the light down at the sloping floor. "Shanna Hudson, meet Tanya Jericho."

She swallowed, hard, trying not to gag as he pointed the flashlight at the piles of bones that had apparently been hidden here ever since Tanya had gone missing. Except that there wasn't a pile of bones. There were metal floor-to-ceiling bars secured toward the back of the cave. And in the middle was a door, open now. That's probably the sound she'd heard earlier, his jailor's keys as he'd unlocked it. But it was what was behind that open door that had Shanna starting to shake again.

Dirty red hair, wide, frightened eyes blinking and turning away from the light. Painfully thin arms lifting to cover her eyes.

Tanya Jericho. *She was alive.*

Shanna's mouth dropped open in disbelief. Then, as if

the two of them were the best of friends and had known each other for years, she ran to the other girl. They wrapped their arms around each other and held on tight, Tanya's tears quickly soaking through Shanna's shirt.

The door clanged shut behind them, startling them apart. The Phantom turned his key in the lock and chuckled. "Enjoy each other's company for a while. I'll even leave you a light." He slid the flashlight through the bars and set it on the ground. "I don't want anything to spoil this day. After all, I have big plans for Jack. Another bully will be taught a valuable lesson before the sun goes down. And don't you worry, Tanya. I'll get the others. They can't hide forever. Just ask your new friend, Shanna. I took care of her bully, too." He laughed and left the cave.

As soon as he was gone, Shanna pulled the shaking young girl down to sit on the ground. "Tanya, I can't believe it's really you. We thought you'd drowned."

"I almost did. Better if I had."

Shanna pushed the girl's hair back from her face. "Don't say that. Don't give up now. Somehow, by some miracle, you've survived for almost a year since you went missing. We're going to get out of here."

Tanya stared at her as if in shock. "A year? I've been here a whole…year?"

"You went missing almost a year ago, yes. Has he kept you here this whole time?"

She shook her head, no. "We move around. Go to cabins when it's cold or he needs to stock up. Or when he says I stink too bad and need a shower." She grimaced. "But I always end up back here." She hung her head. "Others have been here too. I'm always happy to see them, because I'm so lonely. But then I feel guilty." Her eyes brightened with unshed tears. "He'll kill you too. Just like he's done with all the others."

Shanna stared at her in horror. "All the others? How many?"

Tanya ducked her head and shrugged, drawing her knees up and hugging them to her chest.

"Tanya?"

"Hm?"

"He's not going to kill me. And he's not going to kill you. We're going to get out of here."

Tanya sighed as if she'd heard that dozens of times and lifted her head. "Who—who are you? He made it sound like you're someone else being bullied. You're not one of the bullies?"

"I guess that's all a matter of perspective. Everyone has probably treated someone else poorly at some time in their life. Does that make them a bully? In that moment, maybe. But good people sometimes do bad things. It doesn't always mean they're bad people. Don't let that Phantom guy get into your mind, twist you to his way of thinking. Is that what he told you? That he's, what, holding you captive for your own good? That he's punishing those who hurt you?"

She shrugged. "You know about them? Peyton? Her friends?"

"Some, yes. I'm a private investigator, helping your parents find you."

Her eyes widened. "My parents? They don't think I'm dead?"

"They…haven't given up hope of finding you."

"I want to go home." The sudden longing in her voice broke Shanna's heart.

"Then let's get you home. Have you tried working any of these bars loose? They're rusty and corroded."

"The night he took me, I tried them. And for days afterward. Maybe weeks. But I gave up a long time ago."

"The night he took you? Was that at the bonfire, when the others found you watching them and got mad?"

She hung her head as if in shame. "I just thought Peyton and I could be friends if she'd give me a chance. I was watching but didn't know they saw me. They were really upset, said terrible things."

"And this man, the Phantom, he saw them?"

"He lives in the woods. He watches everyone, knows everything going on around here."

"No he doesn't."

Tanya frowned.

Shanna gave her a sad smile. "He's big and scary and I'm sure he tells you all kinds of stories to scare you, to control you. But in the end, he's just a man. We can defeat him if we work together."

Tanya shrugged noncommittally and looked away.

"Peyton told me they pushed you under the water and you never came back up. She and her friends thought they'd killed you."

"They almost did. My hair caught on something in the lake. I couldn't get away. The next thing I knew I woke up here. He—the man—he saved me from them. He got me free and brought me here to—to get justice for me, and for him, too."

Shanna stared at her, dismayed at the words tumbling out of her mouth. She'd been brainwashed into believing the lies this Phantom told her, thinking he'd somehow saved her. But Shanna couldn't set her straight right now. All she could do was keep her talking to see whether she knew anything that could help either of them get away. She turned her attention to the bars and began twisting and pulling at them. "You said for him too. What did you mean?"

"Those bars won't come out," she said. "I've tried all of them."

"It's not like we have books to read to pass the time, right? Might as well try the bars myself," Shanna told her.

"Books." The word was uttered in awe. "I miss books."

The pain was back in Tanya's voice. Maybe there was a chance of reaching her after all, of making her realize the man who was keeping her here wasn't her savior in any way.

Shanna tugged and twisted one of the bars, wincing at the pain that shot through her cut arm. "The man who brought you here was bullied? Is that what you were telling me?"

"He was." Tanya's voice gained in strength as she regurgitated what he'd no doubt told her over and over, feeding her what he wanted her to believe. "He was bullied, just like me. They ruined his life. He couldn't…focus, keep a job."

"He's homeless."

"I guess. But it's not his fault. The kids who were mean to him in school, they're the ones who did that to him." She drew a shuddering breath. "They can't bother anyone else again. That's what he said. And he wants to do that for me, too. I told him everything I knew about Jack and the others. He made plans so they won't hurt me ever again. He's very smart."

"I'm sure he is." Shanna did her best to hide her shock. The Phantom had apparently killed others, when he was younger. And now he was killing again. How many victims were there? She turned back to the bars, tugging and twisting harder now.

"Only Jack and Peyton are left now," Tanya said. "I think. I'm not sure about Sam, if he got him yet."

Shanna stopped and turned around to fully face her. "Got him? Tanya, did he tell you what he was going to do to each of them?"

The young girl's face twisted with despair and tears started tracking down her face. "He told me…he said he'd teach them a lesson. I said… I said…go ahead. I was angry, upset. I never expected him to actually…do what he did. When he brought Tristan here, I—"

"Tristan? Tristan Cargill?"

She nodded and wiped at her tears. "He brought him here, made him apologize to me. I told him I forgave him. Everything was okay. When he was gone, I thought… I thought the Phantom let him go. But then Jessica was here and told me Tristan…that he'd been found in the lake. It's my fault. It's all my fault." She broke down, sobbing.

Shanna held her, trying to reassure this terrorized, confused young girl. "It's not your fault. He's the one hurting people. But we can stop him, together, before he hurts anyone else. We just have to work together to get out of here. Okay?"

She hiccupped, but wouldn't meet Shanna's gaze.

Shanna sighed. She didn't have time for a therapy session. As much as she empathized with Tanya for whatever horrible things she'd suffered in the months since she'd been abducted, helping her get better was only going to happen if Shanna could get her out of this place to somewhere safe.

"We have to get out of here, Tanya. As quickly as possible."

"But there isn't any way out. Not without the keys."

"Start pulling and twisting the bars. If we can't bend or break one, we'll tunnel underneath them. We're both thin.

Two, three bars would be enough. What do you say? Let's at least try. Girl power."

Tanya's lower lip trembled, but she drew a deep breath and something seemed to spark in her eyes lit by the glow of the flashlight.

Hope.

"How will we dig?" Tanya asked.

Shanna picked up the flashlight. "With this. It's made out of metal. We can use it like a shovel. But first, we have to find the weakest bars, the softest dirt. Come on. Let's do this. Let's go home."

Chapter Twenty-One

Kaden slid to a halt a short distance into the mine shaft, shining his flashlight on the ground. There were footprints in the damp earth. One set was large and deep, like a big man might make. The other was dainty and small like Shanna would make. But something was prickling at the edge of his consciousness, telling him to stop. What was it?

The map. The map of the mines from Shanna's computer. Stella had said this was the Cooper's Bluff mine shaft. That shaft went on for a good quarter mile. After that, it opened into the woods. The Phantom had a head start. And the element of surprise. He had to have reached the exit by now. Then what? Would he go through the woods? Or head to the opening of another shaft and continue underground? Where? Where to? The possibilities were endless and he could spend all day trying to find Shanna, only to arrive too late to help her.

Or he could think this through. Figure out where she was being taken. The clues were there, somewhere, niggling at him. He just had to piece them together. Fast.

In spite of his misgivings, he couldn't *not* follow. Shanna had gone this way. He couldn't just turn around and—

"Kaden," Dawson called out. "Wait up."

He turned around, holding up a hand to shield his eyes from the flashlights as Dawson and a group of six state policemen caught up to him.

Kaden pointed to the ground. "He took her through this tunnel."

"We'll find her, sir," one of the officers said as they jogged past him.

"Why did you stop?" Dawson asked.

Shanna's notes. The last ones he'd read. What had she said? "Keep it simple, stupid."

Dawson frowned. "What?"

"Shanna's research, her notes. She knew the mines were around here. She mapped them out. And she studied the topography and…she wrote down KISS."

"Keep it simple, yeah, yeah. What of it?"

"Under that she wrote something about the bonfire clearing. No, not just something. It was specific. She wrote…" He closed his eyes, trying to picture the exact words she'd used. "Tanya. The bonfire clearing. Jack. Tristan. The cove."

"And? What does it mean?"

"I think she was saying to stop making things so complicated. The guy we're dealing with isn't some criminal mastermind. He's a thief and a coward, likely stealing people's food and supplies from the cabins in these mountains when they're empty of tourists and hunters. And for fun, or some kind of misguided sense of a divine mission, he's punishing people he believes need to be punished. Remember what Sam said the Phantom said about bullies? But this guy cheats. He doesn't fight fair. He uses a stun gun, sneaks up on them. Hell, he probably used a stun gun on Tristan to drown him. I'll bet the cuts on his bones were postmortem."

"They were. The ME confirmed it."

Kaden tightened his hand around his flashlight. "Tanya was killed at the bonfire clearing. We know that. It's only a mile or so past Cooper's Bluff. All the others being hurt or killed were at that clearing with her the night she went missing. That bonfire area is his comfort zone. I'll bet he takes all his victim's there to kill them."

"Except Tristan. You found him on the opposite side of the lake, closer to the marina."

"But I don't think he was actually killed there. This guy has a pattern. Abduct someone using a stun gun. He probably uses the mines all the time to transport them where he wants to take them. He's doing it with Shanna. Makes sense he did it with them too."

"That's a huge leap," Dawson said. "We don't know if that's true or not. And there's no evidence to say that Tristan wasn't killed right where you found him. Take Jessica, for example. She was found outside the restaurant. That's nowhere near the bonfire clearing. Is there a point to any of this speculation other than to say he's been by Cassidy's cabin, the restaurant, the cover, and the bonfire clearing?"

Kaden swore and raked a hand through his hair. "I'm trying to play investigator and I don't know what the hell I'm doing."

Dawson put his hand on his shoulder. "Take a breath. The state police are hot on Shanna's trail. They'll find her."

"But will they be too late?"

Dawson remained silent.

Kaden braced a hand on the rock wall of the mine. "Think. Think. What would Shanna do if she was here? Where would she look for someone taken from the B and B down through the mine?" He straightened and turned around. "Trust her. I have to trust the work she did, her notes. Tanya. The bonfire clearing. Jack. Tristan. The cove."

"All right. We'll do it your why," Dawson said. "Trust Shanna's notes, her conclusions. She mentioned two places, right? The clearing and the cove. We can cover more ground if we split up. And we can get to both places way quicker over water than land. You drive to the Tate cabin and get your boat. Head out to the clearing. I'll take the police boat to the cove and radio my officers to split up and cover both places."

"I'm not waiting around for your team."

"I don't expect you to."

They took off running back toward the B and B.

Shanna swore.

"What happened?" Tanya asked. "Are you okay?"

"I think I cut my hand. Wait. Let me get the light on again so we can see our progress."

She carefully felt for where she'd left the batteries after removing them to use the body of the flashlight as a shovel. It took several minutes of shaking the flashlight and using her shirt to wipe out the inside before the batteries got a good enough connection to flood the cave with light again.

"Definitely bleeding. But it won't kill me." She winced at her poor choice of words. "Looks, Tanya. We're getting there. Two bars dug out." But it had taken far longer than she'd hoped. "There's enough room for you to squeeze through. Go on. Hurry. Get out, run and hide before he comes back."

"Wait, leave you? No. I'll help you dig out another bar."

Shanna put her hand on the other girl's shoulder. "A lot's been happening in the past few days. He's escalating. We can't risk that he won't go ahead and kill you when he returns. Killers don't leave witnesses behind."

Tanya's eyes widened. "But I don't… I don't want to leave you behind, either."

"I'll be okay. You'll go get help, right? I need you to do that. If you don't go, we both might be trapped here, with no chance. Go. Hurry. Save us both, Tanya. Go get help."

Tanya's shoulders straightened and a determined look lit her eyes. "Help. Yes. I can do that. I'll find someone to help."

Shanna shoved at the two loose bars. Somehow, they were still attached at the top of the cave. But the bottom parts were free. She shoved them to the side so Tanya could slip through. "Now, go on. Get out of here."

"I'll—I'll come back. With help."

"I'm counting on it. Hurry."

Tanya whirled around and disappeared through the rotten tree.

Shanna braced her aching back against one of the many remaining bars. What she hadn't told Tanya was that the two bars they'd dug out were the only ones with any give at the top. She'd tried to shake and move every other bar before choosing the two they'd dug out. The rest were sunk into the boulder at the top with no movement, which meant even if she dug out more bars from the bottom, she wouldn't be able to move them to the side. And she was larger than Tanya. She couldn't squeeze through the opening the younger girl had squeezed through.

She was stuck here with no way out.

Well, there was one way. She could dig two to three feet down, so she could wiggle underneath the bars without having to swing the bars to the side. But that would take hours. The ground was hard, rocky, and her makeshift shovel was never intended for that kind of digging. Would it even last if she tried?

The only alternative was to sit here and wait for the Phantom to return. As soon as he saw that Tanya was gone, he'd know that Shanna was responsible. He'd kill her, for sure.

Which meant she no choice but to dig. And pray he didn't return anytime soon.

She took out the batteries and set them aside. Then she started to dig.

Her fingers ached from curling around the flashlight, shoving it over and over into the hard dirt. How long had she been scraping with little progress? Ten minutes? Fifteen? More? There was no way to accurately judge the time in the dark. But she couldn't stop, no matter how slow going it was. Tanya had never given up. She'd survived nearly a year in this dark hole. Shanna wasn't a quitter, either.

After shaking out the pitifully small bit of dirt she'd just scooped out, she shoved the flashlight into the dirt again.

A thump sounded from outside.

She froze, and looked toward the cave opening.

"Ladies, I brought lunch." The Phantom's cheery voice preceded him as he shoved his way through the back of the rotten tree. "Did your light go out? Here." Light filled the cave as he switched on a flashlight he was holding.

Shanna smiled. "Back so soon?"

His eyes widened. "Where is she? What have you done?"

She tightened her hold on her flashlight. "Lunch smells good. What did you bring?"

His furious shout filled the cave, echoing off the walls. He tossed the bags of food on the ground and yanked his knife out of the sheathe as he stalked toward her. "I trusted you. You've ruined everything. Now you're going to pay."

Her pulse rushed in her ears. He was going to kill her.

He shoved the key in the lock. "It's time you learned all about Mystic Lake's secrets. Let's go for a swim."

Chapter Twenty-Two

Kaden used every ounce of power the engines on his boat could give, pushing it to its limit. He recklessly passed the marina full of boaters, ignoring the shouts of anger as his wake buffeted the much smaller boats. Channel markers warned of hazards beneath the water that could shred the hull of his boat. He tried to stay away from those areas, but was forced to swerve dangerously close several times to avoid decimating small boats that couldn't get out of his way fast enough.

Still, he pushed for more horsepower.

The mist was still mysteriously hovering over the lake, making it even harder to watch out for potential hazards. But what frustrated him the most was that the mist seemed heaviest at the water's edge. He couldn't see the shoreline to judge exactly where the lake ended and the shore began. If, by some miracle, Shanna was on the shore, perhaps running from her abductor, he wasn't even sure that he would see her.

Forced to rely on his training and experience, he used the boat's instrumentation and the GPS coordinates from his earlier search of the bonfire area to navigate. He was close. Very close. He powered down three of the four engines and dramatically decreased his speed all at once, making the boat rock back and forth like a toy in a bathtub. It creaked and groaned but quickly settled.

According to the GPS, he was fifty yards from shore. The bonfire clearing could be up ahead, in front of those trees, but the mist was too thick for him to be sure.

"Shanna," he yelled, even as he edged the boat dangerously closer. "Shanna!"

A figure appeared, the mist swirling around her. A woman near the tree line. But she was too short to be Shanna. Red hair glinted in the sunlight. What the… Was that *Tanya*?

She jumped up and down, waving her arms. "Help! Help! He's going to kill her. Help!"

Kaden's shock at seeing the young girl alive quickly gave way to dread. He shoved a lever, revving the engine again, rapidly closing the distance. The mist thinned, revealing he was much closer to the shoreline than he'd realized. He turned hard to starboard just in time to turn the boat and avoid grounding it, then returned the engine to idle, bobbing up and down in his own wake.

He stepped out of the wheelhouse and leaned against the railing. "Tanya Jericho?"

"Yes, yes. Please, you have to help her. Shanna. He's got her. I tried to go find help. But he got there too fast. I had to hide. I saw him take her out of the rock."

Rock? He had no idea what she meant. "Where is she?" he yelled across to her.

"There. Over there. He said he was taking her for a swim." She pointed off to her left, Kaden's right.

A swim? Oh, God, no.

"How far?" he yelled.

"Around the next curve."

"Hide, Tanya. Don't come out until you see the police."

She waved in understanding and sprinted into the trees.

Kaden jumped back in the wheel house and gunned the engine again, sending the boat in a full out frenzy parallel to the shore toward the next bend. Another debris marker appeared out of the mist directly in front of him. He swore and jerked the wheel away from the shore. Something hard made a sickening scrape against the hull, but it didn't catch. The boat shot out past it into deeper, safer water.

He quickly turned, powering down again and heading around the next curve where Tanya had said Shanna would be. So where was she?

He scanned the area, swearing as the mist rose thick again, covering the surface of the water. Then he heard it. Splashing.

The mist suddenly opened in front of him like a red carpet rolling out to guide his way. And there, to his horror, in the shallow strip of land at the lake's edge was Shanna with her captor. He had her by the hair and was shoving her under the water.

The gun Dawson had given Kaden was useless. He'd likely hit Shanna if he tried shooting the Phantom. But Kaden had another weapon. *Discovery.* He throttled up, hurtling the boat directly toward shore.

The Phantom looked up, as if just noticing him. He stared at Kaden, smiling as he held a thrashing Shanna under, seemingly convinced Kaden wouldn't hit him.

Kaden gave the engine another burst of speed.

The Phantom shoved Shanna completely under water and scrambled to his feet, desperately trying to get out of Kaden's way.

Kaden jerked the wheel hard to starboard to miss where he'd last seen Shanna. He ran to the port side, grabbing his handheld sonar as he dove into the water. A loud explosion sounded overhead as his boat ran aground and struck the trees. A concussion of power slammed against his body, tossing him against something hard and unyielding. The impact knocked the breath out of him but he managed to maintain his grip on the sonar device.

He struggled against the urge to suck in water as his lungs screamed for air. Pieces of his boat fell into the water, like a hard rain. Then he was kicking for the surface.

He sucked in a lungful of air, then dove back down, immediately sweeping the sonar back and forth. In what felt like minutes, but was probably only a few seconds, one of the lights came on, pointing him toward a shadow several feet below.

Shanna.

Diving straight down, he found her. Her eyes were open and staring. But she didn't see him. His heart seemed to stop in his chest. He tossed the device aside, grabbed her and swam for the surface, but pulled up short. Her hair was wrapped around an old wooden railing of a submerged house.

He savagely kicked the railing, smashing it in two, freeing her. Cradling her lifeless body against him, he headed for the surface as fast as he could go. Once he reached the shore, he laid her on her side and worked to pump the water out of her lungs. A rush of water came out but she didn't cough or start breathing. He rolled her onto her back and began CPR.

"Come on, Shanna. Don't you leave me now, not after becoming everything to me. Don't you dare. Breathe, damn it. Breathe."

He blew two quick hard breaths, watching her chest rise as her lungs filled with air. But just like with Jessica, she didn't breathe on her own. And this time, there wasn't an external defibrillator to help him. He desperately pressed his clasped hands over her heart, pumping it for her, and praying harder than he'd ever prayed in his life.

Please, God. Please. Don't take her. Let her live. Please.

An angry shout was his only warning. He threw up his arm to deflect the blow as the Phantom swung a piece of broken wood from his boat down toward his head. Kaden kicked out at the other man, catching him in the groin.

As the Phantom fell to his knees, cupping himself and groaning in agony, Kaden blew two quick breaths into Shanna's lungs. Still nothing. "Come on, sweetheart. Come on. Don't leave me." He started compressions again.

The Phantom struggled to his feet, glaring at Kaden. His mouth turned up in a feral grin as he slowly pulled out a long, wicked knife.

This was it. He'd probably end up sinking that knife into Kaden. But if he stopped compressions long enough to fight him off, Shanna didn't stand a chance. He had to keep going as long as he could.

Where the hell was Dawson's team?

As if in answer, the distant sound of a boat engine whined out across the lake.

Thank God. His boat disintegrating into a million pieces must have alerted them.

"I love you, Shanna," he whispered, before blowing two more quick breaths.

The Phantom drew his knife above his head and let out the sound a rabid dog might make as he limped forward, still cupping himself with his other hand.

Kaden continued compressions, turning his back to pro-tect Shanna from the coming blow.

The mist suddenly swirled around them, thick and impossible to see through.

The sound of the Phantom's footsteps faltered as he seemed to struggle to search for his prey.

Kaden took advantage of the opportunity, grabbing Shanna in his arms and charging forward to the cover of the trees. He dropped down with her and immediately continued compressions.

And just as suddenly as the mist had come, it disappeared. Kaden glanced through the trees toward the shore.

The Phantom turned his way, spotting him. His face contorted with a victorious smile as he held the blade of his knife and raised it to throw it.

A hail of gunfire sounded from the lake. There, on the small police boat, to Kaden's surprise, was Dawson himself. He held a rifle aimed at the Phantom.

The Phantom's smile turned to dismay and shock as he looked down at the holes in his chest. He staggered toward the lake, then fell facedown into the water, disappearing beneath its murky surface into the depths below.

The sound of a cough had Kaden jerking his head toward Shanna and stopping the compressions. She blinked up at him, her beautiful blue eyes glassy, unfocused.

"Shanna? It's Kaden. Can you hear me?"

Her eyes closed and her head lolled to the side, water trickling out of her mouth.

He swore and turned her, moving her arms to try to clear more water from her lungs. When he rolled her on her back, his panic gave way to relief when he saw that she was breathing. But her pulse was thready, far too weak. And all he could think about was how he'd revived Jessica and she still hadn't survived.

"Don't you dare die on me," he ordered, his voice breaking. "I swear I'll never forgive you."

Her brow wrinkled as if she'd heard him. But her eyes stayed closed.

He lifted her in his arms, cradling her against his chest as he staggered to his feet. Then he was running toward the lake to where Dawson was now idling his boat dangerously close to the shoreline. A body bag on the deck told Kaden what he'd feared might happen. Dawson must have found Jack. But he'd been too late.

Dawson's eyes widened. "Is she—"

"She's alive," Kaden said. "But she's in bad shape. Get the chopper out here. Now."

Chapter Twenty-Three

Kaden stood in his suit outside the hospital behind the others at the makeshift memorial, a tiny plaque shoved into the dirt in front of a sapling that would eventually grow into a mighty oak tree. It was a simple gesture, but heartfelt. If nothing else, it helped everyone here feel as if they'd honored her memory.

He'd have traded it in a second to have been able to save her.

As the small crowd of doctors and nurses began to disperse, he glanced off to his left at some of those who remained. Her family was here, of course. Tanya, surprisingly, was here too, in a wheelchair, just beginning her long road to recovery. Her mother was clucking around her like a worried hen. Beside her, Cassidy Tate, sporting a tan from her recent cruise, fussed over Tanya just as much as her mother. Behind the wheelchair, Tanya's father couldn't stop smiling.

A wave caught Kaden's attention. Chief Dawson stood at the outer fringe, away from the others, waving goodbye. Kaden returned the gesture and Dawson headed toward the parking lot.

He was going through as much guilt as Kaden, maybe

more. The deaths of so many young people in his town at the hands of the Phantom weighed heavily on the police chief whose job was to protect them. No amount of commiseration from Kaden had done anything to make Dawson even begin to forgive himself.

Kaden sighed heavily. Those feelings would only get worse in the coming days and weeks as more of the Phantom's sins were revealed. Tanya was only just beginning to open up to a therapist and reveal the confessions that Phil Gunther—the Phantom's real name—had made to her. Many of the drownings and disappearances throughout the years that had been blamed on Mystic Lake's hazards or some ethereal ghost had actually come at the hands of one bitter, deranged man who'd been bullied one too many times and had decided to take his revenge.

"I'm sorry about your boat," a feminine voice called out from behind him.

He gave one last look at the plaque for Jessica DeWalt and turned around, smiling at the beautiful woman staring up at him from her wheelchair.

Shanna.

He nodded his thanks to Gavin Tate, who'd surprised him by wheeling her out here. Gavin squeezed Shanna's shoulder, then headed toward his wife who was still fussing over Tanya.

"Boats can be replaced," Kaden told her. "You can't."

"Neither can you. And you almost got yourself killed for me."

"Worth it."

She frowned. "Not worth it. I don't want you dying for me." She leaned toward him as if to try to stand, then winced and eased back. "Stupid ribs. They're so dang sore."

He crouched in front of her. "I'm so sorry. Apparently

I need better CPR training. I seem to hurt anyone I try to help."

She shook her head. "Don't you dare apologize. You've done nothing but apologize since I woke up in this hospital. You have nothing to be sorry about. You saved me."

He winced. "That honor goes to Chief Dawson. He's the one who shot the Phantom."

"Who would have already drowned me if you hadn't come along. Dawson merely dealt the final blow. Or, at least, I hope it was final. Have they found the body yet?"

"Not yet. My team's arriving tomorrow morning with another sonar device, and another boat, to search that part of the lake. They won't leave until they find him. The town has suffered enough because of the rumors and myths about the lake. The Phantom has to be found so everyone can truly relax and feel safe again.

"Phil Gunther." She shook her head. "He was a local after all. Or, at least, he started out that way. Cassidy showed me his picture in a yearbook from the school library. He grew up here, graduated from the same school as Peyton and the others. Then he spent the rest of his life stalking and killing. He lived off the mountains, sneaking around essentially unseen to listen in on people's conversations in town, staying one step ahead of the law. I still can't believe it." She glanced at the group of family and friends surrounding Tanya. "Or believe that we actually found Tanya alive."

Her eyes turned misty. "Eleven months of captivity. Torture. She hasn't begun to scratch the surface and tell everyone everything she suffered. If only I'd agreed to help in the beginning, when Cassidy first called—"

"Don't." He feathered a hand down the side of her beautiful face. "You don't know whether you could have helped back then, whether things would have fallen into place like they did for you and me. You might have investigated and given up, thinking she'd drowned. You coming here when you did, at the same time as me, was fate. She might never have been found otherwise."

She wiped at her eyes. "That's one way to look at it, I suppose."

"The only way."

She didn't appear to be convinced, but offered him a small nod. "I haven't heard any updates on Peyton. She has to feel awful with so many of her friends…gone. But knowing she didn't kill Tanya has to help. I suppose."

"I hear she and Sam have been seen together in town since Dawson let her out of protective custody and Tanya refused to press any charges against her. Maybe Peyton and Sam will help each other through the fallout and become better people for it."

"I hope so." She stared at him a long moment, her gaze searching his. "We've talked about everyone else but us. What…what are your plans? You've stayed well past your original plan. I imagine things are piling up at your company."

She drew a shaky breath, as if to hold back tears and turned away.

He gently pressed his hand beneath her chin until she looked at him again. "I'm not going anywhere. Not without you."

She blinked. "I don't…what do you mean?"

"I love you, Shanna Hudson."

Her eyes widened. Her throat worked but no words came out.

He hoped that was a good sign.

Straightening, he pulled the small box out of his pocket

that he'd been carrying around since the moment she'd awakened in the hospital and had been declared out of danger. Then he dropped to one knee in front of her wheelchair.

"Oh, my God," she whispered, staring at him. "Kaden? What are you doing?"

"Solving our long-distance-relationship problem." He flipped open the black velvet box and pulled out the diamond solitaire ring sitting there.

For once, Shanna seemed shocked into silence.

"Shanna Hudson, will you do me the honor of becoming my wife?"

She stared at the ring, then at him. "Kaden, we haven't even known each other for a whole month!"

"And in that time we've been together almost twenty-four seven. I've done the math. We've known each other longer than if we'd just casually dated a few times a week for well over a year."

She burst out laughing. "I'm not sure about your math, but that's a pretty clever argument."

"Is that a yes?"

Her smile faded. "Where would we live? We both have businesses a full day's drive from each other."

"We're both entrepreneurs. And young enough to start over. I can sell my company to my team. They'd love to all have part ownership in it. You could do the same with yours, if you want. We can start our own business together, or retire early on our profits from the sales. I'm not exactly hurting, financially. I've got quite a nest egg saved up. We can go anywhere you want to go. I'll even live in West Virginia if that's where you prefer to be, at the top of the tallest mountain." He searched her gaze. "That is, if I've read you right. I told you I loved you. Now it's your turn. Unless… I'm completely wrong here?"

"Oh, Kaden. How could I not love you?"

Joy and relief swept through him. "One down. One to go. What about my other question?"

She stared at him in amazement. "You're willing to brave driving up a scary mountain road for me? And live at the very top?"

"I'm willing to brave anything if you say yes."

She laughed and held out her hand. "Yes, yes, yes!"

He slid the ring on her finger, then kissed her, far more gently than he wanted, careful not to hurt her cracked ribs. When he pulled back, tears were tracking down her face.

"Happy tears," she assured him. "I love you, Kaden Rafferty. And I want nothing more than to spend the rest of my life showing you." She gave him a sexy wink.

He was grinning so hard his mouth hurt. He jumped to his feet and turned her wheelchair around, then pushed her toward the hospital, racing across the concrete.

"Whoa, horsey," she called out. "Why the rush? Slow down?"

"We have to see the doctor. Right now."

She looked up at him. "Why? What's wrong?"

"I'm going to bribe him to spring you out of here so we can get started on you showing me how much you love me." He gave her a sexy leer.

She burst out laughing and pointed to the hospital doors. "Onward, my prince. Our forever is waiting."

* * * * *

DISAPPEARANCE AT ANGEL'S LANDING

NICHOLE SEVERN

To my husband:

For managing to keep me from going insane during Covid-19 quarantine so I could write this book.

Chapter One

"Quick. Here come one of the pine pigs."

That was a new one.

National Park Ranger Lila Jordan pasted on a practiced smile as she hauled herself up the steep first section of Angel's Landing, the 5,900-ft near-vertical crown jewel that looked out over the expanse of Zion National Park. The name came from some Methodist minister in the 1900s who'd commented that only an angel could land up here and had somehow stuck.

This was the most popular hike in the park for those looking for untamed adventure and that classic photo op, but Angel's Landing had also taken a number of lives over the years. Which was why Lila's legs were currently burning despite years of hiking this particular trail to catch up to two yahoos. While safety was left to hikers—like the two men trying to avoid eye contact ahead of her, probably due to the fact they'd sneaked onto the trail without applying for a permit—she couldn't really let them die out here out of stupidity. Unfortunately for the benefit of mankind. "Morning, gentlemen. Can you please show me your permits and ID?"

"Uh, yeah." The hiker on her left really wasn't anything

to write home about with his bland features, bland brown hair and bland ability to lie his way out of a hole. He patted his pants pockets, then his flannel shirt in a vain attempt to buy himself some time. "I've got it here somewhere."

Lila angled her gaze to the second hiker decked out in nearly every piece of equipment the little town outside of Zion sold. Brand-new boots with a slight film of red dust, a lightweight jacket with the tag still hanging out the back and a backpack most likely stuffed with days' worth of food for a five-mile hike. "How about you? You got a permit?"

His smile flashed wide. All right. Turning on the charm straight away. That had to be a record in her book. "Well, uh. You see, there was a mix-up with the lottery. I got the email we were approved, but I accidentally deleted it."

Right. Anyone applying for a permit on Angel's Landing had to enter a daily drawn lottery so rangers could keep track of how many hikers—and who—were out on the trail. The park had implemented the pilot program during the COVID-19 pandemic but kept it to ensure all hikers made it off the trail in one piece. She couldn't promise these two would.

Lila kept her own smile in place, showcasing perfectly straight white teeth guaranteed to blind given the right angle of the sun. She unhitched her radio from her belt, catching the clip on one of the hot pink jeweled studs she'd hot glued to the faux leather because life was too short to die in a drab gray and tan uniform. It didn't matter how many times the district ranger wrote her up for insubordination. "That's not a problem. We have record of everyone who was approved for a permit today. I just need to see your IDs and confirm your names with rangers on the ground."

The smile slipped, but this guy wasn't going to just admit

he and his friend had broken the rules to get on the trail. Or take her seriously.

She got that a lot. Mostly from men just like him. The ones who only saw her blond hair tucked back into a curled ponytail under her Stetson, the soft pink lip gloss she didn't go anywhere without and the floral pink kerchief tied at her neck.

His head-to-toe leer turned her stomach. "You sure you're a ranger? Way I see it, you're way too pretty to hide out here in the park all day."

"Awww. Aren't you sweet?" She added a rise in her voice on that last word, dipping one leg to shift her weight with a little bit of Southern charm despite the fact she'd come from the middle of nowhere Utah. A little bounce meant to tell prey she was too bashful to take a compliment. It was one of the many weapons in her arsenal to stop anyone from looking past the Ranger Barbie armor.

That was what all the other rangers here in the park called her. In whispers and conversations that stopped short of her approach. In the roll of their eyes and placating words when she volunteered for the most dangerous rescue assignments. She had the same training as they did, with a record number of rescues, yet her penchant for pretty things and pink accessories had somehow put her at the bottom of the list. Like getting picked last in kickball in elementary school.

The only one who let her join in on the ranger reindeer games was her roommate Sayles, and that traitor spent more time with her FBI agent boyfriend than late nights watching crappy romantic comedies with Lila these days.

"Fortunately for you, my looks have nothing to do with my ability to ensure neither of you die on this trail. So you can show me your permits with today's date and your IDs, or I can have you escorted off the trail."

Shock turned the silence between them into something physical. If their eyes could bug out anymore, they'd be rolling down the trail.

"What a bitch." The first hiker took a step toward her, as if she was nothing but a cute yippy dog blocking their ascent to Scout Lookout.

"But you still think I'm pretty, right?" Lila let that sweet smile light up her face as she replaced her radio and unclipped her Taser. Pressing the power button, she let it charge for a few seconds. "Who wants to go first?"

An hour later, Lila handed over both hikers to the law enforcement rangers stationed out of the park headquarters near the Zion National Park museum. They'd pay a fine with a warning not to attempt the trail without a permit again. Wouldn't stop them. No matter how many hikers she dragged off Angel's Landing, another dozen slipped her notice and made it all that much harder for those who followed the rules.

Her radio crackled from her belt before a voice that curdled her insides cleared over the channel. "Jordan, come in."

A deep sigh escaped before she could control it. Here she thought she could lose herself on the trail for a couple hours and avoid any semblance of Rick Risner. Yep, that was his real name, though she and the other rangers preferred to call him by his formal title. Pinheaded F— "Yeah, boss?"

Risner kept her in suspense for close to a minute before responding. It was a tool he kept in his own arsenal to piss off every man, woman and child who stepped into this park. Including his subordinates, which he liked to remind her was every ranger in a two-hundred-and-thirty-mile radius. "We've got a possible missing hiker on Angel's Land-ing. Name is Sarah Lantos. Made her start time at six this morning, hasn't been spotted since. Dark hair, about five foot six, license puts her at thirty-nine years old."

Lila checked her smartwatch. It was close to noon with the sun blazing overhead and working to undo all that care she'd put into her hair this morning. Even the slowest hik-ers made it back to the base of the hike—the Grotto—in around four hours with scenic interludes and photography opportunities along the way.

Six hours. Was the hiker injured? Had she been travel-ing with anyone else? Could she have decided to stay at the peak longer than most? Maybe the woman had forgotten to check in with the permit office or managed to avoid a ranger on her descent. Except none of those reasons eased the acid lodged in her throat. Lila bent to collect the jewel that fell from her belt and pinched the push-to-talk button on the radio. "I'm headed back up now."

"Update me in an hour." No *thanks, Lila* or *be careful, Lila*. Actually, she wasn't even sure Risner knew her first name. He'd only called her Jordan for the past two years since she signed on with the National Park Service. Last named. Unimportant, not worth getting to know as a per-son. Merely a tool. It was the same for the other female rangers on staff, but he certainly made an effort with ev-eryone else, i.e., the men. A true pine pig.

Oooh, she'd have to tell Sayles about the new nickname tonight.

The hot pink jewel reflected back at her in the center of her palm. There wasn't time to fix it now. She'd have to wait until her shift ended. She tucked the good little soldier into her slacks pocket. She hadn't moved out here to the middle of nowhere with a lot of luxuries, but she'd made damn sure her hot glue gun and bedazzling kit made the cut.

Lila grabbed two bottles of water from the park head-quarters' break room along with a couple of protein bars for the trek back to Angel's Landing. Breakfast of champions… four hours too late. Okay, so she probably should eat more vegetables, but convenience was the name of the game.

Summer in Zion had hit full force, and the heat never let her forget it. Storms broke up the days, but this was the busiest time of year in the park. Kids were out of school and driving their parents crazy. What better way than to force them up a mountain—or three—to burn off some of that energy? No time for home-cooked meals in these parts.

Smooth red rock resembling melted taffy acted as stairs as she ascended the first section of the trail. Hikers could climb the first two and a half miles of the West Rim Trail without a permit. It was the second half of the overly popu-lar, adrenaline-inducing, nothing-but-chains-to-hold-onto, 6000-foot drop Angel's Landing was known for. There were days a line of people started at the base and grouped at the end.

Thankfully, she could move at her own pace through Walter's Wiggles—a series of twenty-one switchbacks leading to Scout Lookout—without pushing anyone off the side of the cliff today. Rock turned to sand under her boots and added an additional layer of burn. She'd always been in shape, going from yoga to biking to marathon train-ing and rock climbing over the years when she needed a change, but hiking would be the one to kill her in the end.

Mountains surged upward from every angle as she navi-gated the incessant rise of rough terrain. Chains signaled the beginning of the most difficult portion of the trail, the one leading straight to eighteen people's deaths in the past fifty years. Even as a ranger, she wasn't invincible. Or stupid. She used the chains to propel her up the incline, the metal biting into her palm.

Spots of winter white still clung to north-facing peaks, adding a bite to the air. Jagged surges in rock threatened every step, but she'd hiked this trail more times than she could count. What most considered a once-in-a-lifetime adventure had become part of her daily routine. Sometimes two to three times a day. Barren pines and scrub brush peppered the rock face along the final ascent to the top.

No sign of Sarah Lantos. Though there'd been a couple lookalikes she'd stopped to ask for ID, Lila couldn't dislodge the dread pooling at the base of her spine as she summited the peak. A few hikers snapped photos, a couple getting too close to the chains following the edge of the cliff face and providing unobstructed views of the canyon below.

Sarah Lantos wouldn't have just disappeared off the trail. Allowing herself to feel the fear of falling and forcing herself to do it anyway, Lila stretched out over the near-non-existent barrier between her and certain death. And caught a hint of bright yellow six thousand feet below.

Her chest squeezed—too hard—as she grabbed for her radio. Another jewel abandoned ship, following the projection of the body below. "Risner, I think I found Sarah Lantos."

Chapter Two

People were morons.

Ranger Branch Thompson shoved through the ring of park visitors inching closer to the body. Always pushing to get a better look. As if the woman at the bottom of the cliff was some kind of tick in their to-do list during their national park tour. "Vultures."

Law enforcement rangers were already at work to secure a perimeter around the fallen hiker, but national parks weren't equipped like a regular police force. While rangers followed similar protocols during death investigations, they didn't have crime scene tape, a forensic unit or the manpower to ensure the area around the body wasn't compromised. That was where he came in.

Branch caught sight of a bright yellow jacket—unmoving—in the center of the controlled chaos. Risner, the district ranger, hadn't given him a lot of information on the hiker who'd taken a flying leap off Angel's Landing when he'd ordered Branch to help with crowd control. But Branch noted long red hair and thin fingers splayed out to the hiker's side. Female, from the look of it.

Extending his arms out to either side, he forced the crowd back a couple feet, his expression more than ready to shut down questions. Facing off with two dozen onlookers grated his nerves raw. Why he'd chosen to interact with the public all day in a too-hot box surrounded by things that could eat and kill him, he'd never know. Felt right at the time, he guessed.

And now the park had a death on its hands. Nothing short of a miracle would convince the superintendent to close it. With over five million visitors a year—charged a minimum of thirty-five dollars a vehicle—Zion National Park was one of the most sought-after attractions in the west. The last time the National Park Service had been asked to evacuate Zion had been at the FBI's request during a violent manhunt that ended with an agent and one of Branch's fellow rangers almost dying in the process.

Park Service members had all signed on to protect the park from the people and the people from the park. They knew what they were getting themselves into. Knew the risks. But a hiker who hadn't followed personal safety suggestions before attacking the tallest and steepest trail in the park? This was just another day in Branch's book.

The line of bystanders closed in with their phones and cameras at the ready, questions and whispers and theories flying back and forth. Group mentality tended to do that. It took morality out of the equation. While having a hiker take a dive off one of the country's most dangerous trails wasn't an every day occurrence, Branch wasn't going to give anyone a shot at disgracing the body. "No photos. Step back. I won't tell you a second time."

Pressure built as eyes turned toward him him. Amid the crowd, he noted a flash of pink. A burn that had nothing to do with unobstructed sun bearing down on him lit up under his skin. Heaven help them all if Risner had called her in to help with this mess.

Lila Jordan, or more accurate, the bane of his existence.

The Barbie-like ranger bypassed the crowd and cut straight toward him, a smile plastered on her face. Shiny blond hair had been sleeked back into a ponytail beneath her Stetson, but she'd spent time curling the ends for added bounce. As always. No other female ranger in this park went so far as to wear makeup or keep up her hot pink manicure. And did she just wave at him? "Hi, Branch. Great job on crowd control!"

A growl resonated in his chest as he tracked her to the inner circle of rangers assessing the body. What the hell had Risner been thinking, hiring a woman who accessorized her uniform like Cupid threw up after an all-night Valentines Day binge?

The district ranger himself followed close on Lila's heels without so much as throwing Branch a glance, his eyes glued to her backside. Risner hadn't been thinking with the head above his belt, that was for sure, despite the thick gold band on his ring finger.

Acid curdled in Branch's stomach at the thought of the district ranger leering at Lila or any of the other female rangers in the service. While Branch would do anything to get out of a shift with Ranger Barbie—her enthusiasm and nonstop talking produced some of the most vicious migraines in existence—she didn't deserve her boss's lewd attention.

Though he doubted Lila hadn't used it to her advantage once or twice. Women like her were used to getting what they wanted through any means necessary, just like his ex-wife, with no concern for the trail of bodies in their wake. Lila had probably manipulated Risner into allowing her to join this investigation with a few bats of those long eyelashes and glossed lips. He wouldn't put it past her.

Couldn't fault her, either, considering Risner's penchant for overlooking female rangers for the high-priority assignments. Zion didn't have more than a handful, but they were as crucial to running this place and keeping visitors alive as their male counterparts.

The burn beneath his skin was on the verge of consuming him at the thought of Lila using her beauty to influence Risner. She probably gave that son of a bitch the same smile she'd flashed him.

Nope. Didn't matter. Wasn't his business.

"Someone fell?" A visitor craned her head over Branch's shoulder to get a better look at the scene, a feat in and of itself. Her cracked lips told him she hadn't drunk enough water in these temperatures. If she didn't rectify that soon, he'd have to haul her out of here when she collapsed from dehydration.

Branch set his unimpressed gaze on her, watchful of any others who might think to break the line he'd created to give rangers the space they needed. "I'm not at liberty to say."

Still craning to see around his large frame, the visitor hiked onto her tiptoes, swaying toward him. She slapped her hand against his arm to catch herself. "Do you know who she was?"

"What part of *I'm not at liberty to say* didn't you understand?" He shucked her hand from his arm.

"Aren't you rangers supposed to be nice?" She landed back on her feet, sweat beading her upper lip. "My taxes pay your salary. The least you could do is pretend you know something about customer service."

"I'll keep that in mind." Branch forced himself to refocus on his job, but Ranger Barbie's incessant high-pitched drone proved too much to ignore. It probably deafened dogs.

He hadn't come up with Lila's nickname. Actually, he wasn't sure where he'd heard it the first time, but the shoe fit with her pink socks, pink jewels decorating her belt, the pink nail polish and the pink bandana tied at her neck. He'd never met someone so disrespectful of the uniform.

He turned back to the hiker. "Drink something before I get called to come collect you off the trails."

Her shock only lasted a second. "You—"

"Branch, want to give us a hand?" Risner's question was more of a command.

It pissed Branch the hell off. He'd been doing just fine all the way over here, as far from Lila as he could get. Though his ears would argue it wasn't far enough. "Any of you move, and I'll have you banned from the park for life." Leaving his post, Branch closed the distance between him and the small ring of rangers staring down at the remains.

The near-6000-foot drop hadn't been kind. The hiker's bright yellow jacket contained most of the mess, but unmistakable brain matter splayed out in a burst of red and pink against the dirt. A hand had survived, at an odd angle, but it was there.

Risner pointed at the body. "The medical examiner is ready to turn her over to search her front pockets. Hopefully get a positive ID. Grab a side and help me lift her."

"How?" Branch's stomach revolted at the idea of…pieces slipping through his fingers, but he wouldn't lose his breakfast. Not here and sure as hell not in front of anyone. Weakness would only cost him.

"You could imagine it's a sensory bin." Lila set brilliant blue eyes on him, the color of which could shift from stormy to clear in a matter of seconds depending on her mood. Right now, they were somewhere in the middle. Most likely due to the fact a dead hiker had interrupted her afternoon of chasing unicorns and rainbows or what-ever the hell she did out here. "Have you ever played with a container of those water beads you can squish between your fingers?"

Branch swallowed back a rush of bile. Did she seriously just compare a dead person to squishing a water bead? Leveling Ranger Barbie with every ounce of hatred in his bones, he let his revulsion for everything she stood for bleed into his expression.

His obvious dislike didn't deter her. "What about slime? Have you ever played with slime? I have some in my trailer. I buy it from a seventeen-year-old named Melissa who makes over three hundred different kinds right from her bedroom. She's an internet sensation. She puts all differ-ent kinds of things in it, like cotton candy scent, crunchy glue, sprinkles and any color you can imagine. And she does ASMR videos, especially when she uses foam beads. I can send you her socials if you—"

"Let's get this over with."

Ranger Barbie's smile slipped slightly, but within a sec-ond, it was right back in place.

Branch stepped up to the body. Definitely not thinking about the kind of noises a broken body trapped in a yel-low jacket might make once they got their hands on her.

He took the fallen hiker's right side while Lila took the left, putting them opposite each other. A hint of her per-fume—one he couldn't seem to stop himself from inhal-ing—tickled the back of his throat. Something ambery and feminine. Like a dual personality. Jekyll and Hyde. Who in their right mind wore perfume in over a hundred-degree heat in the middle of the desert?

Risner took control of the hiker's shoulders, his feet

spread wide to avoid the carnage around him. "One. Two. Three." Risner moved first.

They worked as one, slowly turning the remains, and set the hiker on her back. The body had stiffened some. Rigor mortis was setting in. Not at all like squishing water beads or playing with slime.

Lila dusted her hands, that irritating smile back in place with an exaggerated shoulder shrug. "Well, that wasn't so bad. Not as gooey as I thought it would be. Great job, team—"

"Can you shut up and show some respect for once?" The words snapped out of Branch's mouth before he had a chance to think it through.

The instant flash in her gaze told him he'd at least accomplished breaking through her cheerfulness. Lila cocked her head to one side, all signs of that Ranger Barbie smile buried. "Can you imagine what it will feel like when I open a Nature Valley granola bar on your bed?"

Branch fought against a resulting shiver. He could feel the crumbs already.

"Jordan, knock it off." Risner hiked his chin toward the medical examiner. "Search her pockets. We need a positive ID to inform the family of the accident."

Jordan? Since when did Risner address rangers by their last names?

"This wasn't an accident." Lila held Branch's gaze, almost daring him to interrupt her again. Or planning his murder. Branch couldn't be sure. Crouching beside the body, she pointed to a dark pattern of blood around a hole in the hiker's jacket. She unzipped the yellow abomination, revealing a deeper laceration. A stab wound. She glared at Branch before standing. "Sarah Lantos was murdered."

Chapter Three

She couldn't stop her hands from shaking.

Lila tried to breathe through her mouth as she, Branch and Risner transferred the remains to a black body bag. The squelching in her hands was nothing like a sensory bin or playing with slime. Sarah Lantos's body had basically exploded on impact but couldn't escape the confines of her clothing, so putting a pretty label on the squishiness of bone and sinew didn't do much to ease the nausea in Lila's stomach.

But she wasn't going to let it show. She wasn't about to lose the banana she'd forced down her throat an hour ago. Not here and definitely not in front of Branch Thompson.

His name alone threatened to notch her body temperature a couple of degrees higher. The man had been made of sex appeal. If the National Park Service put together a yearbook of their rangers, Branch Thompson would easily win every Best category: eyes, smile, laugh, athleticism. He had it all.

Sigh. That strong jaw could slice her hand open if she wasn't careful, though she hadn't ever gotten the opportunity. He'd made sure of that.

With shorn hair, an abundance of muscle and a partially

hidden spider tattoo stretching from the left side of his collar, he looked as though he'd stepped off the cover of a military magazine. She couldn't be sure if he'd served. Actually, she didn't know a whole lot about him other than he'd transferred from another park earlier in the year. Okay. Four months, two weeks and six days ago. But she wasn't counting.

Branch tended to keep to himself. She was pretty sure she'd never heard him utter more than two words in a row other than to ask her if she ever stopped talking. All the grizzly vibes in the world told her and every other ranger in Zion he was as cuddly as a porcupine. He wasn't the kind of man to pretend to be someone he wasn't, and that had her wanting to get a closer look. To figure out how he got away with it. He was unforgiving, a little broody. Blunt. Not a guy who would ever look at her twice, let alone take her to that cute coffee shop in town on a date.

In fact, she was fairly certain he hated her guts, based on her few attempts to get to know him and the glares he threw her way anytime she managed get within a couple feet of him.

She wasn't even the sole focus of all that intensity. Zion rangers had all learned to keep their distance, going out of their way to avoid partnering up with Branch as much as possible.

But there were times when she swore she could feel his eyes on her. Watching her every move. It came in goose bumps and shivers throughout the days she worked the trails. But the moment she tried to catch him, he'd be gone. Halfway convincing her she imagined it.

Tanned skin accentuated the rise and valley of muscle in Branch's forearms as he settled the victim's remains in the body bag.

Victim. That was what Sarah Lantos was now. Her fall hadn't been an accident; she'd been stabbed. Another murder to add to the books while the park was just barely recovering from the last one.

Branch shoved to his full height, around six-four. An entire intimidating foot taller than her frame, and every cell in her body took notice. Her brain had no trouble imagining what it would feel like to have all that muscle pressed against her, how he could easily toss her from one end of her trailer to the other. How he'd take control and—

Crap. He was looking at her with those dark eyes again, as if she'd broadcasted her thoughts.

She let a sugar-sweet smile take its place on her face. Innocent. Unbothered. Airheaded. Lila knew exactly what Branch thought of her—what every ranger in this park thought of her, including Risner—and she let them. Despite her unrequited crush on the man currently scoffing at her, it was far better for all of them to keep their distance than to see through the mask.

Risner clapped his hands together as if he'd done a lick of work helping that poor woman into the body bag. "Jordan, I want you to take Branch up to Scout Lookout and see what you can find by way of evidence. Now that we know our hiker was stabbed, there might be something there we can hand over to law enforcement. Get this taken care of and make sure to clear the trail while you're at it."

Noooooooo. It took everything Lila had not to growl. Or to look at the man who frequently starred in the wayward fantasies she used to get herself to sleep every night. Her skin felt too hot and too tight at the same time as she shifted her weight between her boots. Any time spent alone with Branch Thompson would only end in frustration and an emptiness she hadn't figured out how to get rid of. "I think you meant Sayles. Or…" Lila searched for some-one—anyone—she could put in Risner's path, but they'd all taken to crowd control or running while they had the chance. Cowards. "…anyone else."

"Right. Wouldn't want you to chip your manicure." Branch's smirk only served to up her heart rate.

Hot anger pushed to the surface. She didn't give a damn about her manicure. Lila took a step toward him but stopped herself short of pummeling that smirk off his face. She'd built this facade for a reason. She couldn't break, but for some reason she couldn't fathom, he'd somehow gained the ability to pry up her carefully laid scales.

Adding a psychotic twist to her smile, Lila locked her gaze on him. "I've been washing bloodstains off my clothes for years. Yours wouldn't be a burden."

Branch's mouth hitched higher. Almost into a smile. If a grizzly bear summoned from the bowels of hell was ca-pable of smiling.

"Jordan, move. Now. And how many times do I have to tell you to stop altering your uniform? Get rid of the pink, or I'm writing you up a third time. We're federal agents. It's time you start acting like it, or I will find someone who can follow orders." Risner headed after the medical exam-iner and the body strung between her and another ranger. "For crying out loud. You look like someone threw up a bottle of Pepto Bismol."

Her jaw ached from the pressure of her clenched back teeth. Heat that had nothing to do with the arching sun burned in her neck and cheeks. It was true Risner had a dedicated dislike for her pink accessories, but it'd been months since his last reprimand. And she hated that it had to be in front of Branch. The urge to pull at her kerchief brought her hand to her neck, but she caught herself before giving in. The pink was ridiculous. She knew that, but without it…

Lila turned for the trail that would take her and Branch up the ascent. "We better get moving if we want to make it to the top before sunset."

She didn't bother looking to see if he followed. She could feel him at her back. If she was being honest with herself, she could always feel him. Like her body had somehow attuned to his since her crush had started all those months ago. Traitor.

Though he kept his distance. He always did.

Her usual need to fill the silence failed as she ascended the melty rocks leading onto the permitted portion of the trail. *Third time's the charm.* Now that the medical examiner had concluded Sarah Lantos had been murdered, they'd have to ensure every hiker they encountered left the trail as soon as possible. A killer was on the loose. And it could be anyone, but that was for the law enforcement rangers to deal with. All she had to do was search for evidence Sarah Lantos hadn't gone over that cliff by accident.

"Does he always talk to you like that?" Branch's voice cut through the incessant spiral of thoughts in her head.

It took her a moment to remember this wasn't her every day shift. That she wasn't out here alone and that she had a persona to uphold. Dang. She was losing her touch. Or maybe some of Branch's personality had rubbed off on her today. "Who? Risner? He's the district ranger. I think being an ass is part of his job description."

A growl reached her ears, and she found herself searching the trail for a wild animal. Then realized it came from Branch. Why did she all of a sudden want to feel that growl vibrate through her? Oh, maybe she could add that to her sleep fantasies tonight.

She swallowed the groan working up her throat. Pathetic. This whole crush was just pathetic. Nothing would ever happen between her and Branch Thompson. He'd made that perfectly clear by practically inflating a five-foot-wide bubble between him and everyone around him. The longer she deluded herself that she could break through, the sooner she'd have to check herself into a psychiatric ward. "This next section is a lot steeper than the first half. You're going to want to take your time on the switchbacks. Burning out before you get to the top will only slow us down."

No answer.

Lila subtly—as subtly as she could—craned her chin over one shoulder to ensure she hadn't been talking to herself for the past few minutes. Yep. Branch was still there. Not even looking remotely out of breath or sweaty. *All righty then.*

The switchbacks were the worst, in her opinion. Steep angles, lots of effort, with very little actual elevation gain. Though she didn't hate the hardpacked trail that saw millions of visitors.

Within another thirty minutes, the landscape angled upward as they approached Scout Lookout. Her legs shook under the effort. Three ascents in one day wasn't unheard of for a regular shift, but this one felt different. She didn't want to credit that feeling to the man easily keeping pace with her a few feet back. Instead, she'd pretend it had everything to do with the hiker she'd helped put in a body bag less than a few hours ago. She was good at pretending.

Chains swung ahead of her with a rogue gust of wind. No matter how many times she hiked this trail, there was always a chance she wouldn't make it back down to the Grotto, but a sense of calm settled along her spine.

It had nothing to do with Branch. Nope.

They crested the lookout of Angel's Landing, and Lila set out to ruin the days of three groups of hikers while Branch searched the perimeter of the plateau. No one wanted to spend four hours hiking Zion's most popular trail in one-hundred-degree heat only to be told to go back once you reached the top, but she couldn't take the chance of losing something that might point to Sarah Lantos's killer.

Sarah had set off to climb Angel's Landing at six this morning. She could've been stabbed anytime between ten and now, leaving a whole lot of time for visitors—or the killer—to compromise evidence of the attack.

There was only one place Sarah Lantos could've been stabbed: directly above where her body had been found.

"She was stabbed and thrown over here." Branch stared straight down the cliffside.

"How can you be sure?" Lila stretched her gaze over the side of the cliff, just as she had earlier. Except there was no bright yellow marker telling her a hiker had gone over the edge. There was nothing but the shimmering surface of the Virgin River below and the riverside trail. "The medical examiner moved the body."

He pointed between his feet, a couple inches past the chain lining the lookout. "Because the ground here is stained with blood."

Chapter Four

Something had shifted.

Branch couldn't put his finger on it as he studied Lila across the expanse of dirt that was Scout Lookout. Law enforcement rangers were en route to contain the scene and analyze the blood he'd discovered, but with the sun sinking below the horizon, it would take more than the usual four hours before he and Lila could distance themselves from this trail. Leaving nothing but the two of them and a path of budding stars in the east.

The entire hike to this point had coiled dread so thick in his gut he'd been able to taste the bitterness at the back of his throat. Being alone with Lila Jordan had never worked out in his favor. Her impulsivity, meddling in other peoples' affairs and lack of discipline had left him with more than a few migraines at the end of a shift. Every aspect of her personality sat in opposition to his. It was one of the reasons he'd gone out of his way to ensure their schedules never coincided. He'd managed to switch days and trails with the other park rangers, but Risner had ordered the two of them to search Angel's Landing together. Probably to get Ranger Barbie away from the scene down below.

Except Lila hadn't been her normal upbeat self on the

way up. As if she'd forgotten he was there at all, and all that enthusiasm and pink was nothing but a cover. For the first time, his nervous system hadn't been on the defense around her. He'd been able to relax surrounded by the jaw-dropping views and crystal sky. No personal questions, no attempts to bond, nothing. He'd actually been able to think. About Sarah Lantos, the stab wound, her killer. It'd been…unsettling.

It was no secret Lila had harbored a crush on him these past few months. If he was being honest, most of the female rangers did. He tended to have that effect simply due to the fact he had no real interest in dating or relationships after his divorce. Something about wanting what you couldn't have. He'd gotten used to their personal crusades to help him break out of his shell, to be the one who got him to open up. Unfortunately for them and the rest of the female population, there was nothing inside but a whole lot of self-destructive rage that threatened to blow any minute. Something he only managed to keep locked up by avoiding others. Saving them the fallout.

Lila kicked at a patch of dirt across the Lookout, keeping to herself as they waited for the law enforcement unit. For some awful reason that didn't sit well with him. As if he'd become uniquely tuned to her moods. Which was ridiculous. He should be grateful his ears weren't bleeding from her incessant attempts at humor.

Had the death of a hiker gotten to her? Or had Risner's earlier reprimand thrown her off her game?

Dislodging his pack, Branch crouched. They'd ascended and cleared Angel's Landing in five hours and had been waiting for law enforcement for an hour. Not once had he seen her eat anything. Probably some strict diet to control her weight. Wasn't that why most women starved themselves? But she was likely to pass out, and he had no intention of carrying her off this mountain.

"Eat." He tossed one of the protein bars he'd packed in her direction.

Surprisingly, she caught it rather than dodge and squeal as he'd expected. Who was this pod person, and what the hell had she done with Lila? Straightening with the bar in hand, she skimmed her thumbs over the wrapper. "Careful, Branch. Wouldn't want to chip my manicure. I just touched it up this morning."

Ah. There she was. He wasn't sure why he'd bothered. Every ranger in this park was capable of taking care of themselves. They were trained to survive in the wilderness for days on end if necessary and through natural disasters. And yet, by setting aside her zaniness for just a couple minutes, Lila had somehow triggered his instinct to care. A mistake he wouldn't make again. "I'm not carrying you out of here if you pass out."

"Aw." Lila tore into the wrapper, her upper body twisting from one side to the other. A gust of wind whipped her ponytail over one shoulder and consumed his attention as it brushed over her face. "Are you concerned about me, Branch?"

Why did she have to keep repeating his name? His nerves couldn't take it much longer, going from zero to overdrive in the span of a single word out of her mouth. Branch locked his jaw to regain some semblance of control, but that was the thing about Lila. Anytime he found himself around her, that control didn't exist. Like she'd subatomically convinced him to forget years of discipline with her free spirit that left him raw and confused and more than a little angry. He forced himself to focus on cinching his bag and not the way his fingers tingled to brush her hair out of her face.

"I think you secretly like me." She took a bite of the protein bar, chewing with her mouth open while continuing to goad him. "I think all those times you switched shifts with the other rangers to make sure you didn't have to work with me is because you're trying to keep your distance when you really don't want to."

She knew about that? Hell.

Branch shoved to his feet as flashlights flickered down the trail. They were still a ways out, but law enforcement had arrived to take control of the scene. Releasing him from this hell and the demon trying to work her way under his skin. Satan had done an excellent job when he created Lila Jordan. Personalized just for him. "They're here."

"Oh, good. I hope they brought hand warmers." Lila buried the protein bar wrapper in her pack and clapped her hands before heading toward the group of three flashlights. "I'm freezing my butt off."

And what a butt it was. He hadn't been able to avoid getting the perfect view the entire hike up. Say what you will about her eating habits, whatever she was doing had paid off in spades. A tendril of heat spiked through him as he caught another dose. Hell, he was disturbed. In no shape or form should he ever consider Ranger Barbie a good idea. They were coworkers. He'd barely survived his divorce. And she…was everything he didn't want.

Branch settled his pack in place. He hadn't noticed the drop in temperatures, too on edge from maintaining the wall he had to continually reinforce between him and Lila, but the cold seemed to rush him now that she'd escaped his orbit.

"Branch. Jordan." Risner nodded to each of them at his approach. Two rangers Branch recognized from the scene this afternoon moved past, heading to the Lookout with flashlights and field kits. The law enforcement rangers would take control of the scene, gathering the blood for analysis somewhere off-site, and confirm the samples belonged to their murder victim. "I see you two managed not to kill each other. Not sure how you pulled that off partnering with Jordan here, Branch, but thanks for saving me the paperwork."

He didn't miss the few inches Lila added between her and their district ranger. Or the fleck of hurt in her expression before she smothered it with that smile she pasted on. Which only added to the anger he restrained on a daily basis. And there was that name again. *Jordan.* As if Lila didn't deserve to be humanized by her supervisor. And, well, that just wasn't something he could let continue. "Lila."

He hadn't spoken her name aloud before. The effect was something sweet and light, counter to the bitterness he'd swallowed after taking this assignment.

Risner flicked his flashlight straight into Branch's face. "What was that?"

"Her name is Lila. Not sure why it's so hard for you to remember." The tingling in his fingers was back, except it'd spread to his palms. He curled his hands into fists to keep himself from launching one into Risner's face. "Or do you call the female rangers by their last names as part of whatever sexual harassment settlement you're involved in?"

Even in the last waning rays of sunset, Branch caught the drain of color in Risner's face. "You're out of line, Branch."

"Actually, I prefer to be addressed as woman, demon or countess." Lila's smile slipped, her gaze bouncing between him and Risner. Pleading with him to drop this. Parted lips he hadn't realized were a bit fuller on one side than the other jumped right back into place. Then again, he hadn't really let himself get too close to notice. For good reason. His blood pressure had crested a few points in the past minute or so. "Whichever comes with the most amount of fear."

The district ranger adjusted his flashlight beam to Lila, rolling his eyes. "Get back down to headquarters, Jordan. You'll find your write-up in your locker, and HR will be waiting for you to discuss the adjustments you've been making to your uniform in the morning."

She motioned toward the two law enforcement rangers. "But the scene—"

"Your shift is over, Ranger." Risner put an end to the conversation. "Your services are no longer required on this case."

"All right." Lila hiked a thumb over her shoulder. "In that case, you might want to tell the law enforcement division about the rope, anchors and carabiners dangling off the north side of the Lookout."

"What?" Risner darted for the edge, pressing up against the chains keeping him from going over. His flashlight locked on something out of Branch's view. "Well, I'll be damned. How did we miss that?"

Branch realized he had made this an uncomfortable situation for Lila. He'd put her in Risner's spotlight without warning her beforehand. Potentially made her position worse. It was clear she was the only one who would suffer the consequences. *Damn it.* She hadn't asked him to fight this battle for her, but he'd made her a target all the same. A growl resonated through his chest as he maneuvered down the rocky incline. This was why he didn't get involved. Why he kept to himself and made it clear he didn't play nice with others. It took more than a few steps for his control to slip back into place.

"Branch, not you, bud. I need you to show us where you found the blood." Risner's voice was nearly lost to the great valleys absorbing the sound of the wild, but there was no way Branch could ignore it.

Lila unpacked her own flashlight and headed down the decline without looking back. Angel's Landing was easily one of the park's most dangerous trails, but she moved with the certainty of a ranger who'd memorized every threat in the terrain. She'd been dismissed, and the heaviness in her shoulders testified to the treatment she and the rest of the female rangers had become accustomed to under Risner's supervision.

This didn't feel right. Lila was the first to realize Sarah Lantos had been stabbed. Not to mention she'd discovered the rope and anchors wedged along the Lookout that could've been utilized by the killer to escape while Branch guarded a meager pool of blood. Ranger Barbie—as much as he hated to admit it—saw more than she let on, and Branch wanted to know why she let her coworkers and supervisor think less.

Of all the rangers in the park, she should be the one to see this through. She'd earned it. He searched the stars for patience. Finding none, he turned back to the district ranger. Branch nodded toward Lila's retreating flashlight. "Assign Lila to the case."

"No way. You have experience with homicides from your time at the Grand Canyon. You're the clear choice here." Risner hiked his hands to his waist with a clear shake of his head. "What the hell has gotten into you, Branch? I thought I could count on you to keep Jordan in line. Now you're defending her? She's a nobody. You know she doesn't care about this job or take it seriously. Not like we do. You really want Sarah Lantos's family relying on her to get them answers?"

Branch gritted his teeth against the blatant backstabbing and the disrespect of a fellow ranger. Stepping up to Risner, he rode that line between letting the rage surface and walking away. "I'll work your homicide case. Because you're right. Sarah Lantos's family deserves answers, and I've worked homicides in a national park. But I'm not doing it without Lila Jordan."

Chapter Five

Ugh. Feelings.

No amount of Cherry Garcia was going to fix this.

Her body hurt from climbing to Angel's Landing three times in the span of twelve hours of a single day, but worse, she couldn't get back to that lovely space where she didn't have to feel anything. The one place she felt safe. Numb.

The house creaked from another gust. The twelve-hundred-square-foot ranch-style house she and Sayles shared in the Watchman government housing development—when her roommate bothered to sleep here at all—was little more than a cardboard box with two bedrooms and a single bathroom. Updates hadn't been done in years, roaches and mouse droppings weren't uncommon, and a good portion of her sleep terrors occurred right in this very room. But it was only a quarter mile from headquarters.

Despite how often she and Sayles cleaned, there was no getting the stains out of the combination tub/shower or rid of the permanent smell of mildew. But they had put in a lot of effort to personalize everything without painting—that was against the rental agreement.

Risner's Pepto Bismol remark might not fully apply to the flares of pink in her uniform, but it certainly applied to her bedroom. Her twin-size comforter looked as though it'd been skinned straight off a pink Muppet with matching pillows and poofs. Lampshade, check. Curtains, check. Most of her casual outfits? Check. In the famous words of Julia Roberts in *Steel Magnolias*, pink was her signature color.

It was the only thing that kept her heart from turning all the way black.

Risner. She scowled merely thinking of his name. Lila scooped another double spoonful of Cherry Garcia and shoved it into her mouth, relaxing on the secondhand couch she and Sayles had found on the side of the road in Springdale. This place wasn't anything extravagant, but it was theirs. Hers. Someplace no one could find her.

There were those feelings again. The ones she'd managed to ignore since coming to Zion, but the little buggers just didn't get the message she wasn't interested. Chocolate chunks and cherries weren't going to touch this. She needed something stronger.

The romantic comedy she'd chosen for tonight—and almost every night—helped. The lonely, isolated, nerdy main character was getting all dolled up and waxed clean to enter a beauty pageant in order to catch a bomber. She just happened to find love along the way in another FBI agent, and right there was that shrapnel of hope Lila couldn't afford. That her self-isolation and loneliness would end in happily-ever-after.

Images blurred on the screen as her mind drifted back to Branch Thompson for the hundredth time tonight. He'd corrected Risner's use of her last name, though she wasn't sure why. In what world did Branch do anything that didn't involve scowling, growling or prowling? It didn't make sense and had ultimately landed her higher on Risner's hit list. The district ranger had removed her from the investigation in retaliation.

It was just as well. What did she know about murder? Her expertise—as far as her supervisor and coworkers were aware—extended to pairing the right eyeshadow to her uniform, coating herself in sunscreen because *ew, wrinkles* and changing out her boot laces with a pop of color.

No one took her seriously. And that was the way she liked it.

Pounding registered on the front door.

Her entire nervous system flinched at the onslaught, and she nearly dropped her Cherry Garcia on her favorite blanket. Dribbles of ice cream slid down her chin. She wiped it with the back of her sweatshirt sleeve. "Who is it?"

"Branch." His voice was throaty and low.

Nope. Not what she was expecting. Her heart rate shot into overdrive. She scrambled to clean up her face, smooth down her hair and make it look as though she hadn't spent the last three hours trying to drown her sorrows in calories. Then again, maybe he'd feel better she'd eaten, considering he'd gifted her that protein bar earlier.

His presence practically bled through the thin wood door. "You still there?"

She didn't know. Maybe this was an out-of-body experience. Or a dream. Never in all his time at Zion had Branch crossed the development from his house to hers.

"Um, just a second!" Squealing. Sure. That was the way to go. Lila nearly tripped over her extra thick fuzzy socks as she rushed to the front door. She scanned the house with her hand on the doorknob. There was no saving the Netflix-and-chill vibe she'd lost herself in, but at least it didn't smell like animal carcass in here. She wrenched the door inward, setting sights on the mountain of a man she had to remind herself would only visit for official reasons. "Uh, hi. Who died? I mean, who else died? I mean, what can I do for you in the middle of the night, Branch?"

What wouldn't she do was more like it.

He answered with a low growl that could mean anything from *I don't understand your joke* to *I only speak to animals* as he stepped past her into the house.

She gestured over the threshold behind his back. "Won't you come inside?"

He didn't fit here. Though she imagined he didn't really fit anywhere given his size. It worked well for him out in the open, but in her tiny-ass house that she had to share with a roommate to afford? Not so much.

Branch surveyed her kingdom as she closed the door behind him. She'd changed out of her uniform into one of her oversize T-shirts from a secondhand shop in Springdale. Sans pants. This was going really well for her tonight. He watched a few seconds of the movie before taking in the melting ice cream and discarded spoon on the scuffed wood coffee table.

Then took a seat on her couch she was sure struggled to support his weight and grabbed what was left of her Cherry Garcia and the single spoon. That she'd eaten off of. "I love this movie."

"What is happening?" Lila slapped both cheeks, trying to wake herself up. Because there was no way in hell Branch Thompson—Mr. Don't Look at Me if You Don't Want a Tree Shoved Down Your Throat—was sitting on her couch, eating her ice cream and watching her favorite movie. She must've died on Angel's Landing today. Yeah. That made more sense. She was dead, and this was her purgatory.

"Sit down." Branch nodded toward the butt imprint on her side of the couch.

Lila didn't know what else to do. Rounding the coffee table, legs bare and a little prickly, she lowered herself onto the couch beside him, careful to keep a minimum of six inches between them. She sat stiff as a board, her mouth dry. She tried to clear her throat, but two pints of Ben & Jerry's had the unexpected ability to make that impossible.

"As much as I loved our time together today, Branch, my shift is over. I'm a free woman for the next six hours, and I'm curious as to why you're here. In my house. Eating my ice cream."

"Did you want more?" He offered her the container, only to reveal less than a bite left. Rude. Settling back into the thin couch cushions, Branch spread his legs in front of him as though he had nowhere else to be. Or like he made it a habit to visit her in the middle of the night.

"I'm good." No. Her voice did not just crack on that last word. Closing her eyes against the rush of heat in her face and neck, Lila tried to get a handle on herself. Then she set her full attention on him.

Shadows had settled under his eyes, deepening the lines in the corners. Like he was in the kind of pain no one could fix. His shoulders seemed tighter, and it took everything in her not to offer to rub out the tension. He wouldn't appreciate being touched, and honestly, no matter how many times she'd fantasized about this exact moment—having him in her house—this entire situation made her nervous as hell. Maybe she hadn't actually accomplished scrubbing the day off in her too-hot shower until her skin turned raw.

"Are you a serial killer?" She'd never seen an attractive serial killer, but if they were out there, she bet they would look just like him.

Branch turned those dark eyes on her. His mouth twitched at one side as if she'd surprised him. Then again, maybe he got accused of committing murder all time. She didn't know. She didn't know anything about him. The man wasn't exactly keen on engaging with society. "No."

"Okay." She dragged the word out longer than necessary to try to get her brain in drive. "So if you're not here to kill me, what are you doing in my house?"

Setting the now empty pint on the coffee table with a last lick of the spoon, he scanned her house. Though she couldn't imagine what it was he was looking for. All these government houses had the same floor plan and upgrades, which meant he was looking at an identical layout as his. "You're back on the case."

That…was not what she expected to come out of his mouth. Shock held her brain hostage for a minute. Maybe two.

Branch didn't seem to mind the resulting silence.

Then she couldn't stop the torrent as though she'd finally been released from a year-long vow of silence. "I don't… I don't understand. Risner sent me back to headquarters. He wrote me up and told me to make sure I met with HR in the morning. As of three hours ago, I was convinced I was being fired. What could have changed?"

For the first time, Branch met her gaze without so much as a wince at the sound of her voice. And waited for her to connect the dots.

"You convinced him to keep me." She braced herself for the argument, but it never came. The gritty, peeling fabric of her couch rubbed against the backs of her thighs as a whole new level of awareness coursed through her. She didn't know what to think about that, what to do. He'd gone against their district ranger to call Risner out for his blatant sexism she and the rest of the female rangers had to put up with for this job. Now this? "Why would you do that? You can't stand me."

Branch shoved to stand up, pushing the couch back a few inches at the effort. He stared down at her. Not intimidating. Just…there. Like he would sign up to fight all of her battles if he could, even the ones she'd kept to herself. Which didn't make a lick of sense. He didn't answer for a series of moments. She wasn't sure if he would at all. Until all that intensity centered on her. "Why do you let everyone think you're something you're not?"

"Because the truth is too awful." A rush of shame burned hot under her skin. It took longer than she wanted for her to make sense of what he was saying—what he thought he knew about her—and for a split second, she was tired of lying. Of being exactly what people expected of her. If anyone was going to see through the lies she'd sprinkled like breadcrumbs over the years, she'd put her hope on Branch Thompson. Only to have been disappointed over and over again when he ignored and flat out rejected her.

He hadn't fought Risner for her to remain on the case out of some mutual interest or a potential friendship as she'd wanted since the day he set foot in Zion. Branch had done it to figure out what happened to Sarah Lantos. Which was kind of admirable in and of itself. Lila fisted her sleep shirt to get her head out of the clouds.

"The Grotto at six." He didn't wait for her to answer as he suddenly lunged for the door. "Don't be late."

Lila couldn't help but scramble after him. "Why? What's at six?"

Branch pulled up short of crossing the threshold back out into the gusty darkness and locked his gaze on her. "We start tracking the killer."

Chapter Six

Lila Jordan was going to be the death of him.

She was late. But had he expected anything less? It seemed in the years she'd joined the National Park Service, she'd gone out of her way to rebel against any and all authority, protocol and human decency. As far as Branch could tell, her erratic monologues and meddling were about holding onto some kind of individuality while conforming to a group for a paycheck. He imagined she was the child who never followed the rules, managed to bring nothing but chaos within her family and played pranks on her siblings and parents.

But with a smile like the one that haunted his dreams, she probably swayed anyone and everyone into her line of thinking with the promise of a good time and a little spice thrown in.

Hell, even some of their fellow rangers looked at her as though some of her stardust could rub off on them, but no one compared to the enigma that was Ranger Barbie. There were just some things that couldn't be learned. Lila's daring was one of them. In the end, that daring and outright disobedience would only serve to distance her from any real connections. Because how could you trust someone who didn't follow a typical pattern of behavior and made decisions based on their emotions?

But hadn't he transferred to Zion National Park to find that same distance? Maybe Lila had a point.

The cold seeped through his uniform as he stared out over the Virgin River. The current this far into the canyon wasn't as strong as it would be upstream, but it reached depths of well over fifteen feet in some places, and hikers never seemed to have the good sense to follow direction on calm days like this. The sun was already rising in the east but had yet to reach the canyon floor. Everything about the view settled that invisible burn of rage he had to keep at bay for the sake of his sanity. This place—the isolation, the beauty, the work—it all combined to fight against his natural instincts to bring down the world around him. After all, it was only fair after what the world had done to him.

Two taps registered on his shoulder, and Branch spun to face the threat.

"Morning! Sorry I'm a few minutes late, but I thought we could warm up with coffee. It's really more for your safety. I'm not a people person until I hit the bottom of the first cup of caffeine."

Ah. The mask was back in place. This wasn't the Lila he'd met on the trail to Scout Lookout yesterday. Ranger Barbie had returned. In full force it seemed.

Handing off one of the cups she held, she took a sip from her own. She'd tied her hair back beneath her Stetson again, accentuating a sharp, feminine jawline. Thick lashes dusted the tops of her cheekbones, and those almond-shaped blue eyes felt as though could see straight through him. There was no denying the natural beauty he'd noted last night. In fact, seeing her in that sleep shirt with an ice cream stain below her chin had probably been one of the most gut-wrenching experiences of his life. Because for those short minutes, Lila had just been herself. Effortless and open, if not a little paranoid when it came to serial killers. "I had to guess on the way you take it. I figured black. Like your soul."

She wasn't wrong. Branch took the offering. The bitterness of the coffee failed to cut through the sweetness rolling off her in waves. Actually, he wasn't sure if there was anything that could protect him against the onslaught of Ranger Barbie's full powers. He could almost see the sound wall of bubble-gum pink and high-pitched laughter coming straight at him. "Thanks."

That bright smile that felt a little too forced at times transformed her face from morning zombie to cocaine high. Damn, the whiplash between her two personalities triggered a painful knot in his neck. Again, that tendril of curiosity tightened in his chest. It had started yesterday on their hike up Angel's Landing, convincing him he'd witnessed something he wasn't supposed to. The real her.

So what made a woman like Lila go out of her way to lie to bosses and coworkers? Surely it didn't extend to the people in her personal life, so why here at the park?

She hiked her shoulders higher, studying the Grotto with its fifty-foot trees, asphalted paths and worn, wooden picnic tables.

The park itself remained open twenty-four-seven, but the shuttle system to get visitors this far into the park had only just begun for the day. It would be another fifteen minutes or so before this trail was overrun. While Sarah Lantos's death had been determined to be homicide, law enforcement rangers didn't have the pull to shut down the Angel's Landing trail. Their only saving grace would be the lottery system that limited the amount of hikers.

Lila seemed to sense their limited opportunity to get moving without an audience. "So what's the plan, Stan? I've got three days' worth of supplies and sixteen ounces of caffeine in me. If we don't start hiking, I might have to climb the side of the Lookout to burn it all off."

She'd come prepared. Good. Neither of them could risk going into this unprepared, but based on his previous homicide experience, he didn't expect that the killer had remained in the park, either.

"Whoever stabbed Sarah Lantos either climbed the Lookout to get to his victim or used the rope and anchors up the side as an escape after he killed her." Branch was already moving across the road as the first shuttle curved along the main transit vein of the park toward the start of the Angel's Landing trail.

"Don't forget he also pushed her over the edge." Her tone was a bit too enthusiastic for this conversation and time of day. "I'm betting the former. The anchors and carabiners would've already had to have been in place for him to escape without any other hikers seeing him flee, which means he most likely climbed the Lookout and set his route in the days leading up to her murder. He would've had to make camp at the base or use a sleep platform."

She was right. Damn it. Why hadn't he thought of that? "You climb?"

"You don't?" The barb hit as she no doubt intended. There were a limited number of climbing rangers throughout the National Park Service. She obviously enjoyed knowing this was one area she outranked him. Lila twisted her pack to her front and unzipped the top, showcasing a perfectly coiled rope of blue fiber with yellow and green woven in. "It's been years since I've free climbed. We could use the killer's gear, but I brought my own in case we don't want to trust another climber's routine."

"If he escaped down Scout Lookout, why bother inspecting his gear and anchor points?" Branch picked up the pace as he hauled himself up the thin rocks layered one on top of the other. Like melted chocolate. His muscles still protested against yesterday's ascent while Lila looked as though she could run a marathon straight up the damn mountain. In reality, there was no best way to get straight to the base of Angel's Landing from here. They'd have to climb either way.

"A climber's routine can tell you a lot about a person. Fitness level, climbing experience, discipline, how often they need to rest. A good majority of free climbers make national parks their Everest. They want to tick as many as possible off the list, sometimes even forgoing the legal route in order to conquer a mountain. Like Yosemite. It's illegal to climb certain parks, in which case there might be an arrest record. We can take all that information and compare it to past permits at the other parks, too, to get an ID on our suspect." She attacked the rise in elevation without so much as a change in her breathing, as if Mattel's CEO was personally waiting for her at the top with a new Barbie. "I imagine Sarah Lantos's killer didn't bother filing for a permit to make the hike, so we'll have to use other ways to locate a suspect. Don't you think?"

Okay. He hadn't thought of that, either. He'd worked a homicide as a law enforcement ranger in Grand Canyon for years before landing in Zion, but the rest frequency and climbing experiences of solo climbers were beyond his scope. "You were a climbing ranger."

Though not here in Zion. She had to have worked for one of the other parks. Joshua Tree. Arches. Maybe Red Rock.

Except then why would Risner keep her as an entry-level ranger if she had that kind of experience?

"No. Climbing for me was a form of therapy. You know, the kind of therapy that shuts off your brain because you have to focus on not dying, and you don't have to give up your secrets to a stranger. Way better than that psychotherapy crap, in my opinion."

"Can't say I don't disagree." Despite his insistence on attending marriage counseling and family therapy in the months leading up to the end of his marriage, Branch had realized too late he and his ex-wife had passed the stage of help. There'd been nothing left to save. "What else do you use as therapy?"

What the hell did he care? It wasn't like they were partners. They were barely more than acquaintances. Professionals. Nothing more. And yet, he'd somehow deemed it necessary to surprise her at her house in the middle of the night to inform her of her ongoing involvement in this case.

"Lots of things." She easily kept pace ahead of him by a few feet. "Yoga, playing violin, ice-skating lessons. Oh, I ran a marathon a couple years ago, but I wouldn't do it again."

"And now?" Branch wanted to punch himself in the face. He'd spent the past four months keeping his distance and setting the parameters of their working relationship. But since witnessing her slip yesterday on this very trail, the harder he tried to gain back that coldness, the faster it trickled through his fingers. The need to figure out the puzzle she presented called to him on a primal level, and it seemed there was nothing he could do about it until he got his answer. That was all this was: a puzzle he wanted to solve.

They were moving into the switchbacks, making great

time, but there was still a matter of four hours between their position and the end of the trail.

"Now I'm kind of lost." Her voice had dropped, away from the pitch only canines could hear. It'd only been hours since he'd left her in that run-down house the government deemed safe, and he was already craving another glimpse of the woman Ranger Barbie tried to suffocate. "And I'm tired."

Living two separate lives birthed an exhaustion that had the tendency to sink bone-deep and refuse to let up until enough time without pressure passed. He'd felt it while pretending his marriage still had a chance. Showing the world one person—a man happily married and in love with his wife—as reality sucked the life from him.

He wasn't sure how long Lila had been trying to hold it together, but it'd only taken a few months before he succumbed to the crushing fatigue. Life sure as hell hadn't asked his permission before it decided to blow up in his face, and now he was stuck.

Just like Lila.

Chapter Seven

The killer had known exactly what he was doing. He was experienced and knew his route up the side of Scout Look-out better than the rangers who practically lived in this park. The bolts he'd drilled into the cliffside for his anchors were doing a masterful job of remaining in place despite Branch's dangling weight.

Their killer was experienced, but he would've been better off taking his rope with him during his escape to avoid potential DNA testing. So why hadn't he? Had he needed a quick getaway and couldn't afford the extra weight? Or had he left it on purpose?

Lila touched down at the base of Angel's Landing first, her harness digging between her thighs and around her hips. Hands dusted with chalk, she brushed the excess on her uniform slacks. That was really going to piss Risner off.

Having her descend the killer's route had been the most efficient use of their draining energy after four hours of hiking vertically. Using the killer's anchors and carabiners, she'd secured her own rope to the cliff face as Branch lowered her at an excruciatingly slow pace as though afraid he might drop her at any moment. Which had been a possibility, but a part of her trusted him more than she trusted herself.

She couldn't make out his features from six thousand feet below, but she could imagine him using his best grizzly bear impression to scare people off. Unholstering the radio at her hip, she pressed the push-to-talk button with little hope her signal would escape the surrounding mountains. "Ranger Jordan to Ranger Thompson. Your turn. Over."

Static crackled through the speaker. One second. Two. The high whistle of the wind cutting through all these surrounding peaks and valleys cut through her concentration as she stared up at his outline.

"I'm good." A man of few words and even less humor. She couldn't get enough.

Lila allowed herself to relive the gravel in his voice. Was that nerves? Damn, he was killing her down here. She studied him while opening the channel. "I promise not to drop you. If I wanted you dead, I would've used the candles I lit last night as part of a sacrificial ritual in your honor."

"You're not funny." Another crackle from the radio. Or was that a crack in his voice?

Widening her legs to take more of his weight—because she was going to get him off this mountain come hell or high water—she locked the end of the rope near her dominant hip. She couldn't stop the laugh bursting from her chest. She'd never thought there would be a day when the great Branch Thompson showed vulnerability. She was pretty sure the man did anything he could to avoid it, and he sure as hell wouldn't want that vulnerability made public. "I'm pretty funny."

No answer to that.

She kept her squinting gaze on him, noting the position

of the sun. Shade bathed her in cooler temperatures, but time hadn't been on their side since Sarah Lantos's murder. "How do you plan to get down here if you don't trust me to take your weight? Maybe you shouldn't have eaten my Ben & Jerry's last night."

Okay. Now she was just poking the bear, but she couldn't resist getting under that guarded man's skin. Just felt right in the moment.

"You shouldn't shame people for their food choices." The rope tugged in her hand.

"All right. How about this." Why did she suddenly feel like a hostage negotiator? Maybe that should be her next area of study. Something new to keep her mind busy while she tried to figure out how to get this black abyss out of the middle of her chest. "I will buy you your own pint of Cherry Garcia that you can eat in the dark with no one else around. I'll even lend you my DVD of the movie we watched last night."

"You're the only person I know who still uses DVDs." He was stalling, and they both knew it.

But she was going to let that comment slide. It was the least she could do considering she'd discovered a new species of grizzly bear that could speak more than two words at a time. "I've checked all the bolts and anchors. They are perfectly capable of handling your weight."

His outline shifted overhead. They were killing daylight here. Every second he refused to trust her was another second Sarah Lantos's killer remained free. Was it really so much to ask to trust the woman you'd despised for the better part of four months? "Now you're shaming my weight."

She couldn't win. Lila raised the radio to her mouth to counter. But stopped short. The hairs on the back of her neck stood on end, her scalp tightening in warning.

As though she was being watched. Shifting her weight to dislodge the sensation, she searched for the source. There wasn't a whole lot to study, but there were countless ridges, shadows and shrubbery to hide in. A shiver chased down her spine. They'd set out to track a killer, but what if the killer was tracking them? "Get down here."

The change in her voice must have been apparent. Without a response, the slack slid from the rope, tightening with Branch's weight. Exposed to the rope's fiber, the friction against the raw skin of her hands threatened to leave her with burns, but she wouldn't compromise Branch's descent because of a little pain. She'd demanded he trust her. This was him trusting her.

His full weight tugged at the harness strapped at her hips, bringing her to her toes. One wrong move, and she could face-plant against the side of the cliff as he free-fell, though she was fairly certain she wouldn't drop him. Seventy-five—no, eighty percent sure. This was why it was a good idea to climb with a partner around your same size, which begged the question: Of all the rangers at his disposal, why had Branch fought for her to be part of this hunt?

Lila kept her gaze upward. Minutes stretched into hours of repetition: the rope sliding through her gloved hands, the mental check-ins on his progress, the lactic burn in her arms. Sweat built at her temples, but he'd only reached the halfway point. Pressure expanded in her chest and hadn't let up. It was growing stronger. As if whoever was watching had somehow gotten closer without her realizing. Her breath shallowed as she tried to split her attention between Branch and the presence at her back. She couldn't risk a single mistake with his life in her hands.

Her arms shook with the effort to keep Branch from falling to his death, but they were making progress. He was almost on the ground, and the closer he got, the less the pressure in her chest had power over her. The fact that his harness accentuated the muscles running the length of his thighs and rear with every movement didn't hurt, either.

When he touched down, the rope slackened between them—taking both a physical and a mental weight off her body—and she rushed to meet him, throwing her arms around his neck. "Look at that. You did it!"

A wave of tension tightened every muscle under her touch, from his shoulders to his toes. The air charged with something she couldn't name, but it was far from the friendly conversation they'd engaged in during the descent down the cliff face.

Branch shoved out of her hold, expression shut down. Eyes hooded. His chest rose violently. "Don't touch me."

The inky blackness she tried to keep under wraps below layers and layers of pink and bubbles threatened to escape. Air lodged in her throat at the sudden change in his demeanor, and the banter between them a little while ago vanished as though it never happened in the first place. Had she imagined it? She had the tendency to do that. To see connections and relationships as more than they really were. "I'm sorry. I didn't mean—"

"It doesn't matter what you meant." Branch loosened his harness, stepping out of it and leaving it behind. No, shoving it away as though it would come to life and bite him. He maneuvered around her without so much as a second glance at her. Why did that hurt more than his words? "We need to keep moving."

Lila stared after him, not really knowing what to do as he searched the ground around them. She'd made a mistake. Believed he'd started letting down his standoffish guard. For her.

She stopped herself from clenching her hands. They ached from acting as base to his descent. What did she think was going to happen when she hugged him? That he'd suddenly see she'd been right there in front of him this whole time? Forget he hadn't ignored and pushed her away since he came to Zion? A nauseous churn erupted in her stomach. All too familiar and suffocating. Rejection. Shame. Worthlessness.

Shucking her own harness, she folded and packed it in her pack, unwilling to leave it behind as Branch had done with his. The killer. They were tracking a killer. Analyzing what had changed between them from last night to a few minutes ago wouldn't get them any closer to finding Sarah Lantos's killer. It would be okay. She'd survived the mess she'd made of her family. She would survive Branch's indifference.

Her boot caught on a rock, and she pitched forward. The world ripped out from beneath her.

Lila threw her palms out to catch herself, but a massive wall of muscle stepped between her and the ground. Strong hands secured her hips and steadied her on her feet.

Her breath escaped her chest for an entirely different reason than Branch running as though she'd physically disgusted him. But it was the heat singeing her insides beneath his palms that threw her off-balance.

Drawing herself to her full height—at least a head shorter than Branch, his chest pressed to hers—she locked her gaze on his. The hardness had left his expression, leaving the man who'd set himself in front of her TV with her favorite ice cream last night.

She set her hand against his chest to return to the distance he'd set between them. "Thanks."

"It's not personal." Calloused fingers tightened on her hips, keeping her in place. His body heat seared through the thin cotton of her uniform's button-down. It was made worse by the increasing temperatures as the sun arced higher in the sky. "I haven't let anyone touch me since my divorce."

"I didn't know." Divorce—no matter the circumstances—was hard. It changed people. While she hadn't been through it, she'd witnessed friends' entire lives crumple when a marriage ended. Couples she'd admired for their commitment and those stolen glances at each other when they thought no one was looking had suddenly turned bitter and angry and hostile, until they were no longer recognizable. And Branch was one of its victims.

Lila counted off his heartbeats against her palm, steady and strong. Just like him. "But it's a little hard to believe you don't like to be touched when you're still holding onto me."

Distinct lines deepened between his brows as if he couldn't possibly figure out why he hadn't let go. In Lila's next breath, Branch seemed to come back to himself and retreated a step, but the impression of his hands refused to dissolve. "I'm sorry. I'm not… I'm not good at being around people anymore."

"Everyone has cuddle-with-a-toaster-in-the-bathtub days." Brushing invisible wrinkles from her uniform, she set her performance smile in place, trying to lighten the mood. She'd been doing it for so long, it'd become as easy as breathing. Because it was better than letting the darkness win again. She didn't expect him to tell her about his divorce, and she wouldn't push. But the idea of someone hurting this man set her teeth.

Lila readjusted her pack on her shoulders. Unnecessarily, of course, but she'd achieved satisfactory distraction level. There weren't any signs of a campsite around here. The killer must've moved deeper into the valley.

"Don't." That single word rocked through her as Branch ate up the distance he'd put between them. She felt the roughness in his voice deep in her bones.

Time slowed as he raised his knuckles to brush against one corner of her mouth. "Don't put that fake smile on, Lila. You don't ever have to hide from me."

Chapter Eight

What was happening to him? An internal battle raged, pulling him in two directions. One side retreated into the safety of his no-personal-attachments rule, and the other closed the distance between him and Lila.

He'd told her he didn't like to be touched, and yet he couldn't seem to stop himself from reaching out. From trying to rid the world of that protective layer she pasted in place, hiding herself from him and everyone else. What the hell did it matter to him how she lived her life? And why couldn't he get rid of that part of him that wanted to know what had conditioned her to don that pink armor? What didn't she want him to see?

Branch dropped his hand away from Lila's mouth as panic flared in those sky blue eyes.

She slid out of his reach, her disguise back in full force. It was terrifying and impressive at the same time, how easily she could switch from one personality to the other. She hiked her pack higher on her shoulders. That bright pink manicure stood out against the drabness of her uniform.

The gray and dark green washed her out. If anything, the small pops of pink only added to her beauty. How hadn't he noticed that before? Oh, right. Because he was making it his personal mission to never speak to another human being again.

"I'm not seeing signs of a campsite here. We should keep moving. Pick up the killer's tracks before he gets too far into backcountry." Lila raised her hands to her hips.

She was going to pretend he hadn't broken his own rule by touching her. All right. He could pretend, too. Branch growled his approval.

"Oh, good. You're growling at me." She moved ahead of him, pack in place, the rope and gear she'd supplied professionally stowed.

His mouth twitched before he could stop it. Her sarcasm and teasing just hit right. He couldn't explain it.

And he couldn't explain how the nerves that held him hostage on his descent down Angel's Landing had lost their intensity now that he had his feet on the ground. His fingers still ached from the pressure he'd kept on the radio. He'd been hanging on for dear life—physically and mentally—but Lila's encouragement had done something to him. Something he hadn't expected. It was as though his entire body had tuned to the sound of her voice, and all he'd been able to think about was rappelling as fast as possible to get another dose of her brightness and humor. Her half-hearted death threats and ability to distract him from the darkness in his head.

Without her, he wasn't sure he would've made it down at all, and wasn't that ironic considering he'd done everything in his power to avoid Ranger Barbie over the past four months? Deep down, he knew why the distance had been necessary. He'd known how dangerous Lila Jordan was before she'd even introduced herself and offered to buy him coffee as a welcome-to-the-team gesture. He'd felt that danger at the top of the cliff and again as he'd allowed himself that brief physical connection a couple minutes ago, a craving to be near her, to give up this damn fight he'd taken on after his divorce. While he had no intention of ever being vulnerable in a relationship again, Lila didn't deserve his rough side.

"She cheated on me." He wasn't sure he'd ever spoken the words out loud before, but he noted the hitch in Lila's step ahead of him. To her credit, she covered herself well, pushing forward as though he wasn't spilling his guts. "My ex-wife and my best friend. Guess it'd been happening for a few months. Right under my nose. At the time, I thought we were happy. Nothing seemed off until I caught them together."

"I'm sorry." Lila's elbows tucked closer to her rib cage. She kept her head down to the point he couldn't read her. Though, if he was being honest, she wasn't like the other rangers who wore their emotions on their sleeves. Even Risner gave away his moods before he opened his mouth. But not Lila. She was an impenetrable force of nature. "Some people's birthstone is crystal meth, and it shows."

"You're not wrong." Damn this woman. It wasn't enough she felt she had to empathize with him, but she had to go and try to make him laugh. Why did she insist on clawing under his skin when he wanted nothing but to disappear? To stay in the dark rather than chase those flashes of spark she set off inside him. "Worse part was, I found out later she was pregnant at the time I walked in on them. With my baby."

"You have a kid?" Her shoulders tensed as though she intended to turn around to face him, but Lila kept hold of herself. Better than he was doing, that was damn sure.

"No." That single word was all he would say about it.

Shade cast over them as they kept to the base of the

mountain, but it was that permanent inner chill that refused to let up. It was windier here in the valley, setting the surrounding weeds and trees in motion, erasing evidence from the dirt with a simple gust. It'd take a miracle for them to pick anything up from their killer.

Branch forced one foot in front of the other, fighting that cavern of hollowness in his chest. "She chose not to keep it. Said she didn't want anything to tie herself to me after the divorce."

And there'd been nothing he could do. Nothing he'd said had swayed his ex to change her mind. She hadn't given him a chance. While they hadn't talked about starting their family yet due to their separate careers, to have the potential taken from him without warning had sent him spiraling.

"Why are you telling me this?" Lila's voice softened, telling him this was the woman he'd glimpsed on the trail yesterday afternoon. The one who'd realized their victim had been murdered, who'd identified the killer's escape and who'd surprised him with the ins and outs of climbing down the cliff face. The real Lila.

In that moment, Branch wanted to see her face. To memorize every centimeter and commit it to memory in case he never got the chance again. This was a rare occurrence that deserved to be remembered, like a comet that only orbited the solar system every few hundred years. "Because I didn't like the look in your eyes when I snapped at you. Like I'd hurt you. I don't want you to think… You don't deserve my anger."

Lila slowed her tread through the scrub brush. Her shoulders rose on a strong inhale as she swiped at her face. "As much as I appreciate that, you don't have to explain yourself to me. We're not friends. We work together. It's not your job to manage my feelings."

Oh hell. Was she crying? His heart threatened to beat straight out of his chest. "Lila, look at me."

Tears glittered in her eyes as she turned to face him.

"Why are you crying?" Something violent tore through his chest at the sight, and he wanted nothing more than to kick his own ass for putting those tears in her eyes. One step. That was all it would take to ease that animal inside of him demanding he fix this. He fought the urge to capture a rogue tear trekking down her face. There was a reason he hadn't opened up to anyone since his divorce. Because of this, right here. Having his pain reflected back at him was akin to falling to his death, slow and unbearable.

"Because I'm mad you had to go through all that, and it's illegal to kill people, and that shit is frustrating." Lila whipped her hands down from her face, rolling her gaze to the sky to dry the last of her tears.

Okay. That was cute. Her frustration on his behalf seeped into him, a wave crashing against the shore and nearly knocking him under the current.

Ranger Barbie wasn't all plastic as he'd been led to believe. She had feelings, and right now, she'd chosen to take on a pain that didn't even belong to her so he didn't have to feel it alone.

Branch took that step, putting himself in her personal space. Hints of her shampoo slapped him in the face on a gust of wind ripping through the canyon. Light and invigorating, it challenged his senses when most everything had gone numb since his divorce. Just like her. The effect awoke sensations he hadn't allowed himself to feel in a long time. Not only had this pink nightmare barged into his life uninvited, she'd somehow convinced him she was essential to coming back to the land of the living. "It's not your job to manage my feelings, either, but I appreciate the effort."

Her brows, a few shades darker than her bleached hair, drew together as though the idea of taking her own advice had never been spelled out for her. The tears dried, and all that was left was a pool of confusion in those sky blue eyes. "You really know how to give off mixed signals."

Branch came back to himself. Remembered why they were out here, in the middle of nowhere, and who they were tracking. And that he couldn't—wouldn't—put himself in a position to get carved up again. He'd barely survived the first time. He wasn't so sure he'd be able to pull himself back together after a second.

And Lila Jordan was capable of ending worlds with a smile on her face and that laugh that followed him into his dreams. Even if it was all a lie. "Turns out I'm not the only one."

Her mouth parted at the jab. It'd been a cheap shot but necessary to keep the professional distance between them. She'd been right before. They weren't friends. They were coworkers. Nothing more. So why did watching her slide into her Barbie persona piss him off so much?

"With all due respect, Ranger Thompson, intercourse yourself." Lila didn't wait for his response, turning back to the path without seeing the grin splitting his face. Was that her professional way of telling him to—

She pulled up short.

Branch's defenses caught the change in her body language, and he maneuvered around her to get a better look ahead.

A campsite.

Abandoned but clear evidence that someone had been there in the past few hours, possibly as early as an hour ago considering the dying embers of the fire. It wasn't anything much—a few rocks set in a circle with blackened twigs and a dead log in the center. What looked like an empty sandwich bag had caught in a bush nearby. Flattened dirt suggested the killer might've rolled out a sleeping bag or mat. Simple. Purely for survival.

Zion didn't accept backcountry permits for this area, nor did it approve of campfires in any capacity. Which meant they were most likely looking at the remnants of the killer's campsite. Streaks cut through the dirt as though the killer had tried to cover his tracks, and from what Branch could make out, there were no identifying treads in the footprints. Like their suspect had filled his boot treads with something to erase anything that could lead to him. "Stay back."

"I would rather take a trailer hitch to the shins." Lila broke through the barrier he'd made between her and the campsite, throwing him off-balance enough to pitch him to one side. Great. Ranger Barbie had gone feral. This was going to end poorly. For him. "I'm trained in search and rescue. Isn't that why you brought me along on this little field trip?"

Right. Not because he'd been intrigued by the pretty demon. Branch scanned the surrounding landscape, unable to pick up any other signs of life. Defeat coated the back of his throat in acid. "It's too late. The killer has already disappeared."

Chapter Nine

There wasn't much left of the campsite. At least nothing that they could use to identify Sarah Lantos's killer. Why had she and Branch been given that responsibility again? They couldn't be the only ones brought into the search. Zion National Park stretched over two hundred and thirty-two square miles. It would take weeks, if not months, to cover that much ground, and even if they got lucky and found a clue as to where the killer had gone, they were at risk out here in the open. Exposure, rock falls, flash floods… So many ways a national park could kill a person. Which meant they were most likely one of several teams involved in the search.

Lila scanned the campsite for something—anything—to give them a direction. This valley branched into several other canyons, each leading in a different direction. While she had her theories as to where a sane person might go from here, it relied solely on whether the killer had done his research of the area, had come prepared or wasn't completely out of his damn mind.

Could anyone who'd taken a person's life be considered in a healthy mental state? She couldn't answer that.

The boot treads left behind weren't anything she'd come

across before. Patternless. Brandless. Useless. There was no way to prove this campsite belonged to the killer without a *Hey, it's me. I murdered that woman* sign, but what were the chances they had stumbled across a random site after descending Angel's Landing? "Based on the distance between the cliff and this campsite, I'd say we're on the right trail. He was here. Probably within the past couple of hours."

The weight of Branch's attention slid down her spine. He'd been watching her for a few minutes, whether he realized it or not. Any move she made seemed to intensify his presence, but she wasn't going to let him get to her again.

"Why wait?" Two words. That was enough.

She could practically feel the vibration of his voice across the empty space between them, as though he was standing within mere inches, which was nuts. Her mouth dried at the thought of all the other things he could say to her with that deep tone. Things he might whisper in the dark, tangled in her sheets with her secured against his unyielding chest.

Nope. Not happening. He'd made that perfectly clear. He didn't get close to people for a reason, and after he'd told her about his horrible experience with his ex, she didn't blame him. How did a person come back from something like that? From that kind of betrayal?

Blood drained from her face. Wait. What was his question again? "What do you mean?"

"The window of when Sarah Lantos died is between ten and two yesterday afternoon." Branch kicked at the ring of rocks that reigned in the embers still smoldering. "If this site belongs to the killer, why wait until this morning to flee? Why not get as far from the crime scene as possible while he could?"

Lila circled the campsite for the—she didn't know how many times—and followed the streaks carved into the dirt. Trying to cover his tracks? No. That didn't feel right. Not with the lack of treads in the killer's boots. Attempting to erase his presence would be redundant, and leaving a sandwich bag voided all that hard work.

But Branch had a point. Why stay here when rangers and the medical examiner's office would be all over the scene literally less than a half mile away? This clearing acted as a starting point that split into multiple escape routes through the valleys and backcountry trails. Maybe he hadn't meant to stay as long as he had.

Crouching beside one of the divots, she caught the pattern. Not with the treads but in the steps themselves. "Because he was injured."

Branch entered her peripheral vision, the scent she'd always attributed to him—cedar and something clean— driving into her system.

"See?" Guiding her finger over the nearest streak without disrupting the dirt, Lila ended at the empty boot print to the left. Then another streak, complete with a second boot print. Again to the left. Then a third.

"He wasn't trying to erase his tracks. His right leg is dragging behind his left." Branch took position beside her, only inches between them. One shift in her weight, and she'd get everything she'd craved in the past few months. It was as close as he'd ever voluntarily gotten, but Lila had to remind herself there was nothing personal about his proximity. He was simply trying to get a closer look at what she saw. "Would he have been able to scale Angel's Landing with an injury like this?"

"Depends on how old it is." That woodsy scent filled her, warmed her from the inside, and she breathed it in a bit deeper. If this was all she could have of Branch Thompson, she'd die a happy woman. Ugh, that sounded pathetic. Months of this crush must've warped her brain. "If it's a disability, he may have learned to compensate on his climbs over years of conditioning and training, but if it's recent, I don't see how."

"So it's possible Sarah Lantos could've fought back and injured her attacker." Why did Branch sound hopeful about that possibility? Like he wanted the killer to suffer for what he'd done? Deep lines etched between his brows as Branch seemed to memorize the tracks in front of them, and she wanted nothing more in that moment than to smooth them away. To offer him some kind of comfort.

He'd probably bite her hand off if she tried.

"Yeah. I guess it's possible." The breeze kicked up, cooling the sweat at her temples and increasing the intensity of cedar. Lila forced herself to stand, to get some distance on the pretense of searching the campsite for evidence when all she really wanted to do was clear her head of Branch. "Problem is we don't really know anything about her. Whether she was armed or capable of hurting him."

All they had was the driver's license attached to the permit Sarah Lantos had applied for to hike Angel's Landing. The license itself had been issued by the state of Washington and listed the woman's birthday and address, but that didn't mean that was where the victim had called home. The law enforcement division would take that information and run with it, but it didn't tell Lila if Sarah was married, if she had children, what she enjoyed in her down time or what kind of books she liked to read. She'd been a donor, but Lila couldn't imagine any of her organs helping someone else after a six-thousand-foot drop. As of right now, Sarah Lantos was only a body. A piece of a puzzle they had yet to figure out, and maybe that was what had sent Lila into two pints of Cherry Garcia last night after Risner dismissed her from the case.

Everyone needed someone on their side.

"How do you do it?" Branch kept his attention on the revealed pattern in the dirt. "See things the other rangers don't."

"Not sure what you mean, Grizzly Bear." Ice threaded through Lila's veins as she backed away from the treads. Not once in the four months, three weeks and two days Branch Thompson had set foot in Zion National Park had he ever asked her a personal question, and she wasn't entirely sure what to do with it now.

Branch straightened to his full height. That startling difference between them was enough to make her question every single daydream and fantasy she'd ever had. Not just physically. Mentally, emotionally.

Every move he made was calculated beforehand where she jumped at any opportunity that distracted her from the incessant thoughts in her head. He set out to push everyone away—to punish them or himself, she didn't know—when all she wanted was connection. Someone who surprised her with her favorite soda or brought her a cookie because they'd been thinking about her. Someone she could talk to, really talk to, without having to rely on death threats and sarcasm. Someone who knew all the bad but loved her anyway. In what world would a man like Branch choose to be with her?

"I worked homicides in Grand Canyon as a law enforcement ranger before coming to Zion. A lot of suicides, too." He stared out over the campsite. "It was an accident, really. Something I kind of fell into after the divorce four years ago. I didn't really know what to do with myself. I couldn't stay in the house we'd shared, couldn't see myself going back to work at a job she'd pushed me into for the income. Telling me it would be good for our family."

Every cell in Lila's body went still, as if one wrong move would break the spell of him opening up.

Branch scrubbed a hand down his face. "After I signed the papers, I found myself on the road, going from one park to the other, trying to figure out what came next. But standing in the middle of the most beautiful places on the planet, I felt… I just felt. For the first time in months, the anger, the hurt, the betrayal—none of it could get to me."

The half-hearted laugh that escaped his throat shocked her straight to the core. She'd never heard a more freeing sound and set a goal right then and there to make him laugh as much as possible. Just for the effect it had on releasing the tightness in her chest.

"I'd only been on the road a couple weeks, but I walked straight up to a ranger in Acadia National Park and asked how I could do his job. Within three months, I'd graduated the law enforcement training program, got my EMT certification, had a job with NPS and was assigned to work at the Grand Canyon." Turning, Branch set all that intensity on Lila, his expression unreadable but not as hard as she'd come to expect. "In my program, they taught you patrol procedures, enforcement operations, over a hundred hours of legal and behavioral science and firearms. Everything you need to protect people in the park, but even with all that training, NPS can't teach anyone how to pick up on the changes in your environment like you do. That comes from years of being stuck in survival mode. Of being afraid."

Her throat threatened to close in on itself, and the mask she'd become so accustomed to wearing slipped. Leaving her as exposed as a raw nerve. She couldn't seem to force her brain to catch up, the shock holding her hostage.

"Who made you afraid, Lila?" His question didn't come with a lick of expectation or forcefulness but threatened to crack her open all the same.

"I'm not sure there's anything else we can get from this campsite, but if the killer's injury is fresh, we could catch up. He couldn't have got too much farther ahead in the past couple of hours." A tremor shook her hands, and she fisted her fingers to regain just a sliver of control.

Problem was, Branch always seemed to barrel through her ability to keep her head on straight. Lila headed for the man-size space between two bushes, the most logical path the killer had taken into the valley below. As long as she kept moving, she had a chance.

"And I know what you're thinking. It's presumptuous to assume the killer we're chasing identifies as male, but up to seventy percent of female homicide victims are killed by a male attacker, most of those by someone they knew before their deaths."

"Lila." Branch had no problem staying on her heels.

A rumble filtered through the panic clawing into her chest. Like thunder. Though there weren't many clouds in the sky. Keep moving. She just had to keep moving, and everything would be okay. And talking. And—

The rumble boiled into a full-blown roar, and she slowed.

"Lila!" Hard muscle slammed into her back.

Her feet left the ground. Strong arms locked around her chest and hauled her closer to the mountain wall. Pain ignited down her side at the impact. "Branch—"

A shadow blocked out the sun, and a boulder exploded mere feet from her. Right where she'd been standing.

Chapter Ten

Heavy breathing punctured the ringing in his ears. Branch's lungs worked to discharge the dust he'd inhaled. It still danced in the air, clouding him and Lila in their own personal dirty snow globe.

The boulder that'd crashed to the earth mere feet away splintered down the middle. Chunks had broken off on impact, and it was all too easy to imagine the damage it would have caused had Branch not gotten them off the path.

His fingers protested as he loosened his grip on her arms. Damn, he'd held onto her tight enough, he was sure he'd left bruises on her flawless, sun-kissed skin. "Talk to me."

Her coughs vibrated through her pack into his chest. Jerky and irregular. "I'm alive. You can let go of me."

Right. The danger had passed—as far as he knew. So why did it take so much effort to command his hands to let go? Branch peeled his body from hers one inch at a time, instantly aware of the loss of her warmth.

Rockfalls were the most common natural disasters within the parks, but this was his first. Any number of geologic processes contributed to them: weathering, bedrock fractures, earthquakes, erosion. There was no predicting the outcome, and he sure as hell wasn't looking forward to a repeat. If he hadn't noticed the few smaller rocks tumbling down the cliff before that boulder had followed…

No. He didn't want to think about that. Didn't want to consider what would've happened to Lila if he'd let her take one more step.

Lila slapped a hand against the towering cliff face, bracing herself as she brought that sky blue gaze to his. Then she glanced at the pieces of rock that could've crushed her more thoroughly than Sarah Lantos's fall from Angel's Landing. Her face paled. "Thank you."

Shaky but confident. And he was still coiled tight as a spring. Branch didn't trust himself to speak as adrenaline kept its restrictive vice around his heart, nodding instead.

The change was slow this time, as if Lila had forgotten her armor had dropped. Dirt trickled down the rock face under her touch. Then she brought her hand to her head and shoved that practiced smile in place. "If you wanted a reason to touch me, Ranger Thompson, all you had to do was ask."

"You sign legal documents in glitter pen, don't you?" He hated his title and last name coming out of her sweet mouth. Well, as sweet as it could be with death threats every few minutes. Turned out, he kind of liked them. Her playfulness and creativity. Her unwavering determination to make him as uncomfortable as possible in her own way. As much as he hated the idea of letting anyone get under his skin, Lila had a true talent for tricking his defenses into letting her slide on in. Branch couldn't deny the electricity in his veins in the few minutes since they'd escaped death.

"And use pinky promises as a foundation of trust." She winked at him with a twist of her mouth. Showcasing the laceration at her temple. "Shall we find a killer then?"

"You're bleeding." Every cell in his body screamed at him in condemnation. He'd done this. Used too much force and failed to protect her head when he'd practically tackled her against the rock wall.

Branch caught her arm before she had a chance to run from him, spinning her into his chest. Her palm pressed over his heart. Even with their height differences—she was more than a foot shorter than him—she fit against him perfectly. The perfect little murderous creature he hadn't been able to ignore no matter how many times he tried. He prodded at the cut with the pad of his thumb, careful not to inflict more damage.

Lila flinched under the invasion. Or maybe the adrenaline had finally evened out, and her body got the message that something was wrong. "Ow."

"Sorry." Blood was already crusting at the edges. She wouldn't have to worry about stitches. "The cut isn't deep, but we should clean it to avoid infection."

Her breath tickled the underside of his jaw as she looked up at him. "Okay."

It took more energy than he expected to back away from the press of her body against his. Maneuvering his pack to his front, Branch dug for his first aid kit and laid it out on the ground between them. Alcohol prep pads and his water would do the best job of killing bacteria and flushing debris from the wound. "This might hurt."

"Haven't you heard? Barbies don't feel pain." Streaks of dirt interrupted the smooth skin of her cheek and forehead, sharpening her features to an almost ethereal level. Lila Jordan was breathtakingly beautiful, though he'd just started allowing himself to see past that first layer of defense to the trapped woman beneath.

"You know about that?" Branch focused on cleaning

blood from the laceration in small sections. Overall the cut wasn't more than two inches long, but the jagged pieces of skin at the edges made it difficult to ensure Lila didn't walk out of this park worse off than when she started. She took his ministrations like a champ, though.

"You mean what the other rangers say about me? That I'm an airhead, and I only care about my looks? Oooh, how about that I throw temper tantrums if I don't get the shifts I want? I'm shallow and clingy, and I don't take anything seriously. I use my assets to manipulate my superiors, and I was handed this job by performing sexual favors. Yeah. I know about that."

The brightness in her eyes dimmed, and Branch couldn't help but free the anger he'd relied on to get him into this new stage of life. At the hurt in those blue depths. She'd known exactly how their coworkers—how Risner—perceived her, and yet, from his observations, she hadn't done anything to earn their judgment. He'd simply gone with the flow. Never joining in conversations centered around her, but he hadn't done anything to shut them down, either, and he hated himself for it.

"I know I can come on a bit strong." She shrugged. "I know what they all call me and how everyone tries to get out of working shifts with me. I ask too many personal questions. Sometimes it turns people off when I want to know what's going on in their lives, but I only ever wanted them to feel like they had a friend. You know? Someone they could talk to on breaks or meet for a movie. Come to if they needed help. Working on the trails can get lonely. I just wanted to help make it a little more bearable, but they don't need me, and that's okay. Talking behind my back and making up nicknames helps them bond with each other, and who am I to get in the way of that?"

She had to be joking. Lila had to see the damage that had been done by letting people disrespect and devalue her.

He couldn't stop a torrent of memories from the past few months. Her throwing surprise birthday parties for the other rangers in the headquarters break room, complete with balloons of their favorite color and cake of their favorite flavor. Her handing out gift cards from local restaurants with an invite to get together for lunch. The dozens of times she'd brought her coworkers coffee at the start of her shift, including him.

Branch finished cleaning the cut, taping a butterfly bandage in place. Realization hit. She hadn't done any of it for them. Hell, Ranger Barbie was…lonely. "That first time we worked together. You asked me out to coffee after our shift, and I turned you down."

"Not sure a growl counts as a rejection, but you got your point across." She pressed her pink manicured fingertips over the bandage with a half smile of appreciation. "The rangers here have worked together for years. They're part of each other's lives. I just wanted to help you fit in, but I don't hold it against you, not wanting to get coffee or have me show you around Springdale. I'm not everyone's cup of tea."

But she wanted to be. He could hear it in her voice. Saw it in the slip of her smiles. Smiles he was sure covered a pain she hadn't let anyone glimpse, and Branch couldn't let it go. The idea that her detailed perception in this case had been born of someone who had made her afraid, cultivated due to long periods of time spent in her fight, flight or freeze response. It was a coping mechanism of trauma survivors forced to adapt—to anticipate—a threat before it occurred in the name of protecting themselves.

He wanted nothing more than to wipe the face of the

earth free of whatever threat she was running from. While he'd gone out of his way to isolate himself from everyone around him to endure the pain he'd suffered, Lila had never chosen to become an outcast.

Blond hair escaped from her low ponytail beneath her Stetson, and Branch shot a hand out to swipe it back behind her ear.

An indescribable need to ease that dullness in her gaze and fight her battles took hold. "I'm not a fan of tea, but I'm open to recommendations. If your invitation still stands."

Her mouth parted, and the loss of all those defenses she'd kept in place only made her more beautiful. Real. This…this was the woman he'd caught glimpses of under the mask. And, damn, he'd never seen a more perfect sight. She was still holding back, but he could be patient. He had nowhere else to be.

"Sure." That single answer left her mouth as more breath than coherent word, gifting him the slightest hint at what she might sound like pinned beneath him, his mouth on her skin, his hands tangled in her hair.

A swirl of desire caught him by surprise, nearly knocking him off-balance. Shit. He hadn't felt anything close to this since before his divorce, but Lila had somehow made it easy. Constantly presenting a mystery to solve.

Branch ordered his hand to drop away from her face and his feet to add a few inches between them before he did something neither of them were prepared for. "We should keep moving in case there are more boulders looking to relocate."

"Right." Lila shook her head as though he'd affected her concentration.

Couldn't say he was sorry, either. Turnabout was fair play.

"This valley separates into three different canyons.

The killer could've taken any one of them to put as much distance between him and the crime scene, but the most passable is the one heading north." Lila took a step in that direction. "I'm betting if he didn't bother covering his tracks at the campsite, he didn't take the time to make sure we couldn't follow."

The analytical part of his brain—influenced by his training and experience in two different national parks—attacked the heat simmering in his gut and shut it down. He'd only ever reviewed these canyons on a map. He'd have to rely on Lila's knowledge of the area moving forward. "How far north can he get?"

"About forty miles. It wouldn't be difficult. That canyon has seen some flooding, but we're far enough into the summer months most of it would've cleared." Pointing out over the valley, she targeted their next destination. "All he'd have to do is follow the river as far north as possible before he can disappear into wilderness."

"And get away with murder." Branch wasn't going to let that happen. They'd packed light. Certainly not with enough supplies to spend days in the wilderness, but the sooner they caught up with the killer, the sooner he could try that cup of tea. "We need to get to check in with Risner. You okay to pick up the—"

An explosion rocked through the mountain above. Rock spewed in every direction and arched through the sky, and both he and Lila threw their arms overhead to block the debris. In vain. Vibrations shook up his legs as torrents of dirt blocked out the sun. Growing louder. Closer.

"Landslide." Branch shoved his partner ahead of him as the first sheets of dirt rained down. "Run!"

Chapter Eleven

Pain. She couldn't breathe, couldn't think. It felt as though a boulder was sitting on her chest. Or she'd been body-slammed again.

It had all happened so fast: the shaking; Branch's order for her to run; the darkness. She hadn't made it more than few steps before the first rock had knocked her to the ground.

Had it been an earthquake? Zion was positioned near four minor fault lines, but nothing had triggered anything like this in the past. That first boulder could've been a warning.

Exhaustion urged Lila to slip back into unconsciousness—to take away the pain—but there was something she had to do. A reason why she was here. Why couldn't she remember?

Dust caught in her throat, and her body jerked to dispel the invasion. Once. Twice. Searing pain shot through her side as she tried to roll onto her stomach. She couldn't stop the moan scraping up her dry throat. Everything hurt, and she was dying. Curling her fingernails into the ground, she fisted a handful of what felt like gravel.

Dirt slipped into her uniform and rubbed in all the

wrong ways. She pressed one hand into her ribs, prying open gritty eyes. Meeting nothing but darkness. The moan contorted into a whimper as she tried to take a full breath. Her ribs screamed in protest, only allowing shaky, shallow inhales. "H-hello? Can…anyone hear me?"

No answer.

At least not any that she could hear. Sunlight filtered in from above, helping her eyes adjust to the unstable walls threatening to crush her. "Branch?"

Where was he? Was he hurt? The taste of copper filled her mouth. She swiped at it, coming away with something sticky and warm, but she couldn't make it out clearly enough. Blood?

Lila studied the precarious positions of the boulders overhead. One wrong move, and the entire house of cards could come down on her. It was a miracle it hadn't already. Sand trickled between the cracks and stole some of the sunlight, which felt like death in and of itself when she imagined being stuck without a way to see. Being truly alone. Forgotten. She swallowed past the thin coating of dirt in her mouth. Her bottom lip wavered with a held sob. She could do this. She had to do this.

"Help."

Her call barely filled the too small space in which she'd been thrown. No. Shoved. Branch had shoved her ahead of him. He'd saved her life. Again. The sob built in her chest until it consumed what little air she'd managed to hold onto. It was only a matter of time before this dark little hole collapsed or was filled with dirt. She couldn't be here for that. She had to get out.

"Branch!"

Lightning speared through her side and behind her eyes. Tears burned down her face. Every NPS ranger was required to earn their EMT certification. She was trained to remain calm in case of emergency and to assess any potential injuries. Breathe. She just had to breathe. One breath. Two. Both hurt like a mother, but prodding her fingers along the epicenter of the pain in her side, she concluded her ribs weren't broken or cracked. Most likely bruised. She'd live.

Hopefully not in this hole.

"Okay. Step one—don't panic. Easier said than done. Whoever came up with that step clearly wasn't buried under a mountain." Lila swiped at her face, caking dirt and tears to her hands. Focus. There had to be a way out of here, to get to Branch. Make sure he was alive. One step at a time. That was all she could do.

"Step two—assess for injuries." Inventorying the rest of her body, she was grateful to find nothing but a few cuts and bruises in the low light coming through the cracks. A gash cut across her shin, but it was difficult to see the damage clearly.

Working her pack from her shoulders with nothing less than four moans and one scream, she dragged it to her chest and searched for her first aid kit, flashlight and a bottle of water. Three large boulders had pinned her in place, with the largest overhead. Any movement against them and she was dead. One wrong move? Dead. Another earthquake? Dead. Which only made escape that much harder. Great.

She curled her upper body off the ground, holding onto her ribs to contain the gut-nauseating spike in pain and unpacked her kit. "Step three—don't die of infection."

Alcohol pads, a little water from her bottle, her largest bandage and a few tabs of ibuprofen did the job.

"Four—figure out where the hell you are." She hit the power button on her flashlight. She had about three feet of space overhead, a few more to her right and only a foot or so to her left. Smaller rocks acted as nothing but annoyances. It was the big ones she'd have to watch out for. Though how she was going to chest press a two-ton boulder was beyond her. She regularly hit the weights—even managed a PR last week—but this felt a little out of her reach. "Well, it could use some color, but otherwise, not so bad."

Who was she kidding? This place was a hole. Almost literally. But she hadn't cried in a few minutes. She'd count that as a win. Lila shifted onto her stomach, searching for… Okay. She didn't know. Something, anything, that might look like a Jenga piece she could pull without setting the whole tower down on top of her? Dirt grated against her skin beneath today's kerchief as she toed herself closer to the wall of rock ahead. A collection of smaller boulders— the size of basketballs—were wedged tight. The mammoth rock hanging over her head was supported by these smaller ones on this side of the death trap. "Okay. So you guys are off-limits."

Craning the flashlight to her right, she lost count of the number of rocks squeezed into every nook and cranny between two of the largest boulders. Those could work. They were higher off the ground. Very little chance of causing a complete collapse with the larger boulder ready to take the weight. Where was her architectural engineer dad when she needed him?

She stopped that thought in its tracks. She didn't need him. She'd been doing just fine on her own.

More than fine. Maybe a little lonely with no one but a roommate she barely saw once a week—if she was lucky. Her parents and siblings blamed her for the destruction of the family and wanted nothing to do with her, but she had a good job. She got to work in one of the most beautiful places in the world.

Though getting trapped underneath it wasn't great.

She could get a little obsessed with romantic comedies and probably went overboard on the Ben & Jerry's more than she wanted to admit. Her boss and fellow rangers avoided her at all costs, mimicking and mocking her when they thought she wasn't paying attention. Oh, and then there was her unhealthy crush on a man who would never see her as anything more than a coworker because of his whole messed-up past and bad attitude, but damn it, she was fine.

Where was Branch? Had he survived? Was he hurt? She wouldn't let herself believe anything worse.

The fact was no one was coming to save her. If she was being honest with herself, nobody cared she was out here, about to die, and wasn't that a kick while she was down? Risner would pretend to grieve but ultimately just want to get himself some attention. There would be a service. She could see him now, giving some big speech where he went out of his way to tell people how close they were. The sexist asshole.

Sayles might shed a few tears, but she'd have her big, strong FBI agent boyfriend to help her through it. The other rangers would probably use the gift cards she'd given them to go out together. Her family considered her dead a long time ago. And Branch… Her heart tried to tell her he wasn't all grizzly bear and growls, but they didn't know each other. Nobody really knew her. Which meant, even if she got out of here, she had nothing to go back to. No one.

Gravity intensified its hold on her body. Trying to bury her in all the bad feelings. But she had her smile. She had those little pockets of happiness, even if it came bottled from the pharmacy.

"I'm not as mean as I could be, and people should be more grateful for that." Lila got her knees under her, her head bumping the ceiling of her little cave. If she weren't about to die, this would be a great shelter in the middle of a storm, but she wasn't planning on sticking around to test that theory. Her injured ribs squeezed, and she lost the air from her lungs. Another moan slipped free, but she used the pain to keep her in the moment. To focus on reaching for that first rock. "Just like playing Jenga. Nothing to it."

She didn't even believe herself. The rock—about the size of her hand—came quietly, and Lila released the tension she'd held in her neck. "See? Nothing."

The boulder overhead shuddered. Then sank another couple inches.

Her scream triggered ringing in her own ears as she flattened herself against the ground. Dust settled, a few other rocks came loose. And she waited to die with her eyes pinched tight.

Except she wasn't dead yet. Her lungs seemed to get the message, letting go of the need to hyperventilate. She pried her eyes open. Instantly blinded by the increased sliver of sunlight coming from between the two largest boulders. It wasn't much. Definitely not enough for her to crawl through, but a couple more rocks might fix that. "Please, just let me have the chance to kiss Branch before I die."

That was all she wanted. All she'd ever wanted. And if he was out there—hurt, alone—she had to get to him.

She collected the flashlight she'd dropped and shoved it in her pack before threading her arms through the straps. One shot. She had to make it a good one. Lila two-handed a basketball-size boulder and put her weight into dislodging it from its position. The rock tumbled free, landing short of her kneecaps. She pumped her fist gently up at the boulder threatening to end her puny existence. "Yay me."

The next part would be the trickiest. *Tricky. Tricky. Tricky.* Nope. She had to down the urge to start singing Run-D.M.C. Those would not be her last words if this went poorly.

A few other rocks skittered down the slope wedged between the two boulders, but she'd managed to clear a good amount. The breeze trickled into the cave-slash-prison, and for the first time since waking, she could really breathe. For now. She could see trees and mountains and sky. And dirt. An entire waterfall of dirt.

Was Branch out there? Was he looking for her? Was he as worried about her as she was for him?

Grabbing for the next section of rock, Lila set each down peacefully in an attempt to not anger the earth gods. She could do this. Excruciating seconds turned into excruciating minutes as she carefully removed and set down each piece of the very dangerous puzzle.

Finally, a hole large enough she could fit through held strong. Another sob built in her throat, but she swallowed it back. She could have a mental breakdown after she got the hell out of here. Preferably in the shower. With ice cream. And one of her favorite scream-o songs on repeat. Everyone needed a self-care day.

She unshouldered her pack and tossed it through the opening. If she didn't make it out of this, at least someone would know where she'd met her maker. No time to think. She just had to move.

Lila thrust herself through the opening. The ledge of rock under her ribs gave out, and she sank a couple of inches. The next scream was lost on a gust of wind as panic took control. Clawing her nails into the dirt, she shoved through as the boulder shifted down with a rumble. Her toes cleared the deathtrap, and Lila collapsed onto her back.

"Well, aren't you a determined little thing?" The outline of a man cast a shadow over her from above, though she could make out his features as her vision darkened. Strong hands wrapped around her arms. "Looks like you're coming with me."

Chapter Twelve

Drip. Drip. Drip.

Branch cracked his eyes open to an upside-down world. His head thudded hard. Something sticky and…wrong plastered against his face. He swiped at it. Blood seeped into the loops and whorls of his finger pads. He followed the drops to a rock below, the source of the soft ticking that'd brought him around. The headache hit then, strong and disorienting. He closed his eyes against the dizziness, but it was no use as long as he was strung up like a piñata.

His pack pulled at his shoulders, swinging above—or was it below?—his head. He tucked his chin to his chest to get a better look at what kept him from splatting against the rocks at the base of the tree. His boot had caught between two bare branches, but his heel was already sliding free from his shoe. A fifteen-foot drop wouldn't work in his favor. Hell.

The landslide had come out of nowhere. He remembered shoving Lila ahead of him to make sure she cleared most of the rock, but…he didn't remember much after that.

Lila.

Scanning the dirt and rock beneath him for anything coming close to pink, Branch felt the uptick in his heart rate. She had to be here. She had to be okay. He swung his arms out like a starfish, and his boot slid another few centimeters. There was only one way he was getting out of this alive.

He slipped his pack free and let it drop. His supplies hit the ground with a too loud thud that triggered another sharp spear of pain in his skull. Curling his upper body, he grabbed for the branch that'd saved his life. And missed. Every muscle in his torso protested the smallest movement. Oxygen crushed from his lungs. He straightened back out to regain his breath, and his boot took the opportunity to remind him he'd run out of time. A drop from this height promised a slow death if he managed to protect his head. Not an outcome he was looking forward to. "Come on."

Branch curled again. His fingertips brushed the rough tree bark but ultimately failed to grasp hold. The momentum and weight of his body pulled his heel free of his boot, and he shot up one last time. Bark cut through the calloused skin of his palm as he gripped the branch. His legs lost the battle to gravity, and he hung upright above the sloped landscape. With his boot still stuck in the tree. He stared up at it, out of reach. "Traitor."

Though he had to acknowledge he wasn't about to die. Gauging the distance between him and the ground, he took the chance. His stomach shot into his throat a split second before he hit the dirt, rolling to avoid breaking his unsupported ankle. Dirt clung to every inch of his body, worked beneath his clothes. Irritated…places.

Scrubbing a hand down his face, Branch fell against the tree's trunk for support. Shit. How long had he been hanging there draining like a slaughtered cow?

His vision wavered, and Branch grabbed for his pack, sinking to the ground. He had to stop the bleeding. Head wounds usually bled more due to the amount and location of blood vessels, but he couldn't determine how deep the wound was without cleaning it first. His mouth dried as he caught sight of his water bottle, and he took a few pulls to stay hydrated. It would be all too easy to get dehydrated out here in the middle of nowhere in over one-hundred-degree heat. He couldn't do a damn thing for Lila if he wasn't taking care of himself.

Washing the wound and his face with a couple handfuls of water, he set about cleaning the injury with the last remaining alcohol pad in his kit. He didn't have a mirror, no way of telling if he needed stitches, so a larger butterfly bandage would have to do. The same he'd used for Lila after that first boulder had tried to kill them.

He should've taken it for the sign it was. Branch studied the devastation of the landscape around him. Fifty-foot trees had been half buried. Boulders that'd outlasted hundreds of years of storms cracked open around him. Dead logs and dirt had swept through and obliterated everything within a quarter mile.

Landslides weren't uncommon in Zion. A couple of the most popular trails had been closed down in the past few months due to shifting, but he'd never seen anything like this.

He hadn't heard it, either, that telltale roar that sounded the alarm in an event like this. But there had been an explosion...

Branch shoved a protein bar in his mouth to combat the fatigue flooding through him and hauled his pack to his back. Lila was out here. Alone, possibly injured. He had to move fast. The woman wasn't the type to sit around and wait for someone to rescue her.

Despite her innocent facade and obsession with the color

pink, there was something vicious and unpredictable beneath that smile. He'd glimpsed it only a couple times—mostly when she was threatening him—but Lila would go out of her way to prove she didn't need anyone but herself. Potentially hurting herself in the process despite her training and familiarity with the area.

They had that in common. While he could pinpoint the moment in his life when he'd cut himself off from the world and convinced himself he was better off alone, Lila kept that part of her life to herself. There was no telling how far she'd push herself to survive. Better he found her before it came to that.

His muscles burned as he hauled himself up the incline to where the landslide had started, leaving his boot behind. The trail they'd been following was gone, buried under several tons of rock and dirt and trees. The landslide hadn't started with a trickle. It'd come in an explosion of death and destruction, suddenly and violently. From this angle, Branch could just make out the jagged shards where the mountain had been carved apart. Too straight. Too sharp. It looked almost…intentional.

Didn't matter right now. Sucking in deep breaths from where the landslide impacted the trail, he surveyed the scope of the damage. At least a quarter mile of the valley was lost. Had Lila survived it?

Pain that had nothing to do with getting thrown around like a rag doll took up residence in his chest. Branch rubbed his bloodied hand into his sternum to try to ease the pressure, but it was no use. He hadn't known. That meddling little banshee had worked her way into his life over the past couple of days. Now she was just…gone? No way in hell was he giving up.

Reaching for his radio, he hit nothing but an empty belt.

Damn it. It must've detached during the landslide. Two other teams had set out to track this killer, each expected to check in regularly with updates, but how long would Risner wait before suspecting he and Lila were in trouble? Hours? Days? Knowing the district ranger's hostile relationship with Lila, he'd wait until nightfall, rooting for another team to contribute something worthwhile to the investigation.

Maneuvering his pack to his front, Branch unpacked his cell phone from the front pocket. The screen had cracked from his tumble down the mountain, but the device itself still had battery life. But no service bars. He'd have to hike out of the valley to get a signal. He tossed the phone back into his pack. "This day keeps getting better and better."

What he wouldn't give for one of Lila's death threats now. Just to hear her voice. To absorb a bit of her overzealous enthusiasm. She'd list all the ways they were lucky to be alive and try to recruit him into starting a gratitude journal. Which he would do without her knowledge. Just as he'd bought himself a pint of Cherry Garcia after watching her drop an armload into her cart at the only grocery store in Springdale a few weeks ago. And streamed her favorite romantic comedy after she'd referenced it in the break room a month before that.

He didn't know what it was about her erratic daydreaming heart that had caught his attention the second he stepped into Zion. Everything she was—impulsive, emotional, upbeat—defined everything he wasn't, but he couldn't seem to let go. If anything, she'd hooked him deeper over these past couple of days, and he didn't hate it. He'd come to crave her promises of murder and learning about her expertise in everything ranging from ballet to calligraphy.

Following the upper ridge of the landslide, he gritted

against the small punctures of rocks biting into his socked foot. Dust puffed off his clothing with every step, the sun only making the pounding in his head worse. "Lila!"

His shout echoed off the cliff faces standing as sentries around the valley below. But there was no other response.

No glimpse of pink.

No sign she'd survived.

His chest tightened against the possibility of never setting sight on that hot pink manicure she protected with the fierceness of a pit bull. Or watching her guard drop when she thought no one was looking. And he wasn't leaving until he found her.

Tossing his pack to the ground, Branch mapped the most likely place she would have succumbed to the landslide, probably a few hundred feet down from their original position on the trail. His heels sank into loose earth, threatening to pull him under as he descended. "I'm coming, Barbie. Don't give up."

Larger boulders took shape at the bottom of the incline. There was too much ground to cover in the search, and randomly digging would only waste time Lila might not have. He needed a narrower search grid. He needed a clue to her location. "Lila!"

Again, no answer. The anger he'd managed to suppress since this morning reared its ugly head, but with it came a whole new slew of emotions determined to knock him on his ass. Hopelessness. Abandonment. The things he'd nearly lost his fight to after the divorce. It hadn't just been about losing a woman he'd loved for more than fifteen years. He'd lost a future. A best friend. Everything he'd cared about because of the misdirected impulsiveness of a single person.

Maybe that was why he'd avoided Lila for so long, convinced that having any kind of relationship with her would only end up killing him all over again. Why he'd offered favors to switch shifts, turned down her attempts at getting to know each other and sat as far from her as possible in any team meeting. In the end, he'd treated her as everyone else had. Disposable. Overlooked. Unimportant. And, damn it, she deserved better.

Lila wasn't his ex. And he sure as hell wasn't going to lose her. Not like this.

Branch scoured the site, every cell in his body focused on picking out something—anything—that didn't belong. He just needed a starting point. A pink kerchief. A manicured hand. Hot pink boot laces.

Sun glinted off a metallic surface. No. Not metallic. A bejeweled backpack.

His lungs emptied a split second before he dashed down the incline, toward the boulders at the bottom of the hill. Heart threatening to beat through his rib cage, Branch skidded into the pack as though he was rounding home base and clutched the canvas to his chest. It was hers. But Lila…

"Where are you?" Scanning the area, he noted the body-size hole between boulders with a few scattered stones along the ground. As though someone had crawled free of a grave.

A quick inspection told him she wasn't inside. She wasn't here at all. She wouldn't have left her pack voluntarily.

Branch took another look at the dirt around the boulder. Picking up on a second set of prints. No treads. With a drag mark to the right. The same boot prints they'd found at the campsite.

Ice coursed through his veins. Lila hadn't walked away from the landslide.

She'd been taken.

Chapter Thirteen

Her moan pulled her back into consciousness. Or had she been snoring? It was hard to tell.

Pine branches swayed above her, glimpses of sunlight bearing down in between them. The ground was soft beneath her. And sweaty. Like lying on a sleeping bag.

That wasn't right. Last she'd checked, she was about to be squashed like a pancake by a boulder twenty times her size. And then… She couldn't remember anything else.

"You're awake." The voice came from somewhere to her right. Deep and vibrating. Almost…amused? Movement out of the corner of her eye convinced her brain to burn the last of the haze. The owner's outline grew larger as he drew close. Dragging one foot behind the other. "I was beginning to think I wouldn't have any use for you after all, Ranger Jordan."

Oh. Damn it. She'd been kidnapped.

Shadows played across a deeply tanned face as a new gust of wind startled the tree overhead. Dark brows cut across a broad forehead lined with age markers. Midforties at least. Salt peppered through a few days of beard growth and at the temples of dark hair. His eyes were a bit sunken, surrounded by fine lines, but his face overall was soft. Bands of muscle fought to break free of the tight long-sleeved shirt he wore. Polyester if she had to guess, wicking, quick-drying. Something a seasoned climber might use, along with the loose nylon pants currently covered in blood.

It took a minute for her name to register. Then she remembered her uniform came complete with a name tag to make it easier for hikers and visitors to verbally abuse her on the trails. Seemed the landslide hadn't deemed it worth destroying.

Lila rolled to her side, instantly reminded of the bruises across her rib cage. The pain struck as though she'd been kicked in the gut as she settled her weight on all fours over a sleeping bag that most definitely wasn't hers. "I don't know you."

"But I know you." Tipping the point of a pocketknife in her direction, the man she assumed to be Sarah Lantos's killer settled against the trunk of the tree a few feet away. "I know you're the one who's leading the charge to find me. You discovered Sarah's body. You were the one who tested my climbing gear. The one leading your partner straight to me."

Had he been watching her? Creepy. And definitely the killer.

"Where is Branch?" Her chest hurt. She was thirsty, and her stomach felt as though it'd started eating itself. Or maybe she'd developed an ulcer in the past couple hours. Anything was possible.

Searching what looked like a smaller campsite than the one they'd come across earlier, Lila cataloged whatever was in sight. And what wasn't, her pack included. She'd tossed it, trying to let any search-and-rescue rangers know her location, but did they even realize what'd happened? The US Geological Survey monitored every national park for seismic activity. Did a landslide qualify? Would SAR be deployed in time to recover Branch?

"The last I saw of him, he was getting swept away with a whole bunch of dirt." He enunciated a low whistle with a flutter of his fingertips, clutching an apple and the pocketknife in the other hand. Very Bond villain, if she was being honest. All he needed was a white cat to stroke as he revealed all his evil plans. "Can't imagine he survived. Dynamite can be very unpredictable. You're very lucky you're still alive. For a moment there I thought you were a goner with all those boulders. By the way, how did you survive?"

Dynamite? Her heart shot into her throat. No. Branch was still alive. He had to be. Because the alternative…

Lila kept her gaze on the weapon in the man's hand. To give herself something to focus on other than the heartbreak threatening to claw her apart from the inside. "You caused the landslide. You killed—"

"Yes, yes. I'm the bad guy. I killed Sarah Lantos and shoved her over the side of Angel's Landing. I killed your partner. I destroyed part of your precious park. Blah, blah, blah." Leaning forward, her kidnapper waved a hand.

Tears burned in her eyes, though she honestly doubted she'd drunk enough to provide much release. Her kidnapper had brought her deeper into the valley. Flat landscape surrounded this little pine oasis, making her nothing but a target if she ran. The only other option was sprinting for the canyons, but without her supplies, she wouldn't last more than a day. Maybe two. "What do you want?"

"I have a problem." He limped toward her, heavily relying on his uninjured leg. Cutting along the seam of his pant leg, the killer exposed the bloody wound in his thigh. "And you're going to fix it."

"She stabbed you." Branch had been right about the victim fighting off her attacker before she'd gone over the edge of the cliff. He'd probably rub it in her face for days if he found out. "Sarah Lantos. She fought back."

"Not before I stabbed her first." The corner of his mouth quirked to one side, and Lila's stomach rolled. It was nothing compared to the slight twitches of Branch's mouth that told her he found her amusing if not a little exhausting. This one was completely acidic.

She shook her head, forcing her gaze to the killer's face. Memorizing everything she could about it. Though now that she thought about it, he'd probably planned on killing her to make sure she couldn't identify him. Still, hostage or not, sometimes it was nice to be held. "I don't have my first aid kit."

"Then it's a good thing I came prepared with more than a pocketknife." Adjusting his weight, he took a seat on the ground alongside her, his injured leg nearly touching her hip.

She could run. Based on the amount of blood oozing from the injury at the back of his thigh, he probably wouldn't be able to catch her. Then again, he'd obviously been able to stay conscious and alive since stabbing Sarah Lantos yesterday afternoon and managed to drag her to this campsite, so there was a chance she'd only be making her situation worse.

The weight of his attention curdled the coffee she'd substituted for breakfast this morning. "I will catch you, Ranger Jordan, and I won't be as careful with you as I was bringing you here."

One second. Two. She raised her gaze to his, shutting down the shiver working to break free up her spine.

"Get the kit." He nodded toward a pack at the end of the sleeping bag she'd woken on. "Front enclosure."

Her hands shook as she followed instructions. She couldn't seem to get the zipper around the curve of the pack as she searched for the easiest route to run long distance. Years of traversing these trails had blessed her with muscles she couldn't name. She had no doubt she'd be able to outrun this guy on a good day, but that meant leaving Branch behind. Possibly injured.

She got the zipper unfastened and freed the first aid kit inside. This was why she'd petitioned rangers outside of the law enforcement division to carry weapons, but Risner had shut that down real fast. Accusing her of most likely injuring herself with a Taser rather than her intended target. When she got back to headquarters, she'd show him exactly how accurate her aim was for putting her in this position.

Lila made a show of zipping the front enclosure with one hand while prying the larger compartment open. A gun stared back at her. Sitting right on top. She couldn't tamp down the shudder shaking across her shoulders as she shoved it deeper into the pack. Just in case. Crossing the sleeping bag, she settled the first aid kit in front of her and popped the lid. "You got a name?"

His laugh practically took physical shape between them. "Why are you asking?"

"Because saying, 'Hey, asshole, this is going to hurt' is awkward." Tearing a slit up the side of his pants, she exposed the wound farther. Blood crusted around the edges, but whatever his victim had done hit deep, most likely nicking a major vein. He was still bleeding from an injury he couldn't reach at the back of his thigh, and if she didn't irrigate and clean the wound, he would suffer from infection and greater blood loss. Not enough to kill him, though. At least, not soon enough.

"You don't need my name." He flinched at her touch. Baby. She hadn't even started cleaning the wound yet.

"Fine. Then I will assign one for you." She used the gauze pads to scrub as much blood from the edges as possible, using his water to break up the flakes. She tucked the water bottle between her thighs for easy access when the time came. She wasn't trying to be careful or mindful of his pain. In fact, she wanted this to hurt as much as possible, but other than that first flinch, the killer didn't seem to feel anything. Had he felt anything when he'd killed Sarah Lantos? Lila put as much hatred into her expression as possible as she leveled her gaze with his and dug her nails into the sides of the wound. "I'm going to call you Covid. For obvious reasons."

Another laugh startled her. This one had more bite, and it stuck in her body and refused to get the hell out. The smile that contorted his face fell, and before she had a chance to react, the killer crushed his hand against her throat. And squeezed.

"You make jokes to distract yourself from what hurts. All of these additions to your uniform, the pink nails, the makeup, the bleached hair. Everything I see about you makes me think you work so hard to make the outside beautiful because the inside is rotten. What was it, Ranger Jordan? Mommy didn't love you enough? Daddy hit you a little too often? Or was it something much, much more terrifying?"

Air lodged in her chest, and her defenses automatically had her reaching for his wrist to break the hold. But he wouldn't budge. Panic flared, rolling through her and clenching every muscle she owned. He was so much bigger than she was. So much stronger. The pocketknife he'd held was right there. Her gaze darted down to it, then back up so as not to give herself away, but she was getting desperate. For air. For escape. For him to stop.

The killer dragged her upper body over his leg, close enough she could smell the sweetness of the apple he'd been eating on his breath. He scanned her from scalp to chin, those dark eyes seemingly undoing years of defenses. Loosening his hold, he let his fingers brush beneath the kerchief at her neck. Then untied the knot. The fabric fell away easily, exposing her—and the scar beneath—to him in a way she'd never allowed for anyone.

"You want people to take you seriously, but you keep them at arm's length. You hide from them. Lie to them. Like a magician, you keep their attention on one thing while the trick is happening in another place altogether."

"Everybody needs a hobby." Lila tried to pull back, to put those precious inches back between them, but he'd locked his hand around her throat a second time. That unreadable expression focused solely on the marred skin across her neck. Her pulse thudded—too hard—against his hand.

"Tell me who did this to you." His thumb pressed into the scar tissue spanning straight over her throat.

Her training failed her in every regard. She didn't know what to do, what to think about his request. So similar to the one Branch had made of her. *Who made you afraid?*

Lila slid one hand around the metal water bottle she'd used to clean the killer's wound. Then bashed it as hard as she could into his face. His groan punctured through the haze he'd created. The grip at her throat vanished, and she shoved to stand.

Lila ran toward the canyon mouth, unwilling to look back. And hoped she came out on the other side alive.

Chapter Fourteen

There was no other sign of her. The drag marks Branch had noted ended at a section of cascading boulders leading down into the valley. Even from this vantage point, it felt as though Lila had simply disappeared.

The killer couldn't have taken her far. Not with the injury he and Lila suspected he'd sustained, but if they'd been wrong—if the killer had trained and compensated around a disability—Branch feared he might never find her.

But why take Lila in the first place? The killer hadn't gone through her supplies as far as Branch could tell. Which meant he'd needed her for something. But what? And for how long?

His entire body ached with unchecked bruises, muscle strain and exhaustion as he navigated the maze of boulders leading down in the valley. It was the most logical path the killer would've taken. There were no caves in this area. Only sheer cliffs, decreasing blue sky and unending miles of trees and dirt. The canyon that led north was where Lila had predicted the killer would go, and so would Branch.

His socked foot slipped off the boulder beneath him, and his entire body shifted out of alignment. Slapping his hands out to stop himself from face-planting into the next rock, he breathed through the pain streaking up his ankle and into his calf. He dragged his foot from between the boulders. Still in one piece, but there was no telling how long that would last.

He growled to provide his frustration an outlet. In vain. There was no outlet. Not as long as Lila was out here, potentially in danger from the same killer who'd stabbed Sarah Lantos. That core tension would keep winding tighter and tighter until it suffocated him. It would only be released by getting eyes on her. Having her in his arms. Ensuring she'd live another day to threaten ending his.

Branch couldn't help but scan the area for the dozenth time. Sooner or later, Risner and the rest of the rangers would realize something had happened and send aid, but until then, he was all she had. And he wouldn't fail her. He wouldn't abandon her as had so easily been done to him. All he could do was rely on his training to get to her.

Reaching the bottom of boulder mountain, he took another pull of water, but it did nothing for the light-headedness taking advantage. The world threatened to tip out from under him as he took the next step. Then another.

Hell. Maybe he'd hit his head harder than he assumed. The laceration hadn't been deep as far as he could tell, but that didn't mean there wasn't internal bleeding or that he hadn't sustained a concussion.

Didn't matter. He'd push through. He'd been the one to drag Lila into this mess. He'd be the one to get her out of it. Risner had wanted her off the investigation—for no other reason than the man was a sexist son of a bitch—and Branch was hating himself for pulling her back in. She'd had a way out. She'd been safe in her own little bubble, and he should've left her the hell alone.

But he'd been selfish. Wanting her insight, wanting that

addictive perfume of hers in his system, wanting her to cheer for him for something as small as finding the killer's campsite. Wanting…her. All of her. The fake persona she wore in front of him and the other rangers, and the woman she'd been trying to hide as long as he'd known her.

And if anything happened to her, he'd live with the consequences of that failure for the rest of his life. Never letting himself rest. Never granting himself forgiveness. So he pushed himself harder, until his vision blurred and Branch didn't know which way was up.

His boot connected with something metallic, and he launched forward to catch himself against a rotting pine tree. Bark came off in his hands as he blinked to get his bearings. Stinging pain blistered along his fingers and in his palms, and he watched as blood blossomed in the cracks. "Damn it."

A metallic cylinder rolled to a stop at the base of the tree. A water bottle. Crouching, Branch took in the dents and scratches interrupting the dark green exterior coating, then allowed himself to take in the rest of his surroundings. The tree provided shade as the temperature climbed but wouldn't do much else as the sky darkened with heavy clouds. A sleeping bag lay crumpled to his left with a supply pack resting at the far end of a makeshift campsite. And a first aid kit—complete with bloodied gauze—had been discarded a few feet away.

"Lila." He tossed the water bottle onto the sleeping bag and headed for the kit. Every pad of gauze had been used. He avoided touching the blood directly, but from the amount that had soaked clean through each pad, he guessed the injury had been severe. Had Lila been injured during the landslide? Had the killer done something to her? Had her abductor tried to stop the bleeding? No responsible hiker would have left their supplies behind. Which meant something had happened.

Tearing into the main compartment of the pack, Brach ripped through the supplies for anything that might give him an idea of who'd killed Sarah Lantos and taken his partner, but couldn't find any ID. A change of clothes, protein bars, electrolyte powder, sunscreen, matches.

And a loaded magazine to a handgun. As well as a handful of blasting caps.

The metal tubes were meant to be inserted into the end of a stick of dynamite with a fuse tied to the end for safe detonation. If there was such a thing. Dynamite itself was notoriously unstable. Any small movement could set it off. The killer wouldn't have carried it around in his pack, which meant the son of a bitch must've stashed it somewhere else.

An echo of an explosion replayed in his head. Right before the landslide.

Branch dug deeper into the pack, almost frantic to prove his theory. Thin twine had been stored closer to the bottom. A fuse. Hell. The killer had triggered the landslide. But to kill him and Lila, or simply to slow them down? Working with dynamite could backfire at any moment. Literally. And now Lila was in the hands of a man who'd weaponized it against them.

Extra gun ammunition had been stuffed in the bottom of the pack. Federal law prohibited hikers from bringing firearms into national parks, but this wasn't the first time Branch had come to terms with the fact that killers didn't like following the rules. No sign of the weapon itself, which meant whoever'd taken Lila had most likely done so at gunpoint. But for what? To help him escape? To hold her as leverage when Branch and the rest of NPS caught up?

Branch shoved to stand, eyes on what he could see of the valley. He watched for any sign of movement but noted nothing but grassland and juniper trees. She was out there. He could feel it.

Lila might indulge in self-deprecating jokes and laugh off verbal attacks from her fellow rangers, but she was a fighter and influential as hell. At the end of this, he wouldn't be surprised if the killer turned himself in with an expression of regret after she was through with him. Until then, Branch would have to take matters into his own hands.

Narrowing his gaze on the canyon that would lead the killer north, he crossed the perimeter of the campsite. "Where are you, Barbie?"

A glimpse of color pulled his attention to a blossoming prickly pear cactus. The yellow flowers looked almost translucent as the sun crested into the second half of the sky. And caught in its needles, a hot pink floral kerchief.

Lila's kerchief.

Oxygen lodged in his chest. She'd been here. He wasn't sure how long ago, but now he had proof. She'd survive the landslide. Only to be taken hostage by a man who'd already killed a woman within the past twenty-four hours.

Branch practically lunged for the fabric, pulling it free. It was softer than he expected, catching on the cuts and calluses on his fingers. The design fit Lila perfectly with black zebra stripes and a border of fringe. He'd barely managed not to roll his eyes at the sight of it this morning at the grotto, but now he could do nothing but hold onto it as though it would provide him insight into her whereabouts.

Hints of her perfume clung to the fabric, and he couldn't help but inhale her sweet tart scent to replace the acrid bitterness collecting at the back of his throat. The effect shot a renewed charge of energy into his veins. Just as the mere sight of Lila had all these months. The kerchief itself had come unknotted, and Branch scanned the distance between where he'd recovered it and the campsite. At least fifteen feet away. She'd left it here. For him. To tell him how to find her. "Clever girl."

His vision threatened to black out as he navigated beyond the patch of prickly pear cacti and down the incline into the deepest part of the valley, gripping her kerchief with everything he had. To keep him conscious. To remind him of what was at stake.

Branch had spent his entire life judging others for their lack of discipline, for failing to follow through, keep their word and hold people accountable for their actions, good and bad. Every standard he'd set for himself, he expected of others, but walking in on his wife and his best friend in bed together had taught him that devotion didn't mean the same to them as it meant to him.

But all that had gone to hell once Lila Jordan had surgically inserted herself into his life with enthusiastic smiles, ridiculous death threats and frenzied schemes to encourage people to get to know her. She was nothing if not devoted. He saw it in the way she held onto her secrets, how she clung to a personality she'd created, when she went out of her way to make everyone else comfortable at the expense of her own peace.

Where Branch had stood his ground—hoping others accepted him for who he was, but not upset or disappointed when they didn't—Lila moved mountains and parted seas. He'd fought that charismatic influence as long as he could, and it hadn't done him a damn bit of good. She'd gotten to him, and there was nothing he could do to convince himself she hadn't earned a place in his life. Whatever that looked like from here on out, he didn't care. He only wanted her safe.

Forcing one foot in front of the other, Branch picked up the pace as the downhill dragged him deeper into Zion's backcountry. Ponderosa pines jutted up from the earth and cut off his view of the rest of the valley, closing in on him, but allowed enough room for him to pass.

The trees here had burned black, stripped of their foliage and growth for the foreseeable future due to a lightning strike that'd sparked a forest fire two years ago, turning the area into a barren wasteland. He couldn't help but compare these trees with the black remnants of his insides, charred, weak, serving no other purpose than to decompose over time for the greater good. He couldn't deny his desire to steal Lila's light for himself—to give him something to hope for—but there wasn't anything he could gift her in return. He was like these trees. Dead inside, waiting for the last straw to break him completely.

Branch slowed at the smallest glimpse of green at the base of one of the burned trees. There, fighting from the depths of the blackened wood against all odds, a pink-petaled flower had begun blooming. As if in challenge. To prove that even dead things still had the potential to create something beautiful.

Then a scream tore through the valley.

Chapter Fifteen

Pain arched straight down her front.

Rock cut into Lila's chest, palms and hips as the weight on her back held her in place. Agony ripped through her scalp as the killer pulled her hair back, forcing her upper body off the ground. Another scream tore from her throat, echoing down the canyon a mere few hundred feet in front of her.

She'd almost made it. She'd almost escaped.

But despite the wound in the killer's leg, he'd somehow caught up to her. Had tackled her from behind. Driving a knee into her spine, he pressed his mouth against her ear. "Hello, darling."

Tears burned in her eyes, but she wouldn't let them fall. Not for this asshole. Her lungs had yet to get the message to start functioning again. They spasmed from the impact as she clawed at his hand in her hair.

In a move any professional wrestler would be proud of, the killer flipped her onto her back with ease. His knees locked down on her arms, holding her in place. "What did I tell you would happen if you ran, Ranger Jordan?"

The sun glared down on her, blocking his features, but she didn't need for him to see her clearly for him to kill her.

Or to feel the gun pressed against her temple. The metal was surprisingly cold in a landscape toasting at a pleasant one hundred and six degrees.

"It's amateurs like you who give kidnapping a bad name. I mean, come on. Didn't you see the water bottle coming?"

The words were a farce. A desperate attempt to distract her brain from recognizing these were her final moments. Her laugh—something along the lines of hysteric and disassociated—cut between them. "You should've seen your face."

He dragged the barrel from her head down her cheek, clutching her jaw with his free hand. His strength was enough to leave bruises if she walked away from this alive. "That mouth of yours just doesn't stop, does it?"

"I've met scarecrows with more spine than you." The words were garbled due to the restraint on her jaw, but based on the contortion of his expression, she felt he got the gist. Pushing against his knees, Lila fought to free her arms, but he only shifted his weight forward. She bucked her hips. Again, going nowhere. She pinched her eyes shut against the frustrated growl trying to escape. Oh, dang. No wonder Branch growled at her so often. This was aggravating as hell. "Get off me."

"You're exhausting, you know that? No wonder someone tried to cut your throat." He set the barrel of the gun beneath her chin, then dragged it across the scar tissue spanning from the right side of her neck to the left. "They wanted to steal your voice, didn't they? Wanted to shut you up. Maybe I should be the one to finish a job. Hmm?"

His words hurt more than she wanted to admit, and the first tear fell. Shame spiked through her, and she tried to buck him free again, but it was no use. He held her steady, pinned against the very earth she'd worked so hard to protect from people like him. People who didn't appreciate the beautiful things in life. Who saw something fragile and pushed it to the breaking point. Who walked through this world with the expectation for everyone else to fall on their knees in gratitude for their mere presence. People like her brother-in-law.

"No, no, no. Don't cry, Ranger Jordan." Lowering his face over hers, he cocked his head to one side, studying her as the park geologists studied sediment rates under a microscope. His breath fanned down her neck, over her scar, until it was all she could focus on. "Relax. I'll make it quick. You won't even feel a thing."

Don't scream, Lila. Every time you fight me, I'll make it hurt more.

That voice. It didn't belong to the killer. The words played on repeat until the man in front of her didn't exist at all.

She was back in her bedroom in her parents' basement. His hand clamped over her mouth, pressing her deeper into her pillow. It hurt. The way he handled her. She didn't know how it was possible she hadn't heard him come into her room. She'd locked the door, hadn't she? She locked it every night since he'd moved in upstairs, noting the way he watched her do the dishes or how his face changed when she came home sweaty from soccer practice. She couldn't see his face right now, but she knew every angle from their time together over the years. Every line. Even the jagged scar down the side of his face. From a fight, he'd told her, but something about him being in her room in the middle of the night—pressing her into the mattress with his weight and nothing but whispers—made her think tonight wasn't the first time he'd done this. That maybe he hadn't escaped unscathed. He pried his hand from her face, trusting her not to scream. But she'd never taken well to following orders.

Lila screamed into her attacker's face, and he reared back.

It was all the chance she needed as his knees briefly lifted off her arms. She dug her fingernails into his face and scratched downward as hard as she could, her survival instincts consuming logic.

His scream fed into a sick satisfaction a split second before the gun slammed against her head. Lightning exploded behind her eyes as she fell back, but the need to escape had already taken hold. She shoved her bloodied palms into his chest as hard as she could. He fell back, pinned her legs to the ground, but it was enough. The gun went with him. Snapping out of his grip, it landed too far away for her to grab.

Lila flipped onto her stomach. *Run.* All she could do was run. She pushed upright. Her toes failed to leverage packed, cracked dirt, and her boot slipped out from underneath her. She went down but managed to get her balance as the killer fought for his. She pumped her legs as hard as she could. She'd been training for this day. Every single true crime podcast had led her to this moment. With his DNA under her blood-crusted fingernails, she'd give the National Park Service everything she could to identify her killer.

"You bitch!" Pure rage laced those two words. Too close. How the hell did he manage to stay on her heels with that wound?

Aiming for the canyon mouth, Lila maneuvered over a felled tree that hadn't survived the forest fire two years ago. Her hot pink boot lace caught on a branch, and she thrust her leg forward to break through. The overly loud snap gave up her position, but she wouldn't stop. Couldn't. A cool breeze taunted her from the canyon entrance. She was going to make it. She didn't have any other choice as the memories of that night in her bedroom waited for the smallest sliver of her attention.

She hated this feeling. Helplessness. Weakness. Pain. It was too similar to those horrifying minutes a man she was told to trust had turned into a monster. Her throat convulsed as though she was right back there in that basement, a scream trapped in her throat.

Shadows crept toward her as the cliffs took shape on either side. Her skin cooled instantly as she scrambled along the riverbed. Smooth stones and awkwardly angled trees growing out of the rock face threatened to trip her up. The canyon itself offered little protection from the killer at her back, but without the sun beating down on her, she felt more herself. Clearheaded.

She couldn't go like this for miles. She'd already burned through the hit of caffeine from this morning and hadn't eaten more than a protein bar before the landslide. Every step took her deeper into Zion wilderness, where the rangers assigned to the backcountry patrolled few and far between. She was actively running away from help, and the killer must know that. He was isolating her. Keeping her from seeking help. Prey to his predator.

Hide. She needed a place to hide, then she could worry about contacting NPS and making sure search and rescue looked for Branch.

Lila shut down the sob fighting for release. No. She couldn't think like that. He was alive. They were going to make it out of this and meet up for coffee the next time neither of them had a shift to cover. He'd given her his word.

It was all she could focus on as a dark hole took shape in the rock face up ahead.

A cave.

It sat about twenty feet off the canyon floor with a few rocks and trees acting as stairs if she was careful. It was also the first place the killer would look for her. And potentially where she could be eaten alive by the mountain cougars that lived in the park. But she had to take the risk.

Her palms screamed in protest as she hauled herself up the first oddly angled tree. The bark fell away under her weight, and she slammed into the wall at her side. Rock grated against her exposed skin, but she pushed to the next obstacle. This would make a great audition for *American Gladiator.*

Darkness enveloped her as she reached the mouth of the cave. Cold air raised the hair on the back of her neck. It was damp and smelled of carnage and decomposition. Something definitely lived in this cave full-time, and she hoped whatever it was had gone hunting instead of waiting for food to walk right in the front door.

The cave curved deeper into the mountain, cutting off the only source of light at the mouth, but distance didn't ease the tension knotting in her stomach. Wetness clung to the walls and soaked into her uniform, and it took everything in her not to groan out of disgust. It'd take a miracle to get the decomposition smell out of cotton. She could already see Risner's signature drying on another write-up for disgracing her uniform.

Cringing against the sticky substance now coating her hands, she moved deeper into the cave.

"I know you're in here, Ranger Jordan. You can't hide from me."

Movement echoed down the tunnel of the cave, accentuating every word out of the killer's mouth. She hadn't heard him follow her inside. How had he managed to keep his footsteps from bouncing off the rock walls? Or had she not noticed due to the chaos in her head?

"I know every inch of this park." He was getting closer. "Most likely better than you."

Fresh images reserved for her nightmares were right there on the cusp of her waking mind, but she couldn't think about that right now. Lila felt her way deeper into the cave. This was a bad idea, but it was the only option she had right now. She'd brained him with his own water bottle, then scratched caverns down his face. Nope. She wasn't getting out of this alive if he had anything to say about it. "Why did you kill Sarah Lantos?"

His low laugh leaked into her body like a cold drip that stole her body temperature. "Some people deserve to die. Sarah was one of them. She made me suffer by keeping her secret all these years. Threatened everyone I cared about. I granted her a mere taste of my pain by stabbing her. But then she had to go trip on a rock and fall over the edge of the cliff. Ended my fun too soon."

Lila's gut clenched. "Do I deserve to suffer?"

She hadn't meant to ask the question. Didn't want to give him any sort of power over her, but there it was. The one question she'd asked herself a thousand times since the fallout of her actions from that night. Did she deserve to suffer? Her family certainly thought so. Sometimes she did, too. Maybe this was always going to be her ending.

But then why had the universe allowed Branch to come into her life?

"You're just like her, you know." Gravel grated nearby, and then she could feel him. Right in front of her. As though he'd simply thought of her location and appeared. His outline solidified the longer she begged her vision to catch up. As did the gun. "You latch onto your targets by pretending to be something you're not, then manipulate them into following your agenda. And for that, you're going to die."

A gunshot exploded.

Chapter Sixteen

He heard the shot.

It punctured the canyon, reverberating through him as though he'd been hit with the sound barrier. Branch slowed to pinpoint the source.

There was no denying that gut-wrenching explosion. He'd heard it multiple times over his years as a ranger in the parks. Thudding and terrifying. And everything in him froze at the realization. Blood drained from his upper body in a rush that nearly knocked him on his ass. "Lila!"

He hadn't been fast enough. He'd followed that single scream across the valley with everything he had left, and it still hadn't been enough. The pain in his head intensified as Branch navigated the uneven terrain of the dry riverbed. He wouldn't be too late. He couldn't be too late. Because that meant he'd failed her and wasted four solid months trying to keep his distance from her when he should have run at her full speed.

Lila had brought a spark into his life. Gifted him glimpses of color in an otherwise black-and-white world. She'd made him feel when he wanted nothing more than to sink into the numbness left behind by his ex-wife and best friend's betrayal. She gave him purpose. A reason to keep going. This wasn't how it was supposed to end. Two days of standing at her side wasn't enough, damn it. "Where are you?"

The canyon swallowed him whole, rising on either side of him as if leading him into a trap. Walls of red, black and white rock towered above him but gave no indication of where the shot had come from. Cool air rippled goose bumps across his bare arms. Hell, his head hurt. He could feel warm liquid tracking down his face. The butterfly bandage had soaked through with blood, warning him not to push it, but Lila needed him. His heart threatened to beat straight out of his chest with every step. "Come on. Come on."

Dragging his hand through his hair, he did the hardest thing he'd ever had to do during his time as a ranger. Wait. For something—anything—that might tell him where she'd been taken.

A low growl reached his ears. The canyon wall moved. Wait, that wasn't right.

Fur, the same color as the rock, shifted to his right, revealing the powerful body of a mountain lion. And, damn, it was big. Most likely male. Mountain lions didn't normally go looking for trouble, but when you just happened to walk into their territory, you were fair game.

Every muscle down Branch's spine hardened with battle-ready tension. Hell, all he could think about was how Lila would smile and want to pet the beast, and that thought alone helped calm his racing heart. She'd probably want to adopt it and bring it back home. Call it something like Fluffy or Pumpkin just to get a rise out of him. "You don't look like a Pumpkin, which means she'll probably call you Fluffy."

The oversize cat hissed, exposing sharp, elongated teeth

meant to snap one of his arms in half. Branch backed up a few steps as the cat descended from its perch, cutting off his access to the rest of the canyon. To Lila.

Raising his arms out in front of him as though Fluffy could acknowledge his surrender—was he really calling this thing Fluffy?—he brought his pack around to his front. Slowly unzipping the top of his pack, he dragged the un-opened bag of beef jerky—teriyaki flavored, of course—into the open and popped the seal. "You like jerky?"

Mountain lions averaged two to three feet in height, but this one had obviously been eating his spinach. Impressive muscle rippled along the cat's back as it gauged the threat Branch presented. Another growl penetrated the space between them in warning. The animal had to have a den nearby. Potentially behind it. Where Lila could be.

Rangers were trained to deal with wild animals, mostly to avoid them and warn hikers to do the same, but Branch maintained eye contact as he tossed a chunk of jerky behind him a good twenty feet. "Go get it."

Did mountain lions take commands? He wasn't sure. But just as Dr. Grant baited the T. rex, Branch tossed a second helping of jerky and froze. Unwilling to do anything more to provoke the animal. He was going to die. It was as simple as that, but he'd go down fighting if necessary.

The cat stared at him with those black eyes surrounded by yellow, looking for all the world as if he wanted to roll his eyes. Then he gave up the staring contest and ambled straight past Branch and closer to the jerky. Seemed Fluffy really did like jerky. Branch would have to remember that. Then again, one mountain lion sighting was enough to last him a lifetime.

Now a whole new fear had taken root again. Not being able to get to Lila.

Branch took a furtive step deeper into the canyon, not stupid enough to take his eyes off Fluffy as the cat gobbled up the jerky. The cat wrenched its head back and forth trying to chomp down on the meat. Okay, so Branch had broken the cardinal rule of not feeding the wildlife, but it was for a good reason. And if he had to come back here every day with a bag of jerky to make up for it, he would. As long as Lila made it out of this canyon in one piece.

A cave took shape ahead. The perfect den for a mountain lion willing to kill anything that came near it. Fluffy was preoccupied with his free meal. This was the only shot Branch would have. "Lila!"

No answer.

His voice echoed off the canyon walls, and he'd never felt so utterly alone in his life. As though his separation from Lila had torn something important from his very being.

How was that possible? How in a matter of two days had she become more vital than his next breath? He couldn't take it anymore, this emptiness. He'd thrived in isolation, telling himself he was better off alone, that he didn't need anyone, not wanting to infect others with his pain, but Ranger Barbie had patched a few of the holes eaten away by his divorce. And he wanted more. He wanted her back.

Scrambling up the odd footholds leading to the mouth of the cavern, Branch slapped his hand against the rock wall for something to hold onto. His head had other plans. It thudded hard with every breath. Darkness wrapped around him in a sickening blanket, but he pushed on. The reward far outweighed the risks.

Slickness coated his hands as he followed the natural curve of the cave, leaving Fluffy and the safety of the park behind. He hauled his pack forward and extracted his flashlight. Hitting the power button, Branch studied the walls—too close together—and patches of tan fur littering the cave floor. Uneven rock threatened to trip him up as he searched for any sign Lila had sought the cave in a last-ditch attempt—

A wall of muscle slammed into him from the left.

His back hit the wall, crushing the air from his lungs. A metallic barrel pressed into his head, but Branch shot his hand upward.

A gunshot exploded next to his ear, triggering a high-pitched ringing that drowned his groan. The second shot rained rock and dust onto his head, and instinct had him knocking the weapon clean from his attacker's hand. The gun skittered across the cave floor, out of sight.

A forearm locked across throat. Branch tried to breathe around the weight, but the killer had the upper hand. Based on the angled beam of his discarded flashlight, the man at his throat clocked in a few inches taller than Branch, but he didn't have the muscle.

Pressure built in his chest as his lungs worked to supply oxygen to his starving limbs. Spit and sweat combined on his face. Inky black tendrils webbed his vision. He was going to pass out any second. Branch wedged his knee up, colliding with the killer's gut. Once. Twice. Still, the bastard's hold refused to release.

Throwing everything he had left into his right hook, Branch connected with the killer's temple. A responding groan accompanied the smallest of releases across his throat, and Branch sucked in a breath. But then he was weightless, the cave floor rushing to meet him. He rolled into the opposite wall, barely catching sight of the outline descending on him.

"Branch!" Lila's voice filled the cavern. Filled him. She was alive. Rushing toward her abductor with one arm raised, she brought down what looked like a rock in her palm, but the killer managed to avoid it colliding with his head. The makeshift weapon bounced off the man's back.

Branch fought to catch his breath. He dug his fingers into the rock floor when his head wanted to do nothing but surrender. "Lila, run."

The killer turned on her. Faster than Lila could counter, the back of his hand slammed against her cheek. Lila hit the ground hard. She lay there, unmoving.

"Lila!" Branch shot to his feet. every cell in his body on fire. The rage he kept at a simmer unleashed as he tackled the son of bitch to the ground. Fisting both hands in the killer's shirt, he dragged his attacker forward, then rammed his head against the rock floor.

A scraping sound reached his ears. The gun. Catching sight of the weapon's outline, Branch scrambled to get his hands on it. He dove. Realizing his mistake too late.

The killer planted a hand at the back of Branch's skull and shoved his face straight into the nearest wall. Cold metal pressed into Branch's cheek as he worked to regain his bearings, sobering him instantly.

"You're wrong if you think she's worth saving, Ranger Thompson. She's nothing but a liar. A manipulator who will choose her own survival over you. She doesn't care about you. She never will."

His insides coiled as Branch locked his gaze on Lila's unconscious form. That rage bubbled over again, out of control as he set both hands against the wall and pushed back, knocking the killer off-balance. He swept his hand out, latching onto his assailant's wrist and twisted until bone and tendon snapped. The knife fell into his free hand, and Branch pressed the tip to the killer's throat. "You don't know anything about her."

"Do you?" A sickening low laugh filled the cave. "Or do you just think you do?" And he rocketed a fist into Branch's face.

Branch went down, the knife still clutched in his hand. But when he turned in expectation of the next threat, the outline of his attacker was gone. Branch dove for the flashlight, spearing the beam over every inch of the cave. Damn it all to hell.

The killer had gotten away.

Adrenaline drained from his body in a rush as movement shifted to his left. "Lila."

"Branch?" A sob cut off her sweet voice.

Dropping the flashlight, he pulled her lightweight frame into his chest. "It's okay. I've got you. I'm here. I'm here."

The tears turned to full-blown sobs as she wrapped her arms around his neck and held on for dear life. Her perfume—muted through the metallic scent of blood and sweat—settled his high-strung nervous system.

He soothed his hand down the back of her head, noting she'd lost her Stetson. "I've got you. You're safe now, and I'm never letting you go."

Chapter Seventeen

Her body had stopped obeying her commands a couple hours ago. Lila rolled over on the sleeping bag, the material sticking to every inch of her back. The tent Branch had set up once they'd left the canyon wore its age well. The bright orange dye had faded from use in the sun, but the mesh windows, canvas and zippers all did their jobs.

She wasn't sure how long she'd been asleep. Couldn't really remember anything past the cave. Of being in Branch's arms. He must've brought her here, but after a cursory search, she realized she'd woken alone.

Her skin felt too tight and sticky. What she wouldn't give for her crappy, stained shower in her crappy little rented house with her crappy twin bed. Never again would she take it for granted.

A low rumble of a voice drew her attention to the zippered tent flap. She couldn't make out the words, but the cadence and tenor soothed all the aches and stings after a few seconds. Branch. The tent itself didn't fit much more than two sleeping bags with some space at the foot for her pack.

Wait. How did…

A headache speared through her brain at the thought of

all the events that'd led to the cave: the landslide, barely escaping being pulverized by those boulders, leaving her pack for Branch to find...

He'd come for her. He hadn't given up.

Dragging herself from the now-soaked sleeping bag, Lila reached for the zipper and maneuvered it around the curve of the door. Blistering pain seeped down her arm from where the killer's first bullet had grazed her. She'd been lucky. One inch to the left, and she might not have made it out of that cave alive. "Oh, hell. That hurts."

Footsteps ricocheted through her head a split second before the rest of the tent flap was ripped back, revealing the dark-eyed mountain of a man on the other side. "You should be resting."

She didn't have the energy to keep her arm up, even with the fresh bandage secured around the wound. Had Branch patched her up? Well, that was a stupid question. Sarah Lantos's killer certainly hadn't done it. Despite the fact the sun had begun its descent behind the surrounding cliffs, bruising the sky to a deep purple, she blinked against the sensory onslaught, squinting one eye as she looked up at him. "How long was I out?"

"A few hours." His expression refused to give her anything of substance. He'd locked himself up nice and tight. "How do you feel?"

"You remember that skunk that got hit by a car at the visitor's center, and none of the rangers wanted to go near it because the stink sack had exploded?" Using the tent frame, she pulled herself to her feet. Her head swam. Mistake. She'd made a mistake. "Like that."

She practically stumbled into the campsite he'd built while she'd been unconscious. Rangers didn't believe in campfires, so while the killer had arranged a ring of stones to contain the flames and stay warm back at his site, Branch had set up an electric lantern in the center of theirs. He'd emptied his pack, lining his food and supplies out in the open. "You've been busy."

Looking at him—really looking at him—she noted the dried blood at the side of his face, the dark circles beneath his eyes. White crystals clung to the underside of his chin. It happened when the body sweated too much salt. Bruising took shape around his jaw. He was standing, but barely. And had apparently lost a shoe somewhere along the way. "Figured it'll take a day for us to get back to headquarters. I needed to see what we had left in supplies."

"And?" She cataloged what he'd gathered. It wasn't enough between them.

"You should eat something." His shoulders bunched as though expecting an argument, but her stomach was basically eating itself as they stood here and talked about food.

Accepting a protein bar and a banana, she nearly collapsed at the edge of the campsite. Her fingers ached as she peeled the banana skin away, and while she'd never been a fan of the overly sweet—sometimes mushy—fruit, it was possibly the best thing she'd ever eaten in her life.

The pressure of being watched raised the hairs on the back of her neck, and she looked up to see Branch studying her. As though ensuring she got everything she needed before he dared take care of himself. "Have you slept?" she asked.

"No." He moved around the campsite, taking up position opposite. As far from her as he could get.

Well, that hurt. Hadn't they just survived a killer together? Hadn't they moved past one-word answers and growls? Or did she really smell that bad? Lila made an attempt to casually check her underarms and cringed at the bitter odor clinging to her uniform…and other parts of her body. But he couldn't be any better.

She shuddered at the physical distance he'd set between them, still feeling his arms around her as he'd carried her out of that cave. He'd saved her. Fought a killer for her. And now… Lila focused on one bite after another. She'd survived the landslide, a kidnapping, a gunshot wound and the crushing hopelessness that came with all of it. At some point exhaustion had won out, and right now, she didn't have the energy to chase Branch's affection. "The killer knew Sarah Lantos. Said he was punishing her for making him suffer."

Branch kept his attention on his metal water bottle, the light from the lantern carving deeper shadows along his handsome face. And, damn it, her ovaries had donned war paint and started metaphorically chucking eggs at the man after everything he must've faced to get to her. "What else?"

"What do you mean?" She had to snap herself out of this haze. Being in Branch's thrall was far more danger-ous than having been taken hostage by a killer in a lot of ways. Sure, Sarah Lantos's killer could do physical dam-age, but her partner had so many weapons at his disposal to destroy her in every other way.

"What else did he say to you?"

Her throat dried. Emotion lodged where she was pretty sure she'd killed it off years ago, but she just couldn't tell him the truth. Not without risking him looking at her like every other ranger had over the years. And she couldn't go back to that. Not with him. Not after everything they'd survived together. "I don't remember a whole lot, but the little I do, it seems our victim isn't who we thought she was. This is also coming from the man who stabbed her, so take that with a grain of salt."

Branch let that sit between them, and she hated his silence. His distance. It made the grime coating her skin burn and itch, but there was nothing she could do to wash it away. After a few minutes and seeing that she'd finished her dinner, Branch shoved to stand, tossing his water bottle at his feet. "I need to assess your injuries."

It was easy to paste her practiced smile back on and slip into that protective layer she'd created to block out all the bad. Spreading her arms wide, Lila leaned back to get a better view of his face in the last offering of sunset. "Have your way with me, Ranger Thompson. I promise not to bite. Unless you're into that."

"You were nearly killed." A scowl contorted his face, a sucker punch straight to the gut. Ah, there he was. The grizzly bear had returned, and everything they'd been through together suddenly didn't seem so bad.

That was okay. She was used to people running the other direction once they realized she was more than they'd bargained for. She'd just wanted things to be different with him. "In my defense, I was left unsupervised."

His fingers splayed across her skin, right over the ring of gauze on her arm, but he was careful not to prod or poke anywhere that might hurt. The lines between his brows deepened as he unwrapped her like a delicate piece of china. Or the way she unwrapped her first helping of Cherry Garcia. Either way, heat spread under her skin at his touch. "Did you pick up anything that might identify the killer?"

Right. This wasn't personal. He'd made that very clear by keeping his distance unless absolutely necessary. Like making sure she didn't bleed out in the middle of the desert on his shift. "Does his astrological sign count? Because that man is definitely a Sagittarius. Egotistical, impatient, boastful. Pretty sure him and Ted Bundy would've gotten along well together."

He didn't have an answer for that. Pain flared up her arm, and she tried to drag herself out of his touch, but Branch held on tight.

"He didn't really introduce himself, but in my head, I called him Covid." Lila tried to even her breathing, but it was so much harder when a six-plus mountain of eye candy insisted on groping her.

Branch's mouth twitched at one corner. So…he wasn't entirely as unaffected as he was trying to be, which only pissed her off more. The break in his composure didn't last long as he raised his gaze to her throat. To the ugly, thick scar she couldn't bear to look at in the mirror. He brought his hand up, his thumb brushing the underside of her neck. "The kerchiefs."

It took her a second to realize he was talking about her attempt to hide her shame from him and the rest of the world.

"Who hurt you?" Those three words again. That was all it took to shake the dragging haze of exhaustion free.

Her skin boiled under his touch, and Lila couldn't take much more. She pulled free of his hand, not bothering to rewrap her wound. Probably a stupid choice, but her choice all the same. Her poor heart slammed against her ribs at the concern in his voice. The anger on her behalf. Compared to the bruises on her ribs and the massive headache telling her she hadn't had enough to drink while running for her life, she'd take another bullet graze than face this conversation. She headed back for the tent, not really sure where else to go. It wasn't as though she could just run for the hills. Those hills had a killer in them. One who'd already gotten too close. "No one."

"Lila." Her name on his lips pulled her up short. Had he ever called her that?

As much as she hated the idea of him joining in the other rangers' Barbie games, she wasn't sure her heart could handle him seeing past the persona she'd designed. Through the smiles and the makeup and the pink kerchiefs. There was a reason she felt safer as Ranger Barbie. Most people—Risner, Sayles and all the other rangers, hikers even—made their assumptions and avoided taking the time to look deeper. Like the glitter she'd applied on her cheeks would infect them. Herpes of the craft world, for the win.

But Branch said her name as though he intended to do just that. Become infected. Dig deeper. And she was scared of what he might find. Would he still want to meet her for coffee after this investigation was over? Would he be able to look her in the eye when he learned the truth? How truly broken she really was.

"Barbies don't feel pain, remember?" If only that were true. The memories that had held her captive more so than the man with the gun threatened to resurface.

A hand clasped over her mouth. Threats in her ear. The weight of her attacker in a room where she should've been safe. It wasn't that night that gave her nightmares or had led her to pasting on the smiles Branch seemed to see right through. It was everything that happened afterward, and at the lowest point in her life, stripped of everything and everyone she'd ever loved, she'd stretched out a hand to find something to hold onto. In a mess of blood and hopelessness in the very room where she'd been made a victim over and over again, her fingers had folded around a Barbie doll from her childhood. And she'd felt…happy. For the first time in years, she had something good in her hands.

It only made sense to carry that feeling with her to fight back the demons closing in. "Nobody hurt me, Branch. I did it to myself."

Chapter Eighteen

In this new concept called caring, Branch was finding quite a few things to hate. Mostly the changes in himself.

He'd waited outside the tent while Lila had changed into a new set of clothes, presumably wanting to be free of blood and grime after she'd helped irrigate the wound at his temple. He'd waited as her movements slowed. Waited as the night grew cold and her breathing grew even. He hadn't been able to face her.

Nobody hurt me, Branch. I did it to myself.

The jagged scar across her neck was unlike anything he'd ever seen. At least not on a person still walking the earth. The moment he'd dragged her from that damn cave and into the open, it'd stared back at him. Crystallizing a deep need to destroy anyone and anything that'd had a hand in marring her perfect skin. He hadn't trusted himself to get near her, afraid all that rage would burn her if he got too close. So he'd set himself up on the opposite side of camp, to protect her, but he'd only managed to feed the hollowness in his chest to the point he couldn't breathe.

Except there was no one to fight.

She'd done it to herself. Why? What could've possibly happened to convince her the only choice she had was death?

Branch pocketed the protein bar wrapper, not really tasting the ingredients. His senses had dulled in the time he'd been separated from Lila and had gone mute since she'd zipped herself inside the tent. Damn it. What he wouldn't give to go back to pretending she didn't exist. To shutting himself away from the rest of the world and avoiding this new rip in his heart that focused entirely on Lila's well-being.

His skin prickled as temperatures dropped. Branch kept his attention on the mouth of the canyon, waiting for the next threat to make another move. The killer had escaped the cave. A quick search for the gun turned up empty.

And it was only a matter of time before his body failed him. He'd driven it to the edge too many times today. Surviving the landslide, searching for Lila, luring a mountain lion with jerky and then fighting off a killer. Worse, at some point, he'd come to accept he wouldn't witness Lila's smile ever again. That he'd lost her. The pinch in his chest had yet to get the message she was alive and breathing on the other side of the stretch of canvas between them. Some part of him was still back in that cave, seeing her unconscious. Unmoving.

Something had split open in him then. Pieces of the man he used to be had surfaced with all the rage, and hell, it scared him the lengths he would've gone to get one more second, one more death threat, with her.

Or do you only think you know her? The killer's parting words had seared into his brain and refused to give him respite. They'd surged with every hyperaware glance in her direction, every move she'd made tonight, every word out of her mouth.

Lila was keeping secrets. She wasn't the person she projected to the world, and while Branch recognized everyone had parts of themselves they didn't want exposed, he thought he'd given her more than enough reason to trust him in the past two days. Everything they'd been through, everything they'd survived—it meant something. Didn't it?

His ex had kept secrets. Had been sleeping with his best friend from work for months before Branch had caught them. She hadn't told him about the pregnancy, about her decision to end it until he'd discovered the truth. Hadn't given him a choice in the matter, and an acidic taste clung to the back of his throat at the idea Lila might do the same. She could hurt him. Whether she knew it or not, Lila had more power over him than he'd allowed anyone to hold since his divorce.

Scrubbing a hand down his face, Branch stopped the thoughts in their tracks. There wasn't a single similarity between Lila and his ex-wife. Exhaustion had won out. The killer had merely tried to get into his head, and hell, the son of a bitch had done a fantastic job. He stood, collecting the electric lantern on his way, and slowly unzipped the tent door.

The sound of Lila's even breathing reached him as he stepped inside. Soft and feminine and bordering a little on snoring. It was cute. He set the lantern at the opposite end of the tent to keep from waking her. After everything they'd been through today, she deserved the rest. But tomorrow they'd have to return to headquarters. They'd have to admit they lost track of the killer, that they didn't have any identifying markers other than his appearance—and maybe his astrology sign. Branch wasn't really looking forward to that conversation with Risner, but he'd sure as hell take it over the silent treatment Lila had given him since retreating to the tent.

He undressed, leaving himself in his undershirt and

briefs, before crawling over to his sleeping bag. The tent allowed two people to sleep side by side, but there wasn't a whole lot of room for him to keep his distance. He could still catch hints of Lila's perfume, feel her body heat as he settled on his back.

A soft moan filled the tent, and he froze. Waiting. Every nerve ending he owned had tuned to her movements, those little sighs she made in her sleep. It was enough to stir his insides with something he hadn't allowed himself to feel for a long time. After a few minutes of strained silence and a whole lot of inappropriate thoughts on how to get her to make that noise again, Branch rolled onto his side, away from her, and closed his eyes.

A coldness that had nothing to do with the temperature set in, his skin tightening to the point of pain around his bones. His head pounded. Even after the way he'd treated her—as nothing more than an inconvenience—Lila had insisted on taking care of his wound and watched him force down a couple of ibuprofen from his first aid kit. Though she'd given talking a break.

That was how he'd known how deeply he'd hurt her by pulling away, and he hated himself for it. After everything they'd survived, she still felt the need to put his health first. Freaking hell. How did she keep going? The looks and whispers behind her back from Risner and all the other rangers, the obvious trauma she'd suffered at her own hand, whatever had driven her to take that step, her brush with a killer in that cave, Branch's disregard and flat-out rejection. How hadn't life beaten her down as thoroughly as it'd beaten him?

Lila was strong. Stronger than him, that was for damn sure, and he couldn't stop whatever this new connection was between them in its tracks. But he didn't know how to do this anymore. Have…feelings for someone else. The blackened organ in his chest had stopped trying after the divorce, but then Lila had come along with the promise of light, and his entire being had latched onto it and refused to let go. And crossing that line, admitting he needed her…

His ex-wife had taken his trust and utterly destroyed it right in front of him. Years of good memories and laughs and future plans instantly ash. And he hadn't seen it coming. Marriage had always been the plan, ever since they'd met in high school from their too-small hometown in the middle of Montana. They'd graduated together, gone off to college together, gotten married a couple years afterward and planned their entire lives together. Vacations, late nights filled with sex and promises and *I love you*s, sacrifices for each other's careers.

An entire life built with the one person he'd trusted instantly shattered the day he thought he saw his best friend's car driving down his street as Branch left for the office. His gut had told him to turn around, just as it was telling him to trust Lila now. What would've happened had he not followed his intuition that day? What would happen now if he did?

Awareness spread down his spine as he brushed against Lila's knee. Without checking over his shoulder, he felt she'd turned into him. Seeking him out unconsciously, and hell, if that wasn't adding kindling to the fire. He'd spent so long proving he didn't need anyone. He wasn't sure how to let himself rely on another person again.

A growl resonated in his chest as a result of the battle occupying his head.

Lila shifted at his back. Closer? "Do you want to know what Barbie taught me?"

Her sleep-graveled voice dragged him over hot coals,

to the point every cell in his body focused solely on the heat building low in his stomach. It was a rush of fire that would take one very specific thing to put out. One specific woman.

"What?" Branch angled his head over his shoulder. He didn't have to see her clearly for his brain to fill in all those sharp features he'd memorized since setting foot in Zion. The shape of her mouth, a little fuller on one side than the other, the arch of her brows, how much of her dark roots had grown in. The only thing he hadn't committed to memory was that scar, though he couldn't banish the sight of it from his mind.

"Barbie. I used to play with them as a kid. I had a whole collection with the Dreamhouse and the cars and the campers, all the accessories. People think Barbie gives little girls poor body image, but those dolls taught me that you can't reattach a head once it's been removed from the body." Her voice vaulted from one extreme—carefree and light—to deadpan. "So be quiet and let me sleep."

He couldn't hold back the chuckle rumbling through his chest. Hell, this woman hit all the right buttons. Testing his patience, challenging everything he thought he knew about her. He'd been wrong to disregard her as nothing more than a shallow, teasing, high-maintenance diva. Lila Jordan might have a free spirit, but she was probably the most sincere, upbeat and imaginative person he'd ever met. She had to be to come up with those death threats on the daily. "Good night, Lila."

"Branch?" The confidence in her voice wavered.

His name leaving those perfect lips threw his insides into chaos. He bit down his inclination to repeat himself. Found himself not wanting her silent treatment anymore. "Yeah?"

"Thank you. For coming to get me." Her touch trailed

across his shoulder, light as a feather, barely recognizable as anything significant but triggered a rush of sensation down his spine all the same. "I know it would've been easier to call in search and rescue and wait for them to lead the search, but I think they would've been too late. He wanted me dead, and you stopped him."

He couldn't avoid looking at her anymore. Rolling onto his other side, Branch faced off with the beauty before him. Her mascara had flaked and run down her cheeks, her lip gloss gone entirely. Even her eyeshadow, once accentuating those compelling blue eyes, had worn off throughout the day. But she was still the most beautiful thing he'd ever set sights on. "You held your own."

She flattened her mouth into a thin line, biting down on the pillowy cushion of her bottom lip. He smoothed his thumb over it to force her to release. A shimmer of tears reflected in the low light of the electric lantern at the other end of their tent. "I couldn't accept you were dead. I was going to go back to look for you, but he wouldn't let me go."

"I'm right here." Branch closed the short distance between them, crushing his mouth to hers.

Chapter Nineteen

Well, that escalated quickly.

Branch's mouth moved over hers in a frantic, almost consuming pace. It was rough and demanding and everything she'd imagined all those nights she couldn't fall asleep.

Matching every ounce of his urgency, Lila threaded her hands into his hair, nearly dragging him onto her sleeping bag. The hard planes of his body weighed on hers. Not to intimidate as she'd felt that night in her childhood bedroom, but to comfort. Security. This was Branch. She was here, with him, in his tent.

His hands framed her face as though he was afraid she would slip through his fingers, but she had no intention of going anywhere. Of being anywhere other than right here. She'd dreamed about it for so long, but nothing compared to the real thing. His woodsy cedar scent teased her senses, the expert strokes of his tongue drove her body temperature higher and higher, and she could taste the slight hint of peppermint toothpaste they'd both eagerly used for some semblance of normality.

The simmering burn she'd fought off all these months roared to a full-blown inferno as Branch shifted a knee between her legs. A moan charged up her throat. She would've been embarrassed if she wasn't delirious with a need to prolong this moment as much as possible.

There was too many layers between them. Her fingernails found purchase at the small of his back, dragging his T-shirt up between his shoulder blades, and he kissed her deeper. Like he'd been starving for this as much as she had. A growl resonated through his chest as his tongue swept over hers, and from there, she was lost in him. No pain in her ribs, no nightmares waiting to ambush her, no hint of a misdirected killer holding a gun to her head.

There was only Branch. He was everything.

Pulling his lips from hers, he peppered openmouthed kisses along her jaw, slowly making his way down her neck, over her scar. She'd gone out of her way to hide it beneath chokers, kerchiefs and scarves throughout the years, but for the first time, she didn't feel the need to shrink back. Or to distract him from the damage she'd done. Lila worked to catch her breath, aware he'd somehow managed to push the top of her sleeping bag out of the way, but it was quickly lost again as calloused hands memorized her hips and thighs in a furiously slow journey.

An unholy gasp rushed up her throat as his thumb trailed along the waistband of her sleep shorts. Her mind raced with guttural pleas for him to touch her where she needed him the most, but then his hands were gone. A protest built on her lips as he stared down at her, and the fire that'd lit her up from the inside died at the expression on his face.

He'd stopped kissing her.

He'd stopped touching her.

"Branch?" She drew herself onto her elbows, trying to get a better read on what had changed.

Drawing back on his haunches, Branch left her aching and cold. They sat frozen for a few seconds before he squeezed his eyes shut. Severing the connection they'd explored in the past few minutes. And when he looked at her again, not a single trace of his desire for her remained. "Go to sleep, Lila. You'll need your energy to get back to headquarters in the morning."

Acid burned her throat as he took up position on his sleeping bag, rolling away from her. Her heart thudded hard against her ribs. Desperate to know what had changed. What she'd done wrong. Rejection fueled the spiraling thoughts into a tornado she couldn't keep up with. She'd been here before. Every time he'd declined her invitation to check out Springdale, every shift he'd negotiated with other rangers to avoid working with her, every unreturned smile or acknowledgment of her presence.

No matter how hard she'd tried to be his friend, she was always the one left a little more depleted and empty. Lila sank back onto her sleeping bag. Tears burned in her eyes, but she hadn't had enough water today, and she'd already cried so much. She didn't have the energy to let them fall. She rolled onto her side, her back to his, and stared at the tent canvas.

But it wasn't enough.

The shame, the vulnerability, the rejection—it all combined to tighten a sickening knot in her stomach, pushing her from her sleeping bag. She couldn't breathe without getting hints of his cedar scent. Couldn't look anywhere in this tent and not see him. She couldn't stay in this enclosed space when he took up so much space.

Sweat cooled on her neck as she tore through the tent flap and out into the open. The first breath should've cleared her head as she broke the perimeter of the campsite, but it only stoked the uncomfortable feelings further. As if her very being had come to rely on his proximity and couldn't survive without him.

She'd handled rejection before, but there was only so much she could take. Forcing one foot in front of the other, she put as much distance between them as she could while keeping the tent in sight. Predators patrolled this valley, both of the animalistic and humankind, but she couldn't stay at the campsite, either.

She automatically scratched at her neck, desperate for the feel of her kerchief between her fingers as a distraction from the fiery prickling sensation, but she'd lost that in her attempt to escape the killer. Her fingertips only met scar tissue. Grotesque and jagged and uneven. Ugly.

The killer had been right before. When he'd accused her of putting so much effort into her outward appearance to distract from the nastiness on the inside.

"Lila." Branch's voice broke on her name. He'd sneaked up on her. Or maybe she'd been too stuck in her head to think he'd leave the tent to come after her. Didn't matter. He'd said enough. Not in so many words—because Branch Thompson preferred to speak in growls and disdainful looks—but he'd been easy enough to read. He didn't want her. Nobody wanted her. And maybe that was what hurt the most.

"Go back to the tent, Branch." Her throat clogged with tightness as she pressed her fingers into the largest section of scar tissue, her back to him. She couldn't face him without her armor in place, and it wasn't coming as easily as it should. What she wouldn't give for a seventy-two-hour psych hold right now. What a wasted vacation opportunity. "Otherwise, I'm going to assume you want me to hand out your phone number to every kid in the park and tell them it's their direct line to Santa."

Footsteps scuffled over dirt. Getting louder, closer. And then he was standing next to her, looking out over the very park that'd tried to kill them. Well, to be fair, it'd had a hand. Damn it, why did he have to look so put together when her entire world felt like it was closing in on her? "I'm here. You can talk to me or not, but I'm here."

"Santa's hotline it is." Tearing her hand away from her scar, she folded her arms across her chest. Stars and ripples of the Milky Way swept across the velvet blackness above them. Out here, light pollution couldn't reach them, almost making her feel as if she were part of the universe.

He slid his hands into his sweatpants pockets. "I'm sorry. About before. In the tent. I shouldn't have—"

"If you tell me kissing me was a mistake, I will give you a firsthand look at my emotional support knife collection." They were pocketknives from all over the country and spanned decades, starting with her dad's knife from when he'd been a kid, but Branch didn't need to know that. "What's so wrong with kissing me anyway? I brushed my teeth. I got all the dirt and blood out."

His laugh only served to piss her off more. "There was nothing wrong with kissing you, Lila. Hell, I... I enjoyed it."

"Then what is it?" Now she was on a roll. That internal ball of fire she'd managed to mask with glitter and lip gloss and faux happiness had reached its capacity. "I've been nice to you since day one. I've tried to be your friend. I asked you to movies and lunch and coffee. I tried to make you laugh. I shared my Cherry Garcia with you, but none of it's good enough, is it? Nothing I do will ever be good enough, and I'm just...tired, Branch. I'm done. I give up. You win. Congratulations, you've successfully pushed everyone who gives a damn about you away."

She moved to retreat to the tent. She couldn't take this

anymore. Wishing he would notice her, accept her. Want her. At some point she had to read the writing on the wall.

She only made it a few steps before strong hands spun her into his chest. His expression softened in the light of a full moon as his gaze ping-ponged between her eyes. His voice was nothing more than a whisper but was still so loud out here in the middle of nowhere. "Is that what you think? That you're not good enough for me?"

What was she supposed to say? That she really was that pathetic? That would really send him running in the other direction. No death threats or cute quips came to mind under his intensity, so she said nothing. She let him assume whatever he wanted.

His thumb brushed along her neck, over the numb scar tissue she never meant for him to see, and her stupid vagina started screaming for attention all over again. "Tell me how you got this scar."

"Telling you won't change anything." It was much harder to breathe when he was touching her like this, like he cared. She darted her tongue across her dry lips, and his gaze honed in on the small movement, signaling the rest of her body to note how close he'd gotten. Silence became a physical force between them, and she'd lost energy to keep fighting him the minute she'd escaped that too-small tent. "It'll just make things worse."

His thumb skimmed along her jaw, back and forth, back and forth. Hypnotic and soothing. "How so?"

But a flood of emotion still lightninged from her forehead to her toes as she realized what he was really asking for. He wanted everything under the sarcasm and self-deprecating humor. Under the pink kerchiefs and sweet perfume. Past the hot pink jewels on her belt and the boot laces she'd special ordered. He wanted the real her, and that right there was more terrifying than facing off with the killer's gun. "You'll see how broken I really am."

Hesitation interrupted his path along her jaw, but to his credit, he recovered quickly. "Show me."

Had he earned the right to know? Branch had searched for her after the landslide, he'd pushed himself to his limits with a head injury to save her from Sarah Lantos's killer. He'd risked his life for hers.

It would be better to finally break the fantasy of them being something more than coworkers once and for all. She owed herself that much. Lila forced her attention back to the night sky and how the tops of the cliffs met that endless velvet, grounded by his touch. "I didn't lie to you before. This scar… I did it myself. I used a knife from my collection. That's why it's so messy. The blade was dull. It took a few tries to do any damage."

"Why on earth would you do this, Lila?" His voice sounded pained, as though she'd physically stabbed him in the chest with the very same knife she'd taken to her own skin.

Her heartbeat thudded too hard at her throat, and she was sure he could feel it in his palm. "Because I deserved it."

Chapter Twenty

There was no way he'd heard her right. She'd deserved it? No one as sweet and innocent as Lila Jordan could deserve this kind of damage. Especially delivered at her own hand.

Branch swept his thumb along the ridge of her scar, memorizing every pucker, every dip. But it was the anguish in her expression that held him captive. "I can't imagine that's true."

"You're wrong." Her tongue darted across her mouth again. A nervous habit he'd noticed in the past few minutes. A coping mechanism meant to distract her brain from oncoming pain, and Branch could do nothing but hold her here in the present. "When I was seventeen, my sister and brother-in-law lost their house. He'd been fired from his job and couldn't seem to get his foot in the door anywhere else. They had to move into my parents' house, but they didn't want to be down in the basement away from everyone, so I volunteered to move into the room downstairs."

Branch had to make a conscious effort not to tighten his hold around her neck as her voice turned disconnected. His breath became rougher, jagged shards of air cutting into the soft tissues in his chest. She was standing right in front of him, and yet she felt a million miles away.

"I'd always been on good terms with my brother-in-law. We joked around, you know. Like brothers and sisters were supposed to. We hit the movies and watched soccer. I'd never had a brother before. It was fun. At first." Her voice wavered, and he couldn't help but hold his breath at the change. Usual permanent smile lines smoothed over, and right then, Branch didn't recognize the woman in front of him. "My sister worked full-time to try to get them back on their feet. She mostly worked nights as an ER nurse. Her schedule was all over the place, so my brother-in-law was around a lot while he was applying to jobs, and I just had school, so I was home most nights. It was just him and me a lot of times while my parents lived their own lives, but after a couple weeks, something changed."

An edge of concern singed his nerves. As much as he craved to learn all the little things that made Lila tick rather than the perceptions of what everyone else believed, he had no intention of retraumatizing her, of making her live through what was obviously a topic she hadn't shared with anyone. His mouth dried as quickly as the desert around them. "Lila, you don't have to—"

Her eyes raised to his. "He started sending me texts."

His intuition kicked in, but he wouldn't jump to conclusions with her again. He wouldn't let anyone or anything tarnish the free spirit digging her nails into his forearms. It took more effort than it should have to ask his next question. "What kind of texts?"

"The kind a brother-in-law shouldn't be sending his sister-in-law, or a minor." Lila sucked her lips into her mouth. Her jaw clenched, meaning she was biting down. Hard. "I never responded. I thought he was just playing some kind of sick joke on me that I didn't get, but the longer I ignored him, the worse it got. There were demands. Pictures he'd taken of himself shirtless, sometimes pants-less. Videos while he…" She shook her head as though she could burn the images from her mind. "One night, I woke up with a hand pressed over my mouth and his weight on top of me. I was so sure I'd locked the door, but he somehow got into my room. And he…forced himself on me. Multiple times."

Removing his hand from her throat altogether, Branch put some much needed space between them as the rage he'd kindled since his divorce took hold. And he couldn't take it out on her, would never forgive himself for hurting her. Devastation contorted her features, and his still-healing heart cracked all over again. The muscles in his jaw ached under the pressure of his back teeth, and all he could see was red. "Then what?"

Tears glittered in her eyes, and he felt like such an asshole right then for not being able to hold her the way she deserved. But it was too much. The violence that he wanted to inflict was on the brink of taking control, and he had no business coming within a foot of her.

"He threatened to hurt my sister if I told anyone, but the bruises… My mom noticed them. She walked in on me changing after one of my soccer games. I told her everything." Lila wrapped her arms around herself, like it took everything in her not to fall into a million pieces right here in the middle of the desert, and Branch couldn't keep his distance. Adding his strength to hers. Tremors wracked her upper body, and he only wanted to hold her tighter. Setting his forehead against hers, he took an exaggerated deep breath in an attempt to help her remain grounded.

Closing her eyes, Lila rolled her lips between her teeth. "She didn't believe me. Thought I'd made it all up to get the attention they'd been paying to my sister. Of course, my dad found out. Then my sister. My brother-in-law denied everything. I showed them the texts he'd sent, but it didn't matter. I was a seventeen-year-old girl who'd played pranks on my family from the time I could talk."

He…hadn't expected that, and a visceral red coated his vision. The only thing keeping him from marching back to headquarters and getting his hands on the name of the man who'd done this to her was the near-death grip she kept by fisting his shirt in her hands.

"I got kicked out of my house. I came home from school and found all my stuff on the front lawn." Lila stared past his shoulder to the great expanse of sky above, but her voice had lost some of its strength. "I pounded on the front door for hours, trying to get them to listen to me. Begged them to believe me. My mother answered after a while, and I thought she'd finally see the truth."

Branch's gut tightened. And then his heart broke all over again. Only it wasn't for himself this time. It was entirely for her, for the betrayal and the loss and the hurt she'd endured to get this far. "But she hadn't."

"She told me I wasn't her daughter anymore. That I needed to leave and never come back and that I was destroying our family." Her gaze slid back to his, but Lila wasn't really there. This was a ghost. Not the Ranger Barbie persona she'd created. Not the woman he'd glimpsed at Angel's Landing. He didn't know this person. She was a disassociated stranger. "I didn't find out until a few months later that my father started drinking after that. The alcohol… He took it out on my mom. My sister and brother-in-law had to move in with his parents, but she filed for divorce a few weeks later. I'd get text messages from her. Nasty things I never thought my sister would say to me."

She looked at him as though he could fight these demons for her, and Branch wanted nothing more than to drive them back, but that wasn't how reality worked. "My dad died in a drunk driving accident. He didn't have any savings or retirement after spending it all on booze, so my mom lost the house. She had to stay with one of her sisters. In the end, I think she was right. I destroyed our family."

"No, you didn't." Branch bent at the knees, putting her in his line of sight. The rage kindling under his skin took a back seat to the blatant pain in her expression. "None of what happened was your fault, Lila. The fault lies with your brother-in-law. He put you in that position. He put his hands on you. He hurt you. No one else."

"It doesn't matter, though, does it? My family wants nothing to do with me, even to this day." She shook her head, a little more awareness coming back into her blue eyes the longer he held onto her. "One of my friend's parents took me in. They made sure I had food and a roof over my head until I graduated high school, but it was never the same. There was always this…hole in my chest where my family was supposed to be. It's still there. Making it hard to breathe."

Tilting her head, Lila nonverbally begged him to ease that emptiness, and he could do nothing but trace her jaw with as much understanding as he could manage. Because he knew this pain, too. "My mom was supposed to help me shop for a prom dress. My parents were supposed to cheer for me as I crossed the stage to get my diploma. They were going to help me with college applications, and I'd planned on throwing my sister a baby shower once she got pregnant, but all of it was suddenly gone. Just gone."

Branch had never felt more connected to her than right in that moment. He felt that same hole resonate in his chest as she brought hers into the light. One soul, two bodies. Hadn't Plato or Socrates been one of the first ones to describe soulmates that way? Once whole before being rent in two by Zeus, leaving humankind to wander in loneliness and longing, searching for their other half. The way his body had tuned to hers so quickly, the way he hadn't been able to ignore her or keep his distance from the beginning despite his best efforts, how her voice and her smile resonated with him on a cellular level. No one had affected him the way she had, not even the woman he'd spent his entire adult life with up until the divorce.

He skimmed his thumb across her bottom lip, loving the way his calluses caught against the soft skin. "I'm sorry. For all of it, Lila." But none of this explained how she'd come to the point where her only option was a way out of this life at her own hand. "You blame yourself for your dad's death. Your mom's problems. Your sister's marriage. Is that why you tried to end your life?"

"Wouldn't you?" She swiped at her face with a half laugh that didn't hold an ounce of humor. She'd found her way back into the present, with him, and hell, he'd never seen a more perfect creature in his life. Strong, resilient and so damn beautiful it hurt to look at her and not touch. "I could've told my mom the bruises were from soccer. I could've deleted the messages my brother-in-law sent. I could've prevented all of this. Maybe then they would still love me. Maybe someone else could love me, too, broken pieces and all."

Shit. He wanted to be that someone. The person who could gather up all her pieces and put her back together. Stronger than ever before. Branch skimmed his hands down her arms, careful of the bullet graze on her arm. There was a reason his ex-wife had cheated on him, left him, divorced him. He wasn't good enough for Lila, and it'd never been clearer than right this moment. "Most nights

I ask myself what I could've done differently in my marriage. What would've happened if I'd been a little more attentive? Was there a single moment where she fell out of love with me, or was it a lot of moments put together that went over my head?"

Forcing a deep breath, he sank into the feeling of Lila. The way she looked to him for answers, for safety. He might've gotten her out of that cave, but he'd failed her in other ways, and right then, he wasn't sure he could ever be the man she needed. The one she deserved. "I think it's natural, to take on some responsibility for the circumstances we find ourselves in, but we tend to blame ourselves for the bad while forgetting to give ourselves credit for the good."

He swept his thumb along her arm. "You're not broken, Lila. I see you. You're everything."

Chapter Twenty-One

I see you.

It was exactly what she'd wanted to hear, yet Lila hadn't been prepared for the full impact of the words. Her bones felt too big for her body, heart still thundering after Branch had led her back to the tent last night and tucked her into his chest. Safe. Accepted. Supported. Where she'd always wanted to be. He had a power over her that would be death of her. Because when he talked to her like that, when he held her and comforted her after spilling her darkest secrets, she could almost believe the man of her dreams—and countless fantasies—wanted her in return.

Ugh. Why did she have to be so…broken?

Why couldn't she accept maybe he had meant everything he said last night? And why couldn't she stop staring at the ceiling of the tent as if it held all the answers?

"I know you're awake." His voice was gravelly, deeper than usual, and her lady bits were the first to take notice. Holy moly, the man could do some damage with few words.

Branch pressed his chest against her back, shoulder to knee, though he was so much bigger than her. She loved it, this sudden need for him to get as close as possible, despite a whole lot of reasons why he shouldn't. Number one:

morning breath. His hand slid over her hip, across her low belly, and she wanted nothing more than to melt into him. To forget all the bad outside these crappy canvas walls and live out one of the fantasies she'd built in her head. Years of therapy had gotten her to a place of being able to hold her own in any given situation with a man, but there was something visceral that convinced her survival instincts that Branch wouldn't ever hurt her. "Your stomach announced your presence before the rest of you stirred."

Traitor. Her stomach vaulted into her chest as Branch planted a kiss on her shoulder. Forget butterflies. An entire Cirque du Soleil act had started up behind her ribs. While they'd done nothing more than share that one kiss and fall asleep in each other's arms last night, Branch Thompson had made her feel a whole lot of dangerous things that scared the crap out of her.

Pushing her upper body off the unyielding ground, Lila added a few inches of breathing room between them. Didn't help. Because looking at his face first thing in the morning was suddenly all she wanted to do with the rest of her life. "You're one to talk. I fell asleep to an entire orchestra performing in your intestines."

Okay. Those words were not sexy. At all.

But his laugh sure as hell was. It filled the tent with a warmth the sun couldn't touch as it crawled over the horizon. His touch fell from her hip as he rolled onto his back.

"Touché." Muscles flexed across his stomach and chest as he hauled himself upright. And what an impressive show it was. In fact, Morning Branch just might be the new star of her unachievable fantasies from here on out. If this whole investigation left her—and her heart—in one piece. "I'll get us some breakfast."

Yeah. There was little chance of getting out of this without more bruises.

They'd lost track of the killer and the gun that could've killed her, but Lila knew in her heart the hunt wasn't over. The man who'd killed Sarah Lantos might've convinced himself of his heroic role in this mess, but that didn't mean he deserved to get away with murder. One way or another, NPS was going to find him, and she wanted to be there when they did.

Grabbing her pack, she kept her attention on changing back into her uniform rather than watching the way Branch had jumped at the opportunity to feed her. No one had really done that for her. Sure, her parents made sure she'd been fed as a kid, but once she'd hit ten or eleven, her mother had taught her to cook her own meals apart from dinner. Even then, her mom had made it seem like feeding the family was more a burden than anything else. None of her past boyfriends—however few and far between—had made the effort to ensure she ate. Rather, they'd expected her to feed them. But Branch... He was taking care of her.

And maybe that was the scariest part of all. She'd gone so long taking care of herself, she wasn't sure how to let someone else do it. And that kiss? Wow. It'd been deep and slow, and oh so intense, she was still feeling it in her nerve endings. His touch, his weight—all of it combined into a dangerous cocktail. That kiss had whispered promises of something she'd dreamed about since she'd met him. It promised forever, but she and Branch didn't have that. Not with the gaping wounds she'd exposed.

The smell of cinnamon and apples hit her a split second before Branch offered a small plastic bowl and a spoon. "Can't say it's as satisfying as Cherry Garcia, but oatmeal should hold us over until we reach headquarters in a few hours."

Right. All this was temporary. The real world wouldn't wait forever. Soon or later, search and rescue would set out to see what had become of them, and she and Branch would have to give their statements about the past twenty-four hours. And explain why they'd failed to hold onto Sarah Lantos's killer. She could see Risner's winning smile now—part hyena, part snake—as he found the last reason he needed to dismiss her from the service. Ugh. Lila stared down into the over-sugared mush in her bowl and closed her eyes. "I will not stab him for talking about ice cream. I will not stab him for talking about ice cream."

"Not a morning person." Branch settled himself on his sleeping bag as she peeled open her eyes. It was admirable the way he tried to fold his legs crisscross-applesauce with his size, but there didn't seem to be any obstacle that held its strength against him. Especially her ovaries. "Noted."

Her heart hiccuped. He said that as if he planned to wake up next to her after today, which was just straight-up ridiculous, but if he could read her mind, he would either be traumatized or turned on. Both, if he was as awesome as she believed him to be.

They'd return to headquarters, Risner would fire her, she'd pack her crap as Sayles looked on, and she'd never see Branch or any of the other rangers again. They'd get what they'd wanted since she started working in Zion: a great view of her ass on the way out. The end. She swallowed the groan in the back of her throat along with a chunk of apple.

"If you don't terrify people a little bit, then what's the point of all of this?" Shoveling oatmeal into her mouth— and not thinking about the two pints of Ben & Jerry's in her freezer in her soon-to-be former shoebox of a house— Lila finished off breakfast and shoved her hands into her uniform top over her sleep shirt. The less they dragged this out, the better. Then again, she never could rip off a Band-Aid without crying.

Within a few minutes, Branch had cleaned and packed their dishware. They each rolled and stored their sleeping bags with a mental inventory of the supplies they had left between them. It wasn't much, but the hike back to head-quarters shouldn't take more than five hours if they kept a steady pace, though their injuries would add some time.

The sky had darkened some since she'd woken, but it wasn't until Lila shouldered her pack that she caught a whiff of rain in the air. Storm clouds had started gather-ing in the north, bringing a gust of frigid wind. She hadn't packed any long-sleeved protection.

Branch followed her gaze on the incoming clouds. They were moving in fast, rolling over each other and bringing nothing but dread. "Let's move."

The banter they'd shared evaporated as the wind picked up, rocketing her nerves higher. It wasn't as though they weren't trained to survive in severe weather. Both she and Branch had gone through hours of wilderness survival be-fore signing on with NPS. They both knew the potential of getting wet and suffering hypothermia despite the sum-mer temperatures. Additionally, search and rescue would call off any attempts made to recover her and Branch due to the storm.

Lila caught the briefest flash of lightning in her periph-eral vision, and soon a backing track of thunder ricocheted off the surrounding cliffs. The hairs along her arms raised on end, driving her up the bowl-like incline of the valley.

Her legs screamed protest with every step, her bruised ribs limiting her breathing. She'd never met a mountain she couldn't conquer during her reign as a park ranger, but this little molehill would be her undoing. Not to mention the fantastic view of Branch's backside on the way up. But she had to slow down. Her body had yet to recover its run-in with a landslide and a killer, and it was showing. "What fresh hell is this?"

"Almost there. Come on." Reaching back for her, Branch intertwined his fingers with hers, pulling her to his side. He kept one hand at her low back, and his warmth instantly assaulted the nerves scraping up her spine. Then it was gone. "I've got you."

"You say that now, but four of the five voices in my head think you're too good to be true, and the fifth is deciding where to bury you." She sucked down a deep breath tinged with humidity that hadn't been there a moment ago. Rain was coming.

She was gifted another one of his laughs, but this one didn't have any feeling to it. Not like the one back in the tent. Still, she couldn't help but engrave it into her brain for recall later when he finally realized she wasn't worth the effort. Or maybe he already had.

Static punctured through the silence between them, right before a low voice sounded over Lila's radio. "Thompson, Jordan, come in. Over." Another round of static.

Lila pulled up short, unthreading her arm from one shoulder strap, and pulled her pack forward. They'd reached the rim of the valley, but the mountains and the incoming storm should've kept them from contacting headquarters. Unless help was closer than she thought. Pulling her beaten radio from the pack, she clamped down the push-to-talk button as Branch took position in front of her. "Jordan here. Risner, is that you?"

Two seconds. Three.

"Jordan, it's about time. Where's Branch?" Cold slithered through her at the district ranger's instant demand to talk to someone who wasn't her.

"He's here. We're approximately three miles northeast from the base of Angel's Landing and headed back." Apart from the very real possibility of not having a job when they returned to headquarters, she couldn't deny the relief of knowing someone had been searching for them. "Over."

"Stay put. We're a mile out from you, and I want answers. Seismometers picked up a reading eighteen hours ago, but the geologists are telling me it wasn't an earthquake." Risner's voice cut out on the last word. "What the hell is going on out there? Over."

A mile? Another dose of dread prickled in her gut. This was it. Once SAR recovered her and Branch, they'd be separated to give their statements, she'd be dismissed from NPS, and all of this would be over.

Lila struggled to respond. The past twenty-four hours had changed her in ways she couldn't explain. For better and worse. And Branch had been there through it all, but she'd known—deep down—this fantasy she'd created between them hadn't ever been a real possibility from the beginning. It was only a matter of time before he realized how much work it would take to put her back together, and he'd barely made it out of his divorce in one piece. His heart couldn't afford another bond with the wrong soul. And she was…wrong. In every way.

Taking the radio from her, Branch lifted it to his mouth, his attention locked on her. "Ranger Jordan ensured we got out alive. Other than that, we're going to need additional rangers to aid in the search. Over."

Lila's lips parted on a strong inhale. Oh, no. Branch Thompson had taken her entire heart, and she was pretty sure he'd never give it back.

Chapter Twenty-Two

Something had changed. In the span of a mere twenty-four hours, Branch had been cracked wide open all over again. Only this time, the pieces were coming together without the need of isolation, hiding or avoidance. All because of the woman standing in front of him.

She'd washed her face free of makeup, leaving nothing but the imperfect beauty beneath. Hair frizzing free from the ponytail she'd dragged it into, Lila stood against the backdrop of thunder and lightning and the promise of torrential summer rain. And, damn it, she was perfect. Her uniform had worn through over her ribs, revealing her sleep shirt underneath where bruises darkened smooth skin, and in an instant, he recalled the feeling of the fabric between his fingers. Recalled how his palm had fit perfectly against her hip, those little breathy sounds she made in her sleep, the guttural moan as he'd kissed her last night. He'd fallen asleep to the rhythmic rise and fall of her back pressed against his chest, and it'd been the most peaceful night's sleep he'd gotten in years.

Hell. He could still taste her. A driving, ravenous need to kiss her—to absorb her into his very bones—sucked the oxygen from his lungs, and Branch pushed himself to add another foot of distance between them. He prided himself on discipline, on control, but everything about this woman urged him to discard every stupid rule he'd set in place to protect himself. The mere thought terrified him beyond facing Sarah Lantos's killer.

A smile caught at one corner of her mouth, sending an SOS straight to his nervous system as she studied him. But even with as much as she'd revealed about herself last night—the assault, her parents' reaction, her attempt to take her own life—he couldn't rid himself of the feeling there was something Lila had left out. That he was being left in the dark.

That same feeling had been there in the days leading up to catching his ex-wife with his best friend, then afterward when his ex had admitted she was going to seek an abortion. It burned low in his stomach, acidic and uncomfortable. But what could Lila possibly have to keep from him? They were rangers, had worked together for a mere four months. They'd only recently crossed the line into something akin to friends—maybe more—and there wasn't a single cell in his body that believed she owed him a damn thing.

Unless it had something to do with this investigation.

Shit. That thought shot his brain into hyperawareness, assessing every interaction they'd had over the past two days and deconstructing the meaning behind every word out of her perfect mouth. The paranoia and betrayal he'd shoved in a box made of rage burst free, and in an instant, he was in too deep, drowning. On the verge of putting himself right back where he didn't want to be: at the mercy of someone he trusted.

Lila dragged her ponytail over her shoulder and twisted the ends between slender fingers tipped in that chipping manicure. He wasn't sure how long she'd been hiding underneath all the pink and rhinestones, but it would take months, if not years, to crawl out from the persona she'd built to shield herself from judgment, hurt and backstabbings. She'd need support. She'd need him with her every step of the way, but she didn't trust him. "I'm not sure anyone has ever stood up to Risner and lived to tell the tale."

His mouth dried. Thunder exploded overhead as the clouds moved in. The first rain drops pattered against his scalp and shoulders, and Lila, in all her glory, stared up into the sky as if daring the torrent to do its worst. She closed her eyes against the onslaught without a care in the world.

And wasn't that kindling to the fire raging inside of him? That she could go through life relying on her impulsiveness, her emotions and meddling without bothering to acknowledge the consequences? How did she get a pass when everyone else had to pay the price for their choices?

Somehow this woman had crawled beneath layers of armor and made herself at home as though she owned the place, and damn it, he was pretty sure she owned him. After everything she'd been through—everything she'd suffered—she'd managed to bury it all with a smile, cheer for her enemies and push back despite the odds.

But it'd all been a lie. A manipulation.

And if he took that step to keep her, she would only end up breaking him completely. Branch fisted both hands to stop himself from reaching for her, to feel her rain-slickened skin and wipe the drops from her lips with his mouth. This resilient creature had shown him what life without pain could look like. Shown him how to feel comfortable in his skin and move on while driving his invisible knife wounds deeper.

The muscles in his jaw ached under the pressure of his

back teeth as he surveyed the storm overhead. To keep himself from memorizing her all over again. Or witnessing Lila break from what had to come next. "Why did Sarah Lantos's killer want you dead?"

"Well, you sure know how to make a girl feel special." Lila's smile slipped as she opened her eyes to study him. Rain plastered her hair against her face, and Branch's fingers itched to set it back behind her ear. To have one last touch. But it would only make this so much harder on both of them. Her mouth parted on a rough exhale, and she diverted her attention to the ridgeline where the SAR unit would approach from. As if hoping they would intervene and save her this conversation. That was only one the red flags Branch noted. "I don't presume to know the inner workings of murderers, but I'm guessing I was standing in his way."

The lie shoved a bitter, acidic sensation up his throat. "Then why didn't he just kill you? Why drag you to his campsite?"

"I told you." Dropping her hands away from her hair, she squared her shoulders to him. "Sarah Lantos fought back. He needed me to patch up a stab wound to his thigh. You were there, weren't you? Didn't you see the bloodied gauze?"

Yeah. He had, and it'd driven him nearly out of his mind imagining Lila had been injured. That her abductor was trying to save her life, but it'd turned out, she'd been trying to save his. Branch took that step forward, more determined than ever to uncover what she was hiding. "But you ran. And he followed, even with a stab wound and the risk of bleeding out. He could've just shot you. He had the gun. Why did he chase you down? Why follow you into that cave?"

"Branch, don't do this." Her eyes widened, begging him to back off, and right then, he knew. He knew there was something she hadn't told him about the man they were hunting.

"Why did he want you dead, Ranger Jordan?" Using her title and last name suddenly made it far easier for him to keep his emotions out of this, and physical pain registered on her face. A flinch of the worst kind. Was that why Risner insisted on calling his female rangers by their last names? To distance himself from giving a damn about them? Maybe the man wasn't sexist, after all. Maybe he'd just learned to not to get emotionally involved.

No, that guy was still an asshole.

The rain picked up, but it did nothing to mask the swell of tears in her eyes or the sweet scent of her skin. Her tongue darted across her bottom lip. Only this time Branch wouldn't let himself get taken in. "He said I was just like her. Sarah Lantos. That I deserved to suffer for manipulating people into doing what I wanted by convincing them I was something I wasn't. Is that what you want to hear?"

His gut somersaulted, and he countered his advance. Her lie had been right there, staring him in the face, but he'd refused to let himself see it because of the feelings she'd stirred in him. "You lied to me. When I asked, you told me you didn't remember anything else from the cave."

"I didn't…" She shook her head, then stilled. Branch watched as she connected the dots. Realized her mistake and what it meant. Lila took a step forward but halted as he took one back. Her face drained of color, voice softening. "I didn't mean to lie to you, I swear. I just—"

"You just what? After everything I told you about my ex-wife, you ended up being just like her, didn't you? Willing to do whatever it takes to get your way at the cost of the people around you. I trusted you to be up front with me, but you may have just compromised this investigation. The killer's motives can tell us about the types of victims he targets or his next move. That information might've given us a clue as to where he's going, and you kept it to yourself because, what? You didn't want to confirm what everyone else already knows?" Branch didn't wait for an answer, stalking past her. He was well aware he was searching for an excuse to sever this gut-wrenching need for her out of fear, but he couldn't afford to risk his heart again. Ending it now was the only way to protect himself, no matter how much he hated himself for it. "Wait here for the search party, Ranger Jordan. Tell Risner I'm still on the killer's trail."

"You can't go out there alone. Branch, please. You're not in any condition to face him again." Threading her hand between his arm and rib cage, she fought to stop him in his tracks.

He turned on her with every ounce of disgust he could muster in his expression.

She dropped her hold as if she'd been burned. Her throat worked on a deep swallow. "I'm sorry. Okay? I didn't want you to think I was that person he accused me of being, the one everyone accuses me of being. I can't lose you, too."

"Too late." Branch lowered his voice, hating himself more than ever before. "Were you even telling the truth about that scar, or was it another way for you to get attention? To make me and the other rangers feel bad for you?"

The words achieved the impact he'd wanted. He'd used her mother's accusations against her, and Branch couldn't help but feel he'd gone too far.

"You said you see me." Her voice barely reached him

over the storm throwing her hair in her face. "That I'm not broken."

This was how he ended it. How he kept what'd happened leading to his divorce from happening again. Every muscle in his body stiffened with self-hatred, but he'd already made the jump. He had to see this through to the end. "I was wrong."

It took less than three seconds for Ranger Barbie to make an appearance, and he couldn't stand to watch her rebuild those impenetrable walls. "You've exceeded the limits of my medication. So enjoy your next twenty-four hours, Branch Thompson."

Lila turned on her heel, soaked to the bone, and headed in the direction of Angel's Landing. Never one to follow orders. Then again, he'd liked that about her. Her penchant for doing whatever the hell she wanted had put her on his radar in the first place and secured her position in the investigation into Sarah Lantos's murder. But now… now his gut warned him not to let her trudge through the desert during an increasingly violent storm alone. Without his protection.

But hadn't that been the point? To add this distance— physically and emotionally—between them? So why didn't he feel better about his decision?

He dug his fingertips into his palms to stop himself from calling after her. Risner would intercept her in the next few minutes. She'd return to headquarters, give her statement of the past two days and go back to the way things were supposed to be. And he'd…move on. Once and for all.

Branch couldn't go back. Ever. He couldn't see her patrolling the park every day and not want to get a dose of that smile she seemingly reserved for him or show up at her front door with a couple pints of Cherry Garcia and a romantic comedy from the 2000s.

No. He was going to finish what he started by ensuring the killer didn't come for Lila again.

Chapter Twenty-Three

He'd given her the one thing she'd wanted most. And then he'd taken it away as though it meant nothing.

Lila's boots slogged through mud and puddles, getting sucked down into the earth with every forced step forward. Cold rain slapped against her face but did nothing to cool her rising body temperature, prickles punctuating the vile words circling her head.

She couldn't breathe properly, couldn't think of anything other than the pure disgust written all over Branch's face as he'd accused her of being the very thing so many others had. A joke, a tease, a liar. Her heart broke all over again as she followed the valley's upper rim. Reds, oranges and tans bled together through the tears in her eyes. She hadn't lied to him. She hadn't. Omitting what the killer had said to her had been nothing but an attempt to convince herself how wrong he'd been. Instead, she'd ended up hurting the one person she'd trusted.

Branch had every reason to despise her. After what happened with his ex-wife, she didn't blame him for shutting her out. Lies of omission were still lies, and there was nothing she could do—nothing she could say—to fix this. No matter how much she wanted to. She'd done exactly as she'd feared. She'd manipulated him into believing she was something she wasn't. A magician, as the killer had called her, and she never felt so alone.

An all-too-familiar, sickening twist cut through her stomach. Lila slapped her hand against the nearest rock wall and emptied her stomach of the oatmeal Branch had made her this morning. How had everything gone wrong in such a short amount of time? How could she have let herself screw this up after everything she'd been through with her family? Wasn't she supposed to learn from her mistakes? She'd had everything she wanted. And now...

She felt as though she was sinking and wished the earth would swallow her whole right here. Her heart pounded loud in her ears to the point not even the breaking thunder overhead could penetrate through the haze. The storm seemed to mimic the suffering inside, which only drove her deeper into the spiral.

Her knuckles ached as though she'd spent the past few hours pounding on a bright yellow door that would never welcome her again. Begging to be let in, for someone— anyone—to believe she didn't deserve this.

But she did, didn't she?

A sob broke free of her throat, and Lila heaved again until there was nothing left. Rejection and bile left her mouth sticky and dry, but she wouldn't unpack her water bottle. She deserved to sit in this emptiness, to taste nothing but ash on her tongue for the rest of her life. To go back to being that seventeen-year-old unlovable girl no one wanted.

Her mother had been right all along. Losing Branch proved it, didn't it? There was nothing she could do—no one she could be—that would make anyone want her. Her brother-in-law had destroyed her, ripped away her sense of self and broken it into a million tiny pieces that could never be recovered. She was nothing. Unimportant, overlooked. Not even pretending to be the bubbly, enthusiastic cheerleader who loved pink and meeting up for coffee convinced people to give her a chance.

Lila swiped her mouth with her hand and sank her back into the cliffside. Rain soaked through her hair and smeared down her face, anything but cleansing. A shiver chased across her shoulders as lightning struck overhead. Risner and the search and rescue team should be here any minute, but as she took in the towering cliffs overhead, she realized she must've taken a wrong turn in her desperation to put as much distance between her and Branch as possible. Damn it. There was no way the SAR team would find her unless she got back on the main path to Angel's Landing. Right then, she felt as airheaded as her fellow rangers believed her to be.

Peeling herself away from the rock face, she trudged back the way she came, following her own treads as a guide. Her throat hurt. Her head hurt. Her heart…hurt.

Branch had effectively drawn her in with promises of understanding and desire and something more and then crushed that hope with nothing more than a few words. Bitterness coated her tongue, and no amount of swallowing got rid of the taste. He'd accused her of trying to kill herself all those years ago to get attention. Just as her mother had before excommunicating her from the family, all the while messaging her photos of herself and her son-in-law going out to lunch together, catching movies together, meeting for coffee.

She'd wanted that. So much. To the point she'd tried to recreate it with her fellow rangers, but something must be… wrong with her. All she'd wanted was someone to choose her, and she'd almost convinced herself Branch had been that person. Her person, but he'd stabbed her heart instead. Used her greatest shame against her and successfully killed off the last shards of hope she'd held onto all these years. Tears burned in her eyes, though she tried to breathe around them. She wasn't sure she could ever forgive him for that. "If karma doesn't kill him, I gladly will."

No. She couldn't hurt him. Not the way he'd hurt her. Despite the hollowness taking up more space than it had before, a part of her had been dedicated to him since the moment he stepped into Zion. Had fallen in love with him. And that was what hurt the most. Her crush had become something…more over the past few days. Not the numb never-going-to-happen fantasy she'd lived off of. She'd shared trauma with him, shared a bed with him. She'd fallen asleep in his arms and given him a glimpse of the darkness she'd carried. She'd imagined a future with him, trusted him. He'd made her feel alive in a way no search and rescue or climbing assignment or hyperfixation had.

But she tended to overreact to anyone who showed her the slightest hint of kindness. That was what trauma did. It brought her expectations of human decency so low, that even wishing "bless you" after a sneeze urged her to sign over her savings in gratitude.

And she could see now that'd she handed over the most sacred parts of herself to Branch because he'd pulled her out of that cave. He'd saved her life. And while it made sense for her to offer something in return, she'd allowed herself to forget the months of growls, annoyed glances and one-sided conversations between them. He'd made it clear from the beginning, hadn't he? He'd wanted nothing to do with her since day one, and yet she'd somehow ended up giving him everything that mattered. "Now I get to fill his bed with Nature's Valley granola bars."

Lila stepped back onto the main trail that would lead her to the base of Angel's Landing. The search and rescue team's position didn't matter in this storm. They would hunker down until the worst passed, which, judging by the way the wind had picked up and thunder exploded overhead, would be a while yet. She'd get out of here faster—away from Branch sooner—by meeting the team where they were now.

A warning teased at the back of her mind. She knew better than to trek the park alone in the middle of a storm like this, but the need to get back to her crappy little house, eat a crappy lunch of ice cream and pack her crappy belongings drove her along the trail. The truth was, even if Risner somehow didn't dismiss her from the NPS or reassign her to another park, she wasn't going back. There was no way she could face Branch on the trails or in staff meetings or in the break room after he'd used her deepest regret against her.

And explaining this all to Sayles… That just wasn't going to happen. Her roommate had her own life, her own person in the form of an FBI agent who melted anytime he set eyes on Sayles, and Lila wasn't going to mess with that. "And this is why you never date anyone from work."

Her fingertips brushed the scar across her neck. The skin tingled there as she recalled Branch's touch, how he'd been so gentle and caring when he'd asked her to tell him what'd happened. How he'd held her as she exposed every nasty detail of an event that had turned her into a fraud.

But she didn't know him. Not really.

The man she'd come to know these past two days never would've accused her of using this scar for attention. But then maybe she hadn't really known him at all. Growls, rejection after rejection and negotiating shifts that didn't involve her had kind of made it hard.

Didn't matter. Once she met up with the search and rescue team, she'd give Risner her notice, and Branch Thompson would be nothing more than another rhinestone on her
mud-caked belt.

The rain washed her boot prints from the mud ahead,
but another set took shape. Larger, more widely spaced.
She slowed, studying each one. Had the SAR team already caught up with her? The storm should keep them
pinned down.

Crouching, she feathered her touch over the ridges
breaking apart with each pit of rain. "No treads."

Lila stood quickly, turning back the way she'd come.

Pain erupted in her gut as the killer's outline took shape.
She looked down. Watched her blood spread across her
uniform from where the small knife penetrated. A hand
slapped against one shoulder, holding her in place, forcing
her to feel every twitch of the knife he held.

"Hello, Ranger Jordan." The killer slid the knife free of
her low belly, still holding her upright. "I've been looking
for you. There's still so much more for us to talk about before we were rudely interrupted."

"You." Stumbling back, Lila clutched her hand over the
wound, free of his hold, but there was no stopping the blood
leaking through her fingers. Her entire body swayed as the
onslaught of pain intensified. It took everything she had
not to compare this moment to the night of her assault, to
relive it rather than stay in her head. To fight back. The
heels of her boots dipped down as she met the upper rim
of the valley.

"You're a liar like she was, Ranger Jordan." Sarah Lantos's killer stepped into her personal space, skimming his
breath along her jawline. "And I intend to make you suffer."

One push. That was all it took for her to go over the edge.

The world tipped on its axis as she fell. Her legs dropped out from under her. Gravity sucked her down to earth as she rolled. Rocks speared into her bruised ribs and cut through the fabric of her uniform. Her hair caught in cacti and bushes and ripped free again and again, tearing chunks from her scalp. She landed at the base of the incline, flat on her stomach.

Blood filled her mouth. Rushed to her head. Thudded too hard in her chest. Stretching one arm out, Lila reached for a palm-size rock a few feet in front of her. Not to escape. She knew that was impossible, but she wouldn't make this easy for him, either. Something warm and sticky dropped into her left eye, interrupting her vision. More blood. It dripped from the same incision she'd sustained when Branch had saved her from becoming a human pancake, mixing with rain and puddling beneath her chin.

A boot pressed down onto her forearm as her fingers brushed the rock. The killer crouched beside her, crushing her arm beneath his weight. But it was nothing compared to the agony in her chest. Of knowing Branch wouldn't be coming to save her again.

"Looks like it's just you and me now, Ranger Jordan."

Chapter Twenty-Four

The rubber band around his heart snapped harder than ever before.

Branch struggled to take his next breath as he met up with the mouth of the canyon that would lead north. Lila had been right before. This was the only escape that made sense to get the killer out of the park as fast as possible and without ranger interference. It was also the most dangerous. Though he hadn't caught sight of Fluffy yet, flash floods weren't uncommon in the area. With the storm bearing down, he could get swept away without more than a few seconds' warning. There was a chance the mountain lion had sought shelter during the storm, which just went to prove how out of it Branch really was.

Or maybe he was looking to punish himself.

He couldn't stop the accusations he'd thrown at her from circling his head. Every step punctuated by another vile word. He'd accused her of lying to him. Not just about what she'd kept from him during the investigation but of using her past to manipulate him. Like her mother had. Like the other rangers had. Like the killer had.

Damn it, it was the most detestable thing he'd ever done. Worse than taking a baseball bat to his best friend's car the minute Brand caught him and his ex-wife in bed together. It'd felt good at the time—like lifting a weight he hadn't realized had been crushing him for months—but he didn't have that feeling now.

All he could think about was Lila's flinch, as though he'd physically struck her. The dullness in her eyes. The way she'd hugged herself to keep from breaking in front of him.

Branch pushed himself harder, wanting nothing more than to ease the regret churning in his gut, but the relief never came. He'd messed up. He'd taken something beautiful and delicate and crushed it the moment he got attached.

That was what he did though, wasn't it? He took and took without giving back. And then he took some more. It was why his ex-wife had started looking to his best friend for intimacy. It was why she hadn't told him about the pregnancy immediately. Why she'd made a life-changing decision without considering what he'd wanted. At some point, she'd felt he couldn't be trusted.

The moment Lila had given him her trust by telling him all the ways her family failed her and the blame she'd shouldered alone for so long, a switch had flipped. He'd shut down any part of himself that allowed emotion and connection, but with her… It'd all come rushing back.

It was as though he'd been standing outside his bedroom door, right back on the edge of that cliff, knowing one more step would change his life, and he'd been afraid of falling. Moans of pleasure puncturing through the thin wood, his hand on the cold doorknob, his heart in his throat. Out there in the middle of the desert with Lila, he'd been back at that door. One step away from claiming the support and connection he'd wanted since the divorce or retreating to safety where he didn't have to worry about corrupting another woman into resenting him. Where no one could touch him.

He'd made his choice.

Only now, Branch couldn't stop rubbing his chest. Knowing if he allowed himself to slow down, the ache would consume him from the inside. He'd survived losing the woman he'd planned on spending the rest of his life with, but this…this was different.

Somehow, deep down, he understood this pain would only get worse the more distance he added between him and Ranger Barbie. And, damn it, he deserved to live in it. To feel every twinge of agony for what he'd said to her. He wasn't good enough for a woman like Lila Jordan who put everyone else before herself, who cheered for the very people working to tear her down, who never gave up. He was hard where she was soft, demanding where she compromised, unforgiving and intolerable where she accepted every facet of his grumpy ass. And he'd thrown it all in her face out of fear. Fear of destroying every good thing that made her the beautiful creature she was.

The tug to turn back intensified until it stole his next breath. Sarah Lantos's killer had targeted Lila. It made sense for him to make sure the son of a bitch couldn't come back for his partner, but there wouldn't be a woman to save if he left things like this between them. Branch pulled up short of the very cave he'd found her cornered by the killer. He had a choice. Duty to his job and this park or choosing Lila. It wasn't much of a choice.

Turning around, he navigated the smooth riverbed, his pace picking up once he reached the mouth of the canyon. That invisible thread connecting him and Lila had grown taut, pulling him back to Angel's Landing. To her.

The valley stretched out in front of him. Lightning struck the ground about a half mile away, raising the hairs along his forearm as he stepped out into the open. His nervous system screamed danger as he navigated forgotten boulders and exposed roots. The trees here had already burned due to a lightning strike two years ago, but that didn't mean another fire couldn't erupt without notice. The first few drops of the next storm spit against his face. His legs ached under the weight of his pack as he jogged across the expanse. Lungs on fire, Branch ignored the pounding in his head.

Seconds stretched into minutes. Minutes into hours. Every single one of them etched deep into his skin as he closed the distance between them. Lila had most likely already met up with the search and rescue team, but the storm would slow them down. He could still catch her. He'd beg for her forgiveness, then let her go if that was what she chose. It would hurt, but it was nothing short of what he deserved. To live the rest of his life alone and regretful.

The ache in his chest doubled in size, spreading like a wildfire through his arms and legs as he crested the bowl-like incline of the valley. Angel's Landing wasn't too much farther, and it would take time for the entire SAR team to ascend the cliffside leading to the lookout with their gear. Just another mile or so. His pulse thudded in rhythm to his steps as he followed the curved upper rim of the valley.

Then he saw them. The search team.

An added burst of energy shot down his legs. Within seconds, he closed in on Risner huddled under a rocky outcropping blocking out the rain, but he couldn't pick out the pink nightmare he'd been searching for in the group. Every ranger had donned their Stetsons, throwing him off, but it was clear within a few seconds that Lila wasn't among them. Had she pushed ahead?

The district ranger raised his attention, setting beady dark eyes on him. Risner's thin frame towered over the others in the team, most likely providing the supervisor with a power trip he hadn't earned. "Branch, it's about time. We've been waiting for you. What the hell is going on out here? I got reports of a landslide but no seismic activity. You know anything about that?"

"The killer used dynamite to trigger the landslide." Trying to catch his breath, Branch studied the canyons ahead, hoping to catch a glimpse of her. He'd told her to wait for the SAR team, but knowing her, she'd decided to head back to headquarters alone. Despite the fact that was where she would be safest, he couldn't help but wonder if she'd be there when he returned. "Ranger Jordan and I were caught in the fallout. We've been tracking the killer. We barely escaped with our lives. You got anything on this guy? A way to identify him?"

Risner jumped at the opportunity to take the lead. "The medical examiner concluded Sarah Lantos was dead before she hit the ground. The stab wound to her side severed the superior…mercenary artery. Something like that."

"Superior mesenteric artery." Another member of the team tossed out a tarp to set up a temporary campsite.

"Right. That. The victim bled out in seconds. The ME says the killer must've had some knowledge of anatomy or he just got lucky killing her that quickly. I'm thinking the latter, considering he's messing around with dynamite. Nobody mentally stable risks their own life with materials like that." Risner swiped the back of his hand beneath his nose to catch the water dripping off the birdlike cartilage. "The blood found on the lookout belongs to the victim. There were no traces of the killer left behind, not even on the gear and ropes. Killer must've worn gloves. Best we can tell, Sarah Lantos was in the wrong place at the wrong time."

That didn't feel right. Not after everything he and Lila

had gone through. "Lila said the killer wanted Sarah Lantos to suffer, that she deserved to pay for what she'd done to him for years. She thinks this is personal to him. Did you run a background check on the victim? Does she have any priors, incidents or family members with records?"

Branch was with Lila on this. He didn't have a whole lot of experience studying motives and modes of operation, but he knew there were warning signs leading up to someone taking a life. Something that might pinpoint who'd killed the victim. And tried to kill Lila.

"She thinks this is personal, huh? Well, since your partner isn't here, we'll have to operate on the assumption the people who actually investigate homicides around here are right." Risner scanned the landscape beyond Branch's shoulders, hands on his hips as though ready to dole out long-awaited punishment for his metaphorical punching bag. "Where is Jordan, by the way? You were both supposed to wait for the SAR team."

Branch's heart stopped cold for the briefest of moments. He searched every team member's face, desperate to recognize the blue eyes he'd woken to this morning in the tent. "What do you mean? I told her to wait here to meet up with you."

"Haven't seen her." Risner angled his arms out, palms up in a shrug. "Damn woman can never do anything right. I warned you not to bring her in on this investigation, but I guess you just couldn't keep it in your pants, Thompson. Don't blame you. Jordan's got that look in her eye that says she'll do anything for attention." The district ranger lowered his voice, barely audible over the pounding rain on the tarp the others had raised. "I expect details when we get back to headquarters." Risner winked. Stepping back, he widened his stance, thumbs hooked into his belt. "We're moving out as soon as this storm passes. We can't wait for her to catch up."

"You can't just leave her out here on her own." His nervous system shot into overdrive as he closed the distance between him and Risner.

The slight widening of the district ranger's eyes told him every preconception he'd had of Branch had been wrong, that he didn't know who the hell he was dealing with. And Branch couldn't argue. He was an entirely different person from two days ago, changed in more ways than one because of a woman who enjoyed threatening to make his life hell.

"And if I ever hear you talk about an employee, especially a female employee, like that again, I'll have the superintendent ship you to Gateway Arch for the rest of your pathetic career. As for Lila never doing anything right, have you bothered to ask yourself if you're the kind of leader employees respect enough to follow orders? Because from where I'm standing, there's a lot to be desired."

Risner's jaw snapped shut as he puffed out his chest, just begging for someone to knock him down a peg. "Whether my employees respect me or not doesn't matter. I'm her superior."

"You're an idiot, and if you aren't going to make the right call to recover one of your rangers, I am." Branch hauled his pack higher on his shoulder. "I'm going after her."

Chapter Twenty-Five

Lila couldn't keep her blood where it should be. In her body. The blade hadn't hit anything major, but it was only a matter of time before she bled out if she didn't get any kind of medical help. Except she wasn't sure how to do that. Her legs weren't working. The killer had confiscated her radio. And no one—not even Branch—knew she was here.

"What do you think of my kidnapping skills now, Ranger Jordan?" That voice, tinted with a slight accent she still couldn't place, filtered in through the darkness.

Thunder rumbled up through the ground. Or had it come from above? She couldn't tell. Something sharp set up residence in her chest, shortening her inhales. Wave after wave of dizziness had tossed her brain in a blender and refused to relent. "You've got the incapacitating your victim part down. Kudos. The cave is also a great touch. Spooky."

Her throat ached with every attempt to speak, draining what energy she had left faster. Another bubble of blood burst from the wound in her stomach. Sarah Lantos had been stabbed just like this, but she imagined it would've been too much work for the killer to get Lila to the top of Angel's Landing with an injury like the one in his thigh. Which seemed to have been patched up as he approached her, discarding the shadows of whatever cave he'd dragged her into.

His laugh rolled with another explosion of thunder. Ugh. She hated that laugh. Bet it'd become the star of her nightmares after this. The storm was still going strong, but it did nothing to drown out the killer's intentions. "Thank you. I've learned a lot since the last time you and I were alone together."

"Is this the part where you open up your case of torture devices and detail your master plan while explaining how I don't fit into it?" Pain spiked through her middle as she tried to push herself upright. "Or am I part of the plan? I can't tell."

"I don't need an entire case of torture devices when I have you right where I want you." Crouching beside her, the killer withdrew that very same knife he'd introduced to her soft tissues, setting it against her cheek, and she froze. The metal was warm despite the drop in her body temperature and the imposing elements. She could still feel flecks of her blood crusted to the blade. "You know, through all your noise and jokes and distractions, you're really just a scared little girl with no one around to protect her."

Scared? Yes. Little girl? No. Though compared to his size, she didn't blame him for making that assumption. Lila reverted into the overly upbeat persona that'd kept her from breaking apart so many times before. Her cheek pressed into the blade as she smiled. "Haven't you heard? Women are allowed to vote now. We have jobs, can choose not to have kids and fight our own battles."

His responding smile set in place as he framed her chin in his free hand. Right before the tip of the blade cut into her skin. Stinging pain ticked her heart rate higher. In a single move, he'd nearly sliced that fake smile off her face.

Blood dripped down her chin and hit the cave floor. "How are you going to fight me when you're bleeding out all over the ground?"

That was a good question. One she'd have to come back to as he released her and took position standing over her. Her weight dragged her back to the hardened, rocky floor. At least this cave didn't smell like decomposition. "Just get it over with."

"Get it over with?" He cleaned the blade with his jacket. Much thicker than the long-sleeved shirt he'd worn before. Which meant he'd prepared for all kinds of weather before shoving Sarah Lantos off that cliff. "Are you really that eager to die?"

She had been once. And while that cavern of loneliness and Branch's rejection had spread to the smallest crevices of her body—clawed her into a thousand little pieces—she didn't want to die. For the first time in years, the numbness had receded, leaving her raw and exposed to the slightest stimuli. The feel of the rain on her skin, the sound of the wind roaring through the cave opening, the scent of something akin to burnt wood.

"The big villain speech. Obviously, you're not going to kill me until you've made me suffer like Sarah Lantos." Lila tested her brain's command of her fingers and toes. The blade hadn't caused enough damage to sever her connection to her limbs, but she'd sustained multiple injuries being tossed down that hill. Coupled with the bruises on her ribs, she was pretty sure she'd broken something. "That's a good place to start."

"It doesn't matter what I say. What matters is my plan for people like you. People like my sister." The killer looked down on her as though she was nothing more than a patch of mud under his shoe. "She tortured me for years, you know. In little ways at first. Pinching me under the table at dinner, adding hot sauce to my food when I wasn't looking. Her face would light up every time she got a reaction out of me, but when I told my parents, no one believed me. She had this uncanny ability to cover her tracks. She moved onto testing her skills with knives while I slept, slicing between my toes and the bottoms of my feet. Still, my parents wouldn't believe their daughter could inflict such harm. After a while she found threatening me to stay quiet by hurting my dog worked just as well as physical torture. I loved that dog more than anything, and she took it from me for fun. All while pasting a smile on her face to deflect suspicion. Much like you do."

The comparison was delusional. There was no other way to describe it. She'd never hurt an animal, let alone another person. She'd never gone out of her way to inflict pain and suffering, but to the man standing above her, she might as well have been the one to commit those unforgivable sins he'd survived.

"Sarah Lantos was…your sister." The pain in her torso intensified with every word. She wasn't sure how much blood she had lost, but she didn't have an endless supply. The longer she laid here, the sooner she'd lose her fight to escape. Lila leveraged her weight into her elbow, cataloguing her injuries from head to toe. Too many. She wanted nothing more than to sink back to the floor and lose herself in unconsciousness, but that would mean giving up. She wasn't ready to die. She'd just started to live despite the heartache that came with Branch's accusations.

"It wasn't until we were in our teens the psychologists recognized her antisocial personality disorder, but by then, the damage had already been done to me. My parents, they realized their mistake when they found me bleeding out all over the kitchen floor after I took the remote from my sister to watch my show after school one day."

Retracting one arm from his coat, the killer exposed his forearm. A thick, jagged scar trailed from his inner elbow to his wrist. The tissue hadn't healed well, much like the scar across her throat. Or maybe the damage had been beyond the physicians' capabilities. Her scar almost seemed to burn in response.

"They finally faced the monster they'd created. The way she hurt others without any kind of remorse, how she went out of her way to push their boundaries, the manipulation tactics she used to get away with her behavior. Years too late. Still, they went out of their way to get her help instead of locking her up where she belonged."

Acid churned in Lila's gut at the realization she and this killer had more in common than most. How the people who were supposed to love and care for them had betrayed them, refused to believe them, ignored their pleas for help.

But trauma didn't erase the violence he'd inflicted on his sister or her, and it sure as hell didn't justify it.

"She kept torturing me." The killer's voice lowered an octave, freezing her in place. "Drove away any woman who might show interest in me with lies of abuse and infidelity. Got me fired from multiple jobs by sleeping with my superiors. Even after my little stint in a psychiatric ward based off a false police report she filed, she set out to destroy me for no other reason than I was something in the way of her having my parents' full attention."

Lila didn't know what to say to that, what to think. She wasn't that person. But because she'd relied on a persona to bury all the bad and hide from the pain she couldn't rid herself of, he'd equated her with the nightmare of his past. She could see it now, the slight manic gleam in his eyes with what little sun broke through the storm clouds. Nothing she said would convince him he was suffering from a delusion. Not even her death. He would kill her, then he'd move onto his next target. And the next. Until the police finally caught up with him. "So you killed her."

So many innocent lives destroyed, all because no one had believed him when he'd needed it most. She couldn't help but wonder what would have happened had she not kept her pain all bottled up as Ranger Barbie but instead unleashed it on the people around her. Would she have become a killer as he had? Would she have met Branch and found her dream job? Would she still have fallen in love or let the darkness consume her?

"You think she didn't deserve to die for what she's done to me?" He was right back in her space, putting himself on her level, sliding the tip of the blade across her throat. Almost lovingly.

"I think you like listening to yourself talk." Lila pressed one palm into the ground. She could stop him. She just had to figure out how to get her body to stop bleeding. And ignore the gut-wrenching agony ripping through her heart.

The truth was, none of those questions mattered. She had buried her pain underneath layers of pink and glitter and bleach because the idea of taking it out on others as her brother-in-law had taken his domination out on her had sickened her down to the bone. She'd found the safety she'd been craving since she was seventeen years old by getting lost and finding small pieces of herself in Zion National Park. And she'd fallen in love with Branch because he'd been the first person to make an effort to understand her, broken or not. He'd taken a good long look at all the darkness she hid from the world and held her anyway. And she loved him for it. Stupid heart. "To be fair, I did ask for the villain speech, but I really don't want your voice to be the last thing I hear before I die."

Her scalp burned as he fisted a hand in her hair. "You really don't know when to keep your mouth shut, do you?"

"No." Lila brought her boot between them and slammed her heel into his groin as hard as possible. The blade nicked her skin as he fell back with a scream of agony. It bounced off the walls and drilled deep into her soul. "That's more like it."

Getting her feet under her, she fell forward toward the exit, as though her body knew exactly where to go. That sense only lasted a second before a hand wrapped around her ankle, and she hit the ground. The breath knocked out of her as she reached for the cave's entrance. It was right there. All she had to do was run.

Her vision blurred as the killer flipped her onto her back. "Let's see how loud you can scream this time."

Chapter Twenty-Six

He'd waited. And waited. But there was no sign Lila intended to meet up with the SAR team.

But while Branch was more than ready to admit she liked to disobey orders to get under Risner's skin, she wasn't stupid. She wouldn't risk her life in a storm like this to make a point, and the rangers back at headquarters hadn't seen her.

Lila was missing.

Which meant something had happened in the time he'd left her in this very spot and when he'd pulled his head out of his ass to come back and apologize for the way he'd treated her. And Branch had an idea who might've been involved.

He scanned the ground in circles, frustration building each time the rain corrupted evidence of her boot prints. The first print had been protected by an overhang, pulling him down a narrow slot canyon worn into smooth curves over the years. He'd recognized it from their two days together. The subsequent prints had washed away in the storm. Every shred of evidence, every clue telling him where she might've gone erased in a matter of minutes. He couldn't fight back the desperation that'd nearly destroyed him after the landslide.

The killer had come back to finish what he'd started. Branch didn't have proof. It was literally vanishing right in front of his eyes, but he'd always trusted his gut. He followed the slot canyon, recovering mere divots of her footprints. Until they just…stopped. She must've taken a wrong turn. Doubled back.

Crouching to get a better look at the patterns left in the mud, he tracked Lila's divots. But her prints weren't the only ones lingering. Another set had followed her in. Deeper. Harder to wash away despite the storm's relentlessness. No ridges or treads. Just impressions. Bigger than his partner's.

And right in the center of one, rivets of brown mixing with rainwater. Like slicked oil refusing to give up the fight against a more soluble opponent.

Blood.

Fire burned up Branch's throat as he shoved to stand. Lila didn't carry any weapons, which meant she'd been injured. He couldn't tell how badly, but enough for the killer to abduct her a second time. Damn it, he should've been there. He should've known the son of a bitch wouldn't let her go. Lila had tried to tell him. The killer was convinced she was just like Sarah Lantos, that she deserved to suffer for her sins, and Branch had left Lila to fight this alone because of some warped sense of protecting himself.

His blood pumped too hard. His throat raw from swallowing the growl clawing through him.

He marched straight out of the slot canyon. She wasn't here. The killer wouldn't have left her body out in the open. He'd want Lila to suffer as promised, secluding her. Branch had returned to the trail in less than thirty minutes after he'd turned his back on her and hadn't seen any evidence of anyone until Risner showed his pinched face. Which meant the killer would've taken her someplace nearby. Somewhere he could take his time but distant enough no one on the trail would hear her scream.

Branch ran through his knowledge of the area. Lila was better at this kind of thing. She was just…better.

In every way.

And he loved her.

More than he relied on his fear. More than his isolation. He loved every inch of her, complete with her shame, her secrets and unwillingness to bend. He loved her meddling and impulsiveness and the way she made decisions based solely on her mood. He loved the flares of pink on her uniform and the way she protested Risner's control by be-jeweling her belt against regulations. He loved the way her body had melted into his when he'd kissed her, as though she'd always been the missing piece of his soul he'd lost in the divorce.

But he mostly loved how she'd dragged him back into the light with her unending invitations to show him around Springdale, to meet for coffee and when she'd thrown him a surprise birthday party in the break room. He still couldn't figure out how she'd learned about his birthday, but it didn't matter. She'd stood in the middle of that linoleum-coated corner of the office with balloons and a cake made just for him with that gorgeous smile on her face and daring in her eyes.

He loved her.

And he would do whatever it took to get her back.

Branch rushed from the slot canyon, taking in as much detail as his brain allowed. Rain pummeled the tracks he'd followed into the canyon, but he could still make out the increasingly rare divots she'd left behind. None of them faced the direction of the valley, wider on one end compared to the other. Had she backed up? Stumbled away after being injured?

His boot met the edge of the upper rim. And then he saw it. The drag marks about ten feet down. They were similar to those he'd found in the landslide. Scrambling to get a better look, he scrubbed water from his face. These marks were much deeper than the ones he'd come across before, and he gauged the distance between this position and the top of the rim.

She'd been…pushed. Branch scanned the surrounding area. And found another set of drag marks. Rocks and bushes acted as obstacles between the first point and the second, but there was no denying the pattern. He descended the incline and froze. Blond hair clung to the branches of a scrub brush. Her hair must've caught on the way down, ripping free from her scalp. He untangled the strand, too many images assaulting his brain as he played the scenario marked in the earth out. The killer had injured her, then pushed her down the hill.

Blood seeped in the stone there. Another cluster of hair suctioned to a prickly pear cactus a few more feet down. His heart worked overtime as the pieces of her disappearance came together. Pushing himself down the last few feet, he crouched at the base of the incline. Next to the largest impression cast in mud, where she'd landed. "What happened to you, Barbie?"

Standing, Branch circled outward from the point of her last known location until another set of tracks took shape. A smooth boot tread with a slight drag behind it. Son of a bitch. He'd taken her. But where?

He didn't have time to think of a strategy. Only time to act. But the radio was already in hand. He called through to Risner and relayed his location. He'd burned through whatever calories the oatmeal from this morning had provided. His legs ached, his energy levels had gone well beyond exhausted, but he couldn't stop. "Hang on, Lila. I'm coming."

The fear he'd given into that had driven him away from Lila had no room in his chest as it was slowly replaced with need. For her. To have her within reach. To hear that rare laugh she reserved for certain people. To absorb that inner sunshine to counter his darkness. In that moment, Branch was convinced he'd die without it. He needed her more than he needed his next breath.

Blackened tree branches clawed at his face, clothes and pack as he navigated the base of the valley, but the sting was nothing compared to the agony tearing through him at the thought of being too late. Each track in the mud he recovered was lighter than the one before it. Soon, he'd lose the trail altogether. Lose her forever.

Not an option.

Branch broke through a dense collection of trees ahead, into some kind of clearing he'd never seen before. Desert grass had overtaken the area, camouflaging evidence the killer had dragged Lila through. The trail here was a little more worn without the protection of trees keeping rain from corrupting the boot prints. There was no next step to follow. As though the killer had vanished into thin air.

In an instant, he was lost. About what to do next, where to go. Except that invisible thread that'd developed over the course of the past few days—the one tied directly to Lila—tugged harder.

He had no other choice than to follow it. He was her last resort. The only person who hadn't given up on her. The storm was only growing worse, pinning Risner and the SAR team in place. Lila's family had betrayed and shunned her when she needed them the most. Their fellow rangers wanted nothing more than to see her fail. And he…he'd turned his back on her.

That connection—however bruised and broken after what he'd said—was still there, guiding him forward. His feet were moving without conscious effort, leading him straight ahead.

A rise in the valley wall took shape to his left, and he slowed. To listen. To wait. Despite everything she'd faced, Lila Jordan was without a doubt the strongest person he'd ever met. Stronger than him. And she would figure out a way to stay alive until help arrived. He just hoped she didn't give up before then.

Grass parted as he maneuvered through the clearing. The rain lightened into a drizzle, slowing the destruction of evidence, but the damage had already been done. Mere rings of mud bled through trampled grass every so often. Branch pulled up short. The grass. Broken and bent stalks of wheat-like feathers swayed under the influence of the wind, revealing the path the killer had taken through the field.

A second burst of adrenaline filtered into his veins. She was close. He could feel it, feel that tug in the center of his chest. He didn't know how to explain it, and he didn't care what it meant, but as long as it was there, he'd follow. He'd fall to his knees for his woman. Hell, he'd crawl if she asked him to.

He'd cut himself off from everything and everyone to keep himself from getting attached to another human who could hurt him. Love had ruined him once. He'd done whatever it took to avoid it from happening again, but he'd never been a match for Lila. Not chasing it was impossible when it came to her. He wanted Lila to ruin him. Because she was worth whatever chaos she brought into his life.

The trees grew dense along the outer edge of the clearing, the grass thinner. He was on the verge of losing her again, but he wasn't about to give up. Not when everyone else had. Lila Jordan had crawled beneath his skin and carved her name with manicured nails on his heart. He was a marked man. Entirely hers.

Movement rustled through the blackened forest about a hundred yards ahead, though he couldn't make out what had disturbed the trees. Then came a dull pounding. Unsteady, hurried. Footsteps? Every cell in his body hardened with battle-ready tension. Branch ducked behind one of the larger trees. Waiting.

Then he saw it.

That flash of familiar blond hair.

Lila. She threw her attention over her shoulder, one arm clutched to her side. Her uniform had torn in places, streaked with blood and caked in mud. But he'd recognize her in the dark or completely blind.

"Lila!" Swinging himself into her path, Branch secured his arms around her middle, bringing her into his chest. Where she belonged. Hints of her scent drove into his lungs and released the vice in his chest. He could breathe easier, see clearer, think better with her here. As though the world had gone from black and white into full-blown color with her mere presence alone. That was what she'd done for him. Bought him back to life after losing all meaning. She was his meaning now. His purpose. "I've got you."

Her fist connected with his jaw, throwing his head to one side. "Let me go!"

Lightning erupted behind his eyes. Damn it all. This woman. Tightening his arms around her, he pressed his mouth to her ear. She was in survival mode. Desperate to escape. "It's me. It's Branch. You're safe."

"No." Tears streaked down her face as she struggled to get free of his grasp. "I'll never be safe. Not from him."

"Look at me." Branch framed her chin in one hand, turning her attention to him.

Lila's eyes rolled into the back of her head. Just before she collapsed.

Chapter Twenty-Seven

She liked the dark. She could admit now that part of her had missed it.

Stab wounds tended to do that. Made you think about all your life's choices and regrets. They weren't lying when they said your entire life flashed before your eyes in your last seconds. Lila could see where she'd gone wrong. How she'd deluded herself into believing—down to her very core—that becoming someone else hadn't fixed her problem. It'd just made them worse.

She was back in her seventeen-year-old body. Sneaking into her childhood home through her unlocked window in the basement window well. Her mom wasn't home. Her dad had gone to work. Her sister and brother-in-law had moved out. And she was hurting. So much. She'd just wanted to go home, for the pain to stop. To be loved again.

She crawled through spider webs and decomposing mouse carcasses that'd gotten caught in the window well and couldn't escape, studied the very bed where she'd metaphorically died that night her brother-in-law put his hands—and other things she didn't want to think about— on her.

Her dad's pocketknife was right there in the nightstand.

Right where she'd left it. Her mother must've missed it when she threw everything on the front lawn that day three weeks ago. The day Lila had been discarded as nothing more than garbage. Or maybe her mom couldn't bring herself to get rid of it. Didn't matter.

Lila knew what she had to do. It would be easy. All she had to do was pick up the knife, and everything would be okay again. She took one last look around the room, catching sight of silky blond hair beneath the bed. Getting on her knees, she got a better look. One of her Barbies, the one with its pink cowboy hat and pink jacket with fringe. The kerchief was stained with marker but was still tied around Barbie's neck no matter how many times she'd tried to take it off. She clutched the too-thin doll like a lifeline, but Barbie couldn't fix this hole inside her chest. She had to do it herself.

And set her dad's pocketknife against her throat.

A rushing filled Lila's ears. Her pulse? She was alive. Barely. But alive. The world tilted as a set of strong arms held her upright. Her vision wavered. In and out. In and out. She could've sworn she'd heard Branch's voice, but that wasn't possible. He'd left her. Just like everyone else.

Her body felt too heavy, her bones too big for her skin. Pain erupted from both sides of her ribs. Throat burning, she peeled her eyes open, and the world exploded with sensory overload. Bark bit into the back of her scalp. When had she sat down?

Movement darkened the edges of her vision. An outline materialized in front of her. Then dark eyes. The darkest brown she'd never been able to recreate in her morning coffee.

Branch's eyes.

"Lila, can you hear me?" His mouth moved, but the

words sounded like they'd been put through a blender. He was here. Or her brain was playing tricks on her. She couldn't be sure. The man whose love language was comprised of growling and glaring set his palm against her cheek. "Where are you hurt? I need to know what to focus on first."

"You're pretty." Her head became too heavy, rolling with the pattern of smooth bark at her back and into his touch. This wasn't real, though. Just a whole bunch of electric pulses her brain fired to make her final moments as pleasant as possible, and she could die in peace. How were you supposed to run from the things in your head? *Good job, brain.* But even if this wasn't real, she'd been wrong to manipulate him with fake smiles she didn't mean, forcing a surprise party he'd hated and trying to get him to open up to her.

All of it had been a lie. A halfhearted one at that. This... The pink, the death threats, the bedazzling... None of it was her.

Bleeding out in that bedroom had rewired apart of her brain that told her if her family couldn't love Lila anymore, all she had to do was become someone else. And Ranger Barbie had been born. But Branch had looked past it. Seen the real her underneath all the makeup and manicures and kerchiefs. He'd seen the unlovable Lila and run in the other direction like everyone else. She didn't even blame him, but holy hell she was tired of being someone she wasn't. And Ranger Barbie hadn't done her a damn bit of good when it'd mattered. She'd still lost the one person she wanted the most.

"You know. You were right." Why did her tongue suddenly feel like she'd licked sandpaper? "I was craving attention. I'd never done that before. Until I wanted yours."

That grizzly-bear expression softened in the smallest relaxing of his eyes. She probably would've missed it if he wasn't a conjuring of her own mind.

His fingers threaded through her hair at the base of her skull. "No. I was wrong, Lila. The things I said to you were abhorrent and untrue. I'm sorry I pushed you away. I've taught myself to become so independent since the divorce, I refused to let anyone in. I thought I could handle it, but it's really a terrifying and empty way to live. Then you came along and blew up my whole world like a pink glitter bomb. You brought color into my life, and the only thing I could think to do was run because I was afraid of how much I'd been missing it. But, damn, woman. Trouble never looked so fine. I want you. More than anything and anyone I've wanted before. Because I love you. All of you. I love Ranger Barbie and Lila and your death threats and the whole pink nightmare. I know you lost your family, but if you give me the chance, I'll be your family now. I'll always choose you."

He pressed his forehead to hers, one hand gripped on the back of her neck. "And I'm going to get you out of here."

It was everything she wanted to hear. Her nose burned with the impending breakdown she'd scheduled after getting stabbed. "I hope you're real because if you aren't, this is a very cruel dream, and my ghost will haunt you until you die out of spite."

His hands slid to her low back and beneath her knees, and Branch hefted her against his chest. "I wouldn't have it any other way, Barbie, but if it makes you feel any better, I'm real. I'm here, and I'm not leaving you ever again."

He took a single step.

And a gunshot echoed off the surrounding cliffs.

Branch jerked forward with a grunt. His hold loosened on

her frame, and she pitched forward. The ground rushed up to meet her—faster than she expected—and a scream burst free of her chest. His weight crushed her into the ground, re-invigorating the pain in her sides. But Branch wasn't moving.

Didn't even seem to breathe.

Digging her fingernails into his shoulders, Lila tried to roll him off of her. Real. He was real. He'd come for her again. And the words he'd said… He loved her. A flood of prickling warmth shot from her head to her toes at the realization her brain wasn't playing tricks on her.

But something else—something hotter and liquid—drenched her uniform shirt. Blood. No. *No, no, no.* This wasn't happening. She'd just got him back. He'd chosen her.

Struggling against the bruises and the stab wound across her torso, she rocked him back and forth. "Branch, you have to get up. We have to move. Please. I love you. I love you, too. Okay? I brought color into your life, but you brought feeling into mine. I was numb before I met you. I thought I had to be something I'm not for people to love me, but it only made things worse. I was scared of the things you made me feel because I didn't want to feel, but I don't ever want to be numb again. So you have to get up. Please."

An outline took shape, peeling away from the black trees surrounding them. The killer. He'd found them. It didn't matter how hard she'd fought to escape that dark little cave or the hollowness in her chest, he'd never let her leave this park alive.

Her hands shook as she set them on her partner's shoulders, but his eyes had slipped closed. He was losing consciousness and too much blood.

"Branch." His name broke on her lips. "Branch, get up."

"There's nowhere you can run that I won't find you, Ranger Jordan." How had the killer gotten so close without her noticing? Or had her body started shutting down? He closed in, standing above her beside Branch's unmoving frame. "My sister thought she could hide once I was released from the mental institution. She was wrong."

He took aim.

Throwing her arms over Branch, she stared at the end of the gun barrel. It took everything she had left to keep her voice even, leaning on that massive confidence Ranger Barbie had always given her. "Just finish it. If you don't, I'll dismember you so completely, the devil won't know what to do with you when you get to hell."

"Always with the jokes." The killer kept the gun steady. This was it. This was where she and Branch ended, just as they'd gotten started. Not how she pictured it in all those late-night fantasies. "You never cease to amaze me, Ranger Jordan, but you're not laughing now, are you?"

A deep warning penetrated through the small clearing where she and Branch had gone down. A blur of tan fur and fangs broke into her vision.

The killer turned the gun toward the new threat, but it was too late. Claws sank deep into the killer's chest, and he vaulted backward. His scream jerked Branch back into consciousness.

A second gunshot tore through the adrenaline-induced haze that'd taken over her body, and the mountain lion that had attacked sank to the ground.

Where had he come from? Cougars rarely attacked unless provoked. Her heart clenched at the thought of the animal sacrificing itself to save her and Branch, but she wasn't about to look a gift horse in the mouth, either.

"Lila, run." Branch's pained voice barely reached her over the hard thud of her heart. Rolling onto his back, he clamped a hand against his shoulder. Blood seeped through calloused fingers and spilled over the back of his hand. Fingers that'd held her with such care and acceptance. Now stained with blood.

Biting against the moan of pain in her throat, she slid her hands under his shoulders and pushed him upright. "I'm not going anywhere. You owe me a coffee date, and you're not getting out of it this time."

His laugh cut short as another growl broke the silence.

The killer launched himself at them.

Branch brought his knee up in time to neutralize the collision, then kicked out as the killer took aim. At Lila. His heel connected with the killer's chest and sent him spiraling backward into a tree. Then Branch was on his feet, his inhales strained and shallow. "You can't have her."

A frustrated scream tore from the killer's throat as he practically threw himself at Branch. Her partner used the attacker's momentum against him, stepping aside and planting his elbow into the killer's back.

The man who'd killed Sarah Lantos—his own sister— turned the gun on Lila, and everything inside of her went cold. "Neither can you."

He pulled the trigger.

But nothing happened.

The killer tried again. And again.

Branch didn't give him time to test it a fourth time. He scooped up a rock from the ground and swung it into the killer's head, knocking their assailant out cold. In the aftermath of adrenaline, Branch's legs failed to hold his weight, and he dropped to his knees.

But Lila was right there. Holding him upright as he'd held her in the desert last night while she exposed all the broken pieces of herself. She swiped her thumb across his bottom lip. "Hello, Grizzly Bear."

"Hello, Barbie." He smiled at her, a genuine, full-blown smile that threatened to unravel her insides. It was the most beautiful sight she'd ever witnessed. And it was all for her. "Do me a favor. Stay with me."

"Always." She clutched his hand between both of hers. Just as Risner and the search and rescue team descended.

Chapter Twenty-Eight

Branch would not go gentle into that good night.

Okay. It wasn't that serious. The bullet wound to his shoulder hurt like hell, though. There'd been no exit wound.

Once Risner and the SAR team had found him and Lila—much to the ego inflation of the district ranger—a helicopter had been dispatched to their location. The ride itself had taken no more than a few minutes, a definite improvement over having to ascend Angel's Landing with a hole in his shoulder. He'd been swept into surgery within minutes short a pint of blood or two. When he'd asked if his day could get any worse, it'd been a rhetorical question. Not a challenge.

And Lila had kept her word after the EMTs had forced her into the trauma surgeon's hands in the Sprindale ER. Once in recovery, she'd stayed outside his surgical suite until the nurses had threatened to have her handcuffed to the bed. But true to Lila's nature, she'd promised to return with straitjackets and a referral to a mental institution for each of them if something happened to him. Seemed she was as reluctant to be apart from him and he was from her. Unfortunately, to the detriment of her own health.

Which only made him love her more.

Branch scooped another spoonful of Cherry Garcia into his mouth, taking his time sucking on the hard-as-bricks chocolate chips. His favorite part. Because once he broke through their hard shell, there was nothing but sweetness and pleasure underneath. Just like Lila. Thank heaven she'd somehow gotten her roommate to smuggle in a couple pints. He was about to throw the next cup of Jell-O he saw against the wall. Though the unending days of lying in a hospital bed were made much better by the blond beauty currently glued to the romantic comedy on TV in the bed beside him.

Bruises darkened the side of her face, a new butterfly bandage interrupted the line of smooth skin along her temple, and she'd sustained a life-threatening injury herself. While the stab wound hadn't hit anything major, she'd bled for a couple hours between facing off with the killer and the time Branch had found her in the grove of burned trees. The damage to her ribs would heal in a few weeks, but it made sitting up and walking much harder. Which she made sure to complain about as often as possible. Turned out, Lila wasn't good at staying in one place with nothing to hyperfixate on, but they would both be out of here in a couple days.

For now, he'd revel in the time they had together right here in this room.

The killer—Jeremy Lantos—was, in fact, Sarah Lantos's brother. Risner and the rest of the search and rescue team had managed to hold him until the law enforcement rangers could make an official arrest and run his fingerprints through the federal system.

Upon release from a mental institution where he'd spent the past ten years of his life, Jeremy had set out to have his revenge against the very woman who'd driven him to kill.

While most of his testimony would remain between him, the Springdale PD and his attorney, it seemed Sarah Lantos had tried to destroy her brother thoroughly and completely since he'd been born. What little Branch had been privy to over the past few days, he understood Jeremy's medical records had shown broken bones, burns, bruises, strangulation attempts and more—all from the time he'd been about two years old. In the end, Sarah Lantos had done such a good job of convincing the people around her of her innocence, she'd actually made Jeremy out to be unstable. It'd only taken manipulating their parents and filing a false police report detailing an attack at the hands of her brother to have Jeremy Lantos legally committed to the institution. Repeated claims he'd been framed and wrongly committed had gone unheard for over a decade before he'd been allowed to step back into the outside world.

Only to become victim to his own delusions.

A knock sounded at the door, and Branch did his best to hide the Ben & Jerry's in case one of the nurses took it upon themselves to confiscate it. But it wasn't a nurse. Suspicion turned sweetness bitter at the back of his throat as Risner stepped inside.

"Ugh." Lila didn't need a mood ring. Her face revealed everything she was feeling, and the painkiller they had her on had stripped away any kind of filter she'd honed over the years. "What the hell do you want, dearly detested? My esteemed rival? My beloved nemesis?"

It took everything Branch had not to laugh, but since he was technically still employed by the National Park Service, he'd see how this played out.

"Now, now, Jordan, is that any way to talk to your superior?" Risner clasped his hands behind his back, taking position between their beds.

"Sorry. What the hell do you want, sir, whose presence I barely tolerate? No. That's not it. Fellow person who has improbably managed to live past the age of nine. No. I can do better. To whom it may concern, because rest assured, that person is not me. Wait. Does that work?" She tried to see the TV around the district ranger's rail-thin frame but must've overdone it. Slapping a hand over her side, she turned her face into her pillow to mutter a few favored curses.

"Stop moving. You'll tear your stitches." Branch had lost count of the number of times he'd had to remind her the pain meds didn't fix everything. She still had to rest to heal, but he also understood memories of the last time she'd been in a hospital brought back feelings of all the hopelessness she must've felt at seventeen.

"Too late." Her groan broke on a shallow whine. "Just leave me here to die. Okay? Live your life. Find new love. See Antarctica. But send me a postcard. I'll be with you in spirit."

"Are you done?" Risner watched with nothing but contempt etched into his expression. Contempt for the woman Branch loved. Strike one. "Good heavens, Jordan, what the hell happened to your neck?"

Color drained from Lila's face, and she stilled. A deer in headlights. No comeback. No death threats. His Ranger Barbie was on the verge of breaking due to the extreme stress they'd undergone during this investigation, the pain medication the doctors had her on and the attention of a man she didn't respect.

All right. Strike three. Branch's defenses snapped into place, and he set the ice cream on the side table, brushing his hands together. "What do you want, Risner?"

The district ranger's gaze snapped to Branch, his eyes

widening as though he couldn't believe an employee who'd done nothing but follow orders might not like him. It took a few seconds for Risner's little rat brain to catch up. "Murray Simpson heads the law enforcement rangers in Zion. He came to me a couple hours ago after reading through both of your statements. He'd like to make a job offer, if you'll have it."

"Not interested." Wherever Lila was, that was where Branch would go. They'd fought like hell to find each other. Battling mountain lions and killers, a landslide and the most powerful storm of the year. Not to mention their pasts. There was no way he'd ever let something as small as a job opportunity keep them apart.

"The job offer isn't for you." Risner rocked back on his heels, gaze directed at Lila. "It's for Jordan."

"Come again?" Lila's voice broke on the last word, and Branch couldn't help but lock his attention on her to gauge her reaction.

"Murray was impressed with the insights you had into the investigation, especially considering you've never had any formal training. He wants you on his team as soon as you're ready to return to the field." Ducking his chin to his chest, Risner lowered his voice. "Without you, we might not have ever figured out that Sarah Lantos was related to her killer or that she'd been stabbed before being pushed over that cliff. Due to the condition of her remains, we might have classified her death as an accident. I was wrong to assume your involvement would only complicate the investigation."

Lila pressed her palms into the mattress, pushing herself upright, the romantic comedy on TV forgotten. "Could you say that a bit louder? I'm going to need all the other female rangers under your command to hear it."

Risner puffed his chest, a defense mechanism that did nothing except make him look ridiculous. The district ranger licked his lips. "I was wrong, and I'm sorry. Do you want the job or not?"

"Count me in." A wide smile—nothing like the fake one she'd been pasting on for everyone around her—flashed across Lila's face. It was genuine and true to the free spirit she'd locked up inside of her all these years. And, yeah, a little terrifying. But Branch would do whatever it took to make it appear as often as he could or spend the rest of his life trying. "I'd say it's been a pleasure, Risner, but I'd be lying. So I'll be filing a complaint with the park superintendent about your behavior toward the female rangers under your command. I'm sure he'll be very interested in talking with you about it. You can go."

Branch made an effort not to roll his eyes. This woman. She'd been to hell and back, but something about the smirk on her face told him she was the boss down there, too.

"Oh, wait." Lila sat a bit straighter. "What happened to the mountain lion that was shot? Is he okay?"

"The vet was able to recover the bullet without any problems. He'll recover in a few weeks, and the vet team will release him back into the wild." Risner left the hospital room with a nod as goodbye.

The second the door closed behind him, Branch was swinging his legs over the edge of the bed.

"What are you doing? You're going to hurt something." That intense blue gaze he'd happily take another bullet for centered on him, and Branch's entire world threatened to explode in vivid color all over again.

"I'm already hurting." He grabbed for his half-full pint of Cherry Garcia and hobbled to her side of the room. Then offered her the goods. "Might as well get some other benefits out of it."

She took the Ben & Jerry's and the spoon, diving right in. Her face smoothed into pure pleasure as the ice cream melted in her mouth, and suddenly he couldn't wait to get the hell out of this place and into his bed. "You know me so well."

"Apparently not well enough." He settled on the edge of her bed, no longer willing to accept the distance between them. Every cell in his body pined after every cell in hers. To the point it hurt not to touch her. To make sure this all hadn't been some screwed-up dream. Threading his free hand over the back of hers, he brought her knuckles to his mouth and pressed a kiss to the scabbed skin there. She'd fought a killer—twice—and lived to tell the tale. Was there anything this magnificent woman couldn't do? "Didn't expect you to take the job."

Her face lit up as though she'd just learned the secrets of the universe and intended to use them to her own advantage. "Do you think law enforcement rangers like pranks?"

Dread pooled in the pit of his stomach. "You cannot under any circumstances pull pranks on rangers that carry guns, Lila."

"You're no fun." Her pout didn't last long as he pressed another kiss to her wrist. Then higher at her inner elbow. Her breathing turned shallow, her pupils growing wider.

"But you still love me." He'd never felt so sure of anything in his life. The past—the divorce, the betrayal, the fear of trusting someone new—could stay where it belonged. He was ready for the future. With Lila, Ranger Barbie and any other personalities she picked up along the way. "And you're going to be an amazing law enforcement ranger."

"Damn right I love you, Grizzly Bear." She smiled for him then. "And you love me, too."

"You got that right, Barbie." His next kiss feathered over her mouth, and he sucked in an inhale laced with cherries, chocolate and cream. His favorite combination. "Forever."

* * * * *

COMING SOON!

We really hope you enjoyed reading this book.
If you're looking for more romance
be sure to head to the shops when
new books are available on

Thursday 23rd October

To see which titles are coming soon, please visit
millsandboon.co.uk/nextmonth

MILLS & BOON

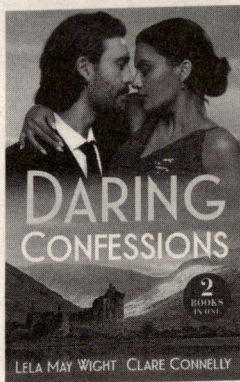

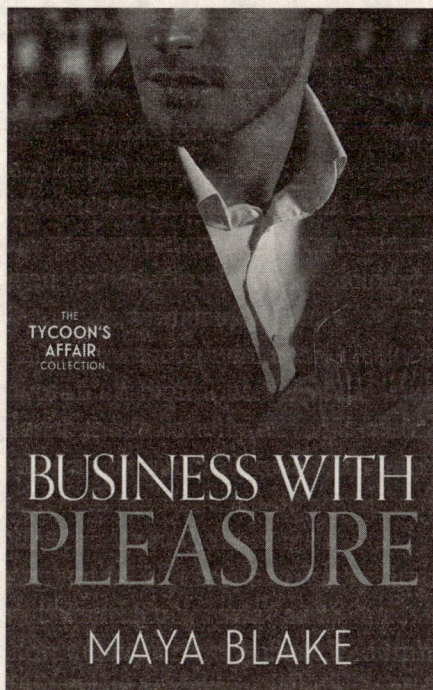

LET'S TALK
Romance

For exclusive extracts, competitions and special offers, find us online:

 MillsandBoon

 @MillsandBoon

 @MillsandBoonUK

 @MillsandBoonUK

Get in touch on 01413 063 232

For all the latest titles coming soon, visit
millsandboon.co.uk/nextmonth